# Little White Lies

**Tattoos and Tears – Jax**
**Book 7**

## By Amiee Louise

I0564377

Copyright © 2025 by

Amiee Louise & Hold Fast Publishing

All rights reserved.

This is a work of fiction. Names, characters, businesses, places, events , and incidents are either the products of the author's imagination or used in a fictitious manner. Any resemblance to actual persons, living or dead, or actual events is purely coincidental.

This book contains sexually explicit scenes and adult language.

All characters in this work are 18 years of age or older.

*Broken is a beautiful place to start...*

# Prologue

## Jax

I don't believe in miracles, but sometimes life just throws you a curveball. As I look into the wide, inquisitive, hazel eyes of my daughter, Thea Ruby Chase, I'm reminded of the woman I lost. *Ruby*. My little firecracker, my reason for living, and the woman I planned to spend the rest of my life with.

Everyone has one great love, a once in a lifetime kind of love, and Ruby was mine. She was my sunshine, my light, my moon and stars, my muse, *my buttercup*.

She is the reason why I can't allow myself to fall in love again, *I just can't*. The thought in and of itself, terrifies the living shit out of me. I can't leave myself vulnerable, I won't open myself up to that kind of heartbreak. I won't survive it, *not again*.

Since Ruby was cruelly taken from us, I'm really fucking struggling. I get what Sam went through when he thought Peyton was gone. The unbearable, soul-destroying, gut-wrenching agony, the crippling sense of loss and the overwhelming grief that consumes you so completely, you can't see another way out. I sat with him through the screaming, the tears, the self-loathing, the booze, the drugs, and the endless nightmares. I watched him torture himself, day after day, night after night, and I found him in a pool of his own blood because he thought he couldn't carry on without her. I resented him for a long time for putting me through that.

After Ruby died, I understood, *I got it*. I understood completely because I felt exactly the fucking same. I was drowning in sadness and guilt; I was in that same fiery pit of hell and I hated myself for not protecting her. I suffered flashbacks, vivid nightmares that seemed so real that in the beginning, I was terrified to fall asleep. I tortured myself for not doing enough to save her and that's what keeps me up at night.

However, fate seems to have other ideas, by throwing an obstacle in my path. A blonde haired, silver eyed goddess, who challenges me, defies me at every turn, and sasses the living hell out of me. She's funny, she's sexy, provocative, she's the total opposite of Ruby, and she's fresh. She's potentially the girl to help me move on from Ruby.

But the fucked-up thing is, she doesn't know me as Jackson Chase, lead guitarist in Rancid Vengeance. She knows me as HandsomeJack0304. For the first time in my thirty-four years, I'm enjoying the chase and the thrill of getting to know someone in the twenty-first century. It's unconventional, it's fun, it's taboo, and it's a little forbidden, but it feels so *right*. Behind the keyboard, I can be whoever I want to be. I can be plain Jack, no fame, no strings, just a regular guy, looking for a little escapism from his reality. *The reality of being a single dad and a world-famous rock star.*

By day, I'm Jax Chase, guitarist extraordinaire and one-quarter of rock band, Rancid Vengeance. By night, I'm Jack, happy-go-lucky, flirty, funny, a little cheeky, the lovable rogue, who can charm the birds from the trees.

However, the stupid thing about fate is that it always seems to catch up with you in the most peculiar and spectacular of ways. Cue the shit storm of deception, little white lies, and overwhelming betrayal, I was about to embark upon.

# 1

## Jax

Life is made of imperfections, impurities, mistakes, and flaws. No tree is smooth, no rock is perfectly formed, no leaf is symmetrical and intact for long. Just as the world around us is changing, so is my daughter, Thea. Every day she is changing, she's learning something new, she's smart like her mum and sasses me in the same way. Her large hazel eyes, wise beyond her years, look up at me and I know she sees the sadness that lies within me.

"Daddy, why do you always look so sad?" she asks in a small voice, and her question takes me aback, punching me straight in the gut.

*Where did that come from? I wasn't fucking expecting that.* I swallow back the tennis ball-size lump in my throat that threatens to choke me where I stand. I take a long sip of my coffee to compose myself before I answer her. She looks at me expectantly and as the door taps softly, relief washes over me. I open the door to Lucas's smiling face, momentarily halting her line of questioning. *Thank fuck.*

"Mornin', man."

He steps inside in his usual running attire of black vest, long black basketball shorts, his favourite Nike running shoes, and black and red Rancid Vengeance baseball cap worn backwards. As Thea sees him, her face lights up and she runs towards him, slamming full-pelt into his legs.

"Uncle Lukeyyyy!" she squeals excitedly, as he laughs and swings her easily up into his arms.

"Hey, little lady! Whatcha' doin'?"

She babbles a million miles an hour and Lucas entertains her, as if they're having a full-blown conversation. *This dude would make an amazing dad someday, if only he met the right person.* I observe their exchange, as she plays with the hair at the nape of his neck and plants a sloppy kiss on his cheek. I swear he blushes! He sets her down in her chair and he casually saunters over to where I'm standing with his hand tucked loosely into his pocket.

"What's up?"

I sigh audibly, leaning heavily onto the marble worktop.

"Tough morning, that's all, mate," I answer honestly, puffing out my cheeks and hanging my head down limply.

"Wanna' talk about it?" He cocks his head to the side; I look up at him and nod.

"Just give me a minute, yeah?" I go over to Thea's drawing desk, pulling out some crayons and some paper.

"Will you draw Daddy and Uncle Luke a picture, please, Princess?" I ask softly and she nods excitedly.

"YEAHHH!"

I smile at her enthusiasm. *She's just like her mum, she is the sun in my dull, grey world.*

"Good girl! Daddy's going to talk to Uncle Luke for a minute, yeah? I'll just be in the other room."

She grins and nods. Even at two years old, she fucking floors me. I never knew love until she was handed to me, wailing her little lungs out. When she grabbed my finger at just minutes old, I knew I was all in and in that single moment, I'd never felt love like that. She took her first breath as her mummy took her last, and even though my life as I knew it was turned upside down, she became the most precious thing in it. She's my whole world, I'd lie down in traffic for her, I'd do serious prison time and I'd sacrifice my life if it meant she was safe. *There's nothing I wouldn't do for her.*

I kiss her on her forehead and head into the living room, which opens out into the kitchen, where I can still keep a careful eye on her.

"Shoot."

I look up to the ceiling, as if it can offer me the answers I seek, but I come up empty. I find myself shaking my head and I'm struggling to find the words to explain.

"I don't know, man, Thea asked me why I always look so sad. It knocked the fucking wind out of me. How do I even begin to answer that question?

I always look so sad because I couldn't save your mummy. I failed as a fiancé, as a fucking man. I had one job and I couldn't even do that right!"

I swipe angrily at the tears that track their way down my cheeks. *Even after two years, it still fucking hurts like it happened just yesterday.*

"Why do you insist on torturing yourself, dude? You can't keep blaming yourself for something that was out of your control. You know it's not good for you, you only have to look at how Sam was back then."

I shake my head. *He has no fucking clue.*

"I didn't know how it felt then, I had no idea how he was feeling, but now I get it because I'm there. I'm in the depths of hell because I couldn't protect her. At least Sam got a second chance, I'm never going to get that because I fucking failed her! I failed both Ruby and our daughter! I wake up night after night and relive that day on a constant loop, in slow fucking motion, frame by frame!"

Lucas squeezes my shoulder in a silent gesture of reassurance. I take a deep breath and he doesn't have to say anything for me to know what he's thinking, *it's not my fault.* Deep down I know that, but it doesn't stop me from feeling hopeless, that in my attempt to shield her, I put her in the line of fire. I'm plagued by that image twenty-four-seven, it makes me feel pathetic and useless. *I truly failed her.*

"Is there a timeframe on how long I should be feeling like this? Is there a limit on how sad I can be? That little girl in there, she's my reason to always keep fighting, to get out of bed in the morning. But it fucking hurts to look at her because she reminds me so much of Ruby. How fucked up is that?!"

I laugh bitterly and Lucas looks at me sympathetically.

"Don't you dare pity me, Luke, I couldn't fucking bear it."

He shakes his head and holds his hands up defensively.

"No pity here, man, I still feel guilty for not doing anything to stop my dad from murdering my mum and my step-father. I was seven years old, I was just a kid, and even though it happened so many years ago, it doesn't stop. It gets easier, yeah, of course it does, time is a great healer, but it's always going to be there, and there's absolutely nothing wrong with that. You deal with it the way you know how, by waking up every day and honouring her memory. Do something that scares you, do something that would make her proud, anything to make that empty feeling go away."

Lucas never talks about his past, even after all these years of friendship, he keeps that part of himself hidden from us and from the world. It's at moments like these, when he's feeling in a particularly chatty mood, that he gives us those rare glimpses of what his life was like before. Before England, before us, before Rancid Vengeance and before his life was turned upside down by the murder of his mother and his stepfather.

His biological dad Fletcher '*Fletch*' Heath was sent to prison for first degree murder and armed robbery when Lucas's mum, Evie Landon, was six months pregnant with him. Fletch managed to escape from prison when Lucas was seven years old. He raped and murdered his mum and he murdered and brutally beat Lucas's step-dad Simon Ford to death with a baseball bat. Lucas witnessed the whole thing after hiding in a laundry hamper. Fletch blew his own brains out with a shotgun after the police surrounded the house. Lucas was taken in and adopted by Kyle and Ava Landon, his mum's sister and brother-in-law, who is a famous movie director. Lucas moved to the UK, and he was mute for two years because of the trauma of witnessing something so brutal and horrific. Lucas only communicated through music for those two years and after working with some of the top child psychologists, he eventually started speaking again.

I have no idea what to say to him because he's never been the forthcoming type, and I think he gets that, as he continues to speak.

"You give that little girl the life she deserves every day, by just being her daddy, by being her hero, by just simply being you. We love you, man," he says sincerely, as Thea comes bounding in waving a piece of paper in the air.

"Daddy! Uncle Lukeyyyy! Looooook!" she says with such enthusiasm, as I take the paper from her and look at the drawing she created.

"*Wow!* Did you do this, Princess? You're so talented! Who's this?" I point to what looks like a stick man with an abnormally long neck on the page and she rolls her eyes dramatically.

"That's you, silly! And there's Uncle Lukeyyyy, and Uncle Sammyyyy, and Uncle Bwodyyyy and that's meeee!" she explains animatedly, waiting patiently while I work it out. I turn the paper and look more closely.

"Awesome! That's the best drawing I've ever seen, Thea! You could totally be an artist!" Lucas steps in and states in an over-the-top fashion. "Good job!"

He hi-fives her and flashes me an encouraging wink. *It's particularly bad days like these, where I treasure his friendship.*

"Shall we go and stick it to the refrigerator with the others?" he asks and she nods, as he takes her tiny hand in his.

"But I'll let you into a little secret, that one is my personal favourite!"

He flashes a grin at her, and her big brown eyes widen. *Bless her heart.* I mouth a silent thank you to him and they go off into the kitchen, as I inwardly chastise myself for being a fucking awful dad. I didn't ask for any of this, I didn't ask to be responsible for a tiny human, who looks like Ruby and has my personality. I love her with all my heart, she's my world, but even after all this time, I still don't know how to be without Ruby.

*A child should grow up knowing both their mother and their father. Every day is a struggle, watching her grow up without you by my side. You've missed so many firsts, her first steps, her first smile, her first tooth, her first word and her first day at nursery. Fuck, I need you, buttercup.*

# 2

## Jax

Ruby taught me a lot of things in the short time we were together. She taught me that love isn't perfect, far fucking from it. Love is messy and complicated, but it lives within us all, love is one quality we were all born with and one that we will all die with. When I met her on that fateful day, it was a day that will be forever etched into the very core of me. I had no idea that I would meet someone so close to my ideal and truly feel again for the first time. I thought she had it all figured out, from the way she strutted into Saint Sinner Ink in her high heels, to the way she winked at me, so bold, brash, and sure of herself. *She was the epitome of sex for me.* Something in me was drawn to that light I saw in her, she shone so fucking brightly, she almost blinded me. Her charm, her complete and utter disregard for *'normal'* is what kept me coming back for more. Every time she refused to return my calls, every time we had sex and soon after, she got her clothes on and left without saying a word. She kept me wanting more of what she was so willingly offering.

In those moments when we were alone, I thought she could see right through me. That I was just the ordinary guy I craved to be, that the fame, the glitz, and the glamour of being a rock star, was a complete fraud. It was so far from the truth, even from the very beginning. Falling for her, hit me like a fucking train, she was so difficult, so high maintenance and irrational, but I just couldn't help myself.

The night I held her in my arms as she sobbed for her best friend, I realised how hurt and utterly devastated she really was. This strong, ballsy woman, who didn't give a shit what anyone thought, broke down so completely. I surprised myself at how naturally I stepped into the role of picking up the pieces and drying her tears. I realised then I cared for her, I think maybe in that moment, I'd already fallen.

Since the day she was brutally torn from me, I've lived my life in the shadows, in shades of grey, never in colour. Living life in the spotlight is becoming a chore, I'm not sure how much longer I can paint on a smile and pretend everything is okay. The only thing getting me through these days, are my daughter and the boys. I don't know what I would have done without any of them. The unobtrusive support of the rest of the boys has aided me. In the early days of coping with the loss of Ruby and being thrust into the world of single fatherhood, was vital to my healing.

\*\*\*

I never put much stock in religion, but as I'm sitting on the bus travelling to our next destination, watching the world go by, I see a neon, illuminated cross and pray to all that's holy to just stop feeling sad. I'm tired of being sad, I'm tired of being the forlorn rocker who lost his fiancée. But every morning when I wake up, the sadness and grief grips me tight and refuses to let go. I have to be strong for Thea, but everything inside me just wants to give in to the overwhelming grief, this fucking soul-destroying loss that never gives me a moment's rest. It torments me and it reminds me in the most brutal way, that *I survived*. I owe it to Ruby and to our daughter, to live, to cherish each day as if it were my last, to be the best dad and the best version of myself that I can be.

After an epic show in Brighton, wired and struggling to come down from the high of performing in front of a crowd of thousands. I find myself staring blankly at a dating site on my iPad screen. After two years, since Ruby was taken from me, there have been a few women... okay, *a lot of women,* don't judge me. I haven't been celibate the whole time, far from it, I'm a virile, red-blooded male, I have needs. It's only ever been meaningless sex to fill the void and satisfy a need, I'm lucky if I remember their names by the time I'm finished. Afterwards, I feel so detached and so... empty, I can't get my clothes on quick enough before I'm running out of the door without a second thought. It feels like so long ago, that I haven't even contemplated what it might be like to meet someone I eventually want to settle down with.

I can't allow myself to think that far ahead, as I continue to stare at the screen. This particular dating site catches my eye, it's a dating site specifically for professional singles. It describes itself as an elite and exclusive members only site. *I can get on board with that.* The tagline of GoMatchPro.com reads *'Find your life partner, or a partner just for the night!' Enter your details and we'll match you exclusively with millions of professional singles. For just £50 per month, get unlimited matches!* I find myself rolling my eyes at the absurdity and the scale of sheer fucking desperation. *Come on, stop being such a pussy, Chase.* It's just a bit of harmless fun. I'm not going to do something as stupid as getting attached. I'd be betraying Ruby, *my buttercup.* The only woman I'll ever be capable of loving, nothing and no one will ever replace her. Besides, I have responsibilities first and foremost. I'm a father to the most beautiful little girl, who reminds me so much of her mum. Her wide, curious, hazel eyes make her look so much wiser beyond her years, her mass of dark brown hair, half me, half Ruby. The way she lights up every time she sees me, it's like I'm her hero and I don't deserve that status. *Not at all.*

Morbid curiosity urges me to press the *'Enter your details'* button. *What harm can it do?* I'm anonymous, besides, I can't give away my true identity, the press would have a fucking field day. I can see the headlines now *'Jackson Chase in online dating shocker!'* The boys would never let me live it down. It asks a selection of questions *'likes, dislikes'* and then it moves on to *'what are you looking for'* and *'what's your type.'* I've never really sat down and thought about the type of women I'm attracted to. Only that the next woman I meet, won't be Ruby. That thought cripples me and I quickly come to my senses. *I can't do this; I can't be disloyal to her.* After all this time, she's the only woman who's had my heart and I'm not willing to give it to anyone else. Not yet maybe not ever. I swipe the screen, close the browser, and snap my iPad case shut. *Not today, I'm not ready.*

# 3

## Jax

Hello, darkness, my old friend, it's been a while. Today is a particularly bad day and even after all this time, I still don't know how to be without Ruby. I still haven't gotten past that grieving stage and I just seem to coast through life, not living, just barely existing. I've learned to cope over the past two years, but it still never gets any easier. As the bus travels down another nameless and endless motorway, I find something silently reassuring and inspiring about the flashing lights, the low hum of the bus engine and the quiet melody of Gorgeous George's music from the driver's seat. Brody is playing *Forza Horizon 4* on the Xbox Series X, grumbling about *'cheating bastards'*, Lucas is tapping his fingers on the table. Sam is murmuring a random tune and writing in his notebook at intervals, breaking the oddly comfortable silence. I lean my head back, as the lights zip past and let my mind drift off to a time when I was actually happy and life for us was normal.

# Jax

# Past

*Ruby,*

*Learn to love what nobody else can love about you, learn to love what I love about you. The way you look in the mornings, all natural and sleep mussed, the way no one can talk to you before you've had your morning coffee. Love the way your shadow looks in the sunlight, love how you dream in colour that you can't describe when you wake up, or love that you dream in greys. Love yourself with the same hatred you have for early mornings, late nights, or spilled coffee. Love the fact that you're still learning to love yourself, forget that you feel naked without make-up and forget that you hate yourself naked. I love seeing you naked, I wake up next to you every morning and I feel like the luckiest motherfucker on the planet. Not only are you beautiful on the outside, but you also have a beautiful soul. You have a life that we both created growing inside of you and that couldn't be any more fucking beautiful, buttercup. I bet you have that cute, stupid grin on your face right now.*

*Well, Ruby Logan, I need you to do something for me, meet me outside Brent Cross Tube Station at eleven a.m. sharp (don't be late because I know you always like to turn up fashionably late!) and all will be revealed.*

*Love you, buttercup, always.*

*Your Jack xxx*

I wrote her a letter, I wanted to write down all the things I couldn't say to her out loud and on the whole journey to the tube station, my nerves were shot to shit.

"Come on, man, like she's really gonna say no!"

My old friend, Travis Cohen nudges me as he drives the one hour, eleven-mile journey from Chislehurst, Kent, to Brent Cross, to assist me with my proposal to Ruby. Travis and I used to busk together every weekend, before Rancid Vengeance hit it big. Trafalgar Square, Piccadilly Circus, Covent Garden, outside tube stations, you name it, we busked there. We made a fair amount of money for a couple of school kids who just loved music, way before the popularity of YouTube.

*Travis is a Club Promoter, but still busks today purely for the love of it. Music has always been an escape for Travis, his mum, Sharon, used to be a barmaid in the pub The Three Cups, that my mum and dad used to run in Bethnal Green, before my mum got back into medicine. His dad, Steve, is a recovering alcoholic and at the height of his addiction, my mum and dad took Sharon, Travis and his brothers Justin and Harrison in, when Steve hit rock bottom and got admitted to rehab. We struck up a friendship over our mutual love of music and even through the fame and the touring, we have kept in touch and seem to have an unbreakable bond outside the madness of Rancid Vengeance.*

"Just sing it like we rehearsed, you never used to let nerves get in the way, dude. It was always purely about the music," Travis says, as I bite down on my nail viciously and tap my hand anxiously on the centre console of his BMW X5.

"That was before YouTube, mate, you do realise I'm sort of a big deal these days! I'm going to go viral, everyone's got access to a camera phone. If she says no, I'll never live the humiliation down!" I state dramatically and Travis chuckles softly.

"You always were a sensitive soul, Jacko!"

I roll my eyes at his nickname for me, no one has called me that in years, except my sister Shay, who thinks it's highly amusing.

"Come on, man, I get this is a big deal, but honestly, you've got nothing to worry about, she's smitten and she's obviously going to say yes." He brushes my arm in a gesture of reassurance and I smile.

"Cheers, mate, I really appreciate you doing this for me," I say genuinely and he smiles back.

"Anytime, brother, anytime, anything for an old friend, you know that. Besides, you owe me one now!"

We both laugh as the car comes to a halt on car park on Highfield Avenue, around the corner from the tube station. My stomach roils and my breakfast threatens to make a reappearance.

"Deep breaths, man, deep breaths." He rests his hand on my shoulder.

"I can't do this, Trav, I just can't."

My breathing becomes laboured, and I'm suddenly overwhelmed with nerves, I feel like I'm going to throw up. Fucking hell, what is wrong with me? I *can perform in front of a crowd of thousands, but I can't propose to my fiancée. What the fuck, Chase? Get it together, dickhead, you got this.*

*Travis regards me intently, a look of pure concern etched on his face.*

*"You good?" he asks reluctantly and I nod.*

*"I got this." I breathe with a wink, I tie my hair up, grab my guitar and my baseball cap, pulling it low over my eyes. Fuck me, who am I kidding? As if a baseball cap is going to shield my identity, I've only got to start playing guitar and if they're fans of ours, they will recognise me and my unique sound in an instant.*

*We head to our pitch and set up off to the side of the bustling entrance of Brent Cross Tube Station. I take out my guitar with a trembling hand and set the open case at my feet. Travis sets up the microphone stand and takes out his guitar.*

*"Good luck, man!" He slaps me on the back, and I clear my throat, as I position myself in front of the microphone. I strum out a few practice chords and Travis does the same.*

*"Like we practised, yeah?" He winks and I nod curtly, as Travis counts me in. "2-3-4."*

*I begin to confidently strum out the opening chords of the song I wrote especially for Ruby, as I see the clock advancing towards eleven a.m. A crowd has formed around us, and my nerves have somewhat dissipated. Like they do when I'm performing in front of a crowd of thousands of adoring fans. I start to relax, as I my fingers dance up and down the fretboard effortlessly. As I play, at least ten people, that I can count, are filming me on their phones. Fucking great.*

*I look up and that's when I see her approach. Ruby, my buttercup. Even heavily pregnant, she still looks so beautiful, it brings me to my knees. Her long dark hair cascading down her back, her black and white maxi dress accentuating her barely visible bump and her rocking curves. My lips curve into a grin, as she positions herself in front of me, gently caressing and cradling her stomach. A look of curiosity and apprehension on her face, I wink and the smile she gives me in return makes my heart skip a beat. Jesus, if only you knew, buttercup.*

*I clear my throat and start to sing, with Travis on backing vocals.*

*"Your flaws are perfectly placed, that no one can replace. They are merely pieces that makeup the jigsaw that is you. I see the full picture, and without all those pieces, those rough edges, I wouldn't have you. My jigsaw, my buttercup, my morning pick me up. Perfectly imperfect, my light, my dark, my morning walk in the park. The sun, the moon, I worship at the temple that is you. My jigsaw, my buttercup, my morning pick me up. My beautiful crazy when you're near, my world is hazy, and I see nothing but you. A picture-perfect memory, for me and for you. My jigsaw, my buttercup, my morning pick me up."*

She watches me with rapt attention and the smile on her face floors me. In that moment, she has never been more beautiful and there's no longer an ounce of doubt in my mind, that I want her to be my wife.

I strum the closing chords of the song and the roar of the applause is deafening. I take off my baseball cap and shake my long blonde hair loose, no longer giving a shit if people know that they've just witnessed Flash from Rancid Vengeance sing for the first time in years. I set my guitar down, as people snap photos and politely ask for selfies with me. I oblige the first four or five people, posing happily, but I need to go to her. I step around the dispersing crowd, until I am standing in front of her.

"Hey," I say casually, feeling everything but casual.

"Hey yourself," she says sassily with a quirk of her perfectly plucked eyebrow. Her hazel eyes full of amusement and mischief. I take her hand in mine, fully aware the crowd are regarding the situation unfolding intently.

"Ruby Logan, from day one, I knew in my heart that you were the woman for me, you blinded me with your absolute disregard for romance and I think that's what kept me coming back for more, time and time again. I remember everything about our first night together. You bring me to my fucking knees every time I look at you, you're so beautiful, inside, and out. When we first met, you weren't sure if you were capable, or worthy of love because you hadn't felt it before. Other men who came before me, illegitimised it and it wasn't necessary to make you happy, but since we've been together, you've seen how being in love can make you whole. You complete me, Ruby Logan, simply by just being you."

I kiss the back of her hand and she's sobbing softly, as I pull out a black box from my pocket and drop down on one knee. I open the box and look up at her, as she realises what I'm about to ask. The crowd gasp shortly followed by a *series of flashes. Fucking wonderful, this is going to go viral, before I've had the chance to even tell my family and the boys.*

*"Will you do me the honour of being my wife? Marry me."*

*She sobs harder now, and she nods as the tears flow freely down her cheeks.*

*"Is that a yes? Because I'm gonna look like a dick if it was a no!" I joke, genuinely terrified that I just imagined her saying yes to my proposal. She nods again, practically squealing her answer in my face.*

*"Yes! It was always going to be yes, Jackson Chase!"*

*Relief washes over me, and my heart is pounding a frantic tattoo, as I get to my feet and take her in my arms, feeling her softness pressing against me. She makes me whole; she makes me want to be a better man, she makes me want to be the best husband and the best father I can be. I crush my lips to hers and whisper against her.*

*"Soon-to-be Ruby Chase."*

*She smiles against my lips, and we stand there for long moments, getting lost in each other,*

*and looking forward to our future together.*

# Jax

# Present

My thoughts are interrupted by my phone ringing. The familiar sound of 'Bon Jovi Livin' on a Prayer' blasting out, signalling that my mum is calling. Jamie-Leigh Chase is my beautiful, intelligent mother. Along with my sisters, twins Shay and Skye and my dad Jude, we were the perfect suburban family, a regular modern day Brady Bunch. My mum is a doctor and runs her own private medical practice called *'Chase Medical'* and my dad runs his own building and architecture company called *'J.C Construction.'*

My sister Shay works in P.R and Marketing, she is the wild one of the family. She is very spontaneous and outgoing. She is the life and soul of the party and would make friends in an empty room. Skye is the complete opposite and couldn't be more different. She is bookish, always has her nose in a book and went to university to study Chemistry. She is currently working as an intern for a research company while working towards her PHD. She is shy, reserved, and is quite socially awkward around people she is unfamiliar with.

"Hey mum."

"Handsome Jack, how's my darling boy doing today?" She greets me warmly and I smile as she calls me by the nickname she's had for me since I can remember, and I can hear the quiet concern in her voice. I'm almost thirty-four years old and she still sometimes treats me like I'm five years old. She can't help it, she mothers everyone, I think it's her maternal instinct crossed with the fact she's a doctor. She cares for people every day of her life, I guess it's hard to switch that off.

"It's one of my bad days today, Mum, but I'm okay, I'll get there. How are you and Dad?" I admit and subtly change the subject. She sighs audibly.

"You know you can always pick up the phone, I'm always here for you, sweetheart, I'm never too busy for my first born!" She chuckles softly and I laugh. "I'm good, so is your dad, he's just plodding on, works busy as always, always sick people to tend to, keeps me on my toes. Your sisters are missing

18

their big brother." There's a wistful tone to her voice and it's my turn to chuckle.

"No, they're not, Mum, I love the bones of them, but Shay and Skye don't miss me. They're probably out causing mischief somewhere, and if I know Shay, she's chasing some boy who isn't interested. Skye probably has her nose in a book and is trying to avoid her problems. Besides, they're not kids anymore, neither am I."

"I know, I know, Jack, but it's nice to know I've got kids that care for each other, I know you're on the road, but it doesn't hurt to check in every now and again. How's my gorgeous granddaughter?"

I smile when I think of my mum with Thea. They adore each other in the sweetest way.

"She's really great, thanks." I don't elaborate, because the tennis ball size lump in my throat is threatening to choke me.

"Come on, Jack, out with it, sweetheart, you're not fooling me with that devil may care facade."

My mum is a force of nature, she reminds me a little of Ruby, with her stubbornness and her ability to know what I'm thinking before I've even thought of it. I let out the breath I didn't know I was holding and get up from my seat, avoiding the sympathetic, burning gazes of Sam, Lucas and Brody. I head to the back of the bus and into the bedroom, shutting the door behind me. I drop down onto the king size bed and lay back staring up at the ceiling.

"Is there a time limit on grief, how long should I be feeling this fucking emptiness? Because I'm struggling, mum. Every day is a constant battle and I'm not sure how much longer I can go on like this. Thea asked why I always look so sad, am I really that obvious that even my two-year-old daughter picked up on it?" I let it all out, without stopping for breath and willing the tears not to come.

"Oh Jack, you've been keeping all this bottled up? Why did you call me before, my darling boy? I could have helped, of course there's no time limit on grief, it's like asking how long a piece of string is, there's no definitive answer. Have you been seeing Kalvin?" she asks, curiosity getting the better of her.

Kalvin is my therapist and has been for a year and a half. I spent six months going through each stage of grief, I experienced denial, anger, bargaining, depression, and acceptance, repeatedly. I was spiralling into a deep depression and there was nothing I could do to stop it. My mum knew Kalvin from her time working as a doctor in our local hospital. He's a therapist and specialises in grief counselling. He is five feet ten inches tall, has skin the colour of espresso, kind hazel eyes, he is always so happy he reminds me of a children's TV presenter. He has a collection of dickie bows that Charlie Chaplin would be envious of and I have never seen him without his signature checked shirt and cords. He was so patient when I had my first meeting with him, he helped me make sense of all the mixed-up feelings I was experiencing. He helped me realise that it was normal, and I wasn't the only person to ever feel like this. Our meetings have been far less frequent lately at just once a week because of rehearsals and touring, but I always feel so much lighter after our appointments.

"Yeah, it's only once a week now, and that's only if I'm not on the road, it's difficult to fit in appointments when you're travelling around the country on a bus full of moody rockers." I attempt to joke, but my mum doesn't laugh.

"Have you considered Zoom appointments? It might be beneficial if you can't get to his office." She says calmly and thoughtfully, and I roll my eyes to myself, feeling more than a little out of sorts.

"I'm not one of your patients, Mum, I'm your fucking son!" Out of nowhere, I snap, and instantly regret it as soon as the words are out of my mouth. She doesn't deserve even an ounce of my anger, my sweet, kind, understanding, beautiful mother. I slam the heel of my hand into my forehead, and I relish the sharp shocking pain.

"Look, Mum, I'm sorry, I didn't mean to snap, it's been a bad fucking day, I didn't mean to take it out on you." I apologise genuinely. *I think I'm overdue an appointment with Kalvin.*

"I can't say I understand what you're going through, and I can't imagine what you went through that day, I'm so sorry I wasn't there for you, darling. But I get it, you suffered a loss, a tragic loss and I can't even begin to put into words what you must have felt. You survived, your baby girl survived, be grateful for that, be grateful that you get to wake up every morning to her beautiful smiling face. Ruby never got that chance, she never got to see her daughter."

There is a temporary silence and I think the call has dropped, until I hold the phone away from my ear and see she's still there.

"It hurts to look at her some days because she reminds me so much of Ruby, is that normal? Is it normal to resent my two-year-old daughter because she's the spitting image of her dead mother?" I blurt out in a rush and as soon as I realise what I've said, I slap my hand over my mouth. "*Fuck me*, I'm an awful human being."

I can't help the sob that escapes.

"Hey, it's normal, you are not an awful human being, you're just human! You love that little girl with every piece of that big old heart of yours. Jackson Chase, I couldn't be more bloody proud of you," my mum says with such quiet conviction and compassion, it causes the tears to come thick and fast.

"I can't do this, Mum, I'm terrified I'll end up resenting her and it's not her fault, she didn't ask to be born into this fucking car crash! It makes me feel sick because I love her like I've never loved anyone!" I babble, unable to make sense of the words that are spilling out so easily to the woman who gave birth to me.

"Listen to me, my sweet boy, you are one of the most kind-hearted human beings I know, you take care of that little girl every day without question, and I have no doubt in my mind that you can move past this."

There is a pregnant pause and I brace my elbows on my knees, leaning forward on the edge of the bed.

"I wish I'd been warned before, I wish people had told me being a dad wasn't always gonna be all smiles & laughter. Being a parent isn't fucking easy, there are days when I genuinely think I've failed as a father. There are days where I just want to run away and just be me again. Plain old Jax Chase, without a care in the world. I'd never change being a dad, ever, but I do wish I wasn't just seen as daddy. Don't get me wrong, I wouldn't change her for anything, I wouldn't, because she's the best thing that's ever happened to me, but she literally terrifies me. She's still this helpless little human who's depending on me to shape her into a decent person and some days, I'm not quite sure I'm fucking capable of it, Mum. I'm scared," I admit and it feels somewhat cathartic to say it out loud.

"There isn't a handbook of how to be a parent, it doesn't come with instructions and even if it did, no one would stick to them. It's trial and error, do you think your father and me knew what we were doing when you came along? Absolutely bloody not! We hadn't got the first clue of how to raise a baby, we spent the first few months walking around like zombies! What I'm trying to say is, don't be afraid to ask for help," my mum reassures me, and, in that moment, I feel confident that everything is going to be just fine.

I say my goodbyes to my mum with the promise that I'll see her when we're back home. I hang up the phone and quickly dial the number I need before I talk myself out of it. It rings three times before the call connects.

"Good morning, Kalvin Jay-Johnson speaking, how can I help you?" he greets me professionally and I clear my throat.

"Hey Kalvin, it's Jax... ummm... Jackson Chase." I stumble over my words, suddenly feeling overcome with nerves. *What the fuck is wrong with you, Chase. Get it together.*

"Ah, Jack, I wondered how long it would be before you called! It's been a while, mate!" he says brightly.

"Yeah, I know, sorry about that, it's been a whirlwind, you know how it is, touring non-stop, the life of a rock star!" I joke with a small, insincere laugh.

"I'm long overdue an appointment, can we schedule something in the diary? I'm touring currently, but I'm willing to do Zoom meetings?" I inquire hopefully and there is a momentary pause.

"Sure, I can do tomorrow? Say one p.m. for an hour?"

I briefly squeeze my eyes shut.

"Can we do two hours?" I ask reluctantly.

"That bad, huh?"

I I exhaled involuntarily, surprised by the deep-seated burden I didn't realise I was carrying. It was heavy and I chose to bear the weight of it alone.

"You have no idea," I state vaguely.

"Okay, that's all booked in, one p.m. for two hours, I'll send you the invite and we can go from there."

I run my spare hand through my hair.

"Thanks, Kalvin. I'll speak to you tomorrow."

I hang up, feeling the grief weighing down on me, hopeful that two hours with my therapist will help ease that crippling burden.

# 4

## Jax

Sometimes the monotony of day-to-day life appears pointless. My morning runs with Lucas, giving Thea her breakfast, doing our daily sound checks, rehearsing with the boys. Everything is laden with these demon voices, they taint every experience. I have begun to understand that the first step, is acknowledging that they are real and accepting the help of others. I know I am not alone and that is the first step to healing, or so I'm told.

We're staying in a hotel tonight, which is a welcome change to sleeping in the pods on the bus. We have some down time before rehearsals start this afternoon, I have set up my iPad on the dressing table and made myself comfortable on the lavish sofa in my suite. I click the Zoom link that Kalvin had emailed me and there he was, his chair was a foot further from mine than usual and his smiling face comes into view. He pushes his stylish black rimmed glasses further up the bridge of his nose and leans forward to adjust the view.

"Jack! How are you? It's good to see you, mate! It's been a while!" he gushes and I find myself smiling right along with him. His charisma and charm is magnetic, almost infectious.

"It has! How are you?"

He cocks his eyebrow and his eyes flick downwards.

"Is there a reason why you avoided my question?" he asks curiously.

"The truth is, no I'm not okay, there isn't a day that goes by that I wake up and feel... normal. Even after all this time, the grief cripples me and I hate myself for it. I can't carry on pretending everything's fine because it isn't, it never will be," I admit, my voice thick with unshed tears.

"Why do you hate yourself? Do you think that there's a time limit on grief? Because you're very much mistaken, it takes as long as it takes, Jack. It could take two years, it could take twenty years, each individual is different.

We all handle grief in different ways, there is no right or wrong way" he explains, pushing his glasses further up the bridge of his nose.

"I'm struggling, Kalvin, I'm not sure how much longer I can keep up the act without cracking under the pressure. I snapped at my mum yesterday, my mum of all fucking people! She didn't deserve that; she didn't do anything to warrant me blowing up like that. She's amazing, she's selfless, compassionate and puts everyone else's needs before her own. I threw my grief right in her face and took out my emotions on the only person that is equipped to understand. I'm a fucking selfish prick because I couldn't get a handle on it!"

I rake my hand viciously through my hair and lean back heavily on the sofa, trying desperately to disguise the tremble in my hands.

"It was never meant to be like this, it's like life is still moving forward at a million miles an hour, but I'm still stuck in the moment she left me... I miss the future I was supposed to have with her and our daughter."

I steeple my hands underneath my chin and my ring glints in the natural light that seeps through the floor length window.

"You still wear the ring she bought you," Kalvin says and it's more of a statement than a question, I nod and look down at the ring on my middle finger on my left hand. A simple white gold band with an inscription engraved on the inside, the co-ordinates of where I proposed at Brent Cross Tube Station "51.5768 N 0.2134"

I twirl it idly around my finger, feeling the cool metal against my skin. I let out a deep sigh and there is a brief but comfortable silence.

"Recently I've thought about the possibility of meeting someone else." I look up, meeting the curious eyes of my therapist on camera. He nods and offers me a smile.

"You said thought about? And how do you feel about that?" His voice void of judgment, which I'm grateful for.

"It makes me feel like I'm betraying Ruby. She was it for me, I never even contemplated a future without her in it and the next woman I meet won't be her. I'm terrified that every woman I meet from now on, I'll try to look for her in every single one."

I feel the familiar tennis ball sized lump begin to form in my throat and I'm temporarily rendered mute.

"Guilt is the strongest emotion in situations like this, but it's normal to feel like that. Only you can determine if you're ready to meet someone, it's not uncommon. Like I said, each individual is different, the right thing for one person, isn't necessarily the right thing for another," he explains and I swallow hard, almost relieved. Our session continues for the full two hours, consistent back and forth between us. I end the call feeling lighter and optimistic that there is light of this long, dark tunnel.

\*\*\*

After yet another epic show, I wake with a start, sitting bolt upright, thick with perspiration, the nightmare clinging to me like a cloak of absolute sorrow and desolation. *Fuck my life.* As I lie in my king-size bed, staring up at the ceiling, my heartbeat thundering in my chest and the silence fucking taunting me. I swing my legs out of bed and pad across the soft, plush carpet over to the drink's cabinet. I pour myself a glass of brandy, my hands trembling violently. The clinking of glass on glass, as I try to stop the liquid from spilling. The only light coming into the room is the moonlight from the floor to ceiling windows. I lift the glass to my lips and take a long, shaky sip, the nightmare still fresh in my mind. I'm damp with sweat, as I gulp the brandy down in one swallow, the warmth instantly settling in my stomach, causing it to roil. I slam the glass down noisily on the neighbouring table and rush to the bathroom, just about making it to the toilet in time for my guts to vacate.

I lean back heavily against the wall, pressing my back to the cold tiles to cool my over-heated skin. I squeeze my eyes shut, as I feel my mind start to spiral out of control. The grief overwhelms me, the guilt all but drowns me and I'm exhausted, but I know I won't be able to sleep, not now. I rest my head briefly on my forearm and tear off some toilet paper to wipe my mouth. I manage to get to my feet and flush the toilet, heading across to the sink, briefly catching sight of my reflection in the mirror above it. I'm almost grey in colour, my skin clammy, with dark, bruise-like circles underneath my eyes and my blonde hair dull, flat and lifeless.

"*Fuck me*, you look like absolute dog shit, Chase," I mutter to myself, as I reach for my toothbrush, turn on the tap, apply some toothpaste and brush my teeth. I spit into the sink and gargle with some mouthwash, as I walk barefoot back into the open lounge area of my hotel suite. I pick up my phone seeing that it's one forty-two a.m., I open my messaging app and tap out a text.

*You still up?*

*J*

I press send and moments later, I receive a reply.

*Wide awake, brother.*

*Gimme 5, but drink?*

*L*

I smile at Lucas's response, as I get dressed into a pair of loose black jogging bottoms, a grey hoodie and I jam my feet into my black Converse. I grab my phone and my room key, stepping out into the long, plush carpeted corridor. We've hired out the whole floor for the night, so it's just us and our entourage. I see two of our security team stationed at intervals down the corridor, nodding to Trey and Kai as I make my way to Lucas' room. I round the corner and stop in my tracks, as I see Lucas standing in the doorway, leaning into the doorjamb and Nick Slade standing outside.

Nicholas Slade is a British actor, and he is one of the U.K's *hottest* exports in Hollywood. He started off acting in low budget Brit flicks and moved to the States, where Damien Valentine discovered him. Nick is also considered 'The British George Clooney'; he is one of Hollywood's richest, most eligible bachelors and has had many encounters with Lucas in the past fifteen years. They have been super careful and secretive about their on/ off relationship, but of late they have both been extremely careless, meeting in public places where they could possibly be caught out and cause a PR nightmare for Tate.

I observe their exchange from a distance, but I instantly notice the off-the-charts chemistry between the two of them. Both men are the same height at around six-foot-tall, Nick is extremely muscular, has lean, narrow hips with dark brown eyes. His dark brown hair, usually neat and styled is mussed, sticking up in all directions. Nick leans in to kiss Lucas on the lips, but he quickly turns his head and Nick ends up kissing him on cheek instead. I see Nick visibly balk at Lucas' cool reaction, as he tucks his hand into his pocket, turns and walks away, leaving Lucas staring after him. I choose that moment to make my presence known and as I approach, Lucas doesn't meet my eyes.

"Don't, just fucking don't," he grinds out curtly and I salute.

"I wasn't gonna say a word, man."

He steps out of the doorway, and I head into the room, Lucas close behind as he shuts the door with a loud click. He picks up a glass of clear liquid and hands me a glass of whiskey. We both take long sips in silence for a few moments.

"So, you can't sleep either?" he implores and I shake my head.

"No, had another nightmare, that's all," I confess and Lucas nods.

"Wanna' talk about it?" He downs his drink in one large gulp and I smirk.

"Probably about as much as you want to talk about Slade," I express wryly and Lucas cocks his eyebrow, pouring himself another drink.

"Touché!"

I place my glass down on the white gloss side table and face him.

"You know he's in love with you, don't you?" I state matter-of-factly and Lucas finishes his drink in one swallow, slamming his glass down next to mine a little more forcefully, grimacing at the afterburn.

"I think I'm in love with him too, I have been for fuckin' years! But it would never work out between us, I'm too jealous and Slade is just... Slade! He's charming, he's everything I could ever want in a partner, but I-I just can't. Plus, I've got the bands' reputation to think of, what would the fans say if I came out as gay? I've been practically lying to them the whole time!"

Lucas briefly squeezes his eyes shut.

"Fuck our reputation! If the fans don't accept you for who you are, then they don't deserve the right to call themselves fans!" My voice level and filled with pure conviction.

"You deserve to be happy, Luke, we've always known about you and Slade, but we chose not to make a big deal of it, because it's not our business and we know how private you are."

He looks at me and pours himself another drink.

"I keep parts of myself hidden to protect myself, I had a rough start in life, rougher than most, it's self-preservation. I dunno it's always felt so... natural and so... right with Nick, ya know? But you didn't come here to listen to me whine on about my shit!" he declares flippantly with a dismissive wave of his hand. I finish my drink and he instantly pours me another, gesturing towards the cream sectional sofa in front of the matching cream drapes. We both sit down, and Lucas puts the bottles down on the table.

"So, shoot," he exclaims abruptly.

"What is there to say? I had another nightmare, it's the same one as before. The one that fucking haunts me on a nightly basis, I'm back in that chapel, Ruby's sobbing and I'm trying to calm her down, when deep down I'm fucking terrified. There's so much noise, so much...carnage, there are bullets flying everywhere and the next minute, I've been hit and I'm collapsing to the floor. I wake up at the exact same moment, every time, it's so vivid, it's like I'm back there all over again."

I run my hand through my hair and down my drink in one swallow with the other hand.

"I wake up drenched in sweat, we were all there on that fateful day, but we never fucking talk about it! Why do we never talk about it, Luke?"

I raise my voice a few decibels and take another long sip of my drink.

"Because we lost so many people that day, man. Every single one of us suffered and gained a scar or life changing injury." He shudders, as if ridding himself of an unwanted thought.

"Something you want to share, mate?" I ask with narrow eyes and come to the realisation that this is the first time we've had this conversation since that day. He downs his drink in one swallow and takes a breath before he speaks.

"I wasn't in the Chapel that day, I was in the bathroom banging Slade."

My mouth drops open at his admission. *Fuck me, I was not expecting that bombshell.*

"What the fuck?!" I say with an incredulous tone to my voice. "What the actual fuck, Luke?!" I repeat, as he drags his hand roughly through his hair.

"I know, I never told anyone what happened. The guilt has been eating me up from the inside out, I was getting my rocks off while my family were being mindlessly slaughtered by some psycho bitch with a grudge!" he snaps.

"I'll never be able to apologise for that, I'll never be able to take it back! How do you think that makes me fuckin' feel, Jax? It felt like I was that scared seven-year-old boy again who hid away in a laundry hamper. I felt helpless trapped in that toilet cubicle with Nick and rather than come out and help we stayed put like fuckin' cowards!" He jabs his thumbs viciously into his chest and a tear slides down his cheek. *Fucking hell, listening to him recount his story, I should feel anger towards him, but my heart hurts for him.* He has some unresolved issues from his childhood that have followed him into adulthood, and I can't imagine what he went through.

"It makes me feel sick! Why do you think I've never told you about any of this before? Because I'm fucking ashamed! I'm ashamed that I couldn't keep my dick in my pants, and I chose him over you! It disgusts me! It's just another fucking reason why me and Slade will never work out."

He leans forward bracing his elbows on his knees and for the first time in fifteen years, I see Lucas Landon sob.

# 5

# Zeppelin

As I sit at my desk in my office, in the comfort of my cosy, but chic, one bedroom flat, overlooking Portobello Road Market. I am wearing my favourite pair of soft, if a bit ratty, grey pyjama bottoms and slouchy top, with my two favourite men, *Ben, and Jerry,* for company. My fingers hover over the keyboard, but I can't seem to get them to co-operate with my brain. The words usually flow so easily, but not today.

The first thing you should know about me, I'm an author. I've been an author for six years, after I quit my job as a Hotel Receptionist, for a well-known, mid-tier, hotel chain. I'd had enough of rude guests, who would act like the world owed them a living, the mundane monotony of unpredictable shift patterns and arsehole bosses, who thought it was ok to talk down to you and give one person the workload meant for three people. I had always been creative and after the first day of being officially unemployed, I started writing my first novel, '*A Perfect Illusion*', centred on a brooding billionaire CEO and a troubled photographer. It took me six months, lots of sleepless nights and coffee by the bucket full, but I finally completed a book that I wanted to read. I approached endless publishers and after what seemed like a series of never-ending rejections, I finally got picked up by an indic publishing house called '*Raven Rebellion Publishing*' and the rest, as they say, is history.

I write under the pseudonym *Z.J Williams;* I was catapulted into the world of erotic fiction and I'm somewhat of a rock star to my readers. My writing affords me the luxury of working part-time as a magazine columnist, for *Core Magazine*. My boss, Amy Lightman-Benedict supports my writing career and is flexible with my hours spent at the office. I mostly work remotely and go into the office once a week to check in with my boss and my work colleagues. I frequently attend book signings and interact with my readers, as much and as often as I can. They say everyone has at least one book in them and I'm currently writing my ninth novel.

The second thing you should know about me, I love music and musical theatre. In particular, country music and as *Luke Bryan Country Girl (Shake It for Me)* blasts from my laptop speakers, I can't seem to connect with Dustin Heath. A dark, but sexy, tortured, ex-alcoholic, country singer, who in a desperate bid to connect with his music, instead connects with a feisty, choreographer, called Montana Silver. She takes him on a journey of self-discovery and becomes his muse, inspiring him to write his best album yet, in his decade-long career in the country music industry.

Montana is the me I aspire to be, she's sassy, a natural flirt and she has the ability to wrap men around her little finger. I, on the other hand, I'm destined to be single. I've been single for five years and my vibrator is the only action I've seen in almost three years. *I'm the eternal spinster.* I'm sad to say, I live vicariously through my fictional characters. *Don't judge me.*

I take off my glasses and rest them on the desk, rubbing the bridge of my nose, to keep the headache I can feel manifesting behind my eyes at bay. My dog leaps up and settles himself on my lap. My Golden Retriever, Labrador cross, Jericho. My ex-boyfriend, Abel, bought him for me as a Christmas gift, after we celebrated our first year together. Jericho understands me better than any human could. He has been by my side when I felt like I had no one, he's been there through the good times and the bad times. He's been a source of therapy and he has aided my emotional and physical well-being; I wouldn't be without him.

He's currently one of two men in my life. The second man being, my gay best friend, Rian. Rian St-James is two years older than me at thirty-two and he's a hairdresser. He used to be a performer on cruise ships and did occasional stints in the West End in touring shows such as, *We Will Rock You, Rock of Ages, Kinky Boots, The Bodyguard* and *Chicago*. He had to retire early because of a cartilage injury in his knee. He's originally from Wales and we met in line at Starbucks on my first morning in London. We bonded over our mutual love for our morning coffee and musical theatre. We found out that coincidentally we lived in the same building, in Notting Hill. We've known each other for five years, but it feels like we've known each other all our lives. I don't make friends easily and I like to keep my circle small. I'm grateful to have him in my life, he's been there when I had no one and I'll be eternally indebted to him for that. I idly stroke Jericho's fur as my phone vibrates, and I find myself smiling when I see Rian's name flash up.

*Heyyy girl!*

*This old queen is bored!*

*Fancy a cheeky glass of wine (or seven) down the road??*

I roll my eyes and smile to myself at his message, which is Rian's code word for wanting to go on the pull. We live down the road from a pub called The King's Arms, which we frequent more often than I'd like. I'm not one for dancing and clubbing, give me a quiet drink in a homely, traditional pub any day of the week.

*Hey!*

*Writer's block driving me insane!*

*Night in with Jericho, I think!*

*Rain check?*

I press send and my phone instantly starts ringing. I swipe the screen and answer.

"Come on, Zep! Fuck that writer's block! A cheeky glass of wine, or seven might help get those creative juices flowing! What sounds better, a night in with a tortured cowboy, or a night out with your GBFF? Come on, say yes, please! You know you want to!" he pleads and I laugh.

"Okay, you've twisted my arm! You big queen! And FYI, he's a country singer, not a cowboy!" I quip and Rian laughs.

"Whatevs, babe! Same diff! Get your cute arse dressed, I bet you're wearing those ratty pyjama bottoms!"

I bite my lip and look down at my comfy, grey pyjama bottoms. *He knows me so well.*

"I take it by the silence I'm right, see, I know you better than you know yourself, Zeppelin Jade Williams, now get bloody dressed! That's an order! I'll be down in twenty! Give you time to make yourself look like the Goddess that we both know you are! Lots of love!"

He hangs up. Maybe he's right, a glass of wine might help the writer's block. *At least that's what I'm telling myself.*

I manage to grab a shower, apply natural make-up and I'm in the middle of styling my short, blonde hair, when Jericho starts barking. I look up as Rian breezes in, without knocking. Jericho starts wagging his tail wildly, as Rian starts petting his head.

"I arrived just in time, girl!"

His dark brown hair is perfectly styled into a side quiff, which shows off his undercut. He is wearing blue ripped jeans, a white v-neck t-shirt and a black blazer with the sleeves casually rolled up. His golden tan completes his look for tonight. I roll my eyes at how put together he looks when I feel just the opposite. He halts me styling my hair and takes over, expertly styling and curling my hair. Rian is an extremely brilliant hairdresser, he works and runs his own salon called '*Simply Hair by Rian.*' He is fortunate enough to still have a lot of contacts in the West End and he sometimes works on touring shows and occasionally with some of the hottest TV, movie, and music stars.

*\*\*\**

The Kings Arms is a traditional English pub. The building itself is old, it oozes history and charm. It looks like an extension of someone's living room, with its dark red and green patterned carpeting, which looks like it has seen better days. It has textured walls which are freshly painted and an odd mixture of ornaments, which are knick knacks that you might find at a jumble sale or in a charity shop. I feel eternally sorry for the poor person in charge of dusting all of those trinkets.

The setting is unpretentious where everyone is welcome. As soon as you walk through the door the landlord greets us with a smile and has our drinks poured. A large glass of white wine for me and a pint of Dark Fruit cider for Rian. It is a little busier for a Monday evening, with a few of the locals participating in a darts match. They nod to us in greeting and in return, I offer a smile and a small wave. We sit in our usual spot towards the back on the soft, dark brown buttery leather sofa that looks like it has seen better days. We take off our coats and settle down with our drinks. Rian crosses his one leg over the other and half turns his body towards me.

"Sooo... what's been happening on Planet Zeppelin?" he asks a little too enthusiastically and I take a long glug of my wine before I answer. He chuckles softly. "That bad, huh?"

I swallow and run my finger idly around the rim of the glass.

"I shouldn't complain really, the book is coming on great, the column is attracting more and more readers each week. Amy's looking at getting me back in the office more than once a week to meet the demand and she's pitching the idea of a weekly podcast. It couldn't be better, but sometimes I feel like, is this it? Ya know?" I say with a shrug and Rian reaches for my hand.

"You know I'm just a phone call and a flight of stairs away, right? All that time stuck in your own head, it's not good for you, Zep. You need to start getting yourself out there, have you even thought of trying... you know, maybe meeting someone?" he states carefully, he knows my stance on dating. A man would just be a distraction and I could do without distractions when I have a book deadline to meet. I'm about to speak when Rian holds his finger up to stop me from continuing.

"Yeah, yeah, distractions, yada, yada! But hear me out, you're a beautiful, intelligent young woman, you've got so much going for you, it just seems... a fucking waste!"

He gestures his hands up and down towards my body. I take another long glug of wine and I'm going to need lots more if this is how the rest of the night is going to go. *Chin fucking chin.*

***

I knew letting Rian talk me into drinking Sambuca shots was a bad idea. I'm lying in bed and the room is fucking spinning. *Fuck me, I'm sloshed.* One redeeming quality of being a self-employed author is I make my own hours, so I don't have to worry about having to be up early for work. Rian is staying over, he stays over on regular occasions and he's lying in bed next to me, softly snoring. I lie still, willing the room to stop spinning and soon, I'm a slave to sleep.

*Breathe, you are going to be okay. Breathe and remember that you've been in this place before and you've survived it. Breathe and know you can survive this too. I know it feels unbearable right now, but just keep breathing and always keep fighting.*

This is my mantra when I wake-up screaming and soaked with sweat, with the stench of burning flesh in my nostrils. My stomach roils and I feel like I need to throw up. *Fucking hell, not again.* This is the fourth time since last week. Rian gathers me in his arms and holds me, pushing my damp, sweat-drenched hair behind my ears.

"Shh, it's going to be okay, I'm here, you're safe, babe, I've got you."

He soothes softly, as Jericho comes bounding in my bedroom. He barks once and climbs up into my bed, as if he knows it's what I need. He curls up in my lap, practically pushing Rian aside.

"Alright, buddy, I know when I'm not wanted," he grumbles and I chuckle softly, as he gets to his feet.

"Don't go, please, Ri, I can't be on my own right now," I plead softly, as he settles back down, pulling me to him and dragging the covers over us. Jericho adjusts himself and resumes his place by my side.

"Do you want to talk about it, honey?" Rian asks curiously, I shake my head and tell him what I always tell him.

"Not tonight, maybe some other time," I state quietly, he nods in understanding and kisses me on the forehead.

"Night, night, Zeppelin."

"Night, night, Ri, love ya."

"Right back atcha', gorgeous."

We say good night and turn out the light, but I lie awake for the longest time. Even though I've been drinking, I've never been soberer. My mind active with novel ideas and character names.

I listen in the dark, as Rian's breathing evens out. When I know he's fallen asleep, I swing my legs out of bed and pad out into the living room, feeling a little more sober. I grab a glass of water to soothe my dry throat and gulp it down. I grab my notebook, settle down on the sofa, pulling the blanket made of old concert t-shirts that my nanna made for me around my shoulders and Jericho climbs up and gets himself comfortable at my feet. Sometimes I curse myself for being so creative, and other times, I wouldn't have it any other way. I always keep my notebook beside my bed, but for some reason, tonight was a rare exception.

*'Some days, I feel everything all at once. Other days, I feel nothing at all, and I don't know what's worse, drowning beneath the waves, or dying from thirst.'*

I idly scribble in my notebook, and I've never written truer words. *Dustin Heath, why do you understand me more than most men?* After what seems like hours of meaningless scrawl, my eyes start to feel scratchy. I'm exhausted, but sleep evades me, as I lay my head back on the sofa. I start to think how long I've been single; five years is a long time and looking back, it feels like it was a whole other life. My heart breaks all over again, when I think of the Abel, I fell in love with all those years ago. I try desperately to push that thought down, as my eyes start to feel heavy and soon, I drift off.

***

I'm woken the next morning by the smell of coffee, a pounding head from far too much wine and the sound of Rian humming softly to *John Mayer Perfectly Lonely*. I must have made it back into bed at some point in the night, as I find myself stretching out like a cat in my Queen size bed. He steps into my room looking like something you'd see in Vogue magazine. Even at this ungodly hour, he still manages to look like a million dollars, in his designer, white and baby pink floral Ted Baker lounge wear set and matching slippers. He has my favourite mug in his hand, which reads *'Careful or you'll end up in my novel!'*

"Mornin' sleepy head." Rian smiles and hands me a steaming cup of the good stuff. I take it hastily from him and instantly feel the warmth around my hands. *Pure bliss.*

"Are you ever going to tell me the full story about what happened?" he asks, regarding me intently and I shift my gaze to the floor. Moving to Notting Hill was meant to be a fresh start for me, I didn't want the past haunting me here. But it haunts me on a nightly basis, proving that it doesn't give a shit where I am. It still plagues me, and it keeps me awake every single night. I pat the space next to me and he settles down, with his feet tucked underneath him, as I begin to purge myself of my past.

# 6

## Zeppelin

They say a problem shared, is a problem halved. As I allow the tears to flow down my cheeks, I start to tell Rian the ugly truth of my past.

"My mum, Genesis, died while she was giving birth to me. My dad, Ronnie raised me on his own. It wasn't easy for either of us, but we were a team, we were the two musketeers. There wasn't a day that went by that he didn't miss her, they were childhood sweethearts, together from the age of fourteen. I guess it was kind of easier for me to deal with, because I never met her, but my dad, he knew her his entire life, she was his whole world. He didn't cope well, but he did his best. He held down a job as a security supervisor and managed to juggle raising me too. I always had food in my belly and clothes on my back. We lived in Southend back then, in this close-knit community, where everyone knew each other. It could be annoying that everyone knew our business, but it felt...safe. He used to drink, a lot, I'd find him passed out on the floor most mornings. I'd just go to school and pretend everything was normal. It went on like that for years, but he got worse as the years went on. He got sacked from his job and after that, I practically raised myself."

Rian squeezes my hand in a gesture of reassurance, and I smile softly.

"It was on my fifteenth birthday when I found him, hanging from a rope in the garage of our house, he took the fucking cowards' way out. I had just turned fifteen and suddenly, I was on my own. I resented him for years, how fucking dare he leave me all alone to fend for myself. Luckily, my nanna and grandad, Pru and Jimmy, who lived in North Finchley at the time, we were so close growing up, they took me in. I stayed with them, until I was eighteen, then I went to university to study Journalism for four years, graduated with honours and got a job in a hotel in the city. That's when I met Abel."

Rian cocks his perfectly plucked eyebrow.

"I knew it! There's always a man involved!" he says dreamily and I chuckle softly, as he nods for me to continue.

"He was... everything, the perfect man, literally. He was one of those old-fashioned gentlemen, who believed in holding doors open. The only problem was, he was sort of... famous." I bite my lip and Rian's eyes widen, he cups his hands over his mouth. *He's a bit of celebrity gossip whore.*

"*Shut the front door,* really, Zep? You bagged yourself a famous boyfriend?" he shrieks and I nod, almost nervously.

"Don't sound so surprised!" I say mock-offended and Rian hi-fives me.

"How famous are we talking here, baby girl?" he presses, bouncing with anticipation and I avoid his gaze.

"Abel Creed from The Poison Puppets," I confess and Rian's jaw drops to the floor.

"*Jesus' fucking Christ,* the band who..."

I swallow back the lump in my throat and nod.

"The band who all died in a boating accident, yeah, the very same. Him and his band were staying at the hotel I used to work at, that's how we met. It was intense between Abel and me from the very start. It was so full on, he pursued me relentlessly, it was such a whirlwind, but he was so charming, loving, and romantic. I saw past that, which you kind of have to when you're dating a famous rock star. He was fun and sweet in the beginning; I enjoyed being with him, the thrill of the chase and the way he made me feel when we were together. It was like nothing or no one else mattered, just us, there in the moment. But towards the end, he allowed the fame to swallow him up. It got so bad I didn't even recognise him anymore, he wasn't the man I fell in love with, he was a total stranger."

I blink back tears, as Rian reaches for my hand.

Abel Joshua Creed was the blue-eyed devil that tore my heart out and presented it to me on a silver fucking platter for all to see. We were together for four years and in those four years, I watched him go from a genuine, charming, yet loving man, to someone I didn't even recognise. The fame swallowed him up and spat him out, he didn't care who he had to tread on, or fuck, to get to the top. He pissed a lot of people off and pushed away those close to him. Even though I was the only one who stuck around when everyone else abandoned him, he still managed to push me away and destroyed our relationship in the process.

Abel died, along with the four of his fellow band members, in a fire, onboard a luxury yacht and I was there. I was one of three sole survivors, the band and their entourage perished somewhere in the Tyrrhenian Sea. To this day how the fire started and events leading up to it are still unknown and even though I was present at the time, it's hazy and still haunts me. I have no idea how I survived; I just know I'm grateful for my life being spared.

His mum Aubrey, his dad Robert and his twin brother Carston, all blamed me for Abel's death. I was the scarlet woman, who was unworthy and wasn't good enough for their precious boy. The truth was, I was just as much of a victim as Abel was and I've never talked to anyone about it, only my therapist.

"He'd just finished a European tour on the night of the accident, Abel invited me to the gig. I took time off work to go with him, I was the rock star girlfriend. It was so glamourous; like something off a movie. Him and the boys from the band were staying on this luxury super yacht in **Marina di Capri, in Italy.** The bands manager had called in a favour from some rich, billionaire guy he knew. Abel asked me to join them, and he got drunk, we argued, and he started shouting about how I was holding him back and forcing him to settle down, he told me he felt trapped. I burst into tears, and I started yelling about how I felt he chose his career over me. He called me pathetic and needy, then he stormed off, telling me it was over. I ended up chatting to one of the other band members girlfriends, I can't remember her name. We chatted, we did shots, and we were so drunk. I passed out drunk and was woken by the smell of smoke. The next thing I knew, the yacht was on fire, and I was trapped, I couldn't get out, I was fucking terrified."

I start to sob, and the tears keep coming. The yacht was anchored in Marina di Capri and investigators believe the fire started on the upper deck, but how is still unknown. The Italian Fire Investigation Unit 'Nucleo Investigativo Antincendio' (The NIA) tried to figure out what sparked the blaze. They completed their work, without ever finding the true cause and pieces of the boat were sent to labs for testing, which came back as inconclusive.

"I never saw him again and I never got to say sorry for all the horrible things I said, Ri."

He pulls me against him and strokes my hair, as I continue to sob. Every time I think about Abel, I can't help the guilt that devours me whole. He died thinking I hated him and that is the thought that dominates my every waking hour. That thought, stops me from moving on with my life, the guilt crushes me to my very core.

"It's okay, shhh, none of this is your fault, Zep. You must know that? You're such a pure soul, you're here living on your own, living in your head, living through those fictional characters of yours. Maybe you're just barely surviving, but you're here, and you're whole. You can't be half a person; you can't be half a heart. If you lose someone in the wreckage of love, you are still here, as you were before it all. Abel just happened to be the one you lost in that wreckage. You were both young and reckless, he could have come back and apologised, but it was his choice. He should be held accountable for his own actions; he knew you loved him and it's on him if he didn't see that."

I listen to his words, and for the first time since I met Rian, his wise words make sense. I'd never thought of it that way before and God bless my best friend for making me see that, after four years of punishing myself.

The Poison Puppets were a big deal, and their sad demise was high profile. I was hounded pretty much twenty-four-seven for a while, but I didn't come out of it unscathed. I endured months of skin grafts, due to the third degrees burns I suffered, but I made it out of there alive and I'll be forever grateful for being spared that day.

Abel's family, his mum, dad and his twin brother all blame me for his death because they didn't believe the official conclusion. They hired their own private investigator and they were certain I had something to do with it. They dragged me over the coals for months, while I was recovering from my injuries. When the private investigator couldn't prove anything, he came up with the same conclusion, but they weren't content with that. Five years on, they're still hellbent on proving I had something to do with their precious son's death. They're convinced I have blood on my hands and it makes me feel sick that they would think that of me.

"It's impossible to become empty when you're already whole, Zep. I have faith in you, and you should start having some faith too, in life and in love. Not all men are Abel Creed, you have to believe that it's been four years, babe, it's time you moved on."

He squeezes my hands in a gentle gesture of reassurance. At that very moment, I start to think that maybe there is life after Abel? Can I really get back out there and start dating again after all this time? *The answer to that is yes, yes, I fucking can.*

# 7

## Jax

To the fans and to the public, I'm Jax Chase, blonde hair, brown eyed, boy next door, guitarist from Rancid Vengeance. To the boys, I'm friend, brother, confidant. To Thea, I'm daddy, her hero, her whole world. I'm so many different personas, yet I couldn't be lonelier. World at my feet, women on tap—*literally*. But I feel so fucking alone.

It feels like so much time has passed since Ruby was taken from me, but in reality, it's been no time at all. It's like the world has moved on and I'm still in the same place as I was two years ago, standing still, never moving on. I wake up every morning on autopilot and I just exist, I don't live anymore, the only person I live for, is my daughter. She'll never know how hard it's been for me to raise her, every time I look at her, it hurts physically, she reminds me so much of her mother. There have been nights where I've just wanted to just leave and never look back, and I've never felt more guilty. She deserves the universe and more and I intend to raise her the right way.

I had spent two years, going over what happened in Vegas in minute detail, and I'd spent countless hours talking about it with Kalvin. I know in my heart of hearts; it wasn't my fault and I know there was nothing I could have done to save her. She was on borrowed time as soon as that bullet pierced her skull. We all suffered that day, we lost people closest to us and our lives were turned upside down, never to be the same again. The newspapers and the press considered us all *"lucky to be alive."* But I don't see it as lucky at all, I see it as just existing. It wasn't lucky, it was a sick, twisted blood bath and every single one of us who were there that day suffered and continue to suffer. I still wake up drenched in sweat with the metallic smell of blood permeating my nostrils, the stench so strong, I can't breathe. The memory, so strong and vivid, takes me right back to that day.

# Jax

# Past

*Hospitals are full of people who are having the best day of their life, the worst day of their life, the first day of their life, or the last day of their life. As Ruby had the last day of her life, our daughter had her first. Life is unpredictable, it can change in the blink of an eye. Everything that keeps you alive, can cease to exist within seconds. The life that you've been building, can collapse when you least expect it, and it can catapult you into the pits of pure despair that you can't see a light at the end of that long fucking tunnel.*

*The blood was pounding in my ears, my heart thudding violently in my chest and my hands trembling. My feet were tingling, and my vision was distorted, as if I were looking through a fish-eye lens. This isn't real, any minute now I'm going to wake up and Ruby is going to tell me this is all a dream. I blink slowly in a desperate attempt to try to focus on my surrounding. My eyes scanning the room for something, or someone familiar when they land on Remy, Ruby's older brother. His face pale, sombre and tear-stained, he looks older than his thirty-three years.*

*"Jackson?"*

*I don't register him calling out to me, until I look up and find him regarding me with expectant eyes.*

*"Jackson?" he repeats with a sniff, limping over to me, leaning heavily onto a crutch. I'm rendered mute, I'm so overcome with grief, the words "I'm sorry, Mr Chase, but your fiancée didn't make it" still ringing in my ears. He rests his hand on my bicep and my eyes follow to where his hand is resting. He has dried blood under his fingernails, my stomach roils at the sight, and I can feel bile rising in my throat. Unexpectedly, I vomit unceremoniously all over the floor. I stagger back, wiping the vomit from my mouth with the back of my hand, a tear slipping down my cheek.*

*"Jackson?" Remy says again and I lift my finger up to halt him. A look of concern marring his features, which remind me so much of Ruby. My heart slams against my rib cage and I shake my head vehemently, silently pleading with him to stay quiet.*

*"I'm so sorry." He chokes on a sob, as I back out of the room to a gut-wrenching wail of despair.*

*I'm in shock, I'm dazed, and I can't comprehend the sick, twisted turn of events. As much as I crave solitude, I can't be alone right now, I just can't. I have to find Sam, the boys, anyone who feels familiar. I make my way down the corridor subconsciously, with no particular destination in mind. My head feels like it's going to explode, and my heart fucking breaks that little bit more with each step I take. I see Kai up ahead, head and shoulders above the doctors and nurses who pass him. He is standing outside the glass windowed door, and he nods curtly as I approach.*

*"Jax."*

*He greets me, but I ignore him, managing to swing the door open and almost falling through it. I can't fucking do this. Marlowe manages to catch me before I hit the floor and strangled sob that rips from deep within me, takes me by complete surprise. I can't fucking speak, if I say it out loud, it all becomes real, and I can't deal with that. Not now, not yet. Without warning, I fall apart and break down so completely in Marlowe's arms.*

*"It's alright, son, I've got you," he soothes, and I look up. He looks at me with such sympathy and swiping angrily at my tears, catching sight of Sam. I blurt out.*

*"I'm a dad, Sam."*

*Sam shifts uncomfortably in his hospital bed, and he winces in pain, letting out a laboured breath, as his eyes widen in shock.*

*"Ruby... died, but they managed to save our baby... I've got a daughter."*

*I almost choke on the words and the impact seems to render him speechless. You and me both, mate. Fuck me, I'm a dad.*

*** 

*I wanted to drink this moment in, I wanted to share this joyous moment with my wife-to-be. As I stand outside the ultra-modern neonatal unit staring blankly through the large window at the dozens of babies. It hits me like ten double decker buses. Ruby's gone; she's really gone. I swipe angrily at a tear that makes its way down my stubbled cheek. I hear the sound of squeaking wheels approaching, followed by a familiar voice.*

"Jax?" Sam rasps, but I don't turn around.

"I can't get my fucking head around any of this." His gruff voice thick with pure anguish. "I'm so sorry, mate."

I squeeze my eyes shut, desperately trying to quell the tears I can feel stinging my eyes and I shake my head.

"Don't," I warn, my emotions suddenly overwhelming me and threatening my composure. He moves his wheelchair and comes to a stop next to me. I steal a glance at him, and he looks awful. His complexion pale, he looks almost grey in colour. His green eyes troubled and red-rimmed. His raven hair a wild, untamed mess and he looks less than his usual put together self. We're silent for long moments, before I speak again.

"I don't fucking know how I'm gonna do this without her, Sam," I admit, swallowing past the lump in my throat.

"I-I don't know what to say, man." His voice full of sorrow and uncertainty, as he drops his head into his hands.

"I've got a daughter," I state incredulously, still not quite wrapping my head around the fact that I'm a dad.

"Congratulations?" He phrases it as a question and my lips quirk into a half smile.

"Thanks." I squeeze his shoulder firmly and he winces. "Shit, sorry, mate."

He shakes his head, his teeth gritted, as the short, plump nurse with kind eyes pops her head out of the doorway.

"Would you like to come in and meet your daughter, Mr Chase?"

I nod and Sam gives me a smile of encouragement.

"I'll leave you to it, Jax, congrats again."

I enter the room and the nurse wheels the incubator into a small connecting room, pulling up a chair and closing the door, until I'm left alone with my baby girl.

"Tell me what to do, buttercup. I don't know what the fuck I'm supposed to be doing," I say to an empty room and our daughter, still yet to be named stirs in her incubator. She's over a month premature, they're keeping a careful eye on her, but she couldn't be more perfect. Five fingers on each hand, five perfect, but dainty toes on each foot. A tiny button nose that reminds me so much of Ruby and she has the Chase chin.

*"It's just you and me now, Princess. I can't promise I'll be any good, but I promise you, I'll try my best," I say softly and she grabs my finger, squeezing gently. In that moment, I know I'm all in, as I look down at this beautiful, tiny, helpless human, I make a silent vow to love and protect her with my dying fucking breath, just like Ruby did.*

# Jax

# Present

I'm snapped back to the present by the bell ringing on the shop door, as I lean back in the leather tattoo chair at Saint Sinner Ink, waiting to be tattooed by Peyton. She appears from the back of the shop, looking every bit the rock star's wife.

"Hey Jax! So good to see you, babe!" She greets me brightly and enthusiastically; I can't help but smile. *Everything about her is infectious.*

"Hello, lovely, you literally saw me less than twenty-four hours ago!" I greet her in return, and she leans in for a hug, giggling girlishly. I hug her and she smells of Calvin Klein Deep Euphoria perfume. She instantly calms me, pulls me in for one her famous bear hugs and kisses me tenderly on the cheek. She makes me crave the softness of a woman and I can't help feeling jealous of the unbreakable bond her and Sam have. *He'd walk through hell for her, and she for him.*

Sam has *'My Angel'* tattooed in elegant flowing script across his chest. It was a memorial tattoo for Peyton. She was and still is, his angel, just like Ruby was my buttercup. Today, I am getting my own memorial tattoo. I want a tattoo to symbolise her and the feelings she evoked in me. Ruby lived her life by the seat of her pants, as if every day were her last and her motto was *'why put off tomorrow what you can do today.'* She was also spontaneous and did things impulsively sometimes, which drove me fucking insane, but I wouldn't have had her any other way. She taught me to just put one foot in front of the other, one step at a time, which is why I can't listen to *Four Year Strong One Step at a Time*, because it reminds me so much of her. She used to play it loud and often, which is why I'm getting a big, bright yellow buttercup and the words *'Breathe in, breathe out, it'll be OK, one step at a time'* tattooed on my neck and round my throat.

The ink on my skin reminds me of the places I've been, the people I've loved and lost and the adventures I've been on, in my tumultuous journey through life. The buzz of the tattoo machine lights me up from the inside, out, there is no feeling like it. There's something about the constant hum

49

and the delicious burn of the needles piercing my skin, that calms me and centres me like nothing else.

"You good, babe?"

Peyton breaks the comfortable silence and temporarily halts her tattoo machine. She looks at me with concerned eyes. *Bless her heart, she's become the gentle matriarch of the Rancid Vengeance family and she looks after everyone else, without a second thought for herself.* Her and Sam couldn't be happier, she's pregnant again with their third kid. She's glowing today, wearing quirky dungarees, a black and white striped t-shirt, black Converse, and her hair is secured in a black bandana. Her small bump just about visible under her dungarees.

"I'm good thanks, love, how are you doing? How's baby Newbolt cooking in there?"

She chuckles softly, sitting back for a second, placing her hand on her stomach.

"All good thank you, I'm managing to keep my breakfast down, which is a great start! I had to resort to using my womanly wiles on Sam this morning, just so I could leave the house!"

I roll my eyes. *Possessive much?* Peyton bites her lip and I cock my eyebrow.

"Go on, you *obviously* want to tell me! What did you do?" I smirk, as she looks up at me mischievously from beneath her lashes. I can see why Sam fell for her, she's pretty, relatable and she's so easy to get along with.

"I kind of... sort of... erm... handcuffed him to the bed," she stutters, biting her lip to stifle her giggles and I burst out into hysterical laughter. As I think about the time Ruby handcuffed me to her bed all those years ago.

# Jax

## Past

*After a marathon sex session with Ruby, I pull on her baby pink silk kimono and she giggles.*

*"Suits you!"*

*I wink.*

*"Matches my eyes, babe! Is it okay if I freshen up?" I ask, as she pouts and narrows her eyes.*

*"Anyone would think you're ashamed of me, Jack," she grumbles. I'm still getting used to her calling me Jack, the only person that calls me that these days is my mum.*

*"Of course not, why would I be? It's just... fun, that's all," I say nonchalantly and I see her visibly wince at my words. I roll my eyes to myself, as I head into the bathroom and turn the shower on.*

*After a hot shower, I feel refreshed and ready to face the day. I'm breaking my own rules with Ruby, I almost never spend the night at a woman's place. Usually when the deeds done, I'm out of the door, but she's hot as hell, fun to be around and she's not like any of the other women I've been with. It's a bonus that she seems happy to just go along with casually meeting up for sex and the occasional booty call when I'm in town. I head out into the bedroom, towel drying my long hair. I'm taken by surprise with what greets me, she launches my phone at my chest, and it lands on the carpeted floor at my feet. What the fuck?*

*"Who's Donna? You said we were exclusive! You fucking lied to me! You absolute prick!" she screeches. Fuck me, she went through my phone? Fucking women!*

*"Babe, listen, yeah? I never made any promises, I'm in a rock band, we're always on the road, I've got fucking needs! Needs that you're not always around to meet, so what do you want me to do? Seriously?" I say defensively and she stalks towards me, jabbing her long slender finger threateningly at me.*

*"I thought you were different to all of the other men, Jackson Chase! Turns out you're just like the rest of them! You're a filthy, pathetic, fucking liar!"*

*With each step she takes towards me, I take one back. I don't need this shit right now, Peyton's in hospital after some psycho cut her brakes on her car, we're all a little on edge. As I step back, the backs of my legs collide with the bed, by this point we're standing toe to toe, and she jabs a single blood red nail in my chest. Her eyes turn smoky, and she moves closer to me, until I can feel her hot, sweet breath gust against my lips and her scent envelopes me. I take her in, she's tall, slender and her dark hair cascades around her shoulders, she couldn't look sexier. She is wearing an almost see-through white baby doll negligée and matching French knickers, the white looks almost virginal and sets off her olive skin. I swallow hard at the sight of her. Fuck, this woman is going to be the death of me. She pushes me down on the bed with one hand and as her hand makes contact with my skin, I'm a total fucking goner. I'm at her mercy and at this moment I'll do anything she says. You're a sucker for a beautiful woman, Chase. She stalks towards me like a hungry lioness, and I move up the bed until I'm laying back against the headboard. She straddles me and grinds herself on my growing erection. Shit, if she carries on like that, I'm going to come like a horny teenager.*

*"Jack, fuck me like I'm the only woman you'll ever want," she whispers seductively. Fuck me, she's beautiful.*

*"Condom?" I swallow, as she reaches over me and pulls out a foil packet, along with a set of handcuffs and a black scrap of material. Kinky bitch. "Fuck, that's hot, you sassy little minx!"*

*She unclips the handcuffs and like a desperate, panting dog, I willingly lift my arms up, allowing her to cuff me to the metal headboard. She lifts my head up and ties the blindfold, taking away the second of my senses. I hear the sound of a foil packet opening and sheathes me with the rubber. She runs her nails down my chest and I growl. Shit the motherfucking bed. She drops down onto my throbbing cock. I'm at her mercy, she's in total control and it's taking everything in me to let her. She's controlling the rhythm, the pace and with every drive, my cock buries deeper in her tight pussy.*

*"Oh God, Jack!" she moans, as she continues to ride my cock like a fucking porn star.*

*"Oh fuck! Ruby, that feels so fucking good!" I cry out, as she increases her thrusts again, and I can feel that she's close to finding her release.*

*"Fuck, you're close, I can feel you pulsing around me, it feels so good," I growl.*

*"Oh, Jack, fuck! Oh God! Fuck! Yes! Yes!" she screams, as she lifts herself up, dropping back down on my cock, controlling the rhythm. She increases the pace and that's all it takes to tip us both over the edge. She lets out a strangled scream, and I explode. My orgasm washing over me, causing my body to tremble beneath her.*

*"FUCCCKKKK!" I grind out, as she climbs off me. She yanks the condom off with a loud snap and I clink the handcuffs against the cool metal of the headboard.*

*"Are you gonna uncuff me and take off this blindfold, babe?"*

*I hear her make her way into the bathroom.*

*"Nope!"*

*What the actual fuck? Is she for real?*

*"What do you mean no, Ruby? Come on, stop fucking about, babe. Uncuff me."*

*There's a pregnant pause.*

*"No! You've got no idea how it felt for me to see all those messages from all your fucking conquests, Jack! You promised me we were exclusive! You said there was no one else! You fucking lied to me! Over and over again!" she shrieks. For fucks sake.*

*"Babe, come on, let me loose, we can talk about this properly."*

*I clink the handcuffs a little more vigorously.*

*"You can't be fucking serious! Come on! You can't leave me here all day!"*

*There's another pause, as I hear the rustle of clothes being pulled on.*

*"Fucking watch me, you prick!" she spits venomously.*

*"Please, come on! I'm sorry, look, I was a complete dick, I know that now, forgive me. From now on, we can see each other, exclusively. There'll be no other women, just you, Ruby, just you," I say genuinely and sincerely.*

*"Promise me, Jack? I can't be with someone who's looking for his next conquest, my heart can't take it anymore."*

*I wish I could look her in the eye, but I don't think I've ever been surer of anything in my entire fucking life.*

*"I promise you, now please, uncuff me."*

*She finishes getting ready.*

*"I don't think so, I've changed my mind, I'm not uncuffing you. I'm going to be late for work! Toodles!"*

*"RUBY! FUCKING GET BACK HERE AND LET ME LOOSE! RUBY!" I shout, as she breezes out of the flat, leaving me writhing on the bed. Fuck my life.*

***

*I'm not sure how long I've been here, but I hear the door opening.*

*"Ruby! Is that you? Have you finally come to your senses, you kinky bitch!" I call out and I'm met with nothing but silence.*

*"I'm sorry, okay, you've made your fucking point, please just undo the cuffs, babe."*

*I clink the handcuffs against the frame, the cool metal biting into my skin.*

*"Ruby? Come on, it's not funny anymore, stop teasing me, honey, please."*

*I hear someone clearing their throat.*

*"Jax?"*

*I jump at the sound of Peyton's voice. Fucking hell.*

*"Peyton! Fuck! Shit! I'm sorry!" I curse, and she bursts out into hysterical laughter. Fucking great.*

*"What the hell happened here, Jax?"*

*I swallow, as I begin to explain. Jesus Christ, this is awkward.*

*"Erm, Ruby handcuffed me. I stayed over, and she said she was teaching me a lesson. I didn't for one minute think she'd go to work and fucking leave me here."*

*She tries to stifle her laughter, failing miserably, as I clink the handcuffs against the bed frame.*

*"Please, Peyton, babe. You need to un-cuff me," I plead and I hear the amusement in her voice. I'm glad my situation is amusing you. Bitch.*

*"Honey, where are the keys? And how long have you been here?" she says softly, I squirm on the bed before answering through clenched teeth, "Erm, I don't know. She left my phone where I couldn't fucking reach it," I say through clenched teeth, and I feel her throw a cover over me.*

*"Hang tight, sweetie, I'll call her, just give me a sec."*

*She goes out into the living room, as I hear muffled voices. One distinctly male. Fuck me, it's Sam. I hear a burst of hysterical laughter.*

"Jax! What the fuck, man!"

*Fucking hell! This is all I need! Wanker! I thrash wildly against the cuffs.*

"Sam! Get the fuck out!"

*Sam laughs.* "The boys have got to see this!"

*Oh no, you're not, Newbolt! I hear the click, click of a camera shutter. Fucking prick!*

"Sam! You fucking dare send that to the boys they'll never let me forget it!"

*Sam laughs hysterically. I hear Peyton walk back in with the phone to her ear, I feel her drop down on the edge of the bed and open the drawer, rooting around until she finally finds the keys.*

"Found them. I'm staying at Sam's for a few days. I'll call you... right back at ya, Rubes, bye."

*She hangs up and she unlock the handcuffs, releasing my arms. They hang limply for a few moments before I struggle free of the blindfold, my eyes adjusting to the bright daylight streaming through the window.*

"Christ, I need to take a piss." *I leap off the bed still naked and bolt to the bathroom, cupping my manhood with both hands. Fuck me, this is a story for the grandkids.*

# Jax
# Present

She continues to tattoo me, the look of concentration on her face makes me smile. I've lost count how many times she's tattooed me over the years and she's still the best in the business. Her and Sam have become rock's power couple, she's got her own make-up line, she writes a column for a popular mother and baby magazine, she's started selling her artwork and she's just about to launch her own alternative fashion brand, as well as working part-time as shop manager and lead artist at Saint Sinner Ink.

As I observe her doing what she loves, I notice I see it in her eyes sometimes, that faraway look she gets in those troubled eyes of hers. She remembers Ruby and the times they shared together. She smiles, almost as if she's in the moment again. Then she realises, and I feel her heart break all over again. She leaves the room, and no one questions her, and I know, because I feel the same. We don't talk about it, hardly ever, the only time I really talk about it, is to my therapist and even then, it's fleeting, just a sentence here and there, nothing ever really in depth. I can't, because if I talk about it for any length of time, it becomes all too real and when the reality finally sinks in, I'll crumble. I'll be lost to the grief, and I can't let myself do that. I have my daughter to think of, I must be strong for her, I have to raise her to be the best version of herself that she can be, which includes parts of me and parts of Ruby.

In one month, it's the anniversary of her death and every year, I deal with it the exact same way. I try to pretend it's just a normal day, but it never works, I just end up getting absolutely shit faced, because I can't seem to deal with it in any other way. My thoughts are interrupted by Peyton's melodic chuckle.

"Something you want to share, babe?" she asks curiously and I let out an audible sigh.

"I was just thinking about Ruby, that's all."

Her smile fades and at that moment, I know she just gets it. She gets it because she grew up with her, she shared the good times and the bad times.

I sometimes feel guilty for grieving when she knew her so much longer than I did.

"In a month, it's the anniversary of her death," I say, as if the words are going to choke me at any second. She sets down her tattoo machine and pulls off her gloves, opening the bin beside her with the toe of her shoe.

"It doesn't get any easier, does it, babe?" she states rhetorically, as she reaches for my hand. I let her take it, feeling the instant warmth of hers. She gets up from her chair, pulling me with her and I blindly follow her.

"Seb, I'm taking Jax into the back," she calls out and he looks up from his client, giving her a one-handed salute.

"You okay, honey bunny?" he asks with narrowed eyes and concern in his voice. She smiles brightly at his affectionate nickname for her, as she turns to look at him and nods.

"Yeah, all good, thanks, pumpkin." She flashes him a wink, as he carries on tattooing his client, who looks awestruck as he looks up and realises who I am. *Fucking hell.* Peyton catches my gaze and rolls her eyes, dragging me into the kitchen area. She closes the door and switches on the kettle.

"*For fuck's sake*," she curses softly. *Bless her heart, she hates the whole fame thing as much as we do.*

"Make yourself at home, I'll make you a coffee."

Instead of sitting down, I move to stand to the side of her.

"Shouldn't I be the one to do that for you?" I offer, as she spoons the coffee into the cup, clanking the spoon loudly on the rim. She leans on the worktop. *If looks could kill, I think I'd have died a painful death by now!*

"*Oh please,* you're as bad as Sam. I'm pregnant, not fucking ill!" she snaps and I hold my hands up defensively.

"Okay! Okay! Don't get your knickers in a twist, love, that was my poor attempt at chivalry!"

We both laugh.

"Sorry, I didn't mean to snap," she apologises.

"He's being his usual mercurial self, he's having another episode, they're becoming far too frequent lately. He's refusing help and he's stopped taking his bi-polar meds, ever since we found out about the baby. It was fucking shock to say the least, I think he's still punishing himself because he wasn't there when Freddie was born. It's just so fucking exhausting, Jax."

Since he was diagnosed with bi-polar, he's been medicating, and he takes his pills religiously. His episodes used to occur frequently, one minute he was flying and the next minute we couldn't drag him out of his hotel room because he'd taken to his bed or trashed yet another room we'd inevitably have to pay for. Over the years, it's become easier for us to spot the signs. He hides it a little too well sometimes, but after almost twenty plus years of friendship, he's developed a pattern. They haven't occurred often since his diagnosis and since his marriage to Peyton, she seems to calm him somewhat.

# Jax

# Past

We all pile off the bus after a small, intimate gig is at the O2 academy; it was a sold-out venue. The after- show party has been organised by the venue and we make the ten-minute journey to a club called The Polo Lounge. Sam has his arm slung around Peyton's shoulders and the doorman nods to us each in turn and lets us through the red velvet rope.

"What are you drinking, angel?" Sam asks her and she leans into him. They're so in love it makes me want to vomit. My relationship with Ruby is complicated and rocky at best right now.

We head into the V.I.P section and sit down on a large, brown-leather seating area surrounded by glass tables. I drop down next to Brody, who's laughing like a hyena. Fucking dick, I don't get why he feels the need to be high, all the damn time. The music is pumping, and the club is packed with people. A few minutes later, Sam joins us; He sets the drinks down on the table, and a waitress in skimpy shorts and a gold bikini top puts four buckets down with four bottles of Cristal champagne in. She smiles an all-too-bright white smile, and Brody shoves a bunch of twenty-pound notes in between her breasts. He winks, and he pats his lap. I roll my eyes at his over-the-top antics, sometimes I wonder how and why we put up with him. Sam sits down on the other side of Peyton and all of our entourage have joined us. Including Donovan, Caleb, Blu, Tate, Skip, Cole, and Lex. J.D also joins us, much to Peyton's dismay. I can't help but wonder why, I take a long welcome sip of my Southern Comfort and coke and quietly observe my surroundings. Peyton gets up from her seat next to Sam and he doesn't take his eyes off her.

"She's not going to disappear, you know," I say sardonically over the pounding beat of the music, and he cocks his pierced eyebrow at my statement, his eyes still firmly fixed on her.

"The mere thought of it makes me feel fucking violent. I can't contemplate my life without her in it, Jax. I don't know what I'd do if something happened to her and I couldn't protect her, ya know?" he explains and the depth of his feelings for her are reflected in his troubled eyes. I don't like the look in his eyes,

*I'm almost certain he's in the midst of one of his episodes, but I don't voice my concerns out loud. Suddenly, his nostrils flare and a tic begins in his tight jaw. I follow his line of sight and a tall, muscular man is leaning in close to her. I reach over and place my hand gently on Sam's arm.*

*"Sam," I say in warning, but he ignores me, shrugging me off him like an annoying bug as he gets to his feet. His six-foot four frame menacing and foreboding. I make an attempt to get up from my seat and J.D grabs my arm.*

*"Relax, Jack, everything's fine, just leave it, yeah? Sam's a big boy, he can take care of himself."*

*Something in the way he says those words doesn't sit right with me, but I nod curtly, obeying his request as I observe the muscular man hold his hands up in defence at Sam and walk off.*

*"Are you okay, angel?" I see Sam mouth and Peyton nods, letting him plant a kiss on her cheek. I watch him lean into her; his jaw clenched. I take another sip of my drink, as I see Peyton yank her arm free from his grasp, her eyes flashing with ire and her teeth clenching.*

*"Stop fucking suffocating me, Sam!"*

*Even over the music, I can hear her desperate scream. They exchange another few heated words before she storms off towards the exit, leaving him with a truly dumbfounded look on his face. I get up and make my way over to him, running his hands anxiously and frantically through his hair. He starts pacing the floor, attracting the attention of the bar patrons.*

*"Sam?" I say with an almost placating tone to my voice and the look of pure anguish in his eyes terrifies me. "Are you sure you're okay, mate?" I ask carefully and he turns to face me.*

*"Why does everyone keep fucking asking me that! I'm fine! Just find her, Jax," he snaps, a tic beginning in his jaw. I'm about to tear him a fucking new one, as he takes a deep breath.*

*"Please, Jax, you have to find her. I'm scared she's going to do something stupid."*

*The look of terror in his eyes has me nodding and heading off toward the exit. I salute the security guard on the door and ask.*

*"Did you see a woman come out here, mate, slim, quite short, long dark hair?" I describe, as he shrugs and shakes his head. I sigh and call out her name.*

*"Peyton."*

*I soon spot her step out from the alley, and rush over to her.*

*"There you are, Sam is about to tear the walls down in there looking for you."*

*She takes a laboured breath.*

*"Take me back to the hotel, Jax, please. I really can't be around him right now, please."*

*The pained look on her face causes my protective streak to kick in. I've got sisters, I recognise the signs and I don't argue, I know better. I nod, brushing her arm reassuringly.*

*"I'll be right back, babe, I need to get my phone, and I'll make sure he doesn't follow. Trust me."*

*I flash her a wink and head back inside. The pounding beat of I head straight for our group, J.D is on his knees in front of Sam. Why does it not surprise me? Sam's in the midst of an episode and J.D is at the epicentre whispering words of comfort in his ear. Fuck, it makes me feel sick. He controls Sam like a puppet, he has for years. I swallow down my disdain for the man who has been our manager for our entire career.*

*"Sam."*

*He looks up as I say his name, his eyes full of fear, concern and something else I can't quite put my finger on.*

*"I managed to find her, she's fine, I'm taking her back to the hotel."*

*I explain, and he goes to stand up, but I shake my head.*

*"She doesn't want to see you, she's angry and upset, I've got sisters, I know when she wants to be left alone. Look, I'll look after her, I'll make sure she's okay and I'll come straight back. I'll call if there's any issues, I'll talk to her."*

*He practically shoves J.D out of the way.*

*"I have to see her, Jax," he snaps, ignoring my earlier statement, as I place my hand on his shoulder, feeling him trembling beneath my hand.*

*"Well, she doesn't want to see you, what part of she wants to be left alone can't you get through your fucking thick skull? She's hurt and she's angry, just trust me, yeah?" I try desperately to placate him, as J.D joins us.*

*"Sam, listen to Jack, yeah?" he says tenderly and I have to stop myself from saying what I'm really thinking. Sam looks from me to J.D and back again. He turns to me and finally nods in agreement.*

"If anything happens to her, I'll hold you personally fucking responsible!" he yells, jabbing his finger in my general direction and I nod.

"I wouldn't expect anything less, dude."

I muble calmly, as I turn and head back outside.

I join Peyton in the back seat of the taxi idling at the kerb, as we make our way back to the hotel. She leans her head on my shoulder.

"Hey, do you want to tell me what that fuckwit did this time?"

A tear rolls down her cheek and I momentarily regret asking.

"A woman called Lyla showed up."

My eyes widen. Lyla fucking Hudson, Sam's crazy ex-girlfriend. She used to be in one of the biggest female rock bands, Hell on Heels. They supported Rancid Vengeance on tour, and we performed at several rock festivals together. Her and Sam got to know each other pretty well. They had a fling of sorts; it was just sex to him, but it was quite clear Lyla didn't see it that way. She went off the rails and had a highly publicised fall from grace, the band split up, and she lost everything. She hit the booze and the drugs hard and did several stints in rehab. She blames Sam for it all.

"Lyla? Lyla was here? Are you sure, babe?" I ask, an incredulous tone to my voice and she nods, eyeing me warily.

"She was at the gig as well; she kept telling me not to trust him. What's he hiding, Jax? Who is she?"

She tries hard to sound unaffected, but she sounds irritated and angry. I put my hand to my head.

"Fuck." I curse and take out my phone. This isn't good at all.

"Jax, don't call him, please," she pleads and I look up at her, the look in her eyes causes my heart to slam against my ribcage. I wrap my arm around her, pulling her into me. She doesn't argue and snuggles up closer to me, resting her head on my shoulder.

"He needs to know she's here, babe."

She sighs in defeat, as she nods in agreement against my shoulder. I type out a text to Sam.

FYI Lyla is in town.
Seems she's been dripping poison in Peyton's ear.
Just thought you should know.

J

*I hit send and ten minutes later, we are pulling up outside the hotel. Luckily, there are no paparazzi here, relieved, I pay the driver, and we both stride into the hotel foyer. I press the button for the lift, and I run to catch up with her.*

*"This isn't his fault, babe, at least hear him out, he deserves that. I've never seen him the way he is with you ever. It's a first for him, he's... happy."*

*We both step into the lift, she pushes the button for the fourth floor, and the doors slide shut.*

*"What's going on with you and Ruby?" She swiftly changes the subject, and I smile as she mentions her gorgeous, tenacious and feisty best friend. I lean back against the mirrored wall and tuck my hands into my pockets, as I think of Ruby.*

*"I'm falling for her, Peyton, she's... incredible. She doesn't stand for my bullshit. She doesn't expect anything from me, I know I slept with someone behind her back, and I'm so fucking sorry for that. We never made promises to each other, I thought we were clear on that. Now she keeps blowing hot and cold, I can't keep up with her. Her mood swings are literally giving me whiplash," I admit in a rush, seemingly terrified at the depth of feeling I feel for Ruby. I sigh long and loud, as the lift comes to a halt. We step out into the corridor, and I gesture for her to step out before me. She complies and I follow a few steps behind her, as she slows down, falling into step with me.*

*"Do you want me to talk to her?" she asks curiously and I smile at her thoughtfulness.*

*"Thanks, Peyton, that's really sweet, but I'm a bit old for the whole my friend fancies your friend!" I quip wryly and Peyton's face turns serious.*

*"She's been hurt so many times, Jax, but she must have some feelings for you; show her how much she means to you. I see how she is around you; she plays down her feelings, and she hides behind the tough girl act," she explains and I cock my eyebrow. If only she knew.*

*"Just like you, you're more alike than you realise."*

*She smiles shyly and fidgets with her hands.*

*"Maybe, but this isn't about me."*

*I stop outside her and Sam's room.*

*"But it was about you; until you changed the subject, remember?" I raise my eyebrows and she holds her hands up defensively.*

*"Okay, you caught me!" She laughs.*

*"Look, I've seen Sam at his lowest points, he has bounced back every single time, but I don't think he'll bounce back so easily if you run from him again. You were the reason he got up on that stage tonight. Talk to him, he's...fragile right now. Please don't break his heart."*

*My voice is pleading, and she nods. The way she looks at me and bites down on her bottom lip, tells me that she has so many things she wants to ask me about Sam's past, but she chooses not to. Not that I would tell her anyway, it's not my story to tell.*

*"I won't," she says softly and I brush her arm.*

*"I'm going back to the boys at the club, text me if you need anything, love," I say quietly, and she nods.*

*"Thanks, Jax." She kisses me on the cheek, and I smile, saluting as I turn to walk back down the corridor. My phone starts ringing, as I head out into the cool night air.*

*"Yo?" I answer and I'm greeted by the low baritone of Cole's voice.*

*"Jax, it's Cole, where's Sam? Is Peyton, okay?" he asks in a panicked rush, he's usually so calm, so his clear apprehension sets my nerves on edge.*

*"She's fine, I delivered her safely to her hotel room, as promised. I thought Sam was with you?"*

*Cole curses. "Motherfucker, he must have dodged me, little shit."*

*I chuckle at his grumbling. "Must be losing your touch, Benedict!" I joke and he growls, as I hear muffled conversations in the background. Cole mutters his thanks and I hear the distinct sound of a car door slamming.*

*"You lot are a pain in my fucking arse! I'm on my way back to the hotel, the bouncer on the door of the club said he saw him getting into a taxi about fifteen minutes ago. Is there a back entrance to the hotel?"*

*I look around, carefully surveying my surroundings, which are unfamiliar to me.*

*"I think so, I'm heading out the front, I can see the paps gathering, shit!"*

*A bright flash goes off in my face, the sound of the paparazzi excitedly catcalling me. I walk slowly backwards up the stairs, pushing my way back through the main entrance. I knew this would happen. Fuck my life.*

*"Jax? Jax?" I hear Cole impatiently calling my name on the other end of the phone.*

*"I'm here."*

*I reply wearily with a sigh.*

*"Move you fucking prick!"*

*I hear him wildly honk the horn of his car, as he curses at the traffic, and I smirk to myself.*

*"I'm five minutes away, meet me around the back and don't fucking ever go anywhere without security! You boys will be the fucking death of me!" he chastises, as the line goes dead. I try to make a mental note of my surroundings, all while looking for any signs of a stairwell, or a back entrance. A few minutes passes and I'm still none the wiser, I make my way to the large marble reception desk and the receptionist greets me a little over-enthusiastically.*

*"Good evening, sir, and how may I help you this evening?"*

*I clear my throat. Come on, use some of that Chase charm.*

*"Good evening, love, I'm in a bit of a situation."*

*I use my brown puppy eyes to my advantage and flash her my cheekiest grin.*

*"The press are out front, and I've got no way out of here without being seen, could you point me in the direction of a back entrance, my driver's on his way." I ask hopefully and she giggles girlishly.*

*"Of course... Mr Chase?"*

*I nod.*

*"Call me Jax, love," I say with a grin, and she points a long finger in the direction of the bank of lifts.*

*"Well, Jax, you're in luck, the stairwell that leads to the back entrance is the door next to those bank of lifts. Follow it down to the basement level, turn left and there's a fire door that leads to the back of the hotel," she explains, pushing her small chest out further and I try not to allow myself to get distracted. Come on, Chase, focus.*

*"Thank you so much, darlin', I really appreciate your... discretion."*

*I wink and I swear to God she's reduced to a puddle. I make my way over to the door, pull it open and sprint down the stairs, taking them two at a time. I get to the bottom, turn left, push my way through the fire door and out on to the street. The cool night air hits me as soon as the door swings open and I see Cole's car pull to the kerb. The headlights temporarily dazzling my vision. His car turns off and he gets out, slamming the door behind him. We make our way back inside the hotel and prepare for the worst, as we head up to Sam and Peyton's room.*

***

*Cole bangs on the door and we look silently between ourselves. After a few moments pass, Peyton gingerly opens the door and moves out of the way to let us both in. We step into the room and close the door quietly behind us.*

"Are you okay, Peyton?" *Cole asks softly, and she nods, as I look at her apprehensively. I know he'd rather hurt himself than hurt her, but I can't help subtly looking for any signs that she's been harmed.*

"Where is he, babe?"

*She points to the bathroom and pulls the sleeves of Sam's Rancid Vengeance hoodie over her hands. Cole takes charge of the situation.*

"Do you want to tell me what happened, Peyton?"

*She bites her lip, looking almost embarrassed and Cole rolls his eyes. Her face flushing an adorable shade of pink.*

"Believe me, darlin', I've heard and seen far worse from these guys, so please don't be embarrassed."

*She takes a breath, and Cole folds his arms awaiting her answer.*

"He came back to the room, he started acting weird, and we had sex. He was so distant, rough and forceful. He's never been that way before, he scared me."

*Her voice trembles, Cole puts his hand to his head and looks at me. Fucking dick. What the fuck was he thinking?*

"Motherfucker! Did he hurt you?"

*Cole moves closer to her with a concerned look on his face and checks her over, while I stand back not knowing what to do with myself. She shakes her head, and Cole lets out a relieved breath.*

"He's having one of his episodes. You need to pack your stuff right now, sugar, no arguments, please. You're going to have to trust me on this one, Peyton, ask no questions, and I'll tell you no lies. I'm going to stay here with him tonight; you're going to take my room down the corridor. Jax will stay with you, is that okay with you, mate?" *Cole says calmly, and I nod. It's obvious it isn't a request, more of an order. Okay, so this is how it's going to go?*

"*It's room four-twenty-four. I'll deal with Sam, I'm the only one who can handle him when he's like this.*"

*Her eyes glaze over, and she nods, struggling to process what is going on. Cole hands her his key card, and she takes it with shaky hands. She pulls up her suitcase on the bed and starts packing her stuff.*

"*Trust me, darlin,' he is going to get a whole lot worse before he gets better, it's best that you don't see him this way.*"

*The door of the bathroom opens, and Sam strides out with a towel slung low on his hips.*

"*Well, well, well, is this a private conversation or can anyone join in?*"

*His green eyes are dull, wild, and agitated.*

"*Don't mind me,*" *he says flatly, dropping his towel. We've seen it all before, we've shared rooms over the years. We don't get bothered by each other's nakedness, or states of undress. He pulls on a clean pair of boxers and a pair of loose-fitting combat shorts.*

"*What the fuck is this, some sort of intervention?*"

*Sam laughs sardonically, and Peyton zips her suitcase up. Sam's eyes widen at the sound, as he looks between Cole and me.*

"*Come on, babe, we need to go now,*" *I say softly, and I pick up her suitcase.*

"*You can't take my girl,*" *Sam says, his voice trembling.*

"*I won't let you take her from me, you can't fucking take her. Peyton, baby, please, I can do better, please don't leave me.*"

*A tear rolls down her cheek, and Sam goes to step towards her, but Cole is so fast and exudes pure strength as he holds him back with an iron grip.*

"*Sam, mate, it's just for tonight.*" *Cole tries to placate him, but Sam's having none of it.*

"*No, no, no, you can't fucking take her. I need her, she needs to stay with me. She fucking promised me she wouldn't run anymore.*"

*He breaks free of Cole's grip, collapses in a heap on the floor, and sobs uncontrollably. His hands run frantically through his still damp hair. Peyton pushes past me, and I think better of trying to stop her, she kneels in front of Sam, cupping his face in her hands.*

"*Sam, baby, I'm here, I'm not running,*" *she says softly, as he looks at her.*

"*I fucked up, please don't leave me.*"

*Sam reaches for her hand, but Cole touches his shoulder and stops him.*

*"Mate, just let her go with Jax, yeah? It's just for tonight; she's going to be right down the corridor."*

*Sam stands up and moves towards Cole until they are toe to toe, Sam raises his voice.*

*"You can't fucking stop me from being with my girl, you've got no right!" he shouts.*

*"Sam, please, mate, you need to calm down."*

*Sam's nostrils flare, and he has gone from uncontrollable sobbing to boiling rage in a matter of seconds.*

*"Jax, get the lady out of here now, please," Cole bellows and her eyes widen.*

*"He needs me, look at the fucking state of him!" she yells impatiently and Cole shakes his head.*

*"You don't need to see him like this, darlin,' trust me."*

*He gives me the nod, and Sam moves forward.*

*"Jax, please I'm begging you, don't do this, mate," he pleads, and I shake my head, holding firm. I lift her up and throw her over my shoulder as Cole holds Sam back.*

*"Jax! Fucking put me down now!" she screams and I stride out of the hotel room, slamming the door behind us. I can hear Sam's raised voice, as we walk the ten yards to Cole's room with her pounding on my back, yelling for me to put her down. I manoeuvre the key card and kick the door open with my boot. I enter the room and set her down on her feet.*

*"You didn't need to throw me over your shoulder and act like a fucking caveman, Jax!"*

*She narrows her eyes and shoots daggers at me. I find the whole situation amusing and shrug, as she sits down on the edge of the king-size bed. I walk over to the other side of the room, open the mini bar, and takes out a miniature bottle of whiskey. I pour it in a glass and hand it to her. She takes it, nodding her thanks.*

*"You look like you need it."*

*She manages a small smile and takes a long sip, wincing as she swallows. I crouch down in front of her just for something to break the awkward silence.*

*"Listen to me, that wasn't Sam back there, he is not himself right now. You need to understand that he has some... erm... issues. He gets like this every now and then," I explain, trying to appear vague. A tear slides down her cheek,*

*and I reach forward, rubbing it away with the pad of my calloused thumb. She finishes her drink quickly and puts the glass down on the floor at her feet.*

*"Hey, none of this your fault, you have to trust me on that one."*

*She looks up expectantly at me and the tears don't stop falling. I get up from the floor and sit down next to her, pulling her into my arms. I stroke her back reassuringly.*

*"Shhh, everything's going to be all right, I promise."*

*She pulls away from me briefly, but I keep her tucked safely in my arms.*

*"What's wrong with him, Jax? Why was he acting like that? Please don't fucking lie to me, I need you to start telling me the truth, I can handle it."*

*She sniffs and I close my eyes for a second, wondering how much I can tell her without violating Sam's privacy. Why the fuck hasn't he told her? She has a right to know, but it isn't my story to tell. For fucks sake. I'm conflicted, as I open my eyes, our gazes lock, blue on brown.*

*"Sam's ill, he has been for years. Day to day he is usually okay, he manages it, he takes his meds like second nature, and he is totally fine. Since he met you, he decided he didn't need his medication anymore, and he has been off it for a few months. He's—fuck, he's going to kill me for telling you this, but I can see it's getting serious between you two and you have a right to know. I have been on at him for a while to tell you the truth, but he was terrified you would run from him again. Sam has severe manic depression, we thought he was handling it until you had the car accident, then he started behaving oddly, being stupidly possessive and very aggressive. We noticed he wasn't sleeping, working out excessively, self-medicating with the drugs, not eating properly, and burning himself out. Cole knows how to handle him in these types of situations; the guy is a total fucking legend. He has been around at some of Sam's lowest points, and he is the only one who he listens to for some reason. If anyone can get through to him, it's Cole. You need to let him work his magic, and he will be back to being regular Sam in no time at all, I promise you, babe. He thinks you're more of a tonic for him than his medication. I begged him to carry on taking it, but you know Sam well enough by now to know that he is extremely fucking stubborn and ridiculously pig-headed."*

*I shake my head, desperate to say more, but realising I've said more than enough. I run my fingers through my hair and let out an audible sigh. She yawns and looks over at the illuminated clock on the nightstand.*

"*You should get some sleep, love, you look exhausted.*"

*She smiles, takes off Sam's hoodie and climbs into bed, pulling the soft, plush duvet over her body. I kick off my boots and pull off my jeans, laying down on top of the duvet next to her, I didn't realise how knackered I was and soon, I'm a slave to sleep.*

*I'm startled awake by the sound of Pour Some Sugar on Me by Def Leppard, I look to the empty space next to me and curse out loud. Where the fuck has she gone? Her phone is lit up like a Christmas tree and dancing all over the nightstand. I see Ruby's smiling face on the screen and as I go to answer, it goes off. It immediately starts ringing again and I swipe to answer.*

"*Oh My God! There you are! I've been so fucking worried! Peyton? Are you there?*"

*Her panicked voice sounding shrill, and I chuckle softly.*

"*Well, hello there, beautiful lady.*" *I greet her and she audibly grumbles.*

"*Why the fuck are you answering Peyton's phone?*"

*She asks in a rather accusatory tone, before I can get a word in.*

"*Is she okay? Oh God, please tell me she's, okay? She's okay, isn't she?*" *she babbles in a rush.*

"*She's absolutely fine, babe, relax, you've got nothing to worry about. Sam's had one of his manic episodes, that's all,*" *I explain carefully, without giving away too much.*

"*Manic episodes? What's that supposed to mean? Oh fuck! Has he hurt her? If he's laid as much as one hair on her head, I'm gonna' rip his balls off and make him wish he'd never been fucking born! Actually, fuck that! I'm coming to get her, I'm gonna' get dressed, drive to Glasgow right now and bring her home where she belongs! She doesn't belong on tour buses with unruly rockers!*" *she shrieks and I laugh out loud at her fierce protectiveness of her best friend.*

"*Look, listen to me, he hasn't hurt her, you don't need to come and get her! Stop stressing! For fuck's sake!*" *I state incredulously and she sighs.*

"*Well, why didn't you bloody say that in the first place?*" *she snaps. I swear this woman's mood swings are literally giving me whiplash.*

"*I was trying, but you wouldn't shut up, woman!*" *I snap back and I hear her sharp intake of breath.*

"*How fucking dare, you... you... man child!*"

*I snort at her lame insult.*

*"Wow! Is that all you got, buttercup?" I try to sound seductive, and she laughs.*

*"Was that your attempt at sexy, because it sounded rather like one of those creepy phone calls?"*

*We both laugh and there is a brief silence hanging between us, but it's not uncomfortable.*

*"On a serious note, is she okay?" she asks.*

*"She's fine, just upset, she's never seen him like this before, it was a shock to say the least, but I explained to her, and she seemed to understand. She was asleep, but I woke up and she's gone, so I'm assuming she's gone to him," I state wearily, suddenly feeling exhausted by tonight's events.*

*"Do you need to go to her? Call me when you can and let me know, I won't sleep if I don't know she's okay."*

*I smile softly at her quiet concern.*

*"I'll call you as soon as I know and I'll get Peyton to call you too...Look maybe we can...you know, go out when we get home?" I ask expectantly, fully expecting her to tell me to go kick rocks.*

*"Yeah, sure, okay. I'd really like that... a lot," she accepts and I can't hide my surprise.*

*"Awesome... okay, well, I'll call you and I'll see you soon."*

*We say our goodbyes and I hang up. I pull on my jeans, jam my feet into my boots and go in search of Peyton.*

*\*\*\**

*There is a lamp smashed on the floor, glass everywhere, and all the furniture is upturned. Sam's large, muscular frame is passed out on the bed with his arm slung across his bare, tattooed chest. I take in the state of the room, it's completely trashed, fuck me, this must have been a bad one. Peyton steps out of the bathroom, her face tear-stained followed by Marlowe. Marlowe sits on the edge of the bed and lets out a sigh. Shit, it must have been bad if Sam's dad is here.*

*"Was it bad?" I ask apprehensively, my face marred with concern for my best friend.*

"*Pretty bad, the state of the hotel room is a clear indication, mate,*" Cole replies and gestures to the mess on the hotel room floor.

"*Fuck!*" I curse and run my hand over the stubble on my chin.

"*Bollocks!*" I curse again. "*Shit! I need a fucking drink.*"

I stride quickly over to the mini bar.

"*I think we all need some sleep, it's late. Things always look better in the morning,*" Marlowe says matter-of-factly. I take a long sip of a large glass of vodka and relish the burn as a warmth settles in my stomach.

"*I should stay with him,*" Peyton says softly. Marlowe stands up and brushes her arm.

"*It's better that you stay with Jax, sweetheart. We don't know what mood he'll be in when he comes around.*"

Peyton looks at Marlowe, and he smiles reassuringly at her. I can't help but think something else has gone on that I'm not privy to.

"*Go with Jax, flower, he'll look after you. I'll call you in the morning.*"

Marlowe kisses her forehead and I finish my drink, wrapping my arm around her.

"*Come on, love.*" I lead her out of the room, down the corridor and open the door of Cole's hotel room, and we both step in, before I close the door behind us.

"*I was woken up by Ruby calling your mobile, repeatedly. That's when I realised you had gone. Ruby was fucking frantic. You hadn't called her back, and she said she was worried about you. I had to talk her out of coming to get you.*" I smirk.

"*Christ, that woman is a fucking force of nature.*" We both laugh for a moment before my face turns serious.

"*Seriously, though, babe, I was genuinely concerned when I woke up and you were gone.*"

She has the sense to look to the floor.

"*I'm sorry, I had to go to him, Jax, I was terrified.*"

I sit down on the edge of the bed and pat the space next to me. She sits down beside me.

"*He finally opened up to me, Jax,*" she explains.

"*Believe me, that's a good thing. Sam keeps things bottled up a lot. It usually takes a lot of fucking vodka for him to say what he is really feeling. He is lucky to have you, love, you're good for him.*"

*She smiles and there's a light tap on the door. I get up to answer it and Marlowe is standing outside.*

"*Can I come in, Jax?*"

*I nod and he steps into the room, closing the door behind him*

"*How is he, Marlowe?*" *I enquire, and Marlowe nods.*

"*He's still asleep; he should be fine by the morning. I actually came to speak to Peyton, if that's okay with you?*"

*I nod.*

"*No worries, I'll go to Lucas's room, he should still be awake. Will you be okay?*" *I direct my question to Peyton, and she nods.*

"*I'll be fine and thanks for tonight, Jax,*" *she says gratefully.*

"*You don't have to thank me, you're one of us now. I programmed all our numbers in your phone, if you need anything at all, love, call me.*" *I wink and leave the room. I shut the door and lean against the outside. Fuck me, it's been a long arse night.*

# Jax

# Present

Peyton puffs out her cheeks, deep in thought, as the kettle finishes boiling. She pours the water in the cup and stirs it, as if she might find answers in the bottom of it. She pushes it towards me and gestures to the sofa. We both sit down, and she regards me intently, unscrewing the lid from a bottle of water. She takes a sip before she begins to speak.

"Why do you never talk about her, Jax?" she blurts out and I smile at her tenacity. *Straight for the jugular.*

"Because if I talk about her, if I even allow myself to remember just for a second, it becomes real, and I know that sounds fucking pathetic." I take a sip of my coffee, wincing as the hot liquid burns my tongue.

"It's not pathetic at all, babe, it just takes time, I still struggle to accept she's gone. I still go to dial her number when I need someone to talk to. Even after just two years, there's still a Ruby shaped hole where she should be. She had her whole life ahead of her, she deserved to see her little girl grow up, she deserved to have a long and happy life with you."

Her voice trembles.

"I feel fucking responsible for it all, Jax. I feel responsible, because I fell in love with Sam, none of this would have happened if it weren't for me."

She breaks down and sobs hard. I put my coffee down and wrap her in my arms. It takes everything I have in me to stop myself sobbing right along with her. *She's fucking killing me.* After a few minutes, her tears begin to subside, and she looks up at me, smiling a watery smile.

"I'm sorry, fucking pregnancy hormones!" she tries to make a joke and I shake my head.

"Don't do that, Peyton, don't you dare blame yourself and don't dismiss your grief. Don't pretend everything's fucking fine, because it isn't, and it never will be. We all lost a piece of ourselves that day and we'll never get it back. As difficult as it's been, I've learned to accept it. I don't talk about it because I feel like a total fraud, you knew her your whole life and I knew her for a fraction of that time," I admit, as she swipes her tears from her eyes.

74

"It's not about the amount of time you knew someone, it's not a competition! It's about the feelings they evoked in you. Ruby was a force of nature; she was hard-headed, stubborn, and she was a fucking pain in the arse most days, especially when she hogged the bathroom in the mornings and left the milk on the worktop!" I laugh and pick my coffee up, smiling at the memory.

"Thea reminds me so much of Ruby, some days I can't look at her, her mannerisms, the way she sasses me. She's exactly like her mum, and that, terrifies the shit out of me. I've been thrust into parenthood, and I didn't ask for any of it. Ruby should be here because I haven't got a fucking clue what I'm supposed to be doing! I read all those baby books while Ruby was pregnant and as soon as I held Thea in my arms, all the crap I read went out of the window! I'm barely functioning most days, I don't know how to be a single parent and I don't know how to be without her, Peyton."

She reaches for my hand, as our moment is interrupted by the door opening, the scrape of metal across the floor and someone clearing their throat. I turn my head to see a murderous Sam looking dishevelled in the doorway, with a metal headboard attached to his welt-covered wrist. *Fuck my life.*

# 8

## Zeppelin

Every morning, I'm greeted by my reflection in the bathroom mirror, and I can't stand the person staring back at me. She's a shell of what I used to be before Abel extinguished the light inside me before the accident. After the chat with Rian, I feel lighter, it's surprising how talking about it helps and getting someone else's take on the whole situation. Abel was responsible for his own actions; he was the master of his own destruction. None of it was my fault, it's taken a long time, but I know that now.

Today is day one, a fresh start, a brand-new day, a brand new me! Which is why I'm starting my weekend with a steaming cup of coffee in bed, laptop in front of me, trying to write, but getting wildly distracted by browsing for dating sites. For the first time in five years, I think I'm ready to start dating again. I don't have the time to meet guys the conventional way, so online is the next best thing, it's anonymous and it's a little taboo. Besides, if I don't meet anyone, it can always be classed as research for my next book, right? I type in *'dating sites for professional singles'* in my search engine. I figure if I go for an exclusive one it could potentially reduce the risk of meeting weirdos and absolute nut jobs. I hit enter and a plethora of options load at my disposal.

I curiously click on the first one at the top of the list, GoMatchPro.com, it sounds harmless and straightforward with its £50.00 per month subscription for unlimited matches with a seven day free trial. It asks for the basics, a name, so I use my nickname and the year I was born, I go for ZepW92. It asks for my age, hobbies, likes/dislikes, the usual questions and then it goes on to ask for looking for. *What am I looking for? Am I looking for casual hook up? Just fun? Just sex? Friendship? A long-term relationship?* I lean back on my pillow deep in thought, as Jericho starts to bark at the light tapping on the door. I push my laptop to the side and place my coffee down on my USB mug warmer, as I pad out of my bedroom and across the living room to the source of the noise. Jericho is wildly and haphazardly scurrying around my legs.

"Hey! It's probably just Rian! You furry pest!" I playfully chastise him with a small chuckle, as I open the door to Rian waving a brown paper bag in the air.

"Morning, beautiful! Guess what I've bought? Breakfast! Hurray for *Uber Eats,* baby girl!" he sings and I roll my eyes at how dramatic he can be! I step out of the doorway, and he breezes past me in his usual designer Ted Baker pyjamas and matching slippers. I close the door behind him, as he makes his way into my bedroom, forgetting that I didn't close the dating site down. *Fucking hell.*

"DATING SITE! You kept that one quiet, you filthy harlot!" he squeals and giggles animatedly, as he settles himself on the bed. I go to close my laptop, embarrassed at being caught, my face flushing furiously and he stops me with a gentle brush of my hand.

"Ah, ah, oh no you don't! Not a chance, come on, spill it, sister." He waggles his finger accusingly, as I sit down next to him on the bed, and he wraps his arm around my shoulder.

"I just... I'm *done* with being sad and single, Ri. It's been five years since the accident and since Abel died. I'm done with mourning for him, I have to move on, it's not healthy, I know that now," I explain and let out an audible sigh, as he chuckles softly.

"About fucking time!" he jokes and applauds theatrically. I laugh along with him, as he cocks his perfectly groomed eyebrow at me.

"Come on, what have you got so far?"

I turn the screen towards him, and he scrolls through my profile with a frown on his face.

"*Fucking hell,* babe, do you actually want to meet decent guys, or weird creepy serial killers, who keep their victim's teeth as trophies?"

I snort. Rian is obsessed with documentaries about serial killers and conspiracy theories.

"You sound like one of those sad dog ladies, who lives alone in a country estate."

He lifts the laptop onto his lap, shielding the screen from me and starts to type, with a look of pure concentration on his face. After a full ten minutes of sipping coffee and frantically typing, he spins the screen around so I can read what he's written.

*Make each day your masterpiece - John Wooden.*

*I love Sundays spent drinking massive amounts of coffee and lingering over books. My Friday nights? Well, you'll just have to wait and see, won't you? People-watching is a favourite pastime and I live for the moments you can't put into words.*

I look at him open-mouthed, as he sits there looking rather pleased with himself.

"Where did you learn to write like that, Ri?"

He laughs and flashes me a cheeky wink.

"Just call me your fairy godmother! Your attempt was so poor, I couldn't read it without my soul dying!" he says dramatically, with an eye roll for effect, as I stick my tongue out childishly at him.

"Thank you!" I kiss him on the cheek and upload a generic photo of a stack of books and a steaming cup of coffee. I click *'save profile,'* start the free trial and in seconds, my profile is live. *What have I got to lose?*

***

We finish our breakfast consisting of coffee and smoked salmon and cream cheese bagels in front of a re-run of Sex and the City. Rian quietly quoting the lines as the characters say them. He's seen them so many times and I smile softly at one of his many quirks. He sighs, pausing the episode.

"I think I've become more like Samantha Jones as the years have gone on, done with dick! Honestly, it's been so long since I last had sex, I think I might be a born-again virgin!" he admits shamelessly and I'm mid-swallow, almost choking on my coffee. Rian chuckles softly and I quickly compose myself.

"Come on, it's not that bad, what about that guy you met on your last job? Was it Danny someone?" I try to recall his name, but I come up short. A dreamy look crosses his perfectly chiselled face.

"Danny Debonair, even his name sounds sexy. God, Zep, I promised myself that if our paths every crossed again I'd ask him out. But I saw him at that gay bar up West a few weeks ago and I couldn't even bring myself to talk to him without sounding like a sad pathetic loser!" he groans and my heart hurts for my best friend who just craves the love of a good man.

"I'm destined to be alone forever, with my ready meal for one, I might even get... ugh... a cat." He lets out a shocked gasp and I nudge him playfully with my elbow.

"You hate cats!" I gently remind him.

"Exactly!"

We both burst into hysterical laughter, as he takes a sip of his coffee and points to the computer screen.

"So, for now, I can live vicariously through you and your tragic love life!" he jokes and I pout. He blows me a kiss and he knows I can't be mad at him for long.

"Ooh, he's cute!" He gestures to one of the matches. He has dark hair, a dimpled smile, green eyes and reminds me a little of Shawn Mendes. "Send him a message!"

Rian bounces up and down excitedly, causing the springs to squeak and Jericho comes bounding into the bedroom, his tail wagging wildly. He leaps up onto the bed and plants a wet lick across my cheek.

"See, even Jericho approves, don't you, buddy?" Rian laughs as Jericho lets out a bark of approval.

"Quit ganging up on me, you two!" I grumble, as I move the cursor up and the light bulb goes green, notifying me that he swiped up too. I browse his profile for a few moments, and it tells me that we matched on reading and writing. *Sounds promising.* My fingers hover over the keyboard as I think of something witty to say. *You only get one attempt at making a first impression.*

**ZepW92:** Fancy seeing you here, I'm Zeppelin. I see that you write, I'm a writer too :)

**HunterXY85:** Based on your profile, I think we'd hit it off, want to meet for sex?

My mouth drops open at his blatant forwardness and Rian snorts.

"On what planet does he think that would work?" he mutters wryly, as I type my reply.

**ZepW92:** I'd rather get to know you first...

**HunterXY85**: Let's be clear, you don't have a picture, so I'm assuming you're either pig ugly, or you're a virgin?

I cock my eyebrow, clearly offended at this arsehole's presumption, so I don't dignify him with an answer and move the cursor down, unmatching with him.

"On to the next, baby girl, not all men are neanderthal pricks!"

Jericho senses my mood and sets himself down on my lap, nuzzling his furry face into my neck.

"Well, you'll always have me and Jericho, Zep!" Rian reassures me, and I spend long moments second guessing my decision to joining the world of online dating.

# 9

## Jax

Before I met Ruby, I didn't believe in real love. Real love was what my mum and dad shared, together since the age or twelve years old, they were soul mates, each other's best friend, knew each other inside out. Love was something I thought happened to other people, I had never met anyone I wanted to spend more than one night with, until I met her. She opened up so many possibilities, she was sassy, she made me laugh, she knew things that I hadn't ever told anyone before and spending forever with her, still wouldn't have been long enough.

Ruby Logan was my once in a lifetime chance to finally experience the love my mum and dad felt for each other. She was my endgame, my fucking soul stone. She was Jane to my Thor, she was Wanda to my Vision, she was Pepper to my Tony Stark. *She was everything.*

But life has a nasty habit of being unpredictable. It can change in just a blink of an eye. Everything that keeps you alive, can cease to exist within seconds. The life that you've been building, can collapse when you least expect it and I have spent the last two years rebuilding my life brick by brick. I started from scratch and even though it has been incredibly difficult, I managed to drag myself through, just about. I'm barely surviving, but I'm here and I'm still breathing. *One step at a time.* I idly trace the lines of my new tattoo across my throat, as I find myself attempting online dating for a second time. I can't seem to find the courage to sign up. It feels like I'm betraying Ruby by even thinking about dating again. I sit there staring at the screen for a few minutes when Brody dives into the seat next to me. *Fucking hell.*

"Whatcha' doing?"

I quickly swipe off my current screen and Brody starts to laugh hysterically.

"*Oh, my fucking God!* Were you just watching porn? *Fuck me,* Jax! On a bus full of dudes!" he shouts rowdily, as I roll my eyes and frown at his presumption.

"*Fuck off!* I wasn't watching porn!" I grumble defensively and he nods.

"I believe you, mate, thousands wouldn't!" He folds his arms and leans over my shoulder trying to peek at the screen.

"What?" I turn to look at him questioningly and he cocks his eyebrow. "Come on, man, spill."

I narrow my eyes on him. *Why is it such a big fucking deal?* Maybe someone else's input would be beneficial? I open the browser on my iPad and show him.

"A dating website? Okay, not what I was expecting."

He nods, his face full of curiosity and I puff out my cheeks, tilting my head up towards the ceiling. I try desperately to find the right words to explain what I'm feeling and why I can't seem to find the balls to just sign up. *What have I really got to lose?*

"I can't seem to pluck up the courage to sign up. I can't help feeling like I'd be somehow betraying Ruby. I know that sounds... I don't know, mate. I really don't fucking know."

I feel so conflicted and so... confused. The look of sympathy on Brody's face is evident, as he gestures with his hand to pass him the iPad. I reluctantly hand it to him and after a few minutes of furious tapping and a look of pure concentration on his face, he gives it back to me.

"There! I've signed you up! Best fifty quid I've ever spent!"

He flashes me a wink and my eyes widen. *What the fuck?*

"What the fuck have you done; you prick!" I yell and he chuckles softly. *I'm glad you find this amusing, Hart.*

"Well, you weren't gonna' do it, were you?" he states wryly and matter-of-factly. *I fucking hate it when Brody of all people is right.*

"I get that you're still grieving, man, I do, but for fuck's sake, it's been two years. You need to get back in the saddle and you need to show the world that adorable boy next door Jackson 'Flash' Chase is back on the market and on the lookout for some pussy!"

He waggles his split tongue suggestively and I find myself laughing along with him. *Maybe it wasn't such a bad thing after all?*

"My work here is done."

Brody rubs his hands together, gets up from the sofa and heads towards the back of the bus leaving me curious as to what he's written in my profile. I bring the screen to life and scroll through.

**HandsomeJack0304**

"I don't believe in magic" the young boy said, and the old man smiled.

"You will when you see her..." – **Atticus**

Music fanatic, I've been told I look like a tattooed Thor (but you'll have to be the judge of that) I'm an occasional gentleman who likes pina coladas and getting caught in the rain...

I work hard and I play harder. Intrigued? You should be...

I'm impressed with Brody's handiwork and after a few minutes of curiously scrolling through the pages and pages of single women. I click on the random profile of ZepW92, and I'm greeted by a black and white image of her smiling face and a dog. *Wow, how can she look like that and still be single?* She's a published author and it tells me she is online now. I swipe up and the light bulb goes green, notifying me that she swiped up too. *That's always a good start.* The egg timer goes around once, and I send her an invite to chat, and she almost instantly accepts. My heartbeat kicks up a notch, I'm completely new to this. I feel all kinds of nervous, as I shakily type a message and hit send.

**HandsomeJack0304:** Hi, I'm Jack, male (obviously!) or am I? Joke, I'm definitely all male! Lol! Thirty-three, London born and bred. Your turn!

**ZepW92:** Hi Jack! I'm Zeppelin – my dad was a massive Led Zeppelin fan (unless you hadn't guessed!) I'm twenty-nine and ¾. Originally from Southend, female, last time I checked! Lol! What are your hobbies? (Is that even a thing you ask these days?) It's been a while! I'm so out of practice!

I smile to myself at her innocence and almost playful response. I start to wonder what to tell her, without giving my real identity away. I decide to go with the fun, not too serious, roguish approach.

**HandsomeJack0304:** I'm into music, I'm a guitar teacher, I love pina coladas and getting caught in the rain!

**ZepW92:** If you're not into yoga if you have half a brain! Lol! I'm an erotic novelist and part-time magazine columnist. I love country music, reading and musicals (Don't judge me too harshly!) Lol!

**HandsomeJack0304:** Whatever floats your boat, babe!

**ZepW92:** So, what brings you here then?

**HandsomeJack0304:** Curiosity, I guess.

**ZepW92:** You know what curiosity did to the cat don't you?

**HandsomeJack0304:** Yeah, poor cat, I was quite fond of the little guy.

**ZepW92:** I'm more of a dog person! Lol!

**HandsomeJack0304:** Me too! I just don't have the time to own one!

**ZepW92:** So, apart from music, what other things do you like doing?

This woman behind the keyboard has my curiosity piqued and before I can talk myself out of it, I type back a reply.

**HandsomeJack0304:** My life isn't really that interesting! But if you really want to know, I love nothing more than playing guitar, writing songs, and just hanging out with the guys.

**ZepW92:** Your life sounds way more interesting than mine right now! I'm supposed to be writing my next novel, but I keep getting distracted and think writer's block is setting in! Every writer's worst nightmare! What kind of songs do you write?

*Shit, why did I have to tell her I write songs?* What do I reply? Oh, by the way I've co-written a few number one songs, and I'm in a world-famous rock band. *You didn't think that one through did you, Chase?* Fucking idiot.

**HandsomeJack0304:** Guitar driven rock, some ballads, they're nothing special. I just write purely for myself and to escape reality sometimes.

*Nice save.*

**ZepW92:** I can definitely relate to that; you don't seem like other guys. I'm new to this whole online dating thing. You're the first guy I've spoken to who's taken time out to just chat, without asking if I fancy meeting for sex! Jesus, there's some weirdos out there! I thought this site was meant to be for professionals only! Lol!

I find myself laughing at her easy chit chat.

**HandsomeJack0304:** Well, last time I checked I wasn't a weirdo, so you're safe on that front! Plus, I'm way too squeamish to be a serial killer!

**ZepW92:** Lol! So, tell me more about you. Favourite movie? Favourite food? Favourite song?

*Shit, this is where I must tread carefully.* She can't know my true identity; she can't know I'm one quarter of the world's biggest rock band. *Whose stupid dumb arse idea was this again?*

**HandsomeJack0304:** Favourite film? Easy! Reservoir Dogs, best film ever! I'm a huge Tarantino fan! But I also really love the classics, Snatch, American Pie and Back to the Future. Favourite food? My mum's Sunday roast, there's nothing better than a home cooked meal, cooked by my favourite person in the world! And favourite song? I don't think I have one, there's too many to list! Your turn!

**ZepW92:** Good choices! Okay, my favourite film is Rock of Ages, but I prefer the musical to the film! I'm a total sucker for a musical! Favourite food probably spaghetti bolognaise, pasta instead of spaghetti though! And my favourite song is Luke Combs, *Beautiful Crazy*.

As I type my reply, I begin to think that it looks like this is going to be a long night.

*** 

My mind is my own worst enemy, after my late-night conversation with ZepW92, I tossed and turned and eventually couldn't sleep. I questioned and second guessed every word that was exchanged between us. Even though, it was innocent for the most part, I couldn't help but feel the overwhelming guilt creep into my consciousness. *I'm so sorry, buttercup.*

I find myself sitting on the steps of the tour bus in the large parking area of the Royal Albert Hall. It's our final gig before we embark on our European leg of our tour. Raleigh Storm is performing with us this evening after travelling with us as research for her movie role in Damien Valentine's latest film *'Rocked'*. Brody has been teaching her how to play guitar and they've become inseparable, it's nice to see him happy. I'm hopeful she can be the one to lay his demons to rest once and for all.

It's still early, so I relish the silence and the occasional sound of birds chirping, reminding me that I'm still alive. I'm tuning my guitar, as Lucas approaches with two cups of take away coffee and he hands one to me. He stops in front of me, he is wearing camouflage combat trousers, a v-neck white t-shirt, black army boots, a black beanie hat and a pair of black rimmed glasses. He's been in a rather sombre mood since his midnight confession, and I haven't bought up the subject since.

"You look like you need this, brother," Lucas drawls, as I take it from him and take that first welcome sip. He tucks one hand casually in his pocket and sips his coffee with the other.

"Cheers, mate, appreciate it, could do with something a bit stronger, but this will have to do for now!" I say wryly, that was my lame attempt at a joke, but Lucas cocks his eyebrow, regarding me intently.

"You know you're not fooling anyone, right?" he says in his familiar All-American accent. I hang my head and lean my guitar against the bus.

"I've been in therapy for almost three fucking years and I'm still in the exact same place I was before I started. It's good to talk to someone who's impartial, but he wasn't there, he didn't experience the absolute devastation. He didn't experience the aftermath; he wasn't the one who tried to protect his fiancée and fucking failed. I can't fucking do this anymore, Luke. I'm drowning in grief; I'm really fucking struggling."

My voice trembles and I take a deep breath, desperately trying to push back the memory of Ruby's bloody, lifeless body lying on the chapel floor. I'm about to speak again when we're interrupted by Sam's deep husky timbre.

"Boys."

He lifts his black Ray Ban Wayfarer sunglasses on top of his head, revealing an impressive black eye.

"What the fuck happened to you?" I ask curiously. He throws his head back and laughs.

"You should see the other guy!" He tries to make a joke of it, and I shake my head, worried for my friend, who's going off the rails right in front of our eyes.

"Chill the fuck out, brother, it's fine. Some guy started it, I finished it, end of, it was no big deal." He shrugs nonchalantly with a dismissive wave of his hand and I nod.

"Try telling your wife that," I remind him, unable to keep the venom from my voice and emphasising the words 'your wife.' He looks almost worried.

"Please don't tell her, I don't want to stress her out." He sounds genuinely terrified, as Lucas gets up from his seat next to me.

"Maybe you should try covering up that black eye then, dude. Just a thought," he says acerbically, pointing at his black eye and leaves us to it.

"What crawled up his arse?" Sam snaps.

"Maybe you did, by acting like a complete fucking dickhead! Look, is everything alright with you, mate?" I ask and he laughs bitterly.

"Everything's peachy-fucking-creamy, mate." he says with an unconvincing edge to his voice. I get up and move to stand in front of him, narrowing my eyes on him, regarding him with careful eyes. I'm about to speak, when he cuts me off by holding up his index finger.

"We're done here, Jax, we're not doing this, not fucking now," he rasps matter-of-factly.

"I get you're concerned, I'm grateful and I'm touched, but it's really not necessary. Me and Peyton are fine, we've got two beautiful boys and we couldn't be happier."

He smiles, but it doesn't reach his eyes. I notice he doesn't mention having a baby on the way, but I don't say that out loud. I observe him for a few minutes, he's twitchy and he's agitated. He's fidgeting and he's deliberately trying to distract me. His hands are trembling violently, he thinks he has me fooled, but he forgets how well I know him. We've been down this road before, and it never ends well. It ends up with him inevitably trashing a hotel room, us calling his dad, or with him back in rehab. Either one isn't good for any of us, as I'm instantly transported back to the day, I found Sam in a pool of his own blood.

# Jax

# Past

*Today was Peyton's memorial at Saint Sinner Ink. The place where Sam and Peyton's love story began, the place where she was truly happy. Sam is really struggling; I see it in his eyes when he thinks no one is watching. He's not eating, he's not sleeping, he's not in a good place. We're all keeping a watchful eye on him, but he's spent the past weeks in his apartment, drowning in vodka and hiding himself away from everything and everyone. He's in the midst of a deep dark episode and there's nothing we can do about it. It's like watching a car crash you can't tear your eyes away from.*

*I'm trying to stay strong for Ruby, but it's so difficult when Peyton was close to us all in some capacity. She was a friend, sister, confidant and shoulder to cry on for those close to her. The people who knew her the best stood up and said a few heartfelt words to remember her by, it was truly beautiful. It was Sam's turn to make his speech and he apprehensively approaches the front, almost shyly. He's so at home performing in front of thousands of fans, it's second nature to him, he has the audience eating out of the palm of his hand. But speaking in front of the people who know him best, it's like he's a totally different person. He's shy, reserved and so far, removed from his alter-ego Bolt. He takes a deep, shaky breath and places his visibly trembling hand on the table for support. He closes his eyes briefly, before he begins to speak.*

*"I'm no good at this, so I'll keep it brief. It was in this very shop where I first laid eyes on Peyton. Her feistiness, her big blue eyes, and her sparkling personality was what attracted me to her. When we first met, she hated the fact that I was a rock star. She had read about my man whoring ways, but as soon as I saw her, I knew that part of my life was over. Her razor-sharp wit and her amazing ability to bring me to my knees with just one look, I think I fell in love with her the moment I saw her. She didn't take my crap, and it was refreshing. She was the first woman to ever say no to me," he admits with a small, fond smile and everyone in the room laughs. Ruby wipes a tear away from her eye and leans closer into me. I wrap my arm around her, offering her the comfort she so desperately craves.*

*"She quickly became my addiction, my reason to get up on stage and perform. She was my good luck charm, my angel, and the love of my life. There's not a day that goes by where she doesn't consume my every thought."* A tear rolls down his cheek, and he looks up to the ceiling as if he's speaking to Peyton. My heart breaks for my friend who is clearly struggling and so consumed by grief.

*"Christ, I'm struggling, angel, I need you."*

He breaks down so completely and his gut-wrenching sobs cause my heart to slam against my rib cage. I nudge Ruby and she gives my hand a reassuring squeeze, as she gets up from her seat. She walks confidently to the front, her heels click-clicking across the floor. She takes Sam's hand in hers in a silent gesture and he lets her. There's a quiet understanding between them and the exchange is wordless, but if any outsider were observing, they would know that this was two people who had suffered a devastating loss.

*"Sorry... erm... shit... I really can't do this."* His voice gruff and thick with emotion, as he snatches his hand away from Ruby's and sprints out of the door. The bell ringing as the door opens and closes, Ruby looks to me for support and I shake my head at her.

*"Let him go, buttercup,"* I say, clearing my throat, as she resumes her seat next to me, taking my hand in hers.

*"He just needs some time, that's all. I couldn't bear the thought of losing you, I can't imagine what he's going through."*

I push that dark thought to the back of my mind, allowing the warmth of her hand in mine to offer me a source of comfort.

***

*The rest of the memorial passes in a blur, as the hours pass Sam doesn't return and a feeling of unease spreads through me like a cancer. I lost count of how many times I've tried to call him, Lucas, Brody, Ruby, his mum and dad, his brother, have all tried, but his phone just keeps going straight to voicemail. With every moment that passes, the feeling of unease intensifies, and I can't help thinking that something is very wrong. This isn't like Sam, it's so out of character for him. I swipe the screen on my phone and dial him again, putting the phone to my ear.*

"*Come on, answer the phone, you twat,*" I mutter, as Ruby joins me, wrapping her arms around my waist from behind and resting her chin on my shoulder.

"*Is he still not answering, babe?*" she breathes in my ear, and I shake my head, stabbing at the screen impatiently to end the call again after it goes to voicemail.

"*FUCCCKKKK!*" I curse, aware of the low hum of idle chatter surrounding me from the people closest to us.

"*This really isn't like him, buttercup... I get that he's grieving, he's just lost the love of his life and he's not been coping well... but I'm really fucking worried about him.*"

I run my hand through my hair and tuck my phone back into the pocket of my blazer.

"*Fuck it, I have to know if he's okay,*" I state matter-of-factly, as I pull my car keys out of my pocket and slip away without a word.

The journey back to Sam's is silent except for the low hum of traffic. I become more antsy with every mile travelled and I can't help thinking that something just feels off.

"*Baby?*" Ruby says, her voice thick with exhaustion.

"*Hmm?*" I hum, as she turns her head to look at me, her long dark hair framing her face and spilling down her shoulders, her hazel eyes heavy.

"*He's gonna' be fine, you know? We're going to get back and he's going to be passed out on the sofa drunk,*" Ruby tries to reassure me with a soft smile, but my gut tells me different. After all these years, I know my best friend, and this isn't him. He's had his fair share of manic episodes in the past, but nothing like this. I squeeze her thigh, as I glance at her profile in the muted streetlights. She really is stunningly beautiful; I can't tear my eyes away from her. I shift my gaze back to the road and I hear her mischievous chuckle.

"*And when I'm inevitably proven right, you Jackson Chase are going to fuck me against the window of your apartment with me wearing only my Louboutin's.*" Her voice low and seductive. I growl hungrily at her statement, too anxious and focused on getting to Sam, as I push my foot down on the accelerator. I hear the car roar to life, as I activate sport mode and pray to all that's holy that she's right.

\*\*\*

*After the forty-five-minute uneventful journey from Islington to Greenwich, I swing the car expertly into the underground car park beneath our apartment building and park it haphazardly next to Sam's Porsche Cayenne 4x4. I swing the door open, climb out and slamming the door shut, not waiting for Ruby. I'm too focused on making it to Sam's penthouse to care, my heartbeat quickening with every step I take. We take the lift to his floor in complete silence, the air thick with apprehension. As the lift comes to a halt, I practically sprint out and across the bright marbled foyer. The dark colour of his door foreboding and sending a chill down my spine, something is definitely not right, I know it. I pound on the door frantically, desperate for him to open it.*

*"Sam, open the fucking door!" My voice is pleading, as I listen hard for any indication that he's in there.*

*"I know you're in there, you fucking dick! Open the door, or I'm going to break it the fuck down!" I roar, Ruby places her hand on my shoulder to try to placate me, but I shrug her off impatiently. Unexpectedly, I hear a loud clatter and the sound of Sam's muffled cursing, followed by the high-pitched sound of a mortally wounded animal, that will stay with me for the rest of my life.*

*"Fuck this! Babe, move out of the way!" I state firmly, as Ruby takes a few steps back. A loud crashing sound filling the silence, as my foot connects with the door. I manage to splinter the wood and send the door, still on its hinges, hurtling against the wall with a thud.*

*I step inside, there is an eerie and inauspicious kind of silence. As I move further into the room, it's like everything moves in slow motion. The sight that greets me causing my stomach to roil, I rush over to Sam, who is lying, unmoving on the floor, on his back, his eyes dull and red rimmed. A dark crimson pool surrounding him, to an outsider it would look like I had just stepped into a crime scene. A large bloody knife in his hand, an empty vodka bottle discarded on the floor and a selection of pills scattered haphazardly beside him. My eyes shift to a folded piece of paper and I pick it up, curiosity getting the better of me. I unfold it and read.*

*To whoever reads this?*

*First off, know this: all roads lead to the same outcome.*

*To this very point in time.*

*I am not a coward, and I most certainly am not a quitter; I'm simply just a man.*

*Everything is insignificant, void without her in my life.*

*I am so fucking sorry.*

*Life Sucks. Fuck you, see you bitches on the other side. Peace out.*

*Sam x*

I slap my hand to my mouth and angrily screw up his suicide note. *Sam, what the fuck have you done?* There's so much blood, *fuck, fuck, fuck!* I run my hands through my hair and kneel beside him. The sight of my best friends' body lying perfectly still, completely floors me. I shake him violently, as Ruby drops down next to me, sobbing softly. *Come on, Chase, get your shit together!* I take a few shaky breaths, as I check for a pulse. His breaths are shallow and his heartbeat slow.

"Sam, you fucking prick, what have you done, wake the fuck up! Oh, man, please don't die on me, please, please."

I tap his pale face, tearing falling freely down my cheeks for my best friend. He blinks up slowly at me, groaning low in his throat.

"Oh fuck, baby, please ring an ambulance. Come on, Sam, stay with me, mate," I plead as I shakily pass Ruby my phone, desperate for him to keep his eyes open.

"SAM!" I yell, as his eyes roll back in his head, and he slips into unconsciousness.

"Baby, he's unconscious." My voice is panicked. She takes my phone with shaky hands, as she sobs uncontrollably.

"Get your fucking shit together, buttercup!" I bite out, unable to keep the impatient tone out of my voice. It seems to snap her out of it, and she takes a calming breath, switching almost instantly from panic mode to cool, calm and collected.

"You need to tell them to fucking hurry!" I command and she nods curtly, as she swipes away the tears, dialling nine-nine-nine.

"Don't you fucking dare die on me, you stupid motherfucker! What have you done!"

Both of his wrists have been cut, the wounds jagged and deep, as the blood oozes thick and fast onto the floor. Ruby moves closer to me, holding the phone in front of her and tapping the screen with her acrylic nail.

*"You're on speaker," she says and I can hear the crackle of the dispatcher on the other end.*

*"Jackson?" The woman's soft, sympathetic voice fills the silence.*

*"I'm Angie, I need you to tell me what he's taken, can you do that for me, please."*

*Ruby looks at me and I can't help but think I'm way out of my fucking depth. Ruby moves around him and bends down to pick up the empty pill bottle. She turns it towards me, and I nod curtly.*

*"He's taken Seroxat," I explain.*

*"Good, thank you. The ambulance is on its way, it shouldn't be too far away, you're doing brilliant, both of you, you did the right thing," she reassures us, as I look at Ruby, desperately trying to hold back the tears I can feel threatening.*

*"His...his wrists are cut...fuck...shit...there's so much blood. I don't know what to do."*

*I can't help the tremor in my voice, as Ruby moves closer to me, reaching for my hand. I let her take it, relishing in her warm touch.*

*"Okay, Jackson, I know it's difficult, but I need you to stay really calm for me, can you do that? Do you think you can get a towel, or something to tie around the wound, we need to stem the bleeding, it's likely he's lost a lot of blood?"*

*Her voice is soothing, a stark contrast to the chaotic situation we have found ourselves in the middle of. Ruby sets the phone down on the floor next to me and rushes into the kitchen. She returns quickly with a pile of towels.*

*"We've got towels."*

*There's a brief pause.*

*"Perfect, now, fold the towel length ways and tie it tightly around the wound, it's likely it'll soak right through, but that's fine, it's normal."*

*I do as she says and tie it tightly around his left wrist, the thick blood gushing from the torn flesh. It makes my stomach roil and I feel like I'm going to throw up. The metallic smell permeating my nostrils, as my hands start to tremble. I repeat the action with his right hand and as I finish tying the towel as tight as I can, I hear sirens getting closer. Relief floods through every part of me, as my legs buckle beneath me. I crumple to the floor, the weight of the situation crushing me and the dominant thought at the forefront of my exhausted mind is, please don't die.*

*** 

*It's late and I can't sleep, the images of two nights ago haunting me on a constant loop. My best friend, the man I consider a brother, tried to commit suicide because he lost the woman he loved. The ambulance men said he was so fucking lucky to be alive; he missed severing his main artery by a quarter of an inch. He chose not to talk to me, instead of coming to me and saying he was struggling, he tried to take the easy way out. Fuck you, Newbolt. We're all struggling, we lost her too. I couldn't pretend like everything was normal when he was lying in that hospital bed, I couldn't bear to look at him. I had to leave, and I haven't been back since, call me heartless, call me selfish, but I can't bring myself to face him.*

*Ruby is in bed asleep, and I'm in my kitchen preparing to go on my nightly run. It helps quietly calm me and it helps me fall asleep quicker when I finally fall into my bed, exhausted. I pull on my hoody and tie my hair up in a loose man-bun, which Ruby finds oddly sexy. I unlock the door quietly, aware that she has the hearing of a fucking bat. I step out of the apartment, down the corridor and down the ten flights of stairs. I've barely broken a sweat by the time I get to the bottom and jog across the large open foyer, which is unusually busy for this time of night. I push through the glass doors and breathe in the cool, crisp night air. I put my ear buds in and start off on a gentle jog down the street to the dulcet tones of Disturbed the Sound of Silence. I pound the pavement and make my way through the Green Parks, pushing myself harder with each mile I run.*

*My mind is clearer, as the minutes turn into hours. I've done eight miles around the park and I'm making my way back home, when it starts to rain heavily. The memories of finding Sam in a pool of his own blood, assault every corner of my brain and I can't hold back the dam a moment longer. I lean my back up against a wall, the rain soaking every inch of me, and I break down in a torrent of tears. Why Sam, why? Why didn't you just talk to us? Why couldn't you tell us what you were going through, you selfish motherfucker? I thought we'd lost you, there was so much blood. The sight that beheld me as I kicked the door down, will be forever burned into my retinas and I can't unsee my best friend, my fucking brother, lying unmoving, in a pool of his own blood. Fuck, fuck, fuck, what were you thinking Sam?*

# Jax

# Present

I'm jolted back to the present and Lucas has re-joined us. I can't help the sarcastic edge to my voice, some of the familiar bitterness making an unwelcomed ugly appearance.

"Who are you trying to convince, man? Me or yourself? Because frankly you're doing a fucking shit job."

He cocks his pierced eyebrow and folds his arms across his broad chest. The veins in his tattooed biceps bulging angrily.

"You're not doing too good yourself, do you think we don't hear you crying yourself to sleep. Brody thinks we don't know he's scoring again and he's using sex with Raleigh to distract himself. Lucas thinks we don't know he's signed up to Grindr because he's still hung up on Slade. We've all got demons and we've all got secrets, some of us are just better at hiding them than others."

Lucas clenches his fists at his sides, and I stomp down on his foot to tell him silently to just leave it. Sam narrows his eyes on me, moving his gaze from mine to Lucas. His eyes have gone an unusual shade of forest green. *He's definitely in the midst of an episode.* I open and close my mouth, desperate to shut him down, but everything he has just said is absolutely true. He chuckles throatily.

"Don't look so shocked, dude. Just turn around and move the fuck on." He sniffs, rubbing his finger across his nostrils.

"You're self-medicating, you're off your bi-polar meds, I know that much. Why do you insist on doing that, not just to yourself and to us, but to her, to Peyton? She doesn't fucking deserve that, she's growing a human inside her, for fucks sake!" I snap, as he scrubs his hands wearily down his face. He looks exhausted and he's too fucking stubborn to admit he's struggling. I don't know how much more I can take without losing it completely, so I stop myself from continuing. *Deep breaths, Chase, count to ten.*

"Finished? Because she's not pregnant anymore, she had another fucking miscarriage! And I'm that much of a bad husband that she didn't fucking tell me!"

My eyes widen at his admission and my lips press into a straight line. *Fucking hell.* I don't continue, as he spins on his heel and walks away.

"Fuckin' asshole," Lucas mutters and for once, I don't disagree.

***

We're in the middle of our set, and the crowd are lively tonight. Sam makes his way to the front of the stage; no trace of his black eye and they go wild. He never fails to amaze me, he's a consummate professional. Whatever he has going on his life, he never lets it affect his performance and I've always admired him for that. He's one of the last true showmen. The whole venue seems to vibrate with enthusiastic energy, and I find myself grinning, as Sam leans into the microphone to speak.

"How are you doing, London! Wow! So, I don't know if you know, but for the past month, we've had a special guest, on tour with us, the very beautiful, Raleigh Storm."

The crowd screams, as her name is mentioned. Her and Brody met in rehab and recently reconnected when she joined us on tour. They have become inseparable in the past months, and I think she could be good for him.

"She's been on the road with us, preparing for her brand-new movie 'Rocked' directed by the legend that it is, Damien Valentine. Whilst she's been on tour with us, our very own Snake, has been teaching her how to play guitar. Our brand-new song 'Rock Me' is also going to be featured on the movie soundtrack and we're going to perform it for the very first time live, for you fucking lucky people tonight!"

Sam sweeps his arm out to the side and Brody steps forward to introduce her, the pride on his face evident.

"For the first time, please give a warm Vengeance welcome, to the extremely talented and honorary Rancid Vengeance member, Raleigh Storm!"

Sam grins, she steps out onto the stage and the crowd cheer for her. She's dressed in tiny leather hot pants, a white vest - which emphasises her breasts - and knee-high leather boots, with black and silver accessories. She comes to a stop in front of Brody, and I can see by the look on her face, she's terrified. He leans into whisper something I don't quite catch, and she smiles softly, as he slings the guitar over her shoulder, allowing her to adjust it accordingly. The opening strains of our new song *'Rock Me,'* echo through the arena. I bounce from one foot to the other, strumming out the opening riff and Raleigh joins in halfway through. She's a total natural, she's picked up what Brody taught her so quickly and effortlessly, it is as if she was born to play. As Sam steps up to the microphone stand, gripping it with both hands and begins to sing. He closes his eyes briefly and when he opens them, he looks out into the vast crowd. His green eyes shining, as if even after all these years he can't believe all these people are here for us.

*"Faster than a moving train, enraged like a hurricane. She's half woman, half American dream. Mistress of singing, I'm pulling your strings, twisting your dreams, and thrashing your drum. Rock me until the sun comes up. She's blinded by me, and you can't see the strings. Just call my name, 'cause I'll hear you scream. Mistress, Mistress, just call me by my name, 'cause I'll hear you scream. Mistress, Mistress, rock me, until the suns come up."*

The spotlight moves on to her and bathes her in soft light, as she grips the fretboard a little tighter and begins to strum out the complex riff. The crowd grows more excited, and the atmosphere is electric. She moves to the front of the stage, as the solo ends, Sam growls and begins to sing again.

*"A demon nestled somewhere in time. No warnings, no sign. My pretty little judgement day and slowly the villain arrives. Eventually, they all commit their crimes. Just call my name, 'cause I'll hear you scream. Mistress, Mistress, just call me by my name, 'cause I'll hear you scream. Mistress, Mistress, rock me, until the suns comes up. Yeahhh! Rock me, til' the sun comes up."*

I move fluidly across the stage to stand back-to-back with Raleigh and lean my head back, so my mouth is close to her ear.

"Let's give 'em a show, sweetheart!" I whisper, as I flash her a wink and count her in.

"Two-three-four!"

As the song draws to a close, the crowd goes wild, cheering, screaming, and stomping their feet. There's no feeling like it, I glance over to the front of the stage, Peyton is in her usual spot, front row, centre and I shift my gaze to the woman standing next to her. Her long dark hair cascading down her slender shoulders, as her face morphs into Ruby's. I blink my eyes a couple of times, *come on, Chase, fucking focus!* My stomach flips, as she winks at me, and I'm suddenly assaulted by memories of happier times playing on a loop in my head. As much as I want to remember the good times, I try desperately to push them away, as I turn to Lucas sat behind his drum kit. He tosses his sticks up in the air and catches them, as he looks up at me.

"You good, man?" The concern on his face evident and I plaster a smile on my face.

"All good, mate, all good."

He cocks his eyebrow, and I don't give him an opportunity to say anything more, as I turn back to the woman in the front row, who looks nothing like my Ruby. *It was good while it lasted.*

# 10

## Zeppelin

After my long conversation with HandsomeJack0304 two nights ago, I wake with a start and for the first time in a long time, I'm optimistic that falling in love again isn't entirely impossible. I know it's early days, but I have a good feeling about this. As I pad to the bathroom, I look in the mirror and as my eyes meet my own reflection, I decide I am going to write my own fairy-tale. I deserve the happy ever after, that I write so frequently about. I go out into my apartment, switch on the coffee machine and Jericho greets me with his usual single bark.

"Morning, buddy." I pet him and head back into the bathroom. I turn on the shower and find my morning playlist. I push play on my showerproof sound system and the room fills with *50 Shades of Crazy by Chase Rice.*

I spend longer than my usual twenty minutes under the almost too hot shower spray, welcoming the sting of the water, as it pounds down on my back and shoulders.

When I emerge from the shower, I feel refreshed and ready to face the day. I wrap my hair in a towel and move across to the sink, swiping the condensation from the mirror. I hum along to *Tennessee Whiskey by Chris Stapleton*, as I brush my teeth. I head into my bedroom and set about starting my day. I dry my hair into loose waves and pull on my black dungarees with a plain, slouchy over-sized white t-shirt. I make myself a coffee and settle myself at my desk, ready for a day of writing.

*"I'd rather hurt, than feel absolutely nothing at all, Tana'. You don't understand what it's like for me, what my life is like. I'm constantly hassled by my fans, hounded by the press, I can't go for a shit without someone reporting it! It's ridiculous and I'm fuckin' tired of it! I'm tired of it all, I just crave the simple life, is that too much to fuckin' ask?"*

*The pain laced in his voice, breaks my heart and I'll never understand what his life is like, but I'm willing to give it a shot. The way he makes me feel, the way in a room full of people, he acts like it's just us. He's a beautiful soul and I think I'm falling in love with him.*

As my fingers fly over the keys, I get lost in the world of Montana and Dustin. I often wondered why love was never the same in real life, as it is in romance novels. Women idealise what the definition of a perfect man is. Tall, dark, handsome, with a tragic past, might check all the boxes for most, but I'm not sure the perfect man exists, not anymore. With that thought at the forefront of my mind, I continue to type, believing that he does exist somewhere in the world.

*\*\*\**

Two nights ago, I thought I made a connection with HandsomeJack0304, and for the past two nights, I have waited for him to appear online again, so I could explore the connection that was growing between us deeper. But he hasn't appeared, no online status, no message, nothing, and I'm almost starting to give up hope. I'm sitting in front of my computer writing, with a glass of rose wine to end an extremely productive day, when my computer pings, signalling that HandsomeJack0304 has just logged in. A message immediately pops up and my stomach flips, as my eyes move eagerly over his words.

**HandsomeJack0304:** Hey stranger.

**ZepW92:** Hey yourself!

**HandsomeJack0304:** Fancy seeing you here!

**ZepW92:** Where did you go? I waited.

*Way to sound desperate, Zeppelin, nice one, you pathetic loser.*

**HandsomeJack0304:** Sorry, things got... pretty hectic at work and at home, I haven't had chance to log in, forgive me?

**ZepW92:** I'm not a very forgiving person... but seeing as it's you, I'll make an exception!

**HandsomeJack0304:** You drive a hard bargain, woman!

I smile to myself, enjoying the easy banter and flirtation between us.

**ZepW92:** So, what have you been up to?

**HandsomeJack0304:** Work's just been extremely hectic and full on, that's all. My life isn't really that interesting. What have you been up to?

I can't help noticing how quickly he changes the subject. *Interesting*.

**ZepW92:** Writing, well... trying to and failing miserably!

**HandsomeJack0304:** What's your book about?

I lean back in my chair and chuckle softly to myself at his curiosity.

**ZepW92:** It's about a recovering alcoholic, country singer and an aspiring dancer!

**HandsomeJack0304:** I want to know what it's really about, not the generic bullshit you tell your readers!

I cock my eyebrow at his witty, no-nonsense response.

**ZepW92:** Right for the jugular, like your style, babe! He's a tortured, country singer, who's been in the industry for ten years, he's become a little jaded and tired of the fame. Then he meets Montana, this sassy, no nonsense dancer, who doesn't take any crap from him!

I smile to myself at my answer.

**HandsomeJack0304:** Sounds interesting! How long have you been writing for?

**ZepW92:** I'm currently writing my ninth novel! It's been a while! Around six or seven years, give or take.

I start to think back when I first started writing full time, the newness of not having a time constraint. I didn't have to think about getting up for work and I loved not having a tyrant of a boss breathing down my neck, always telling me I wasn't good enough, that I was destined to be a wage slave for the rest of my adult life.

Abel didn't get that, not only did I write because I loved it, but because I enjoyed having the freedom of spending my days doing something I *actually* liked. Abel loved being the centre of attention, he basked in the glory of his fans asking for photos and autographs. I sometimes thought his ego entered the room before he did! I don't write for those reasons; I write because I love to create characters and see them progress and succeed in their fictional world.

**HandsomeJack0304:** Wow! Ninth novel that's an amazing achievement!

**ZepW92:** How long have you been teaching guitar and writing songs?

The dots start jumping to indicate he's typing. I lean back in my chair and take a long slug of wine. I'm fully aware that I should be writing, but I couldn't think of a better distraction.

**HandsomeJack0304:** Doing both for almost fifteen years, long time! Every day is something new, it's an adventure. I couldn't think of anything I'd rather be doing.

I smile at his thoughtful answer and the sense of pride that comes across through his words.

**ZepW92:** You sound so passionate about it! You must really love what you do! That's truly admirable, have you written anything I would have heard?

**HandsomeJack0304:** No, I'm not that good! I'm just lucky that I can make a living out of teaching guitar, the song writing is just a hobby really.

**ZepW92:** That's amazing! I used to work as a Hotel Receptionist, I hated it! My boss was a total arsehole and some of the guests were so rude! There's nothing worse than doing a job that you hate, just so you can make ends meet. I was lucky that I had the luxury of being able to give up my job to write full time, best decision I ever made!

The conversation was flowing so freely, and I truly believed this connection needed to be explored further. For once, I was looking forward to the future.

# 11

## Jax

Ever since our first sell-out gig, we've all been reluctantly famous. It's always just been about the music for all of us. The fame, the publicity, constantly being hounded by the press, it's never interested us, individually and as a band. Don't get me wrong I enjoy the lifestyle it has afforded me over the years, but it's becoming tiring. After almost fifteen years at the top, it's close to its expiration date, the quiet life is becoming more and more appealing by the day.

It's been over a month since I met ZepW92 online and after performing in front of a crowd of thousands across Europe. I looked forward to the time I stopped being Jax Chase, guitarist in Rancid Vengeance and became ordinary HandsomeJack0304. I counted down the hours, where I could just leave the madness that fame bought with it at the door and be a regular guy, who was getting to know someone without the added pressure.

Online, I was just Jack, happy go lucky, with no baggage. I felt free of the shackles of fame for the first time in a long time. It felt good, it felt like a huge weight had been lifted. I was no longer the Jackson Chase, who lost his fiancée, I was no longer a single dad. I was the me I was before the fame and the horrors of Las Vegas tainted me. In the month that had passed, I found out her name is Zeppelin Williams, she lives in Notting Hill, London, but she's originally from Southend. She moved to London five years ago after a bad break up. She has a dog called Jericho and a gay best friend called Rian. She knows the fictional version of me that I've created online. She knows me simply as Jack, from London, guitar teacher and songwriter. She knows I have two sisters and three best friends who I think of as my brothers. She doesn't really know anything beyond that, she doesn't know about Thea, it doesn't feel right, not yet, I've been extremely economical with the truth.

We've just landed in Barcelona and after a warm shower, I feel relaxed and settled on the King-Size bed in my suite. I grab my iPad, log on, seeing that she was active ten minutes ago and I immediately send her a chat request.

**HandsomeJack0304:** Hey, are you there?

I don't have to wait for long, as she responds almost instantly.

**ZepW92:** Fancy seeing you here! Come here often?

I smile to myself at her flirtatious message and begin to type an equally flirty reply.

**HandsomeJack0304:** A little too often!

**ZepW92:** Would you think it was weird if I said I looked forward to our chats?

I smile to myself at her sweet words and begin to type out my response.

**HandsomeJack0304:** No of course not, it's the only part of my day I look forward to these days...

*Fuck, why did I have to say that?* I instantly regretted typing those words as soon as I'd hit send. The dots start jumping to indicate she's typing a reply.

**ZepW92:** Sometimes you're so... sweet and your personality shines through in your words, but other times, you say things and you seem so... tortured and so sad.

**HandsomeJack0304:** It's complicated...

*Shit, why did I have to give myself away? Fucking idiot.*

**ZepW92:** Aren't we all? I'm a writer, I like to think I'm a perceptive kind of girl, I can read people. The truth is, I like you Jack, I really do, more than I thought possible. We have a connection... and it's weird because we haven't met yet, but I think we could be good together, you make me feel alive.

This is what I wanted to avoid. *Fuck.* I can't betray Ruby; I won't betray her memory and I won't bring temporary women into my daughter's life. *What the fuck was I even thinking? I was a fool to think this wouldn't happen, it was inevitable.*

**ZepW92:** Are you there? Please, don't ignore me, I couldn't bear it if I lost you. Tell me I'm not the only one who feels this? Don't you feel this...connection between us? I want to explore it, beyond just words on a screen.

The desperation in her words cause my heart to slam against my rib cage and I wish I could be what she so desperately craves, but I can't, I won't.

**HandsomeJack0304:** It's so easy to fall for someone's words, I can be anything, or anyone behind this keyboard...

**ZepW92:** You're not... I have a gut feeling that you're a genuine guy, who just wants to be loved, we're the same you and me...

I contemplate her answer for a few minutes, but she doesn't allow me to reply.

**ZepW92:** I'd like it if we could video chat? I know you've seen what I look like, but all I've got is my imagination? I want to know you, Jack.

If I video chat with her, my secret would be out. *Fuck. Why didn't I realise it would come to this?* She can't know my true identity, she just can't. The implications could be potentially... *catastrophic.* I opt to take the cowards way out and I log off. *Fuck my life.*

***

After we performed in front of a three-thousand-person strong crowd last night in Gran Teatre Del Liceu in Barcelona, we all flew back to the UK on our private jet Air Vengeance. We landed back on home soil in the early hours, because today is the third anniversary of Ruby's death and Thea's third birthday. A tragedy of a life lost, and a celebration of a life gained, all on the same day. *How fucked up is that?* Every day that has passed, I try to share something different about Ruby's life with Thea, so she doesn't forget her mummy. Even though they never met, I'm certain that Ruby would have fallen in love with her instantly, just like I did.

Ruby Logan was the best part of me. She was my conscience; the final decision maker and she wore the trousers in our relationship – most of the time and I'm not ashamed to admit it. Most importantly, she was the calming influence in the madness of Rancid Vengeance. She stepped up in the year Peyton was gone and we'll all be forever grateful for her quiet support.

"Good morning, Princess! And what does the birthday girl want for her breakfast today?" I ask her enthusiastically and she giggles.

"Daddy! I want pancakes... pweeeaasse!"

She asks sweetly and listening to her say the word 'daddy' has me turning to absolute mush. There's nothing I wouldn't do for her.

"Of course, anything for the birthday girl!"

She claps her hands excitedly and I set about making her breakfast, as Lucas taps on the back door. His early morning visits have become part of our routine for the past three years, and I relish his company and quiet support.

"Morning, dude, morning, birthday girl!"

Thea gets up from her chair and runs full pelt at Lucas. He swings her up into his arms and she plants a sloppy, wet kiss on his face.

"Uncle Lukey! I'm three today!" She squeals and he laughs, chucking her chin gently. He's been on his usual morning run, he is wearing long black shorts, a grey hoodie with the sleeves rolled up, black Nike Air trainers and a black beanie hat. *He hasn't even broken a sweat, fucking show-off.*

"I know! Wow! You're a big girl now, Thea! Guess what? Uncle Luke has got you a very special present!"

He turns to look at me with a huge grin on his face and I narrow my eyes. *He spoils her way too much!*

"Reeeealllly?" she says enthusiastically, as her big brown eyes, which remind me of Minstrels light up and Lucas nods, flashing her a wink.

"Yeah, but you're going to have to finish your breakfast for me and daddy, then...I'll give you your present, deal?"

He offers her his little finger, as a pinkie promise. *It's become their thing, bless his heart.* She puts her little finger through his and they pinkie swear.

"Daddy! Where's my pancakes? I want syrups and bloobs." She folds her arms and pouts dramatically. I roll my eyes. *Fucking Brody teaching my daughter ridiculous and pretentious slang words.*

"Say it properly, Princess?" I chastise her softly and I swear she rolls her eyes at me. *She's definitely her mother's daughter.*

"Blueberries, pweeeeeeeeeease?" She gives me those puppy dog eyes, and she knows I can't fucking resist. *She has me wrapped around her little finger.*

"Okay, coming up, sweetheart."

Lucas sets her back down on her feet and she runs off into the living room. I instantly hear fucking Baby Shark for the one thousandth time, but at least it's keeping her quiet for the time being. I make us both a cup of coffee, as I set about making pancakes. I haven't got a fucking clue how to make pancakes, you'd think after thirty-three years on this earth, I'd have learnt to make pancakes. They were Ruby's favourite breakfast, but we'd always let ourselves get distracted by sex and then order in or go out for breakfast. *Fuck, I miss those days.* Lucas must see the conflict in my eyes, as he regards me intently.

"Here, dude, let me! I'll make them!" he offers and I'm grateful for his intervention, as he sets about gathering all the ingredients he needs. *He knows his way around my kitchen better than I do.*

The truth is this house has never felt like home. She moved in with me in the year that Peyton was gone, right after Sam's suicide attempt. She was involved in the initial planning of building Vengeance Estates, I left her in charge, and she chose all of the decor, down to the picture of a monkey in sunglasses blowing a pink bubble above the toilet in the en-suite bathroom. She never actually got to see her vision come to life, but I can't look at it without thinking of her. Her ghost haunts me on a daily basis; I see her everywhere I go. Everything in the house is still as she planned; I refuse to change it. I'm terrified it will erase every trace of her.

"So, what's going on?" Lucas probes, interrupting my thoughts and I shrug.

"I've been so focused on getting through today, I haven't really thought beyond that, if I'm honest," I say frankly, taking a sip of my coffee and he nods in understanding, as he mixes the pancake batter in the glass bowl, with an electric whisk I didn't even know I owned.

"Every year that passes, it's like a noose around my neck and it takes everything I have inside of me for it not to consume me. Every year the noose gets tighter, and I can't fucking breathe, Luke, it's suffocating me."

I scrub my hand down my face and lean heavily on the kitchen island, swallowing past a lump in my throat. He switches off the whisk and regards me intently.

"I thought after three years it would at least be easier to deal with, but it still feels like it happened just yesterday. It's raw and it's fucking exhausting," I admit, defeated, as Lucas chuckles softly.

"I know you probably don't want to hear this, but you need to get yourself back into the dating game, dude. It might be a welcome distraction."

I sigh audibly. *I need to tell someone about Zeppelin; I need someone else's opinion on this whole fucked up situation I have seemingly gotten myself into.*

"I've met someone," I say in a rush, and he stops dead in his tracks.

"Really? Wow! That's fantastic, man, I'm super happy for you," Lucas says enthusiastically, looking up at me expectantly and I know he wants me to elaborate, but I don't bite.

"I take it by the silence, there's more?" he asks curiously and I nod. Lucas is extremely observant and very good at reading people. He's an excellent listener and out of the other members of Rancid Vengeance, I consider him to be my best friend, confidant and keeper of all my secrets.

"We kind of... sort of... met on a dating website," I say reluctantly, almost choking on the words and hang my head, as if it's something to be ashamed of.

"O-kay!" he drawls, in his familiar American accent that I have become accustomed to over the years.

"Online dating, that's cool, have you seen a picture? Is she hot?"

I roll my eyes, not wanting to continue this line of questioning and I idly start tidying up around him.

"Don't hold out on me, man! You're killin' me here!"

He laughs and I shake my head.

"I can't do this, not today. It's the third anniversary of my fiancée's death and my daughters third birthday," I say, guilt wracks my entire being and I don't know if I can continue this line of conversation. He moves closer, placing the bowl down on the marble topped kitchen island.

"Don't give me that fucking horse shit! That has absolutely nothing to do with it! You can tell me; come on, there'll be no judgement from me, plus, I know you're dying to tell someone!" he coaxes, as I take a deep breath. I pull my phone out, scrolling to the picture of her she sent me a few days ago. She's looking at the camera, smiling wide and blowing a kiss to the camera. I turn my phone towards him.

"Not your usual type, but she's hot, you did good!" he says with a laugh, as I put my phone back, turning it face down on the worktop.

"We met online on a dating website for professionals, she's an author, and she thinks I'm...a guitar teacher."

Lucas bursts out into hysterical laughter, and I narrow my eyes at his reaction. *Not the reaction I was expecting.*

"So, she doesn't know you're a rock star? Please tell me she knows you have a kid?"

I shake my head. I don't want to introduce her to Thea if she's only going to be a temporary part of my life. What if Thea gets attached to her? I can't do that to my daughter; she's the most precious part of my life.

"Right on! That's gonna' end badly, sorry to tell you, dude!" he says bluntly. *Talk about fucking sledgehammer, cheers Luke.*

"Thanks for the vote of confidence, dickhead!" I grumble and Lucas nods coolly.

"You want me to lie to you now? You know that's not my fuckin' style, man."

He finishes whisking the batter and moves over to the state-of-the-art induction hob that any chef would be proud to own. He sets a pan to heat on the hob and splashes in some oil in silence.

"So, you're not going to say anything? You're not going to discourage me? Or tell me I'm a fucking idiot?"

He looks up at me and shakes his head.

"Not like you'd listen anyway, man! No one ever listens to the drummer!"

We both laugh, as Thea runs towards me, temporarily halting our conversation. I lift her up in my arms and she idly twirls my hair around her finger.

"Daddy."

Thea's first word was *'Daddy'* which isn't surprising but still made me sob like a fucking baby when I first heard her. Every time I hear her say it, it melts my heart.

"Yes Princess?"

She throws her arms around my neck, twirling my long hair around her fingers, as if she's shy to say what she wants to say.

"You're not allowed to be sad on my birthday," she says in a soft, small voice and my heart slams against my rib cage, rendering me almost speechless at her statement. Lucas takes out the pancake he's making and puts it on the plate, placing down the spatula in the process.

"Thea, do you want Uncle Luke to come and help choose a dress for your party later?" Lucas tries to distract her, but she shakes her head.

"I don't want daddy to be sad anymore, Uncle Lukeyyyy." She buries her face in my neck, and I look to Lucas, completely at a loss of what to say to her.

"Princess, look at me, look at Daddy." I coax her face from my neck so I can look at her. The look in her large hazel eyes causes a lump to form in my throat and I swallow past it before I begin to speak.

"Daddy's not sad, it's your birthday for one, that's the rule whenever it's someone's birthday, no one is allowed to be sad!"

I laugh and she offers me a cheeky grin.

"See, Daddy's not sad, plus daddy has lots of surprises for you later at your party."

Her eyes widen.

"Reallllllllyyyy? What surprises?" she asks curiously and I wink at her.

"If I told you, it wouldn't be a surprise, would it, silly?"

She giggles girlishly and she plants a sloppy kiss on my cheek, wriggling for me to put her down. I set her down on her feet and she runs over to the table, climbing on to her chair, waiting patiently for her breakfast. I move over to Lucas, who has a hefty pile of pancakes set down on the plate in front of him.

"So, what exactly does this chick know about you?" he questions, curiosity getting the better of him and I shrug nonchalantly.

"It's not important, man." I sigh, reluctant to elaborate, as he cocks his eyebrow.

"Don't give me that bullshit! You know me better than that, dude!"
I puff out my cheeks, stealing myself for a lecture.

"She knows that I'm a guitar teacher called Jack, who writes songs."
He smirks.

"You do know this is going to end badly, right?" he repeats his earlier statement, and I purse my lips.

"You know what, Luke? Just fucking forget it! I don't even know why I bothered telling you. I was hoping you'd at least give me some encouragement, or at least some advice. But guess I was wrong about that!" I snap and our conversation is over, for now at least.

*** 

Thea comes bounding into my bedroom, as I'm pulling my hair into a low ponytail. Her glossy dark brown chin length hair and wide, inquisitive brown eyes, which remind me so much of her mum. She is wearing a black and white dress, with a rainbow underskirt, black and silver glittery tights and her beloved black glittery patent Doc Martens. Her hair has been curled, and she looks adorable. It is becoming harder to just paint on a smile and pretend everything's fine, I'm not sure how much longer I can keep up the pretence.

My thoughts are interrupted by Thea clearing her throat, looking up at me expectantly. She moves to stand in front of me with her hands on her hips, pouting animatedly.

"*Wow!* Look at you! You look beautiful, Thea! Like a real-life Princess!" I say with a soft smile, and she does a cute little twirl.

"Uncle Lukey helped me choose my dress!" she states proudly and I nod my approval.

"Uncle Luke has extremely good taste!"

She reaches up for me, as I hear the door downstairs slam.

"It's just me, babe," I hear Peyton call out.

"Aunty Peyton!" Thea yells excitedly and runs off in search of her, leaving me alone with my thoughts. I put on some Diesel Only the Brave aftershave, and I pick up my phone, scrolling down my contacts. I still can't bring myself to delete her number. I never realised that the eleven digits that made up Ruby's mobile phone number, would become a lifeline to me. Every time I've dialled the number for the past three years, I've got the same familiar voice message, that oddly bought comfort to me. I haven't bought this up with Kalvin in my therapy sessions, as I know he'll tell me it's unhealthy and he'll tell me to stop. I can't bring myself to stop, not yet I'm not ready to let her go.

"Heyyy, you've reached Ruby Logan, *soon to be Ruby Chase!*"

I smile at my voice in the background and her girlish giggle.

"I'm not available to take your call right now, as I'm probably having hot nasty sex with my super-hot, rock star boyfriend! Leave a message after the beep, bitches! Peace in the Middle East!" I hear the beep and hang up, comforted that I could at least still hear her voice, that's becoming more distant with each day that passes. I'm terrified I'll forget the best parts of her, her laugh, the way her nose would crinkle when she was deep in thought, her deep-seated stubbornness, the way she looked in the mornings all sleepy, natural, and so beautiful I would just lay there and watch her. Not in a creepy way, I've always been an early riser and Ruby was definitely not a morning person. I smile at the memory and check my reflection in the mirror. I am dressed in jeans, black biker boots and a plain white v-neck t-shirt, which contrasts with the bright yellow of the tattoo on my neck. I tuck my phone in my pocket, optimistic that I have the strength to get through today.

I follow the melodic sound of Thea's cute giggles, as I step into the large, bright open space where the party is taking place. My house has been transformed into every three-year old's fantasy. There is pink and purple glittery shit everywhere and Let it Go is playing loud and proud on the state-of-the-art Bose sound system.

"Jacko!" My sister Shay throws her arms around me. She is a petite blonde with brown eyes that match mine, elfin features, and a short pixie haircut.

"Leave off, Shay, no one calls me that anymore!" I grumble, as she smiles mischievously, and I roll my eyes.

"Stop pretending you hate it, you fucking grouch!" she teases and I squeeze her tighter. The truth is, I've missed both of my sisters, we don't see each other enough and if these past few years are anything to go by, life is precious. I vow right there to make more effort to see them on a regular basis.

"Whoa! It's good to see you too, Jack," she whispers softly, as I catch my mum's watchful gaze over her shoulder.

"Is that your way of telling me you missed me, just a little tiny bit? You're getting soppy in your old age, brother!"

She laughs and I nod against her reluctant to pull away. She has an uncanny knack of reading everything I don't say out loud. She's extremely intuitive and as annoying as it is, I can't hide anything from her.

"Aunty Shay Shay!" Thea comes rushing over, as Shay pulls away from me, observing me carefully with narrow eyes. I dismiss her with a wave of my hand and an animated eye roll.

"Look at you, Thea, you've gotten so big! Aunty Shay Shay has missed you lots!"

Shay says enthusiastically and Thea giggles, causing my heart to slam against my rib cage. *Whoa, that was... unexpected.*

"Jacko?" Shay says with concern in her voice, and I quickly hurry across the kitchen and out into the garden. I relish the cool air on my heated cheeks and drop down heavily onto the grey brick wall. I brace my elbows on my knees, as I hear the footsteps of someone approaching.

"Hey."

I look up and find Peyton standing in front of me. She hands me a bottle of beer, and I take it gratefully, as she takes a seat next to me. She reaches for my hand, and I let her take it.

"It doesn't get any easier, does it?" she says softly, her voice full of emotion, I take a sip of my beer and shake my head.

"I still pay the line rental on her phone, and I keep dialling her voicemail just to hear her voice," I admit and she squeezes my hand in a gesture of reassurance.

"I'm terrified I'm going to forget her, forget the sound of her voice, the way she looked in the morning all sleep mussed and gorgeous. In there just now, Thea just giggled, and it reminded me so much of Ruby, how fucked up is that?"

I take another long pull on my beer.

"It's not fucked up, it's totally normal, you're still grieving. We all are, grief doesn't have a time limit, I've heard that too many times than I care to count. I know you're probably fed up of hearing it, but it's true. We all loved her in some capacity or another, she was a huge part of all of our lives, we're not just going to suddenly forget her. She's still here."

She places her other hand over my heart, as a tear slips down her cheek. She swipes it away and flashes me a soft watery smile. I squeeze her hand tighter, and she rests her head on my shoulder, a comfortable silence settling between us.

"I'm so sorry about the baby, love," I say genuinely, as I let go of her hand and wrap my arm around her, pulling her tightly into me.

"That empty feeling never goes away, no matter how many times it happens. I knew something was wrong, but I didn't want to let myself believe that there was, if that makes sense. So, I ignored it and buried my head in the sand, pretended everything was fine. It was the week before the last date of the UK tour, I didn't want Sam to be distracted, he was already spiralling, I didn't want to add to it, so...I just kept quiet."

Her voice trembles.

*"Fuck,"* I curse softly.

"I was at work when it happened, Seb was there, bless him. There was so much blood, it's one of my triggers..."

She doesn't need to explain because I get it, Las Vegas left us all with mental and physical scars.

"I begged him not to tell Sam, but I had a panic attack, and I passed out. Next thing I know, I'm in the hospital and Sam's sitting next to the bed, pale as a ghost, with his head in his hands. All I can do is sob and tell him I'm sorry over and over and over again."

My heart hurts for her listening to her recount her ordeal. It reminds me why I have so much love for this brave, selfless woman, who has been through hell and back and still manages to smile and put others before herself.

"I don't know what to say, you shouldn't have had to go through that on your own! You're one of us, you're family, for fucks sake! Ruby would be kicking my arse all over this garden if she was here, one of us should have been there, you should have said something!"

# Jax

## Past

*I can't comprehend the level of how fucked up this situation is. We spent a whole year thinking that Peyton was dead, we all grieved, we all mourned her, and we all entered the pits of hell because she was gone. We've spent the past year coming to terms with the fact she was dead and slowly trying to move on with our lives without her in it. Walking into that hospital room yesterday and coming face to face with her was... unexpected. It bought the memory of finding Sam in a pool of his own blood, barely breathing, barely holding onto life, to the forefront of my mind. I was so fucking consumed with anger; how could she do this? How could she turn up after all this time? Sam is blinded by the love he feels for her, and he can't help but be led by his dick. Fucking prick.*

*Seeing her so skittish and so... withdrawn piqued my curiosity somewhat and I started to wonder what happened to her in the year she was gone. As I round the corner, I'm halted by the scene unfolding in front of me. Peyton is sobbing, Brody moves around to her side of the table and pulls her into his arms. I quietly observe for a few moments without making my presence known, listening to him whisper words of muted reassurance.*

*"Shhh, you're safe now, sweets, I've got you."*

*Brody always had a soft spot for her, and I can see why. Her personality was magnetic, paired with her stunning beauty and kind nature, she was a triple threat. But for what I was about to say, I needed to push those thoughts far from my mind and hold on to the seething rage I felt on behalf of my best friend who we almost lost because of her selfish actions. I move closer to them, and Brody visibly tenses with her still in his arms.*

*"Now's not a good fucking time, dude," he states softly, but matter-of-factly.*

*"I just need five minutes with Peyton to say my bit, that's all. There's no need to get all protective, man," I explain defensively, as Brody pulls away from their embrace and kisses her tenderly on the forehead.*

*"Are you going to be okay? Yell if you need me, sweets? I'll be just outside the door."*

*He winks reassuringly, as he strides out of the canteen, leaving me and her alone. The only sound is the clanking of plates and cutlery coming from the kitchen. I run my hand through my long blonde hair and tuck my hands in my pockets before I speak.*

*"Answer me one question, why the fuck did you come back?" I spit tersely, unable to keep the venom out of my voice. She balks at my words and clears her throat before she replies.*

*"I had to make sure Sam was all right, I never stopped caring about him, surely you have to know that. I saw what happened on the news. When I heard he had been stabbed, it bought back... terrible memories for me."*

*I chuckle bitterly at her statement. Terrible memories for her? That's fucking rich! She wasn't the one to find her best friend covered in blood.*

*"Bought back terrible memories for you? Fuck me, Peyton, I found my best friend lying in a pool of his own blood, unconscious after he slashed his own wrists and took a fucking overdose. I thought he was fucking dead! So, don't you dare fucking give me that bullshit, I still have nightmares. It terrified the living shit out of me, the blood, the noise he made before I booted the door down, that will stay with me for the rest of my fucking life. And all that? It's on you," I state, a harsh, unforgiving tone to my voice and I see the colour visibly drain from her cheeks. I almost feel bad because Sam quite clearly left that part out. She bursts into tears and the familiar ire I felt previously charges forward, as she struggles to get her next words out.*

*"I'm... I'm..."*

*I smile coldly.*

*"Let me guess, you're sorry? Fucking save it, sorry doesn't make up for the fact you stayed away and hid like a fucking coward. We would have protected you; we could have kept you safe! You were like a Goddamn sister to all of us, and we were like family! Sorry doesn't make up for the fact that my girlfriend, the girl who you called your sister, cried herself to sleep night after night because she'd lost the one person who knew her better than she knew herself."*

*My heartbeat starts to quicken in my chest, as I think of my Ruby. She was devastated when she found out Peyton was dead, I had to comfort her on a nightly basis, I sat up with her and held her because she was so heartbroken. Peyton swipes angrily at the tears rolling down her cheeks.*

*"Sam, my best friend, my fucking brother, tried to take his own life because you were a cold, heartless, selfish bitch!" I yell, unable to stop my tirade of anger and abuse directed at the woman in front of me.*

*"I'm sorry, I'm so sorry," she sobs, which only spurs me on. I am trembling with such rage I can't seem to stop the vile poison that comes out of my mouth.*

*"The ambulance men said he was so fucking lucky to be alive; he missed severing his main artery by a quarter of an inch, but that doesn't make up for the fact he was so fucking devastated, that instead of talking to us, he shut us all out and tried to take the cowards way out!" I bellow, as she sobs uncontrollably.*

*"I should never have come here."*

*I untuck my hands from my pockets and step closer to her, jabbing my finger angrily in her direction. She retreats into herself, but I don't take time to ask why. The truth is, I don't care.*

*"No, you're right, you fucking shouldn't have, and you need to fucking leave, right now. Make your excuses and go, because he doesn't need you fucking his life up anymore. He's a mess, Peyton, and he's fucking broken. He's changed. He's not sleeping, he's drinking, he's..."*

*My sentence is stopped abruptly by the sound of Sam's familiar low, commanding tone.*

*"Jax, that's enough," he rasps, but I shake my head vehemently.*

*"She needs to fucking know, Sam, what she put you through; what she's done. She needs to fucking see first-hand the consequences of her actions," I shout, as Sam menacingly steps forward with his fists clenched at his sides. My eyes lock with his and I challenge him wordlessly.*

*"You need to shut your motherfucking filthy mouth, Jax." He squares up to me, his stance loose. He's a few inches taller than me, but his size doesn't intimidate me.*

*"Stop fucking defending her, for Christ's sake, Sam! We were the ones who were there for you; we were the ones who picked up the pieces. I was there through the nightmares; I was the one who listened to you wake up screaming night after night. I watched you break down and turn into a shell of what you used to be. You have to take pills day after day because you can barely manage to drag yourself out of bed and that's not you! So, don't you fucking dare stand there defending her, not when she's the one who did this to you!"*

*I have to make him see that this is all sorts of fucked up, she has to know what she put him through. She has to understand the impact her actions had on not just Sam, but everyone else involved.*

*"STOP TALKING AND SHUT THE FUCK UP JAX, I SWEAR TO GOD!" Sam snarls and grabs me by my t-shirt with his uninjured arm, pinning me to the wall. I lift my chin defiantly, silently daring him to hit me. Over his shoulder, I see her frozen to the spot, as her breathing becomes erratic. I gesture with my eyes to her, and he lets go of me. Her legs buckle underneath her, and Sam catches her before she hits the floor. The shame and guilt of the last twenty minutes flood my entire being.*

*"Fuck."*

*I observe the interaction between them, her tucked into his arms, the look of sheer terror and panic in her eyes makes my heart slam against my rib cage. You caused that, you absolute dickhead.*

*"Breathe, angel, I've got you, stay with me, deep breaths," Sam says gently. "Breathe."*

*Their eyes lock and the love between them in that one look, blindingly obvious. He is sat back on his haunches in front of her and I feel sick, I'm the one who did this to her.*

*"Breathe with me, angel. I need you to focus. In and out. That's it, eyes on me, just keep breathing."*

*The guilt that barrels through my body makes my stomach twist and I can't watch anymore. I turn and walk away to the sounds of her laboured breaths and Sam's soft words of comfort.*

# Jax

# Present

Peyton laughs bitterly and shakes her head.

"And what good would that have done, babe? It would have sent Sam back into the midst of a manic episode, he would have ended up back in rehab! He wasn't strong enough to deal with it, so I made a decision for both of us not to say anything. Call me selfish, but I couldn't fucking do that to him! Not after everything we've been through!"

I'm in awe of this beautiful, brave woman sat next to me.

"It's not selfish, if anything it's selfless and it's brave, I'm in awe of you, love. I never got to properly apologise for the way I acted when you came back, the things I said to you, that was fucking unforgivable."

I shake my head in disbelief, shame flooding through me.

"You had every right to say those things, Jax. You found your best friend in a pool of his own blood, I can't imagine what you went through, it doesn't bear thinking about," she states incredulously, but our moment is interrupted by someone clearing their throat.

"Sorry to interrupt, darling," my mum says, as Peyton sniffs and unwraps herself from me wordlessly, kisses me on the cheek and rushes inside. I get to my feet and turn to face my mother, Jamie-Lee Chase. Her long blonde hair, the same shade as mine is loose around her shoulders and she is wearing black skinny jeans, heels and a champagne silk blouse, tied at her throat. Her make-up is flawless and her matching champagne heels high.

"What was all that about?" she asks, as I press my lips together and finish my beer in one long gulp.

"Nothing for you to worry about, mum," I say dismissively, as she narrows her eyes on me.

"Hadn't you better slow down?" She points to my empty bottle with her perfectly manicured fingernail.

"Hadn't you better mind your own business? Today's hard enough, mum, I can't deal with it sober," I snap, aware of how rude I'm being, but I can't seem to help myself.

"I'm just worried about you, that's all, it isn't a crime to be worried for your first born! I know you tend to... drink excessively," she observes, as I cock my eyebrow at her and point with the neck of my bottle in her general direction.

"Don't you dare judge me, Mum, I deal with it in my own way. I've been dealing with a lot lately; we're still on tour. Today is just a pit-stop in between shows so I can celebrate my daughter's birthday," I explain, feeling the need to justify myself.

"I look at her some days and think how did we get here? How is she three-years old already? She's growing right in front of my eyes; she's learning new things every day. This morning, she told me I wasn't allowed to be sad on her birthday."

Lucas catches my eye, bringing me out another beer and my mum eyes me warily, as I unscrew the lid.

"She's an intuitive little thing, bless her heart, she's picking up on things," my mum says and I take a sip of my beer.

"Every day she amazes me, mum, and all I keep thinking is her mum should be here experiencing this with us."

I take a breath to quell the tears I feel building behind my eyes.

"I've been away so much lately..."

She cuts me off.

"I know how much your job means to you, darling, but at the expense of your family? When are you going to say enough is enough? When she's eighteen and she resents you for missing out on her formative years?"

I roll my eyes.

"Like you missed out on our formative years?" I state bitterly and she cocks her perfectly plucked eyebrow. *Low blow, Chase.*

"I'll let that go, Jack, because you're upset, but I'm not your enemy, I tried my best, your father and I always made sure you had food in your bellies and clothes on your backs!"

She says defensively and I suddenly feel an overwhelming guilt at taking my anger out on my sweet, loving mother.

"It's not about that! You know I love my job, mum and I'm sorry, but please don't make me choose between my job or my daughter, because it will be her every single time. She's everything to me, there's nothing I wouldn't do for her, I'd burn the fucking world for her if it meant keeping her safe."

Our conversation is cut short by Thea calling out 'daddy' and I go in search of her to find she's wrestled Sam to the floor. She's sitting proudly on his chest, with Freddie and Zachary at her side. They've taken on the roles of her protectors and every time they're all together, I find it so adorable. I can't hide the smirk on my face, as Sam looks to me for help and I shake my head.

"You're on your own, mate!"

I burst out laughing, as Lucas joins me.

"She's a firecracker, dude, she's got us all wrapped around her little finger!" he says with a laugh, and I nod.

"I feel like I'm drowning, Luke. I can't fucking do this anymore."

My voice trembles and I know it's not healthy to still feel like this after three years, but I can't move on. *Not without Ruby.*

"I've tried so hard; Zeppelin asked me to video chat with her last night, and I fucking bottled it! What sort of person does that make me, Luke?"

I gulp down my beer, my feelings suddenly overwhelming me.

"It makes you human, Jax. I get that you're conflicted, it's understandable, but you need to at least give her a chance. I get that the whole online dating thing is... intense and I know you started off on a lie but maybe tell her the truth. Explain why you did it and start over, she'll understand. Maybe start with telling her about Thea, then go from there."

As I listen to Lucas's advice, I glance around the room at the people in attendance, family and those who have become family over the years. They're all here for Thea, to celebrate her third birthday. My eyes scan the room, it is quite the gathering my mum, dad, my sisters Shay and Skye. I spot Sam's family Marlowe, Brandon, Elijah, Willow and the Lightning Bolts, Milo and Seth, as well as Cole, Amy and Addison. Nearby are the boys, Lucas, Sam and Brody, as well as Peyton, Freddie, Zachary, Raleigh, Danny, M.J, Gorgeous George and Seb.

As I shift my gaze around the room, they land on Ruby's mum and dad Pearl, Ray and Ruby's older brother Remy. The man who looked after Peyton and Freddie in the year she was gone. I haven't seen him since Peyton and Sam's wedding, but he FaceTime's with Thea once every couple of weeks. Even though he doesn't see her every day, he still plays an active role in Thea's life, as her uncle. He's like a male version of Ruby; his mannerisms and his facial expressions remind me so much of her. He looks so different to the last time I saw him that I have to do a double take. His usually long dark hair is shorter and brushing his chin. He catches my eye and nods curtly, making his way over to me with a limp. I know that he used to be in the military, and he was stationed in Afghanistan. He had his left leg blown off below the knee by a roadside bomb in the Helmand Province. At twenty-seven, Remy was honourably discharged from the army, due to the injuries he sustained. He received a substantial amount in compensation and has undergone several operations and extension rehabilitation. He suffers from P.T.S.D, he has a prosthetic leg and walks with a slight limp. He moved to America and owns a bar in Santa Monica. He also works as a part-time self-defence trainer, as well as helping other injured veterans.

"Jackson," he greets me formally and Lucas brushes my arm.

"We'll talk more later, yeah?" I nod, as Lucas turns to leave us to it. I reach out to shake Remy's hand and he grips it firmly.

"Really good to see you again." Remy's tone light and genuine, I find myself smiling fondly.

"Likewise, mate, it's been a while," I reply and he nods.

"In person at least, the last time was at Sam and Peyton's wedding, right?"

He falters slightly, as he says Peyton's name. They dated when they were younger, he joined the army and left her behind. In the year she was gone, they reconnected. I don't know the full story, but from what I found out from Ruby, something happened between them, and he tried to win her back from Sam.

"Yeah, so how have you been?"

I grab another bottle from the kitchen island, unscrew the lid and take a sip.

"Not so good, but I'll get there eventually, or so I'm told," I admit honestly and Remy nods in understanding.

"How about you?" I inquire, as he wrinkles his nose at my question and his expression changes.

"So-so, you know how it is, there are good days and bad days," he answers with a shrug, as I pass him a bottle of beer and he takes it gratefully.

"Thanks, I can't believe it's been three years."

He shakes his head incredulously, as if he can't believe how much time has passed.

"It still feels like yesterday," I say, as he unscrews the lid of his bottle and takes a long pull.

"Tell me about it."

His wistful gaze shifts over my shoulder and I turn to see what has him so distracted. His eyes land on Peyton and she stops what she's doing, as their eyes lock. Both unmoving and staring at each other.

"You're playing a very dangerous game there, mate." My voice is stern and full of warning.

"You've got no idea, every time I come back here it's fucking torture. Seeing her, seeing what I could have had. It's like my heart is breaking all over again, I can't stand it."

The emotion in his voice is evident, as he shifts his eyes to the floor.

"You're still in love with her."

It's not a question, more of a statement.

"Even after all this time, but it'll never be enough, I'll never be enough, I'll never be... him," he admits with clear bitterness to his voice, and I feel sorry for the man who was going to be my brother-in-law. He clears his throat and glances up at me regarding him intently.

"I came here for my niece, today isn't about me."

He changes the subject with a dismissive wave of his hand, as Thea comes running up to us and slams into Remy's legs.

"UNCLE REMYYYYY!" she squeals excitedly, and he puts his bottle down on the nearby counter to swing her up into his arms.

"Hey Princess!"

She plants a wet kiss on his cheek, and he laughs.

"You came alllllllllll the way from 'Merica to see me?" she asks with an awestruck enthusiasm to her voice, and he nods with a genuine beaming grin.

"Of course, I did, I wouldn't have missed it for the world, Princess! Your presents are over there with all the others. Will you make sure she gets them and knows they're from me?"

He directs his question to me, and I nod.

"Will you take me to 'Merica one day, Uncle Remy?" She plays with the string on his grey Adidas hoodie.

"Soon, Princess, but only if your daddy says it's okay?"

I smile at their interaction, and it makes my heart swell. She clings to him and flops her head onto his shoulder.

"Tired?"

She nods, her hazel eyes growing heavy.

"It's tiring being a Princess!"

She sighs dramatically and we both laugh at her.

"She's definitely her mother's daughter."

Remy says thoughtfully, his gaze shifting back across the room to Peyton, as she rushes outside, looking more than a little out of sorts. Remy kisses Thea on top of her head and hands her to me. I take her from him, and she wraps her legs around my waist, as she idly starts playing with my hair.

"Don't," I warn him.

"I just want to talk to her, that's all."

His tone defensive and I sigh, as I watch him go after her. *This isn't going to be pretty.*

***

"Daddy? Can we cut my cake, pleeeaasse?" she asks sweetly, giving me those puppy dog eyes, and she knows I can't say no to her, especially not on her birthday.

"Of course we can, beautiful."

I drop a kiss on the top of her head, as I make my way over to the long table with piles of presents for the birthday girl. A three-tier, bright and colourful unicorn cake is the centre piece, Sam, Brody and Lucas are standing around the table. Sam's eyes are darting around the room, as I move to stand next to him.

"Everything okay, dude?" I ask curiously and Sam turns to face me, his emerald, green eyes blazing with anger.

"What the fuck is he doing here, Jax?" he says quietly through gritted teeth and a rather menacing tone to his gruff voice.

"Not now, man, he's here for his niece's birthday, I didn't know he was going to be here, it was up in the air whether he could make it. Just leave it, please, at least for now?"

His nostrils flare, as his eyes land on the two of them outside in the garden deep in conversation. Remy cups Peyton's cheek in his hand, as my hand flies out to grab Sam's arm to stop him from following, his bicep tensing, as he glances down to where my hand is rested.

"Sam, stop. Not here, not at my daughter's birthday... please."

His lips purse, as he clenches his fists at his sides. His wedding band glistening, as the light catches it.

"He's got his grubby fucking hands on my wife!" His jaw is tight, and I flash a warning look in his direction. He turns to me and nods curtly in response to my request. I set Thea down on her feet and everyone gathers round to sing happy birthday. Brody and I are handed our acoustic guitars by Raleigh, and we start to play happy birthday. My dad picks Thea up, as Sam starts to sing to her, and we all watch her blow out her three candles. Everyone erupts into a round of applause for the birthday girl.

"Make a wish, Princess!" my dad says to her, as she giggles girlishly. It is the most adorable sound I have ever heard and my heart slams against my rib cage, as my mind starts to wander to Ruby, to her looking glowing and pregnant, cradling her small bump as she watched me serenade her outside Brent Cross Tube Station. A fleeting image settles itself in my frontal lobe and my stomach roils at the sight of Ruby's large hazel eyes, filled with tears and pleading with me to help her, as a dark crimson hole forms in her forehead. My breathing becomes erratic, and I can't fucking be here. *I can't.* I have to get out of here, I'm aware it's my daughter's birthday, but I need to be anywhere away from here.

"Jack?" I hear my mum's concerned voice filter through my foggy brain, but I don't engage her. I push my way through the throng of people all calling my name and rush out of the front door, the weight of the day bearing down on me like a tonne of bricks.

My heart is beating a frantic tattoo, as I stumble onto the gravel driveway, my knees buckling beneath me. I sink to the ground, my world spinning, as I drag my hands agitatedly through my hair. My chest begins to grow tight with the dull ache I feel, and bile rises up in my throat threatening to choke me where I kneel. *Fuck, come on, Chase, breathe.* My grip on my hair tightened, the mild bite of pain seemed to ground me somehow. I take a long, slow, deep breath desperately trying to quell the tears I can feel burning my eyes. I hear the front door close with a click and the sound of footsteps crunching across the gravel. There's a brief silence, as Sam drops down next to me, handing me a beer and sipping his own.

"Wanna' talk about it?"

I turn to him, his dark hair looking mussed as if he'd been constantly running his hands through it. I take the bottle of beer from him with a trembling hand, and when I don't answer, he nods.

"Fine, if you don't want to talk, then we can just sit here in silence, or you can at least tell me why you walked out of your daughter's birthday party. She's in there sobbing her little heart out by the way, telling everyone how you broke your promise of not being sad on her birthday."

My heart breaks a little more at hearing him say those words. I briefly squeeze my eyes shut, unable to find the words to tell him why I ran out of my daughter's birthday party. *Did I tell him I hallucinated my dead fiancée? Did I tell him that I can't look at Thea without seeing Ruby? Did I tell him the guilt I carry around on a daily basis cripples me and keeps me awake at night?*

"I could cope if it was just Thea's birthday, but it was the day her mum was fucking murdered! How am I supposed to deal with that year after year?"

Sam cocks his pierced eyebrow.

"Really? You're asking me that? You fucking deal with it because she's your daughter! And she deserves her dad to be present! She survived and it's your duty to raise her, to fucking protect her, you selfish prick!"

He snaps and I idly peel the label off the beer bottle. I can't explain how I feel in a way that he'll understand, so I shake my head and get to my feet.

"You know what, just fucking forget it! You'll never understand!" I choke out, as he gets up and grabs my arm, his grip verging on too tight. His eyes flashing with irritation and obvious anger at my careless statement.

"I'll never understand. Are you fucking serious? My sister and J.D were the two people who set all of this in motion, don't you think I blame myself for that? Don't you think I go over and over it in my head trying to figure out if I could have prevented it all? It makes me feel physically sick! So don't you stand there and tell me I don't fucking understand!"

He grinds out, his voice gruff and pained, his jaw tight.

"I've met someone," I blurt out, as he drops his grip of my arm, and he looks at me soberly.

"Are you asking for permission to move on? Is that it? Because it's been three years, dude. No one is going to think any less of you for meeting someone else, if anyone deserves their happy ever after it's you."

His words resonate deep, and I let out a long, laboured breath.

"How can I move on when I hallucinate my dead fiancée on a near daily basis? I see her in every woman I've had sex with! I saw her just now when I ran out of my daughter's birthday, I saw her with a bullet hole lodged in her head, pleading with me to fucking help her, Sam! How fucked up is that? I can't look at my daughter without seeing her, I've met someone, and she doesn't even know my real fucking name!"

I all but yell at him, trying and failing to fight the tears that have tracked their way down my cheeks. His eyes widen at my declaration.

"What? Wait, wait, back up a fucking second, she doesn't know your real name?"

He asks incredulously, cocking his eyebrow curiously. I laugh bitterly, swiping the tears away from my eyes.

"Seriously, dude, that's what you took from that?" He shakes his head.

"I...I don't know what to say, but I know what you're going through, more than most. I hit rock bottom when I thought Peyton was dead, I tried to find a version of her in every woman I had sex with, I saw her at every show we played, that fucking video playing on a loop in my head twenty-four, seven. It kept me awake at night, I hid behind Bolt, when in reality, I felt like I was dying inside. I opened a vein and tried to take my own life, for fucks sake."

He runs both of his hands through his hair, the still visible, large, jagged scars on his wrists a brutal reminder of his suicide attempt. He drops down heavily on the stone step in front of the door, as if he his ridding himself of an unwanted thought. I move forward and sit down next to him.

"I was lucky that I got a second chance, not everyone gets that and I'm so sorry you never got that, Jax. But it still haunts me, the nightmares are less frequent these days, but it's still there, I see it in Peyton's eyes when she thinks no one's watching, I see the scars that sick fuck left her with!" His voice is filled with emotion.

"I don't blame you, Sam, no one blames you, none of this was your fault, this was on J.D and Savannah. I had a lot of suppressed anger towards you, for a long time. I blamed Brody for leading you down that dark path all those years ago, you were my best friend, Sam, but... I feel like I don't know you anymore. I blamed you for making me find you in a pool of your own blood, I went through hell, praying you'd pull through, praying you wouldn't die."

He turns to me and shakes his head; his face filled with such shame and remorse.

"I'll never be able to apologise enough for that, that time of my life, it feels so far away now, but I wasn't in a good place back then, the pain of losing her, it fucking consumed my every waking thought. That feeling, I'd never felt it before, it was alien to me because I'd never been in love with anyone before, not like I was with Peyton. She was it for me, she was my reason, and I couldn't see another way out. I know that doesn't excuse my shitty behaviour, or justify my actions, but I'm so fucking sorry that it was you that found me."

He drops his head into his hands.

"I've never told anyone this before, but I've thought about ending it, then the guilt takes over and I hate myself for thinking it. How could I even contemplate leaving Thea behind? She's... my world, she's everything to me."

I look up at the sky, the blue cloudless sky a stark contrast to the overwhelming darkness I feel deep in my soul. There is a brief silence between us, but it isn't awkward or uncomfortable. Sitting here on the grey stone steps of my house, I find a renewed hope that I'm no longer alone and it's okay to move on with my life. I had to build a life without Ruby, no matter how painful it was and sipping beer with Sam, I had come to accept that.

# 12

## Zeppelin

We've spoken every night for over a month, at the same time, without fail. I am glad I decided to pursue our connection deeper, because I couldn't imagine my life now without him in it. I know its early days, and I haven't seen a picture of him, or even video chatted with him yet, but deep down, I feel it. I feel our relationship growing stronger every time we talk, and Jack could be the one my soul has been searching for, I think he could be the one to end my single days.

I never felt this nervous rush when I was with Abel, or when I've been with a man in general, but I know from his words alone, that Jack is special. He gives away small parts of himself with each conversation we have, and I don't think he realises how important he's become to me. In the month since we started talking, I'm now halfway through writing my ninth novel. He doesn't know it, but he's become my muse and my source of inspiration, which is why I don't understand his reason for logging off, when I mentioned video chatting. *Is it something I did wrong? Has he realised I'm not worth it?* These are the questions that are on a constant loop in my mind, as I'm trying to sleep.

I'm lying in my Queen size bed, in the dark, the moonlight peeking through the slats in the light grey Venetian blinds. I'm mindlessly scrolling through my social media account hoping it will help me fall asleep, when I get a WhatsApp message from him. In the month since we started talking, we swapped numbers. Out of morbid curiosity and with the sole intention of cussing him out, I swipe the message open.

**HandsomeJack0304:** Firstly, I wanted to apologise for being an absolute dickhead. I had my reasons for logging off and it wasn't anything you did, so I don't want you to think that. I've got some issues I'm working on right now and I'd appreciate your understanding. Just know that I'm really sorry for making you think it was something you did, it wasn't. I'd totally get it if you didn't want to talk anymore, I deserve every ounce of your anger, I was a total shit head.

As I read his words, I am taken aback by his honesty and his sincerity. I'm speechless, I opened his message with the sole intention of giving him a piece of my fucking mind, but now I feel bad for even thinking it. I lay there staring at the screen for a few minutes, contemplating how to reply to him. I see the dots jumping and another message comes through. *He must be feeling particularly chatty tonight, and I intend to take advantage of that.*

**HandsomeJack0304:** I know you must be angry, but please forgive me? I look forward to our chats, it's an escape from my normal life. My real life is fucking hectic and full-on, but it's nice to just chat and shoot the shit with someone. It helps me to unwind and forget for a little while.

I smile at his words and start to type my response.

**ZepW92:** I had every intention of cussing you out for just logging off like that. But when I read your message, all the fight was knocked out of me. You seem so sincere, and your honesty took me by surprise. You're not like other men, Jack. I've never spoken to anyone quite like you before and it's refreshing; you're one of a kind. Of course, I accept your apology, I get I was as much to blame as you were. I shouldn't have pushed you like that when we were getting to know each other. I look forward to our chats too, I've been single for far too long, five years to be exact and I'm a little out of practice. But I'd like it if we could practice together?

I press send and mentally slap myself all over my bed when I realise what I said could be easily taken out of context. *Fucking idiot.*

**ZepW92:** Oh God! I didn't mean that! Not in a dirty way, I realise how that came across! Sorry! Out of practice, remember?

**HandsomeJack0304:** Fuck, there was me thinking it was my lucky night! I've been single for three years, there's been the odd one-night stand here and there, but nothing really beyond that. I'm no saint, far from it, but I think maybe I'm ready to move on and start dating again. My life is complicated, to say the least, maybe a little more than most, but I'm willing to give it a shot, if you are?

I turn over onto my side and re-read his response a few times before typing a message back. *Fuck, I was definitely not expecting that.*

**ZepW92:** I'm willing to see where this takes us and get to know each other better. You intrigue me, Jack, and I still don't know your surname!

He goes quiet for a few minutes, then the dots start jumping again.

**HandsomeJack0304:** It's Logan, my name is Jack Logan. I get that this is unconventional, but I'd like it if we got to know each other better too.

**ZepW92:** Yes, I'd like that a lot!

I find myself agreeing all too easily to this sweet, yet mysterious, man behind the keyboard.

# Jax

We continue our chat uninterrupted and I'm grateful the boys have left me to my own devices this evening. I think they realised I must have needed some alone time after my meltdown at Thea's birthday party. She told me she hated me for breaking my promise of not being sad at her birthday and those words cut deep. Every hiccupping sob was like a thousand knives to my heart, and I deserved every last ounce of her anger. I held her in my arms, as she cried herself to sleep and I cried right along with her, feeling like the number one contender for the world's worst father award. At that moment, I couldn't have needed Ruby more, she would have been the voice of reason, and I wouldn't have been lying there in her Elsa from Frozen bed, feeling like I'd failed her somehow.

We had flown back to Spain, this time Valencia to play a gig at La Sala, we were in good spirits and after the show, we'd all opted to go out for dinner and go back to the hotel. It was a welcome change for us because usually after a gig, we're usually so wired that we would want to go for drinks and party until the sun came up. These days it's a little different, we're more subdued as the years have gone on and two out of four of us have settled down. Well, I doubt whether Brody would ever settle down, but Raleigh seems to be good for him, she seems to ground him somehow and he's less wild because of her calming influence.

I headed back to my hotel room for the night, and I Face Timed with Thea, she seems to have forgiven me for now and my heart melted when I saw her with her hair in pigtails. Marnie, the band's nanny is looking after her while we're away. Marnie Breckenridge is Peyton's brother Dexter's girlfriend. He lost his fiancée Grace in the wedding massacre in Vegas three years ago. He took some time off his job as a police officer to grieve the loss of the woman he loved and went travelling for a year. He met Marnie on a beach in Bali where she was travelling too, and they have been together for a year. She is a part-time Instagram influencer with over a quarter of a million followers and a part-time nanny. She looks after Freddie and Zachary while Peyton is at work and when she comes on tour with us. I initially didn't want her to look after Thea because I want to raise her right and be present in my daughter's life. But life on the road with Rancid Vengeance, it isn't always possible, so we came to a compromise. Marnie looks after her when I'm out of the country on tour and Thea seems to have taken to her, which is all I can ask for.

I'm lying on the King-Sized bed in my hotel room and after I apologised to Zeppelin for logging off so suddenly, I decide to take Lucas' advice and tell her about Thea. If we're going to pursue this connection between us, I had to start with being honest with her. I felt like I owed it to her and to myself to tell her the truth, at least a version of it.

**HandsomeJack0304:** I need to start by telling you something... It's pretty important...

**ZepW92:** Hmm... I'm intrigued, Mr Logan...

My stomach flips at her calling me Mr Logan, but oddly, it brings a sense of comfort to me.

**ZepW92:** Don't leave me hanging, you're scaring me...

I gnaw on my thumbnail, my fingers hovering over the keyboard on the screen, contemplating how to tell her that I have a three-year-old daughter.

**HandsomeJack0304:** I don't mean to scare you, but I owe you the truth since you've been so forthcoming with me. I want to explore whatever this is between us and it's about time I was honest with you.

**ZepW92:** Whatever it is, it changes nothing between us, I want you to know that.

I smile at her words and that gives me the confidence boost I need to type the words. *Come on, Chase, what's the worst that can happen?*

**HandsomeJack0304:** I have a daughter...

The dots start jumping for a few seconds and stop abruptly, then the inevitable happens, she leaves me on read with the two blue ticks and doesn't reply to my message. *Fuck my life.*

# Zeppelin

When he said he had something to tell me, him having a daughter was the last thing I was expecting. *What the actual fuck?* It took a few moments for the words on the screen to register in my shell-shocked brain, before I read his message and didn't send a reply, I needed some time to process. *What did this mean for our blossoming relationship?* When a person has a child with someone else, they are inextricably bound together for the rest of their lives. While they may no longer be in a relationship together, they by necessity have to interact and co-parent with that person. I had to ask myself the serious question, did I really want to get into a relationship with someone who was a father? *Did I really have what it took to be a stepparent? What if it didn't work out between us and he introduced us?* Some children adjust well into blended families, but what if I met her and she hated me? Inevitably, he would put her first, what parent wouldn't? My mind was a mess of unanswered questions; it was a riot of self-doubt and morbid curiosity gnawed at me like a swarm of angry bees.

I opened up my social media account and typed in Jack Logan. A barrage of Jack Logan's popped up, but because I had yet to see a picture of him, how would I know it was him? I stared blankly at the screen for long minutes, wondering what the hell I had gotten myself into and allowing the stark realisation of his confession to sink in. *What did this mean for us now? Where did we go from here?* I sit up in bed, contemplating what to do next when Jericho crawls up the bed and drops down on my legs, as if he knows what I need. I stroke his soft fur between my fingers, and he plants a single lick to my nose, it soothes me somewhat, giving me the strength and courage, I need. I lean my head against the grey velvet headboard trying to find the words when my phone pings a notification. HandsomeJack0304 has sent you a photo and out of curiosity I open up WhatsApp. My mouth gaping at what I see on the screen. He's sent me a picture of himself with his daughter.

His face is obscured, it's been taken from an artistic angle, and the candid photo is black and white. He's tall, muscular, lean and he looks genuinely happy, the side view of his face bursting with a cheeky grin. His blonde hair is pulled up into a neat man bun on top of his head and he has a neatly trimmed goatee beard. He is wearing three-quarter length denim shorts, which showcase leg sleeves on both legs, a white v-neck t-shirt and Converse. In the photo, he is throwing his daughter up in the air and the shot has been caught with her in mid-air as if she is floating. She has short jaw length dark hair and the smile on her face tells me she adores her daddy. My heart constricts in my chest, and I suddenly feel like an awful human being for just not responding to his message like that.

**HandsomeJack0304:** These feelings I'm developing for you...perplex me, I can't explain it, I'm so confused and conflicted. I didn't tell you sooner because I'm terrified of how fast and intense this...whatever this thing is between us is progressing. I'm so sorry I didn't tell you, but please understand why I didn't. Forgive me, Zeppelin, please.

The tone of his message obliterates any ill feeling or anger I had towards him after he revealed his secret. It breaks my heart reading his words back and I contemplate what to say to him for a few moments, biting my lip in deep thought. *How do I even begin to follow that bombshell? How do I make amends for leaving him on read and not responding like a complete fucking coward?*

**ZepW92:** I'm sorry too... so fucking sorry.

I try to inject as much remorse into my words as I can, and I curse myself to hell when a hot tear slips down my cheek. Jericho whines and climbs further up onto my lap, nudging his nose against my wet cheek, as if reading my scrambled thoughts. I scratch behind his ears to placate him, and he settles back down again.

**HandsomeJack0304:** You've got no need to apologise; it was on me for not being honest with you. But before I continue, I will not choose between you or my daughter because it will be her every time...

The pure conviction in his words are admirable, as I type back my reply.

**ZepW92:** I would never expect you to choose, what sort of person do you think I am? I would never make you choose.

**HandsomeJack0304:** She didn't have the best start in life, I want to give her the world, I want to shield her from harm, I want to protect her with my dying breath. She's everything to me; she's the reason I'm still breathing.

I start to wonder what happened to him, what happened to her mother? I try desperately to rein in the morbid curiosity, but I fail miserably and before I know what I'm saying I type out my response.

**ZepW92:** What happened? Are you still with her mum?

I ask, suddenly regretting my intrusive reply. He doesn't reply straight away, and his silence sets me on edge.

**ZepW92:** Sorry, I shouldn't have asked, that was intrusive and none of my business.

I gnaw on my thumbnail while I await his reply, and relief floods me as the dots start jumping.

**HandsomeJack0304:** No, not at all. She died in childbirth three years ago; it's just me and Thea now.

My heart slams against my rib cage, as I read the words a few times before I can think of what to say next. That must have been awful for him, suddenly being thrust into single fatherhood. I can't comprehend how that must have felt for him, how it must have impacted his life.

**ZepW92:** I'm so sorry, that must have been hard for you.

I don't know what else to say, I'm struck dumb at his tragic story.

**HandsomeJack0304:** It's been difficult to say the least, there's been night's when I just wanted to run away and never look back and then the guilt overwhelms me for even thinking it. The night's when she was screaming the house down because she was teething, the night's when she thinks monsters are under her bed, it makes me question whether I've got what it takes to be a good father. The night she was born, and she was handed to me, this tiny helpless little thing, wailing and pink cheeked, it scared the shit out of me. I was suddenly responsible for this human being who looked half like me and half like her mum, it wasn't how I envisioned things, it wasn't how I imagined my life would turn out.

I read between the lines, and I conclude that he was in love with his daughter's mother. But lying in the dark, I make peace with the fact that even with a child, it doesn't make me want him any less. In a way, it makes me want him more and I was more than willing to work at it to make that possible.

# 13

## Jax

I felt like a heavy weight had been lifted from my shoulders after I told Zeppelin the truth about Thea. Her initial reaction startled me, and I suddenly regretted my bombshell revelation. I was acutely aware that this could be make or break for us. Even though we had yet to meet, it could have halted our blossoming relationship before it had even begun. The guilt wracks me every time we talk, I so desperately want her to know the real me, but I know once my secret is exposed, she'll leave, and I don't think my heart can take that. I could feel her slowly slipping away from me as soon as I told her, and I sent her that photo of me to prove to her that I wanted to at least try with her. My face might have been obscured and not in full view, but it was my way of letting her see a glimpse of who I really am. I'm staring at the screen of my phone, watching the dots furiously jumping and eagerly anticipating her reply when it pings with a notification.

**ZepW92:** You said you couldn't sleep, me neither. How about we give each other a helping hand with that?

She swiftly changes the subject, and the tone is light.

**HandsomeJack0304:** How might you do that then, gorgeous?

I smile to myself at my flirty tone.

**ZepW92:** You're going to have to use your imagination, babe!

*Am I really going to turn into one of those guys who jacks off with some stranger he meets online?* One quarter of one of the world's biggest rock bands, I've been nominated for greatest guitarist of the 21st century for Guitar Magazine ten years in a row. *For fucks sake.* But this woman, who I've gotten to know over the past month, has my curiosity well and truly piqued and before I can talk myself out of it, I type back a reply.

**HandsomeJack0304:** I'm not sure you could handle my imagination, beautiful.

**ZepW92:** Try me, handsome...

*What harm can it do?* It's been months since I had any sort of action. I've had to make do with Pam and her five daughters.

**HandsomeJack0304:** My cock is rock solid, babe. Think you can help me out?

**ZepW92:** How about we help each other out, handsome, my pussy is dripping wet...

I settle myself back against my pillows and slide my boxers down my thighs. I wrap my hand around my cock and stroke it up and down.

**HandsomeJack0304:** Is it indeed? You're a very bad girl...

**ZepW92:** Then punish me...

**HandsomeJack0304:** Oh, I intend to, gorgeous girl, with pleasure...

**ZepW92:** I'm fingering myself for you...I want you nice and hard for me...

*Fuck me.* I swallow hard and start to pleasure myself. *When did this conversation start getting X-rated?*

**ZepW92:** Show me your cock, I want to see you.

*This could end badly, Chase. Think about the consequences.* I try to talk myself out of it and before I know what I'm doing, I reach over to dim the lights. I adjust the angle of my camera and activate video chat. I'm careful to hide my face and shift the camera down so she can see from my chin downwards. She turns her camera on, and my heart starts a steady beat in my chest. *Fuck, she's beautiful.* Her eyes are sparkling with mischief, her blonde hair perfectly mussed, and her pert breasts pushed up in her black lace bra. She has a tattoo on her sternum, and I can't quite make out the design, as it's hidden.

"I want to see your face," she asks and I chuckle softly.

"I'm camera shy!" I try to joke, hoping she won't push the issue.

"God, you're so fucking beautiful." My voice is gruff with want and she moans audibly.

"Show me your cock," she demands, her voice thick with hunger, as I move the camera, focusing on my long, thick, length.

"Think you can take it?" I challenge.

"Oh God, that's so fucking hot. I think I can take it all," she says in a rush, almost sounding embarrassed.

"Your turn, take off your bra, I want to see all of you," I state, as there is a brief moment of shuffling and then I'm looking at her tits. *Fuck me, they're perfect, just like her. Shit, where did that come from?* I shake that thought away and focus on her.

"I have a tattoo just here."

She moves the camera down to her bare, waxed pussy and I see a tattoo above her labia which is a set of stairs leading down and the words 'stairway to heaven.' I laugh out loud and she laughs too.

"My best friend dared me when we were drunk one night!" I hum and she moves the camera back up to her face.

*"Fuck*, I'm so horny right now, Jack."

*You and me both, sweetheart.*

"Me too, babe," I admit, eagerly anticipating her reply.

"Are you still stroking yourself, handsome?"

I wrap my hand around my cock and stroke it a few times. *Fuck, it feels so good. It would feel even better with a woman's lips wrapped around it.*

"Mmm, feels so good, babe. Are you still finger fucking yourself?"

"Yes, I'm so horny right now, I wish you were here to relieve my frustration, I wish you were inside me," she pants, her voice desperate and filled with pure unadulterated want.

"Me too, babe, but we'll have to make do with this for now, at least until we can do it for real and we will do it for real, I can fucking promise you that. You're making me feel things, Zep."

*Fuck, fuck, fuck, why did I have to go and say that for? Bad move, Chase.* She goes quiet for a few seconds, her face thoughtful and her mouth agape. I fear I've scared her off, until she takes a breath and begins to speak.

"You make me feel things too, Jack. Things I can't explain and things I haven't felt in a long time. Oh God, I think I'm going to come!"

*Fuck, that was unexpected.* I stroke my cock a few more times, increasing the pace, as the familiar feeling rises to the surface.

"Me too, babe, me too, let's come together."

I continue stroking myself, as I squirt all over my chest.

"Fuck, I'm coming, Zep. Jesus Fucking Christ!" I bellow.

"That's    it,    I'm    coming    too,    Jack,    oh    God, FUCKKKKKKKKKKKKKKKKK!"

We both go quiet for a few moments, and I can't think of anything useful to say, so I deactivate my camera without saying another word. The guilt instantly consuming every part of me, and I head to the bathroom to get some tissue, catching sight of my flushed reflection in the mirror. *Fuck me, Chase, what were you thinking wanking off to a virtual stranger on camera? You sad, pathetic, bastard.* I run my hands through my hair, and I'm so overwhelmed by guilt I feel sick. I drop to my knees in front of the toilet bowl and vomit violently, my stomach knotting and roiling. When my stomach is satisfied its empty, I let out a stifled sob, my emotions getting the better of me. *I'm so sorry, please forgive me, buttercup.*

***

I hate waking up in the morning and being so overwhelmed by grief. I hate looking in my daughter's eyes and seeing Ruby staring right back at me. I hate opening the newspaper and seeing our lives splashed front and centre. I hate myself most of all, for being so God damn weak. After mine and Zeppelin's X-rated conversation last night, I went to sleep disgusted with myself and it was a long while before I allowed myself to drift off. I felt an overwhelming sense of guilt, as I caught sight of my reflection in the bathroom mirror. I felt so disgusted I didn't want to be reminded of the pathetic, weak shell of a man I had become in the three years since Ruby's death.

I'm sitting on the stark, white sectional sofa in my hotel suite in Valencia before I head out to rehearsals for tonight's gig at Loco Club. I look at the screen at Kalvin and he's regarding me intently. Stroking his chin, he sits back comfortably in his chair, with one leg resting on top of the other. He's dressed rather flamboyantly today, in a black and white checkered shirt and a black dickie bow. His looks expectantly at me over the top of his black rimmed glasses. We're both silent for long minutes, as he starts furiously tapping at the screen of his iPad.

"Don't do that, you know it makes me edgy when you do that, after almost three years, have you learned nothing?" I say impatiently and he stops, regarding me with careful, wary eyes.

"I apologise, I'm just interested to know what's got you so on edge, you're usually forthcoming in our meetings but it's like you've just clammed up. It's very unlike you, that's all," he asks, his voice full of quiet concern, as I lean back on the sofa and stroke my chin thoughtfully.

"I-I've met someone," I admit and he cocks his eyebrow.

"Wow, that's great, I take it there's a potential but coming?"

*Perceptive as ever, Kalvin.*

"We met online, but she doesn't know me as Jax Chase, she knows me as Jack Logan, guitar teacher," I explain and he nods.

"Ah, so, she knows a fictional version of you?"

I nod, feeling an overwhelming sense of shame and guilt.

"Do you want her to know the real you?" he asks probingly, as I gnaw viciously on my thumb nail, and I contemplate his question with careful thought. *Do I want Zeppelin to know the real me*? In a way, yes but once she knows my real identity, will she still like me, or will she hate me for lying about it?

"In a way, no, because I'm terrified that once she knows the real me, she'll know what happened, what I went through. I can't bear to see the look of pity in people's eyes, I don't want what happened to define the rest of my life, it makes me feel sick."

I take a few steadying breaths before continuing.

"We've been talking for over a month online and the more we've been talking, the more I want to explore whatever it is that's between us, there's a connection. I've been giving her snippets of information about me but being careful not to tell her anything that could give my identity away. She knows about Thea now, and I sent her a photo of me, but chose one that obscured my face."

Kalvin goes to type on his iPad but catches my annoyed gaze in the camera and sets his hands down in front of him.

"Why don't you want her to know the real you? Jackson Chase instead of Jack Logan?"

He asks, his voice full of concern and I sigh.

"I've been in Rancid Vengeance for almost fifteen years, I've been there, done that and got the t-shirt. Once women realise, you're who you are, it's like they've got some sort of radar. I've seen my fair share of gold diggers and women who are just in it for the money, the status and the exposure. Ruby didn't give a shit how famous I was, or how much money was in my bank account, she just wanted me and me alone. It was the first time a woman had gotten to know me, I was always waiting for the other shoe to drop, but it never did, not with her, she was like the fucking sun."

I can't keep the pain out of my voice, as I try to keep it together, the grief so overwhelming I feel like I'm drowning in it. I swallow past the lump in my throat and steeple my hands beneath my chin.

"My motto has always been life's too short for regrets, but my biggest regret is screwing around on her in the early days. She didn't fucking deserve the way I treated her; she deserved to be treated like a Queen. I was a complete prick, I lied and I fucking cheated on her, more times than she knew about. I'll never forgive myself for that because I don't deserve it. It makes me feel guilty every time I think about it."

I admit and Kalvin hums his answer.

"Were you expecting Ruby to be like all of those other women? The one's who used you for your fame and your status. It sounds like you had very low expectations back then and were surprised when Ruby exceeded those expectations, she was the complete opposite of what you'd previously experienced."

I hate it when he's right and I nod.

"She exceeded every single expectation I had, she wasn't like anyone I'd ever met before, she was sassy, she challenged me in every way possible, she was a breath of fresh air compared to those other bimbos I'd let into my bed. She wasn't afraid to call me out on my bullshit."

I explain and Kalvin pushes his glasses up the bridge of his nose.

"So, what it is about Zeppelin that's intriguing to you?"

His question catches me off guard. I open and close my mouth to speak, but nothing comes out. Kalvin smiles sympathetically.

"I apologise, I'm aware my question caught you a little off guard. I just want to understand, that's all."

I nod curtly, taking a deep breath before answering.

"She's the total opposite of Ruby in looks, she's blonde, fair skinned, but her personality is the same, she's sassy, independent and I can tell she's been just as broken as me, but I don't think she quite trusts me to tell me the full story yet, so we're both keeping secrets."

I say with a nonchalant shrug.

"Are you somehow using that excuse to justify why you're choosing to keep your real identity hidden from her?"

Kalvin asks matter-of-factly.

"Not at all, I just...my whole life has been about Rancid Vengeance, releasing albums, performing gigs around the world, signing autographs, doing interviews, seeing sensationalised stories on gossip sites, in the newspapers, it's exhausting. I just want something, someone who isn't exposed to that. Is that really too much to ask? She's going to find out eventually, but I don't know what that will mean for us once she does."

With those words, I'm resigned to the fact that Zeppelin Williams will never truly know Jackson Chase. *At least not yet.*

# 14

## Zeppelin

In the five years since I had moved away from Southend, I had never experienced what it's like to be a single girl living in London. The simplicity of just sharing a bottle of wine with girlfriends while we pamper, preen, and make ourselves look fabulous, whilst listening to cheesy eighties and nineties pop music. I had never experienced the easy banter, or the girlish giggling about boys because I'd never had girlfriends before. I'd written about it on more than one occasion, but deep down it was something I longed for.

I grew up without a mother and didn't really connect with any of the girls in school. Even though I had the unconditional love of my Nan and Granddad, it didn't really compare to having someone to talk to about boys, periods and someone to confide in when I was struggling.

After my dad died, I became withdrawn and preferred my own company. I found it difficult to communicate what I was feeling, and I didn't make friends easily. I was a loner, and I never really fitted in; I was different to the other girls. They liked fashion, make-up and had celebrity crushes. I liked poetry, reading and music, I always had my earphones in because that was my escape from reality. I got lost in lyrics because they spoke to me, they got across what I could never say out loud and that became my happy place.

"Somethin' you wanna' talk about, baby girl?" Rian's soft Welsh lilt interrupts my thoughts, as I'm sat at my white gloss dressing table, applying my make up in the light up mirror wearing my white silk dressing gown with a delicate pink cherry blossom design all over.

"I was just thinking..."

He chuckles softly at my statement, as I swipe my mascara over my lashes.

"That's never a good thing!" he says with a smirk, as he takes a long sip of his cool white wine.

"I've never experienced what it's like to be a single girl living in London," I admit wistfully and he offers me a soft, sympathetic smile.

"I get it, you just want to be a small-town girl, living in a lonely world!" he states dramatically and gives me a twirl, finishing with a theatrical kick of his leg. I laugh at his ridiculousness, as I finish applying my mascara.

"No, on a serious note, you've been so wrapped up in grief for the past five years, you need to start getting out and living your life, you're a long time dead, baby girl."

I catch sight of my dull, lifeless silver eyes in the mirror, and they lack sparkle. The sparkle that hasn't been present since I lost Abel all those years ago.

I've found myself just lately longing for the joyous, tingly feeling I get when I talk to Jack. He makes me feel so alive that I forget everything that made me feel dead inside in the first place.

"You've got that dreamy look on your face again! Is it Handsome Jack by any chance?"

Rian laughs and I chew fiercely on my bottom lip.

"I don't know what it is about him, Ri, he always knows the right words to say, he gets me on a level that no one ever has before and it's so confusing and so... addictive," I admit with a sigh and Rian moves to stand behind me, taking over styling my hair into soft waves.

"I hate to rain on your parade, babe, but do you ever think he's saying those things to you because he knows it's what you want to hear? I get that talking to someone online can be intense and I don't mean to be a bastard, but I really don't want to see you get hurt, Zep."

I look up at his expectant eyes in the mirror and he's chewing on his bottom lip.

"Is that what you really think, Ri? You think that I'm so desperate I've gotten attached to some crazed serial killer? Or doesn't that fit in with your idealised fantasy of how my fucking love life should be?" I snap at him, raising my voice a little louder. He has the sense to balk at my obvious anger and pauses, the curling wand still in his hand.

"He gets me, and I'm terrified of the way he makes me feel, because he makes me need him like I've never needed anyone before. I hate that it's so intense and I hate that we've never met in real life, it almost seems too good to be true."

My voice trembles and I press the heels of my hands to my eyes, as I feel the burn of tears begin to threaten my composure.

"If it seems like it's too good to be true, then it usually is. It might be the cynical old Queen in me, but he fucking lied to you about having a kid! What sort of man does that? And if he's lied to you about that, what else is he lying about?"

Rian's bitter words sting like I've been slapped in the face, and my mouth drops open in shock. There is a brief silence and the guilty look in Rian's eyes almost shatters my resolve, as if he can't believe he just said those hurtful words out loud.

"I haven't felt this way about anyone since Abel, you of all people should be fucking happy for me, Rian!"

I can't hide the quiver in my voice, as he sets the curling tool down on the rubber mat on my dressing table and curses softly.

"*Fuck,* I'm so sorry, baby girl, I didn't mean to upset you, I don't want to see you hurt, you've been through enough. I've sat with you through the tears and the nightmares, I just want to see you happy again, Zeppelin."

His voice is so sincere it hurts my heart, and I reach for his hand squeezing it in mine.

"I love you, Rian, so much."

I catch his gaze in the mirror, and I'm instantly transported back to the day we met.

# Zeppelin
## Past

From the moment I stepped off the train into London, it was the start of an instant love affair. The smells, the fast pace, everything was so big and seemed to go by in a blur of businessmen talking their jargon on mobile phones, teenagers looking down at their phones, hipsters with headphones on and young couples in love walking around hand in hand with stars in their eyes. I was in awe of it all, but I felt like such a fraud. I'd just stepped off the train, I was alone, and I knew no one. This was a fresh start for me, I was in a city where no one knew the real Zeppelin Williams, no one saw me as the ex-girlfriend of Abel Creed, no one knew the tragic story of how I was one of three survivors from the yacht fire that killed Abel's band The Poison Puppets. No one saw the horrific scars marring my body, this was a new start for me in the city of opportunity. Dragging my large suitcase behind me I find the nearest Starbucks before heading to see my granddad, Jimmy.

Jimmy Fraser is my granddad; he's a security guard and concierge for Samson Newbolt from Rancid Vengeance. He lives just outside Camden with my Nana Pru and he's helping me move into my new apartment in Notting Hill. I've landed on my feet, I've got a Notting Hill address, I managed to put down a deposit on the apartment with the substantial compensation I got from the yacht accident.

I push the door open to Starbucks and remove one earbud, temporarily halting Idina Menzel singing about Defying Gravity. I join the queue behind a tall, lean man with dark hair perfectly styled into a quiff. I take out my iPod to stop the music, humming to the song as I switch it off. He turns to face me; his face is just as stunning as the rest of him. His skin is lightly tanned, he has a piercing in his left ear, his blue eyes full of amusement. He is wearing a v-neck white t-shirt, dark blue ripped jeans, black and white checkerboard Vans, and a plain black unzipped hoody.

"Ah, Idina Menzel, good choice, girl!" he says brightly with a grin, and I can't help but smile at his comment.

"Thanks, although it would be better if I were caffeinated! Coffee and musical theatre are two essential ways to start my day!" I quip and he puts his hand to his heart.

"Girl after my own heart!" he retorts with a wink and holds his hand out.

"Rian St James," he introduces himself and I take his hand with a warm smile.

"Zeppelin Williams. My dad was a huge Led Zeppelin fan," I say almost shyly, and he laughs, as he cocks his perfectly shaped eyebrow.

"I never would have guessed! Pleasure to meet you, Zeppelin."

I nod.

"You too, Rian. You're the first person I've met that's actually taken time to speak to me instead of grunting in words of one syllable!" I state wryly and he lets out a bark of laughter.

"You're definitely not from around these parts, girl!"

I laugh along with him.

"You guessed, huh? I'm not doing a particularly good job at pretending!"

My phone starts ringing and I pull it out of my bag, seeing that it's my granddad.

"Hey, Pops," I greet him affectionately.

"Hello love, did you make it into London safe?"

His voice full of quiet concern. Bless his heart.

"Yeah, I'm just grabbing myself a coffee before I head over to you, I won't be long," I reassure him, as he clears his throat.

"That's what I'm ringing for, love, I'll meet you at the new apartment, save you coming here to go back again, I'm sure you just want to get settled."

"Yeah, okay, thank you. Can you text me the address again, please, Pops? So, I at least have some reference of where I'm going, you know I'm useless with directions."

I admit and he chuckles throatily. Rian regarding me intently out of the corner of my eye.

"Yeah course, love, you're as bad as your Nana, I'll text it to you now and I'll see you soon."

"Okay, love you, Pops, see you soon."

I hang up the phone and slip it back into my bag.

*"Useless with directions, huh? You're definitely not a true Londoner!" he quips and we both laugh. I instantly like this man who seems so easy to talk to.*

*"Maybe I can give you directions? I'm not a creepy stalker or a serial killer, I promise, and I know we just met, but you seem genuine."*

*I smile as my phone vibrates. I open the text from my granddad with my new address on. I lift the phone to show him, and he looks impressed.*

*"Ah, well it just so happens that's where I live! Small world! If you want to wait for me, I can take you there? It would be rude to leave a fellow Idina super fan lost and all alone!" he says dramatically, with an eye roll and I find myself agreeing, making my first friend in a new city. Maybe life in London won't be so bad after all.*

# Zeppelin

## Present

I'm snapped back to the present by Rian clearing his throat.

"Whoa, that must have been some thought!" he says with clear amusement in his voice.

"I was just thinking about the day we met."

I smile fondly at the memory.

"Ah, you looked so starry eyed, I knew instantly we were kindred spirits! Now, are we going out out or not? Because it's been far too long since I got laid and quite frankly, I'm fed up with endless re-runs of Friends. I also think my wine stash is long since empty!"

He rolls his eyes dramatically and I laugh at his droll sense of humour.

"So, this old queen needs some action, I'm tired of living vicariously through you and your sickly-sweet online romance with Handsome Jack."

He picks up the curling iron and finishes styling my hair. I get up and make my way over to my walk-in wardrobe, that was one thing I refused to compromise on. I step inside and light fills the vast space, showcasing my clothes and shoe collection. I scroll through my dresses and pull out a black, sleeveless body-con dress with a high turtleneck. Next, I select a pair of black peep-toe Christian Louboutin sky-high heels. I pull on the dress, the soft material sliding up my body like a glove and step into my heels. I turn to look at my reflection in the mirror and the dress shows off my slim, but slightly curvy figure. My eyes are smoky and dramatic with a cat-eye flick. I hear a wolf-whistle and look up to see Rian standing behind me with his hands on his hips. His jeans look like they have been sprayed on, and his long, lean legs go on forever.

"What have you done with the real Zeppelin Williams, because you are looking hot as fuck tonight!"

We both giggle like a pair of schoolgirls, as he hands me a tube of red lipstick.

"The LBD definitely deserves nothing less than a red lip," he says with a wink, as I carefully apply my lipstick, ready for a night on the town with my best friend.

***

The music is loud and pumping out through the speakers, as we enter Neon Nights. Neon Nights is a premier night spot and popular with the elite, rich and famous. Rian called in a favour from one of his clients and bagged us V.I.P entry to a charity masquerade ball. The walls decorated with opulent black and aubergine wallcoverings. The main area of the club is open, with purple plush sofas all around the edges and the tables are black granite and chrome. The fully stocked black granite bar takes up the whole back of the venue and I can't help but look around in awe of my surroundings. The sea of people wearing masquerade masks creating an air of mystery to the atmosphere. I pull my black leather and lace mask into place.

"What are you drinking, baby girl?" Rian says into my ear, the feathers of his black mask tickling my cheek.

"White wine, please," I shout so he can hear me above the music. A few minutes later, Rian passes me a glass and turns to chink my glass with his. I take a sip of the cool wine and smile, as he grabs my hand leading me towards a set of double doors. The doorman asks Rian his name and he marks us down from his list, speaking in a clipped tone, as he lets us through the red velvet rope with a curt nod. Rian turns to me wide eyed and leads me into the V.I.P lounge. It looks exactly the same as the regular lounge, but there are subtle differences in the still plush, sumptuous decor. The music is still pumping and the cool vibe of Ed Sheeran Shape of You fills the room. There are a lot less people in here, but it still has the feeling of a packed club. I hear the distant sound of screams, as I turn to Rian to see what the commotion is and he leans in close.

"Rancid Vengeance are the V.I.P guests tonight."

My eyes widen and he flashes me a wink.

"Did your 'client' happen to be Danny Debonair, that guy who had you swooning all over him?" I ask curiously and he hums, his mouth forming a straight line.

"Maybe! A lady never kisses and tells!"

His voice a few octaves higher than usual and I cock my eyebrow.

"No, you just shag and shout, you slut!"

I throw my head back and laugh, as Rian nudges me with his elbow and laughs along with me.

"Bitch! Another drink?"

I nod, handing him my empty glass, as I observe what's going on around me. I see a couple off to the side getting hot and heavy on the dance floor, I shift my gaze to a drunk man in a suit, his black mask lopsided, he sways from side to side as he pulls his tie loose. He approaches me with his index finger pointed in my direction.

"You, I've seen you somewhere before," he slurs and I shake my head, taking in his dishevelled state.

"You must have me confused with someone else, mate." I try to sound confident, as he continues to advance forward.

"No, I definitely know you, I'd recognise beauty like that anywhere."

I roll my eyes at his cheesy pick-up line, as he lurches forward and grabs me around the waist.

"Come on, beautiful, dance with me." He sways us from side to side and I try to squirm away from him.

"Get off me! I said no!" I say firmly, but he's not taking no for an answer.

"Come on, don't be like that, relax. I just want to dance," he coos, as I try desperately to wriggle from his steel grip.

"I believe the lady said no," a male voice bites out sternly and the man in the rumpled suit let's go of me, holding his hands up defensively. His eyes glossy and heavy.

"Cock tease, you could have told me he was your boyfriend!" he accuses and as I turn, I'm faced with six feet two inches of lean male. He's one of the few people who isn't wearing a mask, I'd recognise him anywhere, he has that air of familiarity about him. Jackson Chase from Rancid Vengeance, the man who I based my first main character on. He was my muse for Stone Gregory, a handsome billionaire playboy who fell in love with his sassy, but bookish intern Raven Hardwick. I take him in, he reminds me of a tattooed Thor with a neatly trimmed goatee beard.

He is lean, tanned and has shoulder length blonde hair that looks perfectly mussed and as he speaks, I see the strobe lights glint on his tongue stud. He is wearing dark ripped jeans, a v-neck white t-shirt, a black blazer with the sleeves rolled up to showcase his full arm and neck tattoos covering his body. He has the cutest, wide, deep-hazel eyes and as he catches my wistful gaze, I instinctively look away shyly. He cocks his eyebrow curiously and flashes me a cheeky grin.

"I don't usually make a habit of rescuing damsels in distress, but I couldn't watch any longer. It was actually painful!" he quips wryly and I giggle girlishly.

"I don't usually let strangers grope me, but he just caught me off guard, that's all!"

He nods, as he takes a sip of his beer. The muscles in his neck contracting as he swallows, the lines of his vibrant, bright yellow buttercup tattoo extending up his throat making it look like it's dancing. I can't take my greedy gaze off him. *I want my lips on that throat. Jesus fucking Christ, where did that come from? It's been far too long since you got laid, Williams.*

"So, what's a beautiful woman like you doing in a place like this all alone?" he asks with a smirk, as I look over his shoulder, desperate to find Rian. I see him leaning in close to a tall, lean man with collar length dark hair and a jawline so sharp it could cut glass. Rian looks positively beside himself with glee and keeps subtly brushing the man's arm. *Ah, so that must be the famous Danny Debonair?*

"Doesn't look like he's coming back anytime soon, love," Jax muses and I let out a long-drawn-out sigh. *For fucks sake.*

"Can I get you a drink? That's if you don't mind? But you look like you need it?"

I nod, as he leads me to a large velvet aubergine booth with his hand at the small of my back. His touch causes jolts of electricity up my spine, and I wonder if he can feel it too. My breathing starts to quicken, as his hand flexes against me, his touch almost burning. *Fucking hell, this is new.* He gestures for me to step into the booth ahead of him and he climbs in beside me, a tall, red-haired waitress is at the table in seconds.

"What can I get you?" she addresses Jax directly and completely ignores me. *Rude, but ok, I get it, he is so fucking hot, I'd ignore me too.*

"What are you drinking?"

His voice tears me away from my reverie and I feel out of sorts, I've never felt like this before. I've never felt this... out of control before. I'm usually so put together, calm and collected, but within minutes of meeting this man, my thoughts are scattered.

"White wine, please?" I say with a swallow, and he nods, placing his order. After he's placed his order, he brushes my hand with his and I instantly feel goosebumps erupt all over my body. The unfamiliar electricity crackling between us and I swallow hard again because it shouldn't feel this... good, this... right.

"Jackson Chase, but you can call me Jax," he introduces himself and our eyes lock, brown on silver. I can't look away; I'm lost in his hazel orbs, and I'm rendered speechless by his presence. He's magnetic, everything about him screams possess me and fuck me until I'm seeing stars. I open my mouth to speak, but nothing comes out, I drop my gaze to the table feeling almost embarrassed at my ridiculous fucking behaviour and he chuckles softly, tipping my chin up, forcing me to look at him. His touch igniting every nerve in my body and setting my blood ablaze with pure, unadulterated need.

"You felt that too, huh? That spark of electricity when I touched you."

His voice is rough as he leans in closer until I feel his warm minty breath against my cheek. He smells so good of mint, Diesel Only the Brave aftershave and faintly of beer. It's a heady combination that makes me feel out of sorts.

"It's okay to let yourself go, love, to let yourself... feel."

He moves closer and I still can't find the words. He must think I'm a fucking mute, or just plain dumb. *For fuck's sake, Zeppelin Jade Williams, get your shit together!* His goatee grazes my cheek, and my heart starts thundering in my chest, as I feel a slick heat pool between my thighs. I feel my face flush and I'm suddenly too warm.

*"Jesus Christ,* you're so fucking beautiful, I can't see your face properly and I don't even know your name," he admits, his voice almost pained. He reaches for my hand and my words die on my lips, as he stands up, pulling me up with him and leads me out of the V.I.P lounge. He leads me down a short corridor and I let him, willingly and blindly following him. His hand

feels so good in mine, all warm as he strokes his calloused thumb over my hand. His touch feels like tiny sparks of electricity, my skin burning for him. He gently tugs me into the ladies' toilets, checking each individual cubicle for occupants by kicking the doors open with his boot, without his hand leaving mine. When he's happy we're alone, he leads me into a cubicle, crowding in behind me and locking the door.

"I don't normally drag women around like a fucking caveman, I am usually a gentleman... on occasion, I promise. But there's something about you that makes me feel... reckless. I want to throw caution to the wind and just say... fuck it."

He presses me against the cubicle wall, the coolness of the smooth wood against my back a welcome contrast to the heat coursing through my body. I desperately want to tear my mask off so he can finally see my face, but it adds an air of mystery to our encounter making it feel almost forbidden. I boldly wrap my arms around his neck, tugging gently at his long blonde hair. Our faces inches apart, his breathing is hitched, and I can feel his heart pounding in his chest beneath the material of his t-shirt. I eagerly press my lips to his frantically, almost desperately. I am filled with pure want and carnal need for this man. I stroke his tongue with mine, the feel of his velvet tongue performing a sensual, erotic dance with mine. He carefully lifts me off my feet with ease, as I wrap my legs around his waist. The heels of my shoes digging into his arse through the material of his jeans.

*"Fuck!"* he curses.

"What are you doing to me?"

His question rhetorical, as he presses his damp forehead to mine, my breath coming out in shallow pants, and I can feel his erection pressing into me. *Fucking hell, I've never been this turned on before.* I nip his earlobe with my teeth and crash my lips against his. He swallows my soft moans, as he moves his hand to cup my breast.

"Oh God!" I cry out.

"You feel so good... almost too good," he breathes.

"I want you, oh fuck, I want you so bad," I admit shamelessly, as he moves his hand from my breast and slips underneath my dress. He shifts my knickers to the side, and I am a slave to his touch. He swipes his finger through my soaking wet folds and pushes two fingers into my pussy. I mewl softly at the feeling of his fingers inside me.

"Mmm," I hum, as his thumb finds my sensitive nub and strokes gentle, leisurely circles. I am writhing and panting beneath him, desperate for his touch, fraught for my release. His thumb circles my engorged clit and I let out a long, loud moan.

"Shhh, I've got you, love, I'll take care of you," he whispers softly.

"Oh God! Jax! Yes! Make me come, please make me come," I pant, desperate to reach my climax.

"*Christ,* I can feel you throbbing against my fingers, you're close."

His voice dripping with seduction, as his rhythm increases, driving me towards the finish line.

"*Fuck,* I'm going to come! Oh God! Jax!"

I bump my head against the wall, as he expertly circles my swollen nub. "*Oh fuck! Jax!*"

He grins, his hazel eyes twinkling with pure lust.

"That's it, come for me, love," he croons, as he increases his pace and my orgasm rolls through me, lighting me up from the inside out. He swallows my moans, covering my mouth with his, as he squeezes every ounce of pleasure from my tightly wound body. I'm boneless, as I come back down to earth and I blink up at him, flashing him a lazy smile. He offers me a bright grin, as his eyes lock with mine.

"I'm not finished, not yet, not by a long shot."

His voice is laced with desire, and he reaches down shift my knickers to the side again.

"*Christ alive,* I'm so fucking hard right now."

There's something oddly familiar about his voice, but I push that thought to the back of my mind, as he reaches behind him with his other hand, pulling his wallet out. He takes out a condom and tears the wrapper with his teeth. He unzips his jeans and pulls his cock free from his boxers. *Fucking hell, he's huge! Long and thick, how on earth is he going to get that... thing inside me?* He sheaths himself, the head of his cock poised at my entrance.

"Tell me you want me to fuck you, love, I need to hear you say the words. I'm not sure I'm capable of stopping this from happening," he grinds out and I'm not sure I want him to stop, he feels so good, unlike anything I've ever felt before.

"I want you to fuck me, Jax!" I demand firmly.

"Correct answer," he says with a lazy, cocky smirk, as he lifts me up in one rapid move, impaling me on his waiting erection. I lock my legs tightly around his waist, as he gently moves me up and down in a slow, leisurely pace, allowing me to adjust to his size.

"Faster! I want you to fuck me hard and fast!" I yell, grabbing his hair and yanking forcefully. He chuckles softly.

"Demanding aren't we? Whatever the lady wants, she shall get!"

He rams his cock deep inside me, pushing me further up the wall, creating a delicious friction and adding to the building pleasure.

"God, you feel so fucking good! Too damn good!" he moans, as he increases his thrusts again, and I am so close to finding my release.

"*Fuck*, I'm so close," I moan into his ear, as his pace quickens, and I feel the familiar flutters of my orgasm cresting to the surface.

"*Shit, FUCK*!" he barks out with a delicious thrust of his hips. We both explode and find our releases at the same time.

"I'm coming, *fuck*, Jax, oh God! I'm coming," I yell, as he moves his other hand over my mouth, muffling my cries. I feel his hot seed spurt inside me, as he jerks out his own release with a low, primal growl and I scream around his hand. I bury my head in the crook of his neck, breathless and spent. He runs his hands up my spine, holding me to him. He feels so good pressed against me, the pure, masculine scent of him drives me crazy with want and I'm reluctant to let go.

"Hey," he whispers softly. He shifts and I wince as he pulls his cock out of my sensitive folds, setting me down on wobbly legs. We both begin to straighten ourselves out and I finger comb my hair. I smile to myself, and he looks at me with lust-filled eyes.

"*Fuck*, I need to be inside you again," he admits shamelessly, his voice gruff. He leans in and kisses me deeply, his kiss instantly taking my breath away, as his pierced tongue softly caresses mine. My body goes lax against his hard, muscular one and I grip his thick biceps to steady myself. He pulls away from our kiss briefly, pressing his forehead to mine.

"I still don't know your name," he whispers gruffly with a soft chuckle and cupping my face in his hands. He reaches behind my head to untie the bow of my mask. I take a step back just out of his reach, and he cocks his eyebrow questioningly.

"I don't usually fuck rock stars in toilet cubicles... and I-I'm sort of in the public eye," I explain and he nods in understanding, as my eyes roam over his body committing him to memory. I notice a tattoo peeking out of the v-neck of his t-shirt and it seems familiar to me as if I have seen it somewhere before. I push that fleeting thought from my mind, as my eyes lock with his again.

"I get it, believe me, I get it more than most, love," he says wistfully and I want him to at least know my name.

"My name's..."

He cuts me off by placing his finger softly to my lips.

"Maybe it's better I don't know your name, if it's meant to be, we'll find each other again."

He stills, dropping his hands to his sides and slowly backing away from me.

"What's wrong? Jax?"

He shakes his head, a stricken look on his face and his hazel eyes haunted.

"I-I... I'm sorry, I can't fucking do this. This shouldn't have happened."

He turns, unlocks the door and leaves me alone and bereft in the toilet cubicle, feeling used and wondering what the fuck just happened.

# 15

## Zeppelin

The next morning, I wake in my bed, and as I roll over sleepily, I feel a delicious soreness deep inside me, reminding me of my steamy encounter with Jackson 'Flash' Chase from Rancid Vengeance. Jericho leaps up on the bed and lets out a single bark.

"Morning, buddy," he barks again, as there is a knock at the door, and I chuckle softly to myself.

"You just came to warn me that Rian was at the door, didn't you?"

He looks pleased with himself, his tongue dropping out of his mouth, and he pants. I swing my legs out of bed and pet his head.

"Good boy, Jericho," I croon, as I pad across the apartment to the door, Rian is standing in the corridor wearing a pair of black booty shorts, a white vest, Ted Baker slippers and his hair perfectly sleep mussed. He has the widest grin on his face and he's way too happy for this early in the morning.

"Morning!" he sings, as he waves two cups of coffee and a white paper bag. I roll my eyes at his flamboyant, yet inappropriate attire. *Typical Rian.*

"I bought breakfast."

He practically skips inside, twirling as he passes me, the smell of bacon making my mouth water. He regards me with narrow eyes and points an accusing finger in my direction.

"And where the fuck did you disappear to last night, Missy?"

I drop my gaze to the carpet, playing with a loose thread on my pyjama top, as if it's the most fascinating thing I have ever seen in my life. But as I take a deep breath, I find myself blurting out.

"Like you care! You dropped me like a hot potato when Danny showed up! You just left me! Anything could have happened, Rian!"

I can't keep the vitriol from my voice, as he cocks his perfectly plucked eyebrow.

"Oh, come on, Zep! Don't be so dramatic! Yes, I admit I left you and I shouldn't have, for that I'm sorry. But I really, really like him, more than I've liked anyone in a long time, if ever. You know how long I've been waiting to see him again. He was on the set of a morning TV show a few days ago, I saw my opportunity and I went for it! You wouldn't have come with me if I'd have told you!" he admits, not a hint of shame or remorse in his voice.

"Damn right I fucking wouldn't have! I can think of better ways to spend my night than being the third wheel!" I chastise him and then come to a not so shocking realisation, rolling my eyes with a wry smirk.

"You shagged him, didn't you?" I say matter-of-factly.

"Of course, I fucking did! And I rocked his world, baby girl! Might even see him again tonight for a repeat performance!" he says with a cheeky wink, as he passes me a cup of coffee. I take off the lid and take a sip of the steaming black liquid. *The caffeine hit is just what I need this morning.*

"So, come on, don't leave a girl hanging! Spill, where did you go? I saw some drunk guy grab you and some blonde God come to your rescue. I figured he had it covered judging by the size of him, so who was he?"

I briefly squeeze my eyes shut, desperately trying to quell the memory of him fucking me hard and deep in the toilet cubicle.

"It doesn't matter, it's not as if I'm ever going to see him again."

I sigh, unable to keep the defeat from my voice, as I pick up my phone and notice the battery is dead. I plug it in and leave it on the arm of the sofa.

"Come on! Don't hold out on me, Zep! Spill!" he presses, eagerly anticipating my answer.

"Jackson fucking Chase! It was Jackson Chase from Rancid Vengeance, okay?" I blurt out in a rush and Rian's mouth drops open forming a perfect O shape.

"OH, MY FUCKING GOD!" he shrieks theatrically.

"Zeppelin Jade! That guy is hotter than Hell on a summer's day!"

He fans himself with his hand.

"So, what happened?"

I puff out my cheeks and lean heavily against the worktop in the kitchen.

"This drunk guy grabbed me; I was trying to fight him off and Jax came to my rescue," I explain, as Rian lets out a dreamy sigh.

"It sounds like a scene from one of your romance novels, so, the burning question is, did you fuck him?"

I bite my lip and feel my face flush, as I think of his long, thick cock sliding into my wet heat. *Dear Lord, that single encounter has ruined me for all other men.*

"You did! You little slut! But I thought you were sworn off rockers, you know, after dearly departed Abel?" he says with narrow eyes, and I take another sip of my coffee. My heart doesn't slam against my rib cage at the sound of Abel's name anymore.

"There was something about him, Ri, I'd never felt like that before... not even with Abel. That jolt of electricity sparking between us when he touched me, he seemed so... familiar, but it felt so fucking good. I've never been fucked like that, God, he was... perfect. He wanted me to take my mask off and I said no, I was about to tell him my name and he said it was best I didn't tell him and if it was meant to be, we'd find each other again somehow. Then he freaked the fuck out and left me standing there like a lemon! I was so humiliated! I'd just had the best sex of my life and he just ran off like I meant nothing!" I admit incredulously, as if I can't believe it happened. Rian flashes me a look of sympathy and wraps his arms around me.

"Oh Zep."

I snuggle closer to him and disappointment envelopes me.

"I tried to find him afterwards, but he was nowhere to be found," I say in a rush, and I can't believe I was so fucking stupid. I mean what did I think was going to happen? We were going to fall madly in love and live happily ever after? That doesn't happen to girls like me. Girls like me are meant to settle for mediocre sex with a man I have nothing in common with. I write for a living, and I write about happily ever after, but I've never experienced it myself. I feel like a fraud to my readers, but they wouldn't read my books if they didn't have the happy ending, right?

\*\*\*

As the day goes on, I cling to that thought as I sit at my desk, the words flowing and *Luke Combs Even Though I'm Leavin'* playing in the background, nursing my seventh cup of coffee.

*I'm an expert at a step-ball-change, but I don't know how to fall in love with a man without failing miserably. Dustin and I are worlds apart, yet somehow my world begins and ends with him. How the fuck did that happen? Montana Silver doesn't do happy endings, she does one-night stands with zero expectations of anything more. I wasn't sure I was capable of more, until Dustin Heath breezed into my life with his Stetson and his sexy-as-hell cowboy boots.*

I lean back in my chair and perch my bare feet on the desk, wiggling my toes and taking off my glasses. I rub my eyes; my stomach growling reminds me of how long I've been sat here. I get up from my chair and go to head into the kitchen. I pick up my phone from the arm of the sofa and swipe the screen to life. I notice it's odd that I haven't had any messages from Jack and guilt suddenly envelopes me, as I let my mind wander to my encounter with Jax from Rancid Vengeance. Everything about him demanded my attention, his chiselled jaw, his long blonde hair, his captivating hazel eyes. It all seemed so oddly familiar, the timbre of his voice, his tattoos, but I couldn't explain why. I'm about to open a bottle of wine when there's a tap on the door, Jericho starts circling me and wagging his tail, letting out his signature bark. I laugh and roll my eyes, petting him on his head.

"You know it's going to be Rian, silly dog! Literally no one else visits us!" I mutter, as I open the door and Rian waves a brown paper bag in the air.

"I bought your favourite Chinese, because let me guess, you forgot to eat?"

I bite my lip guiltily. He sighs dramatically and breezes in shutting the door behind him, the smell of food making my stomach growl loudly. Rian toes his shoes off and heads into the kitchen, pulling out some plates and unboxing the food to serve it. He brings both plates into the living space and hands me mine in silence, the food looks and smells divine, beef chow mein with black bean sauce instantly makes my mouth water. He hands me a fork and we sit cross-legged on the floor, as I take my first bite. He regards me intently with narrow eyes.

"I'm assuming there's more to what you told me earlier. About Jax Chase?" He breaks the silence and I nod around a mouthful of food. I chew for a moment and place my fork down on my plate.

"We had the most incredible sex, he seemed so... familiar, but he was a stranger at the same time, if that makes sense? We had this... connection, it wasn't just a mindless fuck in a toilet cubicle in a club. It was beyond that, it was...real and it made me feel things I haven't felt in so long," I say in a garbled rush and Rian hums, he's silent for long minutes before he speaks.

"So, hear me out, what if... plot twist, what if Jackson Chase is really HandsomeJack0304? I mean, it isn't outside the realm of possibility. You said he seemed familiar somehow, what if that's the connection? What if because through a chance encounter you unknowingly ended up having sex with the guy you were talking to online? Maybe that's why he freaked out? Why else would he have done that?" Rian reasons and I shrug. *He watches way too many serial killer documentaries and conspiracy theory shows. He also has an uncanny knack of making two plus two equal five.*

"Come on, Rian, really? Those serial killer documentaries have seriously messed with your brain! And why would a world-famous rock star like Jackson Chase need to meet single, lonely women online? I bet he has women queuing up around the block for just one night with him."

He chuckles at my reaction and I roll my eyes at him.

"Come on, Zep, stop and think about it for a second, it actually makes perfect sense," he states, crooking his finger in my direction.

"Finally, all the pieces of the puzzle are beginning to click into place. That's why he won't let you see a photo of him, that's why he sent you that picture with his face obscured, so you wouldn't realise he was really Jax Chase from Rancid Vengeance!"

I shake my head, unable to comprehend the weight of his words. *What if he's right? What if there's truth behind Rian's theory? What if HandsomeJack0304 is Jackson Chase from Rancid Vengeance and all this time he's been lying to me?*

"You're wrong," I state matter-of-factly, dismissing his ridiculous notion.

"He's not Jackson Chase, he's Jack Logan, a guitar teacher from London." I try to sound confident, as Rian hums and strokes his chin thoughtfully.

"What part of London? How old is he? Where did he grow up? Has he even told you those things?" He pops a mouthful of food into his mouth and I shift my gaze.

"He's thirty-three and he lives in Kent with his daughter," I say in a rush, hoping to shut down his line of questioning. Rian nods, chewing his food and swallowing, pointing his fork at me.

"And?" He presses for me to continue, I open my mouth to speak, then close it again. He's right, he's hasn't been very forthcoming with what he tells me about his life. I barely know anything about him beyond what he's told me, which is very little in comparison to what I've told him.

"I... know his favourite film is Reservoir Dogs, he has two sisters and three best friends who he thinks of as his brothers," I explain and I know I'm clutching at straws, as Rian lets out a bark of laughter.

"Wow! You really don't know anything about this guy, do you? And how many members of Rancid Vengeance are there? Three, plus him, think about it, Zep."

He taps his index finger to my temple, as I press the heel of my hands into my eyes, coming to a shocking realisation.

"I know I've fucking fallen for him, Rian! It was inevitable, we stayed up until the early hours of the morning talking about anything and everything, I laid myself bare for him! I told him things I've never told anyone!" I raise my voice a few decibels, as I start to sob uncontrollably, unable to keep my emotions in check a second longer. *I've fallen in love with HandsomeJack0304 and there wasn't a damn fucking thing I could do to stop it.*

# 16

## Jax

As soon as I laid eyes on her, I was drawn to her, she was feisty and so full of life that she made me forget Ruby existed. For that split second, I couldn't walk away, in that moment, I was so intoxicated and that jolt of electricity that ran through both of us when we touched, it really was rare. I had to have her at any cost, her smile disarmed me, her eyes captivated me, her curvy body and her pert breasts unmanned me. I wanted to lose myself in her, I wanted to possess her and mark her as mine. I wasn't content with it being a chance meeting in a club, I wanted to know her, I wanted to know her name, I wanted to know everything there was to know about this woman. This stranger who had me feeling things I hadn't felt in three fucking years, I had to see her face. I wanted to explore what it was about her, but I wasn't prepared for the barrage of emotions that came afterwards.

My stomach twisted with guilt, I felt physically sick that I had betrayed my Ruby and I had somehow defiled her memory by committing the most intimate act with a woman that wasn't her. There have been random hook ups over the past three years, but none have evoked this depth of feeling in me before. I had never wanted more beyond sex with a woman before and that fucking terrified the shit out me. The thought at the forefront of my mind at that moment was to run, to run as far away from her as possible. I convinced myself I didn't want to know her name, I was content with it just being a random hook up and I didn't want more than what had just happened between us.

I had to get out of there, I had to be as far away from her as possible. I ran back into the main vestibule of the club, as if my life depended on it and I asked Trey in no uncertain terms to drive me home. We were the special guests at this charity masquerade ball, but I couldn't stay. I hated myself for running, but it felt like it was the only choice I had. I made up some excuse that Marnie called, that Thea was throwing up and I left, a riot of emotions barrelling through my suddenly exhausted body.

When I arrived home, I thanked Marnie for babysitting, kissed Thea goodnight and for once, she didn't ask me to sing to her or read her a story, which I was grateful for. I opened a bottle of Jack Daniels and sat at the kitchen island drinking it straight from the bottle, staring mindlessly at the clock on the wall, listening to monotonous ticking as time went by. I'm not sure how much time passes, but my vision is starting to blur, and my drunken mind is moving at a hundred miles an hour. I pull my phone out of my pocket and pull up the dating app, stabbing at the icon on the screen as if it is my sworn enemy. GoMatchPro.com opens up and I click on ZepW92, her smiling face taunting me, guilt swimming through every nerve in my body and my finger hovering over the chat function. Instead, I close the app and continue seeking absolute oblivion.

*** 

The next morning, my alarm goes off, rolling over and blindly reaching for it to turn it off, the world goes quiet again. My brain feels like it's trying to evacuate my skull, as the dull pounding begins to work its way through my head. I groan, as I turn over to the other side of the bed, the events of last night coming to the forefront of my foggy mind. I pick up my phone, trying to focus on the all too bright screen with one eye closed. I note the ridiculously early hour and make the decision to go back to sleep, at least until it felt like there wasn't a marching band in my head. I hear tiny footsteps approaching and my bedroom door swings open, Thea greeting me with a sleepy smile. She rubs her eyes, her dark hair sleep mussed, and she lets out a long, dramatic yawn.

"Daddy!" she squeals, as she takes a run and a jump onto the bed, bouncing up and down like a jack in the box. *Fuck me, this kid has far too much energy for this early in the morning.*

"Morning Princess."

I sit up and lift her onto my lap, as she plants a wet kiss on my cheek and giggles girlishly.

"Daddy?"

I hum my answer. "Yes, Princess?"

She snuggles closer to me.

"Marnie says she's going to the zoo today with Freddie and Zacky."

I smile softly.

"Do you want me to call Uncle Sammy and Aunty Peyton to see if you can go too?"

Her large hazel eyes widen, and she nods vehemently. I lift her up and set her down on her feet, she bounds across the floor squealing about monkeys, lions and some random, incoherent three-year-old gibberish. I laugh at her enthusiasm and dial Sam.

"To what do I owe the pleasure of this phone call on this fine day?"

Sam greets me in his usual husky tone.

"*Shit,* did I interrupt...?" I reply and I hear Peyton giggling in the background.

"Morning, Jax!"

She calls and I slap my hand to my head.

"I'm so fucking sorry, I'll call back in a little while," I apologise and Sam laughs.

"Na, it's all good, man, what's up?"

I shake my head to myself.

"Thea mentioned Marnie's taking Freddie and Zack to the zoo?" I ask.

"Yeah, and you're calling to ask if she'd take Thea? You don't even have to ask, mate, Marnie was planning to take Thea as a surprise anyway."

I smile at Marnie's thoughtfulness.

"She's coming in half an hour, Trey and Jace are their security detail for the day, under Cole's orders. Listen, is everything OK? You just bailed last night, is she feeling better?"

I'd forgotten I had used Thea throwing up as an excuse. *Shit.*

"Yeah, she's fine, must have just been one of those twenty-four-hour things, or too much chocolate." I try to sound convincing but fail miserably.

"You can't bullshit a bullshitter, Jax. This is me you're talking to; I'm insulted you'd even attempt it after all these years."

I hear the wry amusement in his voice.

"Long fucking story, man." I sigh, leaning back on my pillow and staring up at the ceiling.

"Do you need me to come over?"

I drag my hand through my long hair, mentally and physically exhausted.

"I'm good, mate, honestly, I'll make sure Thea's ready in half an hour. Thanks again, Sam."

I hang up without saying goodbye, hoping I can fix my relationship with Zeppelin.

After I said goodbye to Thea, I step in the shower and turn the water to scolding hot. The hot water feels so good against my skin, and I take longer than usual in the shower, relishing the peace and quiet. I step out of the shower, brush my teeth, and head to my bedroom. I dry off quickly, I get dressed into a pair of ripped jeans that hang low on my hips, a heather grey v-neck t-shirt and black Doc Marten boots. My blonde hair is still damp from the shower, as I head downstairs into the open plan living room, I relish in the silence for long minutes. It feels so quiet without Thea's laughter and palpable, unrelenting energy. I perch myself on the arm of the sofa, I'm restless and fidgety, I can't seem to settle.

I get to my feet and begin pacing the floor, taking in the platinum discs on the walls, the golden guitars and all our album covers. *We've come so far over the past fourteen years and I'm so proud of our achievements.* The silence taunts me, as I find myself pulling on my hoodie, grabbing the keys to my fire engine red Jaguar F-Pace R-Dynamic with tinted windows and personalised number plate CHASE1 and leave the house. I unlock the car and climb into the driver's seat, shutting the door behind me, the silence unnerving. I start the engine and turn up the music until the dulcet tones of *Apocalyptica I Don't Care* fills the enclosed space. I push my foot down on the accelerator with only one destination at the forefront of my mind.

\*\*\*

Her vibrant, carefree life could never be marked by a gravestone. Gravestones are so cold, and so... final. It reminds me that life is temporary, that tomorrow is never promised. What lies in the ground is only flesh and blood, that was never what she was to me. She was the most beautiful spirit I had ever met in my life. I was honoured to know her, even though I knew her for a fraction of time, she made an impact on my entire existence. Life is about moments of impact and when she breezed into mine, I had met my soulmate, my best friend, my equal, the best part of me. She was the mother of my child and the woman I wanted to spend the rest of my life with. As I sink down to my knees on the damp, dewy grass in front of Ruby's final resting place, a single tear slips down my cheek. I run my fingers over the cold marbled stone, crushing guilt bearing down on me like a lead weight.

"I'm so fucking sorry, buttercup, so sorry," I choke out, my voice thick with emotion. I squeeze my eyes shut for a brief moment to quell the torrent of tears I can feel burning behind my eyes. When I open them, I look up into the warm hazel eyes of Ruby Logan.

# 17

## Jax

She looks exactly the same as she did the last time, I saw her. Her long dark hair billowing around her shoulders, her pregnant stomach protruding in front of her. She is wearing a long, white maxi skirt, a black polka dot halter neck, her feet bare. My mouth drops open, as she almost floats towards me and settles herself down on the grass next to me. She's so close I can almost smell her perfume, it calms my racing heart, as she reaches for my hand.

"I'm so sorry," I repeat and she smiles softly.

"You've got nothing to be sorry for, Jack. You deserve to be happy; you don't need my permission to move on."

Her melodic voice comforts me, as I look down at our joined hands, her engagement ring glittering in the almost too bright sunlight.

"I'm not ready, buttercup, I'm not ready to continue my life without you in it, it's been three fucking years! And I'm still not ready!" I raise my voice and she shakes her head.

"Look at me, Jack, I love you, so, so much, I always will, but I see you drowning in guilt, drowning in grief every day and that breaks my heart that it's because of me. I want you to move on, I want you to build a life without me, to raise our daughter in a home full of love and happiness. You both deserve to be happy, she's so beautiful, I would have given her the moon if I could have. I'd give anything to have held her in my arms for just one night, but it's up to you now."

I shake my head vehemently, as a dark crimson bullet hole begins to form in her forehead. *Please God, not again.*

"I can't do this without you, Ruby, I can't." I sob uncontrollably, squeezing my eyes shut.

"I want you to be happy, Jack, she deserves to know the real you and if it doesn't work out, then at least you tried. I'll always be here."

She places her hand on my heart and as I open my eyes, she's gone.

"Are you okay, son?"

Startled and feeling more than a little out of sorts, I look up into the concerned eyes of an elderly man wearing a grey anorak, smart grey trousers, black Oxfords and a tweed flat cap. My eyes darting around the cemetery and I'm fully aware it was another hallucination, but it felt so real I almost felt her touch. I pause for a moment, as I get shakily to my feet. He reaches for my elbow to steady me, but I take a step back, halting his action and not entirely comfortable with this stranger seeing me at my most vulnerable.

"Y-yeah, I'm good, thank you for your concern."

I nod, clearing my throat and the elderly gentleman smiles softly.

"It doesn't get any easier, does it?" His voice is full of sadness, as I tuck my hands into my pockets. I swallow a few times, unable to answer his question. I shake my head, my stomach in knots, as I look up to the sky.

"You're not going to find your answer up there son?"

He moves closer to me, regarding me intently with his head cocked to the side.

"Arthur." He introduces himself and I nod.

"Jack."

There is a brief silence.

"There are so many things I regret, you know?" I find myself blurting out.

"Life's too short for regrets, son," he replies and I shake my head.

"My fiancée was murdered and there was nothing I could have done to stop it; I didn't protect her. As a man, as a fiancé, as a father, I failed her and our daughter."

I explain and I immediately want to take those words back.

"My wife... my Christine, sixty years of marriage and she died in my arms on New Year's Eve, on our wedding anniversary. When she died, I thought my whole world had come crashing down round my feet, I regretted the things I wanted to say but I never got chance. I still miss her; I visit her grave every day."

I look down at the navy shopping bag he is holding and notice he has three bunches of flowers inside, yellow roses, daisies and purple peonies. He catches me looking and offers me a sympathetic smile.

"Sixty years, and I never strayed, I never got bored of waking up next to her, I never got tired of talking to her or just being with her. She was everything to me and she got taken away from me, her heart just gave out, I still love her so much, she was my soul mate."

I smile softly at this old man's tragic story and my heart hurts for him.

"How did you meet?" I ask curiously.

"She was a nurse during the war, she was beautiful long flowing black hair, the brownest eyes I'd ever seen, I'd always been a sucker for a woman in uniform, she nursed me when I got injured in action and I thought I'd try my luck and ask her out."

I start thinking to myself that after sixty years of marriage there was and still is so much love there, listening to him telling me about this woman who he had been married to for sixty years. They were so in love, and they never stopped needing each other. That could have been and Ruby, I saw us growing old together, our kids visiting every weekend with our grandkids running around. I saw it so clearly in my mind.

"How did you and your lady meet?" he snaps me from my thoughts.

"We met in a tattoo shop, her best friend is a tattoo artist, she was tattooing me and my band."

He nods thoughtfully.

"You're in a band? They don't make music like they did back in my day."

I smile at his statement, as I steel myself to continue.

"She... she was murdered... three years ago. She was pregnant, she died, but our daughter survived."

I swallow past the lump in my throat, as the expression on his face changes from curious to pure sympathy.

"I'm so sorry, son, no child should outlive their parent."

I hang my head and let out the breath I didn't realise I was holding.

"There are so many things I regret in life, but she isn't one of them, I look at Thea every day and she reminds me so much of her mum, it hurts to look at her. But I've come to realise, that I'm all she's got, to her, I'm her whole world. Ruby was murdered three years ago, and I've recently met someone online, she doesn't know my real name, she's only recently found out I've got a kid and I'm terrified that I'm betraying Ruby. If she finds out who I really am, that I've spent almost two months lying to her, she'll never forgive me," I admit and it feels so good... so cathartic to say it out loud.

"In my experience, son, take some advice from an old man, don't live your life with regrets, Ruby would want you to move on, to be happy. She never got to meet her daughter, she didn't get the happy ever after, you didn't get to grow old together and that's just life. Sometimes we get dealt crap hands, but it's how you play it that counts, play it to your advantage. This new girl, you like her?" he asks curiously and I nod.

"More than I've liked anyone in three years," I say with a sigh, and he brushes my arm reassuringly.

"Then be honest with her, tell her who you really are, she'll understand. You're not betraying Ruby's memory; you're just making new ones. It's not a bad thing, you can't carry on living your life in the past, you've got to keep moving forward. You owe it yourself and to that little girl."

With those words fresh in my mind, I head home with renewed purpose, and I know deep down what I need to do.

# 18

## Zeppelin

I remember so clearly the trips to Blackpool when I was a kid, back when things were normal. The boring, long monotonous motorway trips, the greasy but oh-so-good food at Little Chef, at the service station.

I always had a cheeseburger and chips, loads of ketchup, no salad, and a banana milkshake. Dad always had a black coffee and a full English breakfast, scrambled eggs instead of fried, with extra mushrooms. *They were his favourite.*

I remember the silly impressions my dad used to do to make me laugh, the endless games of eye-spy and Eddie's and Winkies and I always made sure I took extra batteries for my Sony Walkman. I loved music, back then, it was Take That, N Sync, Backstreet Boys, whoever was the flavour of the moment. It was then my love affair with music began, it can make or break my thought pattern; it can set an idea in motion, or the theme to my current novel. It can set the mood for a particular chapter, or just get me in the zone to actually sit down and write and not become wildly distracted by dog videos on YouTube, or handsome men in online chat rooms. *Well...let's face it, that last one was a complete lie, that was never going to happen.*

After my conversation with Rian, he received a booty call from Danny Debonair and left like someone lit a fire under his arse, leaving me to my racing thoughts. My phone pinging a notification that HandsomeJack0304 had sent me a message. I pick it up, swipe open the screen and settle myself on the sofa, Jericho immediately leaping up on the sofa to lie on my feet.

**HandsomeJack0304:** Hey you, sorry I haven't been around much, stuff got hectic with work and with my daughter.

**ZepW92:** Hey yourself, it's okay, life happens, I get it!

**HandsomeJack0304:** It's hard trying to entertain a three-year-old when you're a single parent! She's currently at the zoo with my best friends two sons, they adore her.

I smile fondly, as I read his message.

**HandsomeJack0304:** So, I've had a really fucking weird day...I visited my fiancée's grave, and I met this old boy. He told me about his wife who died and how they were together for sixty years. I saw myself growing old with her and after she died, I couldn't see myself growing old with anyone else but her. After today, it made me realise that life is so fucking precious, it can be taken away in the blink of an eye. I don't want to carry on living in the past.

The dots continue jumping as I steel myself for the words that follow, waiting with bated breath.

**HandsomeJack0304:** The world hurts less when we talk, I've been in the grief club for far too long, it's the club that nobody asked to join, membership is just automatic after losing someone you love. But the grief is easier to deal with when I know you're there. I want to move forward, and I think I want that with you.

My eyes widen at his revelation, and it takes me a few minutes to process the words.

**ZepW92:** Time's like these I think we're making progress, then you blow hot and cold on me. If we agree to do this properly, then it has to be the right way, we have to be honest with each other. It's easy to fall in love with someone's words, Jack. No more secrets, no more lies, my heart can't deal with anymore deception.

I gnaw on my thumbnail, as I await his response.

**HandsomeJack0304:** What do you want to know?

I nod. *He's at least willing to try, that's a good start.*

**ZepW92:** I just want to know you, Jack. We can take it in turns if you want. You tell me something about you and I'll tell you something about me, it can be a random fact, or just about your life in general.

**HandsomeJack0304:** Or how about we just arrange to meet, in person? I'm ready to share the real me, straight up, no more lies.

My eyes widen at his statement, and I read them again to make sure I wasn't just imagining things.

**ZepW92:** Yes! I'd really like that!

I can't hold back the beaming grin that spreads across my face, as I catch my reflection in the screen of my phone. Jericho starts jumping up and down, wagging his tail, his tongue flopped out to the side. I stroke his ears and pet his head.

**HandsomeJack0304:** Awesome! How about tomorrow at midday, at a restaurant called The Cave?

*I've read reviews on that restaurant, it's owned by celebrity chef, Kit Roman. It's super exclusive and uber expensive.*

**ZepW92:** Sounds perfect! But don't you have to book way in advance at that place?

**HandsomeJack0304:** Don't worry, I've got it covered, meet me at midday and all will be revealed. I want to pursue whatever this is between us and I'm ready to share everything with you. I don't want any more lies or anything else to come between us, I just want us to get to know each other in real life and see where it takes us.

I smile at the sentiment and find myself all too easily agreeing to meet this strange, mysterious man, whose words I have fallen in love with.

# 19

## Jax

After my conversation with Zeppelin, I went to bed that night feeling lighter than I had in a long time and I was finally looking forward, instead of living in the past. We had arranged to meet tomorrow, and I fell asleep with a nervous energy that I hadn't felt in three long years. I was ready for her to know the real me, I was ready for her to know Jackson Chase and not Jack Logan, the persona I had been hiding behind for the past two months.

I'm not sure how much time has passed, but I'm startled awake by a loud, persistent rapping on the door. I sit bolt upright, disoriented and still groggy from sleep.

"JAX! OPEN THE DOOR! IT'S ME! JAX!"

I hear Sam's loud, familiar rasp and he sounds panicked. His rapping turns to full-on banging, and I glance over at the clock, noting it's coming up to one thirty a.m. It takes me a few moments to gather myself, before I swing my legs out of bed and pad down the stairs in the dark. I'm careful not to wake Thea, if she isn't already awake, she went to sleep earlier telling me adorable tales of giraffes with the longest necks she's ever seen and zebras with lots of stripes.

I open the door, rubbing sleep from my eyes and I'm greeted by all six foot four inches of him. Sam's hair is dishevelled, as if he's been running his fingers through it constantly. He has dark circles underneath his eyes, and he looks less than his usual put together self.

"Jax."

His face ashen and the look he gives me is grave.

"Sam, talk to me, what's happened? Is it Peyton, or one of the boys?" I ask, apprehensive of the answer he is about to give me. *Please God, don't let it be any more bad news.* He shakes his head and relief washes over me, unprepared for the words that follow.

"I-it's Brody."

183

His gruff voice shaky.

"He's been in a motorbike accident, it's bad, Jax, really fucking bad."

His eyes glossy with unshed tears and my eyes widen at his revelation. *What the fucking fuck?* He swallows a few times, as if to compose himself before he speaks again.

"He was in a motorbike accident," he repeats, as if he can't believe what has happened.

"Stupid motherfucker took a corner too fast and crashed into an incoming vehicle, it was a hit and run. He was found unconscious in the middle of the road, covered in blood. He's in intensive care."

He drags his hand through his hair, and it takes me a few moments to comprehend the weight of the words, as I'm instantly transported back to a different time.

# Jax

# Past

*It's been two weeks since Sam's suicide attempt and as a band, with J.D's blessing, we have decided to take a year out of the music industry. Ruby has moved in with me, after the pain of losing her best friend, she decided that life was too precious to waste time regretting things and it seemed like the next logical step, after everything that's happened over the past months. Sam's been discharged from hospital and J.D is keeping a closer eye on him, but something seems off to me. It doesn't sit quite right with me. Brody's drug addiction has spiralled out of control and he's using daily, if he isn't careful, he's going straight back to rehab through no fault of his own.*

*We are looking out of the floor to ceiling windows out across London and spot Brody getting on the back of his bike on the street below. He straddles the bike, kicks the kick stand and revs the engine. He's wearing a white t-shirt and jeans, his motorbike is the only thing in his life that he takes seriously, but today isn't one of those days. He isn't wearing a helmet, or any of his usual leather safety gear. Ruby and I have just woken up after a marathon sex session, as we stand in the window observing him, Ruby in one of my oversized Rancid Vengeance t-shirts and me in just my boxers.*

*"Don't you ever worry about him?" she asks thoughtfully and I chuckle softly.*

*"Nah, he's a big boy he can take care of himself," I state nonchalantly, as I wrap my arms around her waist and rest my chin on her shoulder. She leans back into me, her head rested on my shoulder.*

*"Someone's world is on the back of that bike," she says wistfully. She's such a worrier, bless her.*

*"We've never really seen eye to eye, he's too self-destructive, he doesn't think before bringing everyone else down with him. He doesn't give a shit about other people, only himself, he's a selfish motherfucker," I explain with a bitter edge to my voice.*

*"Don't you ever think he's just waiting for the right woman to come along to put him back together?"*

*I cock my eyebrow with a snort.*

*"Na, he's just waiting for his next fix." I state drolly, shifting her back against me and feeling her warmth.*

*"Anyway, I don't think any woman in this world would put up with his bullshit."*

*Ruby frowns and a line jumps between her perfectly plucked eyebrows.*

*"You never know, he might surprise you one day," she states with a sigh, and I smirk. She sees the good in everyone, it's one of my favourite traits of hers.*

*"Once a junkie, always a junkie, he'll never change, buttercup, we've been friends for a long time. He's always been reckless and never gives a second thought to other peoples' feelings. He's more of a do now, think later kind of guy."*

*She cocks her head to the side and regards me intently with a pensive look in her beautiful brown eyes.*

*"What did he do to make you so bitter towards him?" she asks curiously and I shake my head.*

*"I couldn't count on my fingers and toes the amount of times he's fucked up. It's happened time and time again, but the boys and J.D seem so oblivious to his path of self-destruction. Either that, or they just turn a blind eye, it's like watching a car crash you can't quite tear your eyes away from. I've seen the effects he's had on Sam over the years, I see right through his bullshit and Brody knows it, that's why we've never been close."*

*Ruby turns to face me and wraps her arms around my neck, I place my hands at the small of her back, pulling her closer to me. She gently presses her lips to mine. Her soft plump, pink lips against mine feels like heaven. I'll never get tired of kissing her, as she coaxes me to deepen the kiss, teasing and caressing my mouth. I feel my cock stir in my boxers, as she reaches down gripping my growing erection.*

*"Enough about Brody, I want you to fuck me, Jack," she whispers breathily and who am I to deny her?*

# Jax
# Present

The time goes by in a blur and as we arrive at the Queen Elizabeth Hospital, the entrance is full of paparazzi and journalists. *Fucking vultures.* The click-click of the paparazzi's cameras and the glaring flashes, as they continue to photograph us entering the hospital. Heckling and catcalling to Sam, Lucas, Peyton and me. Sam's arm casually slung around Peyton's neck, pulling her closer into him and shielding her from them. Lucas' hand is tucked casually into the pocket of his jeans and it's taking everything I have in me to stop myself from lashing out at the press. *We're fucking human beings too! We deserve a little privacy at a time like this.*

We all head up to the Intensive Care Unit with sombre looks on our faces, my anxiety growing exponentially with each step I take, as we soon find ourselves stepping over the threshold and into the stark, sterile hospital room. An unwelcome feeling of apprehension and dread settles itself in my gut. My stomach roils violently, and I feel the sudden urge to vomit. *Come on, Chase, breathe.*

"You good, man?" Lucas asks, his familiar American drawl seems to settle me somewhat and I nod curtly.

"Boys." Lenny, Brody's sober sponsor greets us with his familiar gruff tone. Lenny is an older gentleman, he's old school and him and Brody are extremely close. He's been like a father figure to Brody over the years. We all greet him and his wife, Nancy in turn, he has his hands tucked into his pockets. He is average height, grey slicked back hair, pale blue eyes, wearing black dress trousers and a baby pink Lacoste polo shirt, with the top two buttons open, revealing a smattering of white chest hair. The look on his face tells us all we need to know, it's bad.

"He's got a fractured skull; he was flung up in the air and hit the ground from a height. He's also got a broken wrist, fractured tibia and fibula, and a broken collar bone."

*Fuck my life, this can't be happening. I know we've never seen eye to eye, but I don't want anything to happen to him.*

"Look, I need to call Brody's lady friend, to let her know what's happened. Sam, my boy, will you pick her up and bring her here? I know she trusts you."

Lenny turns to Sam. It's more of a statement than a request and Sam nods his agreement without question.

"Sure, she was staying over at Brody's last I heard."

Lenny pulls his phone out of his pocket and steps away for a moment.

*"Fuckkkk!"* Sam curses long and low.

"What the fuck was he thinking? Fucking prick!" he mutters and Peyton reaches up on her tiptoes to stroke his cheek tenderly. I quietly observe, as he places his hand over hers and leans into her touch. A pang of jealousy hits me, as Lucas moves closer to me, regarding me with careful eyes.

"How are you holding up? I know how much you hate hospitals," he asks and I let out the breath I didn't know I was holding.

"Is it that obvious?" He smiles.

"Just a little." I find myself smiling back.

"The last time I was in a hospital, my life as I knew it was literally nuked right in front of me and there was fuck all I could do about it. There isn't a day that goes by that I don't wish everything was different," I admit and Lucas brushes my arm in a silent gesture of reassurance.

"I asked Zeppelin to meet me in person," I blurt out and Lucas nods his approval.

"About fuckin' time!"

I smirk, as Lenny re-joins our group.

"She's in a right fucking state, poor girl. Sam, she's expecting you."

Sam nods curtly and turns to leave, as we wait with bated breath whether Brody will live or die.

# 20

## Zeppelin

The dress that had hung so limp and lifeless on the svelte mannequin is the only separation between my skin and the midday chill. I tug it down, conscious that it was far shorter than I was used to, but the bubbly, over-enthusiastic, red-headed shop assistant swore I looked a million dollars. I was beginning to second guess my decision, as the time crept on. I had no time to go home and change into something more comfortable, more...me. You didn't get a second chance to make a first impression, so I'd have to make do. I didn't mention to Rian that Jack and I had arranged to meet in person, it would only have given him the opportunity to talk me out of it. Anyway, he was too loved up with Danny Debonair to care about my love life, to him it was tragic, and I agreed with him. It was tragic, but I finally had a chance of meeting someone who I had connected with.

As I sat at my dressing table applying my make-up, listening to Rachel Platen sing her *'Fight Song'* to me, I swept the brush across my cheek, the nerves settled in my gut and the doubt started to weave its way into my every being. I had to stop myself from picking up my phone and texting him some lame excuse as to why I couldn't make it, but I wanted to meet him. I wanted to know the real Jack Logan, in real life. I pulled up my big girl pants, put on my new white and yellow dress, covered in a cute, quirky lemon print. I jammed my feet into my most comfortable pair of heels, styled my blonde hair into tousled beachy waves and secured it with a white hairband to match my dress and made my way to The Cave. I walked slowly down a hidden path, along the Regents canal, the decadent, flaky, buttery croissant I had for breakfast threatening to make a reappearance, as I finally get to the stylish, uniquely modern restaurant, complete with a bright conservatory.

As I approach the maître D at the glossy white podium, my stomach roils.

"Hi, I'm here to meet someone... erm... Jack...?" I say nervously, the tall, lean gentleman with dark wavy hair greets me with a curt nod, cutting me off before I continue.

"This way, Miss." He gestures for me to follow him, as I follow him into the back, the restaurant filled with what look like paper lanterns as the main source of light. The bar is made of stone and the round tables are covered in black and white striped tablecloths. The walls are decorated in a mid-grey colour, with a selection of different beachscapes. The table he seats me at is towards the back of the restaurant in the corner, shrouded in the privacy of four exotic looking trees that are covered in colourful foliage. I try to appear relaxed, as I pull my shoulders back and straighten.

"May I get you something to drink, Miss Williams?"

*How the fuck does he know my name? Jack must have told him.*

"Erm... yes, yes, please, white wine, whatever you recommend. Thank you."

I try to smile without it looking like more of a grimace and he nods, setting a menu down in front of me before rushing off. I look down at my smart watch, quarter past twelve, he's late and I check my phone for the sixth time in four minutes, anxious to why I haven't heard anything from him since he text me last night.

A few moments pass and the maître D returns with a bottle of expensive looking white wine; he moves the glass on the table towards me and pours a glass in complete silence.

"Would you like anything else while you're waiting?" he asks and I shake my head, as he sets the bottle of wine down on the table.

"No, thank you."

He smiles softly, leaving me to my racing thoughts. *What if he's changed his mind?* I pick up the glass of white wine and take a tentative sip, the cool liquid sliding down my throat and warmth settling in my still roiling stomach. I look at my phone again, noting twenty minutes have passed and I still haven't heard anything. I contemplate sending him a text or even calling, but I don't want to come across as desperate. *Come on, Zeppelin, relax, he'll be here, I'm sure there's a logical explanation as to why he isn't here yet.* I take another sip of wine and try to calm myself down, feeling judging eyes boring into me, as I continue to wait. My phone pings a message, startling me from my thoughts and I immediately snatch it up.

I'm so sorry I should have let you know sooner.

One of my best friends has been in a serious motorbike accident, it's not looking good.

It's touch and go, I'm at the hospital now.

I can't make our date.

Please forgive me.

I'll call you later.

J x

Irritation burns through every nerve in my body. *How fucking dare he cancel on me like that?* He could have at least let me know sooner so I wouldn't have been waiting here like a complete fucking lemon! I feel my face flushing with embarrassment, as I down my glass of wine in one gulp and I get up from my seat, as the maître D rushes over.

"Miss Williams, allow me to escort you out."

I look at him questioningly, as he tries desperately to hide the panicked look on his face.

"Did you know he was going to cancel?"

I can't keep the accusatory tone from my voice, as his lips form a straight line. He remains silent and I can't believe this is happening. Then I think about the unfinished bottle of wine on the table and the glass I drank. I open my bag and start to frantically rummage for my credit card. *Fuck my life.* He places his hand on mine gently, halting my action and offering me a sympathetic look.

"The bill has been taken care of," he informs me, as I let out a relieved breath and smile softly, swallowing past a lump that has formed in my throat, willing the tears I feel burning the back of my eyes to piss off.

"Thank you," I say shakily, I must look pathetic to all of the other patrons in the restaurant, and I've never felt more humiliated. I make my way past all of the diners, out into the cool afternoon air and it isn't until I arrive home, that I allow the tears to fall.

\*\*\*

After changing into something more comfortable and settling myself on the sofa with Jericho at my feet, I flick on the TV and as I'm mindlessly scrolling through the channels, something catches my attention.

*"Rock band Rancid Vengeance's future in the music industry looks bleak and uncertain tonight, as rhythm guitarist and well documented lothario, Brody Hart, has been involved in a major road traffic accident. The extent of Hart's injuries are yet to be confirmed. However, a spokesperson for Rancid Vengeance has been contacted for further comment. Hart, thirty-four, outspoken and hailed the notorious bad boy of the band, has recently been linked to troubled Hollywood starlet, Raleigh Storm, twenty-nine. The reason behind this horrifying incident is still unclear at this stage. We will keep you updated on any developments as this story unfolds."*

As I continue to listen to the awful news story about Brody Hart's tragic accident, I start going over in my head what Rian had said.

*"What if... plot twist, what if Jackson Chase is really HandsomeJack0304?"*

Jack had text me to let me know he couldn't make our date because one of his best friends had been in a serious motorbike accident. This was way too much of a coincidence, as the cogs start to turn in my lizard brain. Maybe that's why he's always been so vague, he hasn't revealed much detail about his private life because he knew I'd eventually make the connection. I lean forward to pick up my iPad from the glass coffee table and pull up the internet browser. I type Jackson Chase Rancid Vengeance into the Google search bar and wait for the results to generate; the first result is a Wikipedia page, and I click on it. As the page opens, his perfectly chiselled jaw and smiling face taunts me.

*Jackson Chase is a British guitarist, also known as Flash. Jackson found fame as one quarter of the rock band Rancid Vengeance, achieving commercial success on a global level. His achievements include guitarist of the year with Guitar Magazine for five consecutive years, a string of number one hits and a series of platinum albums under his belt.*

*Born: West Sussex (Aged 33)*
*Genres: Rock, Alternative rock.*
*Occupation: Guitarist, songwriter*
*Label: Vengeance Records (formally Diamond Records)*
*Spouse: Ruby Logan (fiancée deceased)*

*Children: Thea Ruby Logan (Aged 3)*
*Lives in Chislehurst, Kent.*
*Parents: Jamie-Leigh Chase and Jude Chase*
*Siblings: Twins Shay Chase and Skye Chase*
*Chase, along with the rest of Rancid Vengeance (Samson Newbolt, Brody Hart, and Lucas Landon) have received a record number of Kerrang Awards, including best rock band and best album, eight years in a row and been inducted into Rocks Hall of Fame after almost fifteen years in the music industry.*

I snap my iPad case shut, as if it has burned me. I've read more than enough, as I try desperately to hold back the torrent of tears that are threatening. *How could he do this to me? Why would he lie like that?* He's a rock star for fucks sake, surely, he doesn't have to lie to get a woman to have sex with him. *Hell, I had sex with him!* What are the fucking odds of having a random sexual encounter and it turning out to be the man I've been talking to online for the past few months? My mind is racing at a hundred miles an hour, as I start to think back to Rian's previous words.

*"Finally, all the pieces of the puzzle are beginning to click into place, that's why he won't let you see a photo of him. That's why he sent you that picture with his face obscured, so you wouldn't realise he was really Jax Chase from Rancid Vengeance!"*

I pull up his picture on my iPad and study it carefully. It's a beautiful photograph; it conveys the unconditional love between father and daughter perfectly. It's a deeply intimate and personal photo to share with someone you've never met. I pinch and pull the screen zooming in on the black and white image, enlarging it and moving in close on his face. It definitely looks like Jax Chase from Rancid Vengeance. I look at his face a little longer and decide to reverse image search the picture. I pull up Google images and type in Jackson Chase and daughter. Instantly, the exact same photo appears in the search results. My mouth drops open in disbelief, as I click on the link to the article in OK! Magazine.

*Jackson Chase from Rancid Vengeance introduces his daughter Thea to the world.*

*Jax, also known as Flash, from rock band and rock royalty Rancid Vengeance gives his most candid interview on fame, fatherhood and speaks out exclusively to OK! on the tragic loss of his fiancée.*

*Jackson Chase is almost as famous for keeping his hectic, lavish, rock star lifestyle private, as he is for his expert guitar skills. Introducing his daughter for the first time to the world, in a rare interview with guitarist extraordinaire, Jax describes Thea as the 'love of his life.' He explained 'She's such a daddy's girl, I was overjoyed when she was born. But with the loss of my fiancée and her mum Ruby, it was bittersweet really. It never really gave me a chance to grieve properly, it all happened in such a short space of time, and she was this little human who was completely relying on me. Those first few months were terrifying; I'm not going to lie...'*

I scroll through the series of candid images, including the one he sent to me. My heart slams against my rib cage, as I study the pictures over and over again, taking in every single detail. From the look of absolute adoration on his beautiful fucking face, because there was no doubt, he was devastatingly handsome, in a boy next door kind of way. To the pure unconditional love in his daughters' eyes.

I can feel hot tears stinging the back of my eyes and I try to swallow past the tennis ball lump that has lodged itself in my throat. I can't believe he's been lying to me this entire fucking time! I pick up my phone, my hand trembling, as I dial Rian's number, he answers on the first ring.

"This better be good, baby girl, I'm about to be ravished by—" He greets me brightly, but I don't give him the opportunity to continue.

"You were right, Ri. Jack is Jackson Chase," I say shakily, trying desperately to hold back the torrent of tears that are threatening.

"*Shit*! I'm on my way down."

He hangs up and a few minutes pass, before there is a soft tap on the door. I open it and as soon as I see Rian, I let out a strangled sob. I collapse in a heap on the floor and sob hard, Rian swings the door shut, as he sinks to his knees, gathering me in his arms and pulling me into his warm chest.

"Shhh, I'm here, baby girl, I've got you, shhh," he soothes. I am not sure how long we sit on the floor in silence, but my tears have finally subsided. Rian scoops me up in his arms and lays me down on the sofa. He pulls down the grey fleece blanket and settles himself at the other end of the sofa, our legs entwined. He cocks his head to the side and regards me with wary eyes.

"Don't you fucking dare say I told you so, Ri, I couldn't bear it." I sniff, as he holds his hands up in defence.

"I'm offended you'd think that of me, baby girl," he says with a wry smirk and a dramatic wave of his hand. I roll my eyes at his theatrics.

"But you need to start talking, Missy, what the fuck has been going on with you?" he says with an accusatory tone to his voice, and I let out a long, drawn-out sigh.

"It's all such a fucking mess, Rian, I don't know what to do," I explain the last few days to him, down to Jack's text cancelling our date.

"*Fucking hell*, I should have bought wine, lots of wine! In fact, hold that thought! I'll Uber some!"

He takes out his phone and starts tapping on the screen, a few moments later he declares we have wine and snacks on the way. *God bless him.*

"So, where were we? Oh yeah, you were being stood up by a hot rocker!"

He taps his fingernail against his front tooth, studying me carefully.

"For fuck's sake, just say it, Ri! You're dying to say I told you so!" I whine and he bursts out laughing.

"Don't frown, it gives you premature wrinkles! And what kind of friend would I be if I said I told you so?"

I lean my head on his shoulder.

"After what happened with Abel, I swore off rockers completely. I don't need the drama that goes with it! It was fucking exhausting! Abel was so confident and so at ease with the idea of fame, he handled the attention from the press and from the countless women who'd flash their boobs at him, like it was a second nature! I can't handle that again! The jealousy killed me; I turned into someone I didn't even recognise! Abel was small time compared to Jackson fucking Chase! He's like rock royalty!"

My voice goes up a few octaves higher than usual and Rian wraps his arm around me.

"You don't even know for certain yet, why don't you just call him and ask him?"

I snort.

"Yeah, and how's that going to go? Hi Jack, are you Jackson Chase from Rancid Vengeance? And by the way you're a total prick for lying to me! I've already suffered enough humiliation for one day!"

Rian cocks his perfectly plucked eyebrow.

"Oh please! What the fuck is this? Pity party for one. Come on, where's the ballsy Zeppelin Williams we all know and love?" He gestures in my general direction.

"I'm tired of falling for the wrong men, Rian!"

He squeezes me tightly to him, pulling me closer.

"You don't fall for the wrong men, maybe that's the problem! You don't fall for *any* men! You've been single for five years!" he states incredulously and for once, I don't disagree with him, as I'm instantly transported back to five years ago.

# Zeppelin

## Past

*He's been off for days, distant, and Abel is never distant. It's like he's been replaced with someone completely different. He always has a dimpled grin, or a cheeky wink for me, no matter what mood he's in. After four years of dating, it's been tough at times, especially when he's on the road and touring, but we seem a little more settled now. He still hasn't put a ring on my finger and I'm sick of waiting. Mrs Zeppelin Jade Creed has a nice ring to it and my finger was missing a huge princess cut diamond.*

*I'm spread out on the gargantuan King Size bed of Hotel Mamela, after a marathon sex session. The silk sheets soft and decadent on my skin in the ultra-modern hotel room. I roll over naked, kicking my legs up behind me as I hear the shower turn off. The bathroom door swings open, letting out masculine, scent-filled steam and he looks like a God damn snack, a towel hanging loosely off his lean, tanned hips. His dark hair wet and framing his chiselled face, his tattooed biceps thick and taut, with rivulets of water running off his sculpted abs.*

*"Put some fucking clothes on, for fuck's sake!" he huffs and my mouth drops open, agape at his harsh, unfeeling tone.*

*"Don't fucking speak to me like that, Abel Creed!" I shriek, affronted by his shitty behaviour. After we had sex, he was so loving and attentive, but he had gone from gentle lover to a cold, emotionless shell in the matter of minutes.*

*"I'll speak to you however I please! Now get some fucking clothes on, we're going to be late!" he says through gritted teeth, his jaw clenched tightly and the eyes I fell in love with, void of any and all emotion. My heart slams against my rib cage, as I leap up from the bed, shoving him out of the way. He reaches out to try and grab me.*

*"Zeppelin, baby, I'm sorry!"*

*I slam the bathroom door behind me, ignoring his apology and flipping the lock. He shakes the door handle, and I hear him growl.*

*"For fuck's sake, Zeppelin!" he yells through the closed door, as I desperately try to quell the tears I can feel stinging my eyes.*

*"FUCKING ASSHOLE!" I scream, catching my reflection in the mirrored medicine cabinet above the sink and I look thoroughly fucked. My eyes glossy and wide, my long blonde hair perfectly mussed. In that moment, I make a solemn promise to myself that I will not allow Abel's behaviour to ruin this trip, as I set about getting ready for the night ahead.'*

*** 

*Abel and the Poison Puppets have just performed a gig in Italy. They were supporting The Devil's Henchman. It was a huge deal for a rock band, who had gained a massive following. They had gained mega star status after being signed to High Voltage Records just over five years ago. Despite his flaws, Abel deserved it, he put his heart and soul into the band. He didn't have the best upbringing, but music was his escape, like writing was mine. I always admired him for his motivation and sheer dedication to his music and the band. I supported him wholeheartedly and after our lovers' tiff earlier, he was back to his usual loving and attentive self.*

*The bands manager Jayson Mendoza had called in a favour from a billionaire friend of his and the after-show party was going to take place on a luxury yacht in the Marina Di Capri. It looked like something from a movie, the pink, orange hues of the sunsetting behind the yacht. The shimmer and the soft lapping of the sea around the harbour, it was paradise.*

*The yacht as a two-hundred-and-eighty-foot super-yacht, it screamed wealth. It had three floors, each more luxurious than the previous. It boasted its own helicopter hangar, Olympic sized swimming pool, a private casino, spa, sauna and ten cabins, each the size of a small standard hotel room, complete with en-suite bathrooms. It also had a fully stocked bar, a beauty salon, a restaurant with its own private chef and a huge sitting room, which had been converted into a dance floor for the evening's celebration.*

*"Smile for the camera!" Jayson says with a chuckle, his white linen trousers lightly flapping in the early evening breeze. His navy blue and white striped shirt and no socks combo oddly suited his flamboyant, yet understated look. He pushes his glasses further up the bridge of his nose, his bright white teeth almost blinded, as he points his mobile phone at Abel, me, Rico and Shep. Abel pulls me closer to him, and I cuddle into his side, feeling sexy in my white mini*

*dress, which sets off my golden tan. Abel was wearing a light blue checkered shirt, denim shorts and flip flops. His hair in a neat man-bun and his aviators shielding his eyes. The rest of the band looked cool, relaxed and in good spirits after performing an epic show in front of a crowd of five thousand strong.*

*We had been here for five days and while Abel was rehearsing with the band, I was working on my tan and exploring the new city I had found myself in. I spent countless hours by the pool writing and I had never been more inspired. I was in the middle of writing my fourth book and despite Abel's mood swings in the weeks that had passed, I was happy and content with my life.*

*"Remember this night, always, babe."*

*He presses a kiss to my temple, as we all pose for the photo. The moment frozen in time and captured perfectly.*

\*\*\*

*I was in awe as I stepped onto the yacht. The music was pumping, as Junior Senior Move your Feet blasted from the built-in speakers. We step into the wide-open space of the bottom deck, and I'm struck dumb at the sheer opulence. It really is spectacular; it is decorated gunmetal grey throughout with silver accents. It is the epitome of extravagant, and I felt oddly out of place. This wasn't the world that I was used to, I didn't fit in here, I felt like a fraud. Abel hands me a glass of champagne, snapping me from my reverie and clinks his glass with mine, I can't help but smile at his boyish enthusiasm.*

*"I'm so proud of you!" I shout over the music and we both take a sip of our drinks at the same time. He kisses me tenderly on the lips and pinches my bum.*

*"Is it wrong that I'm turned on by the thought of my come inside you?" His voice is dripping with seductive charm, and I almost choke on my drink, as he chuckles softly.*

*"I'll never not find your shyness cute! Relax, babe! Mingle, let your hair down, have some fun!"*

*He waves to someone across the room and with those words, he's gone. I stand awkwardly for a few moments, gulping down the rest of my champagne and placing it down on a passing waiter's silver tray.*

*I'm swaying to the music, Candi Staton You Got the Love blasting through the speakers. I have lost count how many glasses of champagne I've drunk, and I haven't seen Abel for a while. I go in search of him, navigating my way through the throngs of people. I hear voices and the soft moans of a couple getting heated somewhere in the stairwell.*

*"Ah, fuck!"*

*I'd recognise that voice anywhere. Abel fucking Creed. I stomp up the stairwell, his pants around his ankles.*

*"UNBELIEVABLE!" I shriek, as he pushes the dark-haired woman away from him and starts to pull up his shorts.*

*"Zeppelin! It's not what it looks like!"*

*My mouth drops open. Is he for real?*

*"Not what it looks like? Yeah, it really looked like you were discussing real world issues!"*

*I yell, heading up to the second floor, Abel following close behind.*

*"Come on, Zeppelin! Please, I can explain!" His voice is almost pleading, as I spin around to face him.*

*"What's there to explain? You tripped and fell into her vagina?" I spit and he follows after me zipping up his shorts.*

*"Fuck you, Abel!" I all but scream at him, attracting the attention of almost everyone on board. I'm so blinded by anger and hurt; I don't notice them. Abel catches up to me grabbing my arm and I spin around slapping him hard across his face.*

*"What the fuck, Zeppelin! I've tried so hard these past four years! But the truth is, you're suffocating me! You're holding me back from my music career! I've tried but it feels like we're not compatible anymore, you're so lost in your fictional worlds, you don't even notice me anymore!" he yells over the music and my mouth drops open at his admission.*

*"I'm holding you back! You just had your dick in another woman! I'd hardly call that holding you back! You're a typical rocker thinking you can do whatever you want regardless of the fucking consequences! Is this what this is really about, I don't notice you? Come on, you're Abel fucking Creed! The whole world notices you! You're the poster boy for all those teenage girls, the women want to fuck you, and the men want to be you! You're the new Rancid Vengeance, that's what they're describing you as! So, tell the truth for once in*

*your life, Abel, this isn't about me noticing you, this isn't about you craving attention from your girlfriend! This is about you wanting to have your cake and eat it, I've busted my arse for you over these four years! Jesus, I gave up my shitty hotel job to travel with you after you told me that I was better than that, you persuaded me to take up writing full-time and I did that not only for myself, but for you!"*

*I jab my finger in his direction, unable to stop the tears falling down my cheeks, as I sob.*

*"It's over, Zeppelin, I'm sorry, we want different things and let's face it, you're never going to be the next J.K Rowling, you're a ten-a-penny indie author who dreams of making it big, but it's never going to happen! I want to explore the world, I want to experience what it's like to be adored by thousands, if not millions of fans, I want our fans to sing our songs back to us, I want us to be bigger than Rancid Vengeance! I can't do that with you holding me back, it would never have worked out between us, not long term. I'm sorry."*

*Every word he spoke was like a knife to my already broken heart and in that moment, I knew I was done with Abel Creed. It was fun while it lasted, but nothing lasts forever, right?*

# Zeppelin

## Present

**ZepW92:** Jack, we need to talk

I gnaw viciously on my thumbnail, as I eagerly await his reply.

**HandsomeJack0304:** I can explain... I'm so fucking sorry I had to cancel our date. One of my best friends has been in a motorbike accident. It's not looking good, it's bad, really bad. He's been rushed for emergency surgery, it's fifty-fifty on whether he's going to make it. We're taking it in shifts to be here if something happens. I couldn't leave, I'm sorry, please understand.

My heart hurts for him, his pain coming through in his words.

**HandsomeJack0304:** Look, I know you probably hate my fucking guts right now and I wouldn't blame you one little bit. But I'm just on the way home now, I could maybe stop by on the way home... we could finally meet. I'm tired of hiding, I want to know you and I want you to know the real me.

I'm taken aback by his words, and I stare mindlessly at the screen for a little longer than necessary.

**ZepW92:** I was really fucking angry when I got your message, and I was sitting in the restaurant. I waited for you, Jack!

**HandsomeJack0304:** I'll spend the rest of my life making it up to you, please. Seeing him lying broken in his hospital bed... God, it bought back some awful memories for me. It put things in perspective, life's too short for regrets, it's too fucking precious...

As I read those words, I know what I have to do. I type my address, hit send and wait for the knock at the door. I had to know if Rian's theory was right, I had to know if Jack Logan really was Jackson Chase.

# 21

## Jax

*Brody "Snake" Hart, one quarter of popular rock band Rancid Vengeance, has been involved in a horrific hit-and-run accident. Notorious bad boy of the band has hit headlines in recent weeks for his blossoming romance with troubled Hollywood movie actress Raleigh Storm. Storm, twenty-nine, is currently starring in 'Rocked', directed by controversial British movie director, Damien Valentine. Hart, thirty-four, was identified as the victim at the scene and rushed to a nearby hospital. Sources close to the band say, "he's in a critical, but stable condition." Police are urging the driver of the other vehicle to come forward and are encouraging witnesses to contact their local constabulary with vital evidence. A spokesperson for Rancid Vengeance has been contacted for an official statement. However, the extent of his injuries are said to be severe and potentially life-threatening...*

We were victims of our own success. Rancid Vengeance were a product for J.D and Diamond Records to exploit to their advantage. We allowed it to go on for years and we've continued to pay the high price ever since. Our lives front and centre, hiding our personal lives away from the press, our lives not really our own and repressing who we really are, for recognition and record sales.

We were cash cows, and it destroyed us all in some way or another. We weren't the same naive, starry-eyed young boys blinded by fame that we used to be. We were oblivious to J.D's subtle manipulation and obvious abuse of power. We were hardened to it all, we were season professionals, who had broken free of the chains of our success. But we still held on to the freedom of being signed to our own label, to take back what we had lost all those years ago.

As we sit in the relatives' room, bathed in soft light, awaiting news on Brody, a doctor joins us. The doctor is a tall, lean, balding, middle-aged man who introduces himself as Doctor Cooper.

"I'm Doctor Cooper. May I ask who is Mr Hart's next of kin?" he asks and Lenny steps forward, squaring his shoulders with an air of authority.

"That would be me, doc," he says gruffly, desperately trying to hold it together and be the strong patriarch figure that Brody has come to rely on for so many years.

"Whatever you need to say, you can say it in front of them. They're as much his family as I am, and this young lady is his girlfriend."

Raleigh has taken it hard, her face is pale, her lilac hair lifeless and her eyes dull. I observe her for a few short moments, and I almost feel bad that I haven't gotten to know her as well as I should. The doctor nods curtly, clearing his throat. and smiles sympathetically at Raleigh. She presses her lips together, as she is listening intently to the doctor's explanation.

"We found significant traces of cocaine in Mr. Hart's blood stream and his body went into cardiac arrest."

I can't say I'm fucking surprised, it was only a matter of time before he fell off the wagon from a great height. *Does he not think about how this affects anyone else, but himself?* We've been far from squeaky clean over the years, but every time he's fallen back into a mountain of cocaine, Tate and our P.R team have buried it. There's only so many times it can be swept under the rug before our reputation starts to become questionable. Every trip to rehab, every time we're photographed falling out of clubs and every groupie who sells a story detailing her *'night of passion'* just to make a few quid. It all adds up and I don't know how much more we can take before enough is enough.

"He has some significant internal bleeding, due to the point of impact, which we're certain that the handlebars of his bike caused. He's also suffered a basilar skull fracture and that has resulted in excessive leakage of cerebrospinal fluid. We'll need to operate as a matter of urgency. We're prepping him for surgery now, to hopefully stop it and prevent any further damage. We have to tell you this, I'm afraid, but because of the extent of Brody's injuries, there's a considerable chance he might not make it through surgery."

The doctor continues, as Raleigh lets out a strangled sob and Peyton sobs softly too. Peyton squeezes her hand in a gesture of reassurance and wraps her arm around her shoulder.

"What would happen if he didn't have surgery?" Lenny asks pragmatically, squeezing the back of his neck and clearing his throat.

"He could potentially bleed to death, organ failure, or the oxygen to his red blood cells would be compromised. There's also a risk with any type of brain surgery that he could suffer brain damage or, worse case scenario lives the rest of his life in a permanent vegetative state," the doctor says and I can't wrap my head around any of this. *How could he be so fucking stupid?* Seeing Brody lying perfectly still and broken in his hospital bed, with wires coming off what seems like every part of his body. It put things into perspective for me, we had all just found out that Raleigh was pregnant, and Brody was going to be a dad.

It made me start to think back to a question I got asked once in an interview, what would Jackson Chase's legacy be if my life was cut short, and right now, I honestly didn't know. I couldn't allow myself to think like that, I had Thea to think of, she's my number one priority. I wasn't the reckless, carefree, irresponsible adolescent I once was. I was a grown man with responsibilities, I had an innocent, yet curious three-year-old to take care of now. Being a father was the biggest challenge I'd ever faced, but I was doing better now, I had a great support system around me, and I'd be forever grateful for that.

I had cancelled my date with Zeppelin and even though he sometimes doesn't deserve our loyalty, Brody is family. He's only ever had us in his life, he has no one else and we couldn't abandon him in his time of need. I felt a crippling sense of guilt for cancelling on her, but family comes first and that would have to be enough, for now.

The hours all seem to blur and blend into each other. I'm not sure how long we've been here, but Brody is finally out of surgery. His head injury was worse than the doctors first anticipated. He had several seizures during surgery and to limit long-term damage, he has been put into an induced coma to allow his body to fully heal. The next twenty-four to forty-eight hours are critical and those words terrified me. A man who has partied to excess, lived life to the fullest and taken every drug known to man, Brody, who I call my brother could have his life cut short. We had already lost nine people in Vegas; we couldn't lose another one of our own. The previous tragic events had left a lasting impact, and the news affected me worse than I anticipated, I couldn't be here anymore.

"You good, man?" Lucas drawls, regarding me intently and I shake my head.

"I can't be here anymore, Luke." My voice betrays me, as I drag my hand through my long hair and start to pace the floor.

"Do what you need to do, brother, holler if you need anything and I'll call if anything happens. Give Thea a kiss from Uncle Lukey."

Lucas squeezes my shoulder, and I nod curtly, grateful for the reprieve. I say my goodbyes and leave the hospital, flanked by Kai and Trey. The press and a selection of our hardcore fans had camped outside, the camera flashes go wild, as I step out and I give them a wave. I'm escorted to my car and as soon as the car door slams shut, the silence instantly taunts me. I lean back in the driver's seat, the past twenty-four hours like a lead weight bearing down on me.

I'm about to start the engine, when my phone pings a notification. I pull it out of my pocket, swipe the screen and open the waiting message.

**ZepW92:** Jack, we need to talk.

I contemplate my reply for a few moments, as I begin to type furiously. She deserves a proper explanation as to why I cancelled on her.

**HandsomeJack0304:** I can explain... I'm so fucking sorry I had to cancel our date. One of my best friends has been in a motorbike accident. It's not looking good, it's bad, really bad. He was rushed into emergency surgery; he's been put into an induced coma. It's fifty-fifty on whether he's going to make it. We're taking it in shifts to be here if something happens. I couldn't just leave, I'm sorry, please understand.

I figured honesty would be the best choice in this situation.

**HandsomeJack0304:** Look, I know you probably hate my fucking guts right now and I wouldn't blame you one little bit. But I'm just on the way home now, I could maybe stop by on the way home... we could finally meet. I'm tired of hiding, I want to know you and I want you to know the real me.

**ZepW92:** I was really fucking angry when I got your message, and I was sitting in the restaurant. I waited for you, Jack!

The anger is palpable through the words and tone of her message. *Fuck, I feel like an absolute prick for bailing on her like that.*

**HandsomeJack0304:** I'll spend the rest of my life making it up to you, please. Seeing him lying broken in his hospital bed... God, it bought back some awful memories for me. It put things in perspective, life's too short for regrets, it's too fucking precious...

I was genuinely tired of hiding, if we were going to pursue a relationship in real life, I had to start being honest with her and I figured now is a good a time as any. I wanted to know her, and I wanted her to know Jackson Chase more than anything. I didn't want to hide behind Jack Logan anymore, I owed it to her, I owed it to myself and more importantly, I owed it to Ruby. She would want me to be happy; I had to start building a life without her in it and I had finally made peace with that. Before I can really contemplate the weight of my words, she types back her address.

***

I come to a stop and pull up outside an apartment block in an upmarket area in Notting Hill. I take in the modern grey brick building for a moment and switch off the engine, nerves suddenly getting the better of me. *Come on, Chase, for fucks sake, you can perform in front of a crowd of thousands, but you can't pluck up the courage to meet the woman you've been talking to online for the past two months? Have a fucking word with yourself!* I check my phone; I've definitely got the right address. I unclip my seatbelt and climb out of the car. I lock my car and head up the set of stone steps. I push my way through the gold and glass door entering the vast foyer, catching sight of my reflection. *Fuck me, I look like shit, but I suppose I'll have to do.*

"May I help you, sir?" A concierge greets me, and I nod politely.

"I'm here to see Zeppelin Williams."

He smiles.

"Ah, yes, I believe she's expecting you. The lifts are just to your right, sir."

He gestures to the far-right corner of the vast space, and I smile my thanks. I make my way over to the lift and press the call button. It arrives after a few moments and I step inside, the doors slide shut, and my pulse seems to rise with each floor we pass until the lift comes to a halt on her floor.

I check my phone again to make sure I have the right address, as I make my way down the plush, cream carpeted corridor, which reminds me of pretty much all of the hotels we've frequented over the years. I approach the large looming white door, and I knock twice. As I try to appear casual and confident, when inside I'm all sorts of nervous, on edge and generally an absolute mess of mixed-up feelings. My stomach roils, as I wait for her to answer the door, my foot tapping anxiously.

A few moments pass, as I contemplate knocking again, when she opens the door tentatively and apprehensively. I clear my throat before I speak, as I take her in. She's even more beautiful in the flesh than she is in her photos, her photos don't do her justice. Her short blonde hair frames her face like a halo, the tousled waves making her look carefree, fresh-faced and younger than her twenty-nine years. Her large silver eyes turbulent and filled with an emotion I can't quite read. *Is it familiarity? Lust?* I'm so fucking out of practice.

"Hey," I greet her softly with a smile, as she looks at me like a deer caught in headlights.

"Jack?" she asks questioningly, her throat contracting on a swallow, and I nod cautiously. *Is that a fucking trick question?*

"B-but, y-you're Jackson Chase from..."

Her voice trembling and a few octaves higher than necessary. I tuck my hand into the pocket of my combat shorts and stop her from continuing.

"Rancid Vengeance." I finish her sentence for her, as her eyes widen and her perfect, lush, full mouth agape. She looks positively murderous, as her hand lashes across my cheek and the door slams in my face. *Well shit, that wasn't the reaction I was hoping for.*

# 22

## Zeppelin

I always knew a man would ruin me. Never in a million years did I ever think it would be Jackson Chase, guitarist from Rancid Vengeance. He knew how to use those calloused fingers on something other than the fretboard of his guitar. *Innuendo intended.* I had no idea that he would end up tearing my heart clean out of my chest and shoving it back in without due care or attention. *Jackson Chase was a filthy fucking liar. How could he fucking do this to me?*

The sweet man behind the keyboard, who knew all my deepest darkest secrets, was a total fucking fraud. He lied for months about who he really was and after my fingers were burned with Abel, I'm not capable of forgiving easily. I let him into my heart, and I unknowingly let him into my pants. *You stupid, stupid girl!*

After all those months of chatting, we got way more intimate and deeper than we could ever have done in person. I allowed myself to get sucked in, I fell in love with a lie. *I fell in love.* With his words, with his honesty, he was so sincere in everything we talked about. I don't understand how he could lie like that. *I mean he's fucking famous for fucks sake! As if he needs to bullshit!* He could get a woman into bed by just looking at her! He didn't need to lie! I can't get my head around any of it.

I let myself fall in love with Jack Logan, Jack who stayed online until the sun came up, chatting about everything and nothing, all at the same time. Jack the guitar teacher from London. Not Jax Chase, one quarter of the world's biggest rock band. Not Jax Chase, who won guitarist of the year with Guitar Magazine, five years in a row. I got caught up in his web of deceit and now, I'm not sure I can move on with my life, without him in it.

My thoughts are interrupted by the loud pounding on the door.

"Zeppelin, please, just let me explain!" he calls, his voice pleading.

"FUCK OFF!" I yell in response. *I'm so fucking angry at him right now!*

"Please, let me in and we can talk about this properly!" His tone is defeated.

"What, so you can fucking lie to me some more? No thank you!" I snap, as I hear him sigh audibly through the closed door.

"Fine! Then I'm gonna' sit out here, until you talk to me, and you're done being mad at me! I'm not going anywhere."

I hear what sounds like his head hitting the door and a low curse, I almost feel bad for him. *Almost.*

"Zep, look, I'm sorry, I'm so fucking sorry," he says softly.

"You can shove your sorry up your arse! You still fucking lied to me! Jack Logan... Oh sorry, JACKSON MOTHERFUCKING CHASE!"

I swear I hear him growl. *Fuck him, I'm feeling in a petulant and childish mood right now.*

"I get that you're mad at me but at least let me explain the reasons why and I'd rather not do it through a closed door." His voice is calm and composed. It is the complete polar opposite to the way I'm feeling right now, I'm angry, hurt and upset.

"Technically, I didn't lie to you, I withheld the truth, yes, but I didn't outright lie," he explains and with each word he speaks, I feel the anger building within every fibre of my being. *Is he for fucking real right now?*

"Typical fucking man logic! Did you, or did you not tell me your name was Jack Logan?" I scream through the closed door, and I swear I hear him mutter *'fucking women.'* But I choose to ignore his petty statement.

"Yes, I did, but had you asked me if I was Jackson Chase, I would have fucking told you!" he counters, as I start to pace angrily around my apartment.

"On what planet is that a sound argument? You fucking lied to me! Repeatedly! You kept the fact that you had a daughter from me! That should have been red flag number one! You're covered in red flags, Jack, Jax, Jackson, whatever your fucking name is!"

I know I'm being unreasonable and irrational, but I can't seem to help myself. He's pushed every single one of my buttons, not only did he lie to me about being Jackson Chase, but I've also had sex with him, and he doesn't even realise it was me! *Way to go, Zeppelin. You little slut.*

"Are you done? Because I fucking apologised for keeping my daughter from you! I know I'm in the public eye, but I have the right to privacy too! I'm a human being! Thea is non-negotiable, the press don't get to photograph her because she's a fucking child! Her daddy might be a guitarist in one of the world's most famous rock bands, but she's not fodder for them to feast on. I won't apologise for that, she's three-years-old for fucks sake! She doesn't deserve that!"

Listening to the pure conviction in his voice cools some of my earlier ire and I feel a little calmer.

"Look, I'd really rather not do this through a closed door. Please let me in so we can talk about this properly, like adults."

He lowers his voice, and I feel a little calmer than I did ten minutes ago. I take a deep breath and gingerly pull open the door. I look up at him through my lashes and I'm temporarily disarmed by the sight that greets me. Jackson Chase, all six foot two inches of him, leaning in the door jamb, his bicep tattooed and taut. His long blonde hair cascading down to his shoulders, his deep brown eyes filled with raw emotion, and he has at least a weeks' worth of rough blonde stubble on his perfect chiselled jaw. I'm rendered speechless by this perfect specimen standing outside my door and my mouth opens and closes like a fucking goldfish. *Come on, Zeppelin, get your shit together!* His eyes lock with mine and he offers me his hand.

"Let's start again, I'm Jax Chase."

As my hand connects with his, I feel the familiar spark of electricity as his skin makes contact with mine. I thought that was just the stuff you read about in romance novels, but the feeling is all too real, as I clear my throat.

"Zeppelin Williams."

Our hands linked together a little longer than necessary and I don't want to pull away.

"Pleasure to meet you."

A warm smile spreads across his handsome face, making his eyes sparkle and dance with amusement. I'm the one to pull away from our handshake first and I'm instantly bereft at the loss of contact.

"Please, come inside," I say softly, inviting him in, as I step out of the doorway and he walks slowly inside with his hand tucked into his pocket. He looks instantly out of place, as I shut the door behind him.

I take a few moments to study him, from the full sleeve tattoos on both of his arms, to the vibrant yellow buttercup tattoo, which spans his neck and throat. The way his camouflage combat trousers hang off his lean hips and the bulge of his biceps in his distressed heather grey Motley Crue t-shirt. He's studying me with a similar piqued interest.

He's silent for a few minutes, as he casually saunters around the sofa to the window. I continue observing him in my space, looking every bit the rock star that he is. His profile is striking, he's all hard muscle, his features soft, but angular at the same time. His heavy dark blonde stubble and his long blonde hair hanging limp around his shoulders. *He really does look like Thor God of Thunder!* The dark circles underneath his eyes make him more human in some way and less unreachable.

"When you experience loss, people say that you move through the five stages of grief, denial, anger, bargaining, depression and acceptance. What they don't tell you is that you'll cycle through them all, every day." His voice is shaky with unshed tears and my heart hurts for him, as he says those words. He doesn't meet my eyes, as he leans against the window, before continuing. His thick, tattooed biceps bunching and flexing with the movement.

"When Ruby died, I never thought I'd be strong enough...whole enough to be able to find someone else. I never even contemplated it, until you."

My mouth agape at his admission.

"I'm sorry I kept things from you, I didn't do it intentionally, I had to protect myself and my daughter. God, if I could shield you and her from this...this fucking shit show I call my life, I would! The fame, the fucking press! It's exhausting, it was easier to pretend to be a fictional version of myself than the reality."

He drops his head into his hands, and I move closer to him, placing my hand on his bicep. He tenses as he looks up to finally meet my eyes.

*"Fuck,"* he curses softly.

"You're so beautiful."

He tucks a strand of my hair behind my ear and strokes my face tenderly. I lean into his touch, briefly closing my eyes, as my heartbeat starts to quicken. I open my eyes, as I tilt my head up to look at him and he unexpectedly crashes his lips urgently to mine. As soon as his lips touch mine, every ounce of anger I felt previously at his deception melted away and instantly dissipated. I cursed my treacherous body for betraying me, but I don't push him away, I can't. I wanted him too much, his lips are so soft, the contrast of his rough stubble scratching my cheek. His tongue delicately caressing mine in a sensual dance, he cups my face with both of his hands, as I go lax against him, feeling his solid erection pressing into my stomach. The scent of Diesel Only the Brave, mixed with the faint scent of sweat invading my nostrils, he briefly pulls away and the look in his brown eyes renders me mute.

"Something about you feels... oddly familiar." His voice is rough, and I want to scream in his face that I was the woman from the masquerade ball, but I don't want to ruin this moment between us. He moves closer to me, and I can feel his hot breath tickling my cheek, as he wraps me in his strong muscular arms.

"I wanted to take my time with you, I wanted to take the time to actually get to know you in real life, but as soon as I laid eyes on you, all that got shot to hell."

I find myself smiling at his words.

"And here's me thinking you were a gentleman."

He smirks and the sight causes a slick heat to pool between my legs. A fierce ache begins to blossom within me, and I need him to take it away.

"Jax." My voice is breathy and needy. He shakes his head.

"With you, I'm not Jax, I'm just Jack."

I understand the weight of his words, from an author who creates and writes fictional characters on a daily basis. I find myself nodding and agreeing to a real-life romance with Jackson Chase.

# 23

## Zeppelin

I was a mess of pent-up sexual frustration and as fast as it was moving between us, I didn't want it to slow down. I wanted to be beneath him, I wanted his cock buried deep inside me and I wasn't ashamed to admit it, even if I didn't say it out loud.

I wrap my arms around his neck, as he backs me into the window and presses his lips desperately to mine, kissing the life out of me. He kisses me furiously and breathlessly, and by the time he pulls away, we are both burning with need for one another. I feel my arousal slick between my thighs and a fierce ache began to blossom and pulse within me. It felt like I was on fire, for him and only him.

"I want you, Jack."

My voice doesn't sound like my own, it was desperate and filled with hidden need. He leans forward and I can feel his warm breath gusting against my neck, his scent enveloping me. Every nerve in my body is on high alert and tuned to everything Jackson Chase. His hand snakes down my stomach and reaches in my shorts, as he finds my swollen clit. I moan out loud, as his finger swipes up my wetness.

"*Fuck*, you're soaking wet, tell me it's all for me."

He whispers seductively and I nod, trapping my lip between my teeth.

"Mmm, yes all for you, Oh God!" I moan audibly, as he pushes his long-calloused finger inside me, moving in and out, increasing the momentum with each plunge of his expert finger.

"*Fuck*, you're so wet for me, Zeppelin," he practically growls, as he introduces a second finger, as my breath increases and becomes urgent.

"Oh God! Jack! *Fuck*! You feel so good!" I scream, as I grip his biceps to steady myself.

"Good girl, I want you to come for me," he croons, as he increases his pace with each measured, expert movement, finger fucking me thoroughly and driving me towards my release.

"*Oh shit!* That feels so good, don't stop, please, don't stop. I'm close, so fucking close!"

My breath is coming in short, sharp bursts, as he quickens his momentum, moaning softly at my orgasm builds deep within me. I feel the familiar flutters that I haven't felt in so long, as he twists his fingers deftly inside me and strokes my clit.

"OH JACK! JACK! I'M GOING TO COME! OH GOD! OH GOD!"

My orgasm tears through me like an explosion of weeks of pent-up sexual energy. I want to let him know that I was the woman he fucked at the masquerade ball, but I push that thought to the back of my mind and focus on the pure pleasure he's bestowing upon me. I scream out, as wave after wave of pleasure surges through me like a tsunami. My legs buckle beneath me, and Jack catches me in his arms, as I cling to his thick, tattooed biceps.

"I'm sorry, I don't know what came over me, I don't usually give women orgasms on the first date!"

He sounds almost embarrassed, and I chuckle softly at his statement, relishing in his warmth and being in his arms.

"Don't apologise, that was quite possibly the best orgasm I've ever had, and I don't just say that to all the boys!" I reply wryly, as I straighten myself out and finger comb my hair quickly, suddenly feeling more than a little self-conscious in the presence of this delicious human being.

"And technically we haven't been on a date yet!" I say sassily with a cheeky wink, and he laughs. Something in the way his soft brown eyes dance and sparkle with amusement tells me he doesn't laugh often. It is a sight to behold; he looks younger than his thirty-three years and it makes me want to know more about him. He cocks his head to the side and regards me intently with those captivating eyes, I swear if he asked me to spread my legs right now, I think I would do as I'm bid. I've barely touched the surface with him, but I know in my heart I'd do anything to have his hands on me. I'd give anything for him to be mine and only mine, exclusively. But right now, I don't feel like I have the right to ask that of him, so I don't.

He shifts his gaze to the floor, and I can sense him slowly pulling away from me.

"Hey, I don't blame you, you know. None of this is your fault, you were doing what you had to to protect your identity and your daughter. I have...a tendency to overreact, it's sort of a defence mechanism," I say with a nervous chuckle, and he shakes his head.

"It isn't that." He brushes his thumb tenderly across my swollen bottom lip.

"I didn't think I could ever feel like this again, Zep," he whispers softly and I smile softly in return.

"I was kidding myself to even think I could walk away from you, Jack, from us. From the moment we started talking, I felt... this... connection between us. I'm falling for you, I've tried to fight it, but I can't, I think I'm in love with you."

He gasps out loud at my admission and I instantly regret the words leaving my lips. He drags his hand through his long hair and puffs out his cheeks.

"*Shit!* I didn't mean that... well... I did-b-but."

He silences me by placing his finger on my lips.

"Today is day one, I want to do this right. You mean more to me than... than some hook up in a club."

My eyes widen at his statement, and I look up at him through my lashes. My mouth opens and closes, the words are on the tip of my tongue. I'm about to speak when his phone starts ringing, the loud sound of Linkin Park Leave Out All the Rest filling the room, our moment lost. He pulls it out of his pocket and curses under his breath.

"I'm sorry, I really have to get this," he says in a rush and steps away from me for a moment, I can hear him talking in hushed tones. I watch him carefully, moving casually around my space with one hand tucked in his pocket and the other with the phone up to his ear. He looks like he has just stepped out of GQ Magazine, his tall, lean stature, his long, flowing blonde hair hanging around his shoulders, his tattoos bright and vivid.

"Hmm, yep, I can be back there in thirty minutes. Just say the word... hmm... is Thea okay... Good, that's good... I know, I miss her too. Tell her Daddy will be back home soon... Is he okay? Fucking hell, what was he thinking, love? I don't get it... I know, we need a meeting, I bet M.J is pulling his fucking hair out... Another mess for Tate to clear up, *shit*! How much more can we take, Peyton? As a band, as human fucking beings! I mean... *bollocks*... I'm sorry."

His voice is filled with pure anguish and frustration, it makes me wonder if there's more to the story than what the news said. *Who are you kidding? Your experience with Abel should tell you that there's more than one version of the story.* He glances up at me and catches me staring at him. I look away quickly and walk towards the window. His presence is making me nervous all of a sudden and I bounce from one foot to the other.

"I can't talk right now... hmmm... tell Sam to call me when he's spoken to M.J and I'll be there... I just needed some time; it's a lot to take in... I know... you know how I get where hospitals are concerned... I know... thanks, love, I appreciate it... Give Thea a kiss from Daddy and you take care of yourself... stop it! You're making me blush!"

He laughs.

"Okay, you too, love... speak soon... bye."

He stops speaking and the hairs on the back of my neck stand on end. I know he's near; I can feel his eyes boring into the back of my head.

"Now, where were we?"

He wraps his arms around my waist and kisses my neck. I shiver at the feel of his soft lips and the contrast of his beard against my neck. He kisses a burning trail from my neck, down to my collarbone. My head flops back against his shoulder and I close my eyes, as I feel his hot breath against my damp skin. I feel his erection press into my arse, as his hand moves down slowly and into the waistband of my shorts.

His long, calloused finger finds my swollen nub, and he circles it, softly at first, then increases his pace. I moan softly, biting down on my plump bottom lip, as he takes my nipple between his thumb and forefinger. The rhythm matching the one on my clit.

"Oh, God, Jack!" I cry out.

"*Fuck,* you feel so good, Zeppelin," he grinds out, as he increases the motion, and I find myself panting for him, my heartbeat quickening.

"I want to watch you come this time, where's your bedroom?"

I manage to point across the flat, as he pulls his finger out of me and lifts me up as if I'm weightless. I giggle girlishly as he kicks the door open with his boot Jericho leaping up from the bed and letting out a series of barks. Jack doesn't break his stride, as he enters my bedroom and stops at the foot of the bed with me in his arms.

"It's okay, buddy."

I coo, as he stops barking, trots off into the living room and settles himself on the sofa.

"Now, where were we?" Jack says with a soft chuckle. He deposits me in the middle of my Queen size bed, yanking my shorts off along with my knickers. I take off my top, careful to shield my scars from him, until I'm completely naked and awaiting his next move. I'm watching him just as carefully as he's watching me and it's so fucking hot, like my very own strip show. He peels off his t-shirt and I lick my lips brazenly at the sight of his taut, tattooed abs. He's all clean-cut lines, with a defined, toned six-pack. He takes off his combat trousers, his muscles bunching and flexing with the movement, until he's standing gloriously naked in front of me. His lean, narrow hips and powerful thighs, I can't take my eyes off this God-like creature in front of me. I feel so desperate for him to take me, I am panting with desire, and he hasn't even touched me yet. If he were to touch my pussy right now, I think I'd come on the spot.

"You like what you see, sweetheart?"

I swallow hard and nod, I don't take my eyes off him.

"All, this, it's all just for show," he says cryptically, as he crawls up the bed like a hungry lion claiming his mate and settles himself between my legs. His tongue darts out and swipes up my slit, gloriously assaulting my pussy in the most delicious way.

"Oh fuck, Jack! That feels so good."

He smiles against me, his beard glistening with my juices.

"Tell me you want me, Zeppelin." His voice is hoarse.

"Oh shit! Jack, I want you! I fucking want you like I've never wanted anyone else!" I scream, as his tongue flicks over my sensitive swollen nub.

I feel the familiar flutters, as my pussy floods. My breath comes in short, sharp bursts, as he quickens his momentum. I moan softly, feeling my orgasm building deep within me.

"OH FUCK! JACK! I'M GOING TO COME! OH GOD! SHIT! I'M GOING TO COME!"

I cup my breasts in my hands and roll my nipples between my thumb and forefinger, the bite of pain mixed with the pleasure is a heady cocktail.

"That's it, good girl, come for me. Let it go, Zeppelin, let me watch you fall apart."

With one swift stroke of his tongue, my orgasm barrels through me like an explosion and I throw my head back.

"JACK!"

He looks up at him.

"Don't you dare take your eyes off me," he commands, as I tilt my head forward, my eyes locking with his, silver on brown.

"I'M COMING! JACK! OH GOD! I'M COMING! JACK! OHHH FUCCCKKK!" I scream out in pure ecstasy, as wave after wave of pleasure surges through me, lighting me up from the inside. I tremble with tiny aftershocks, as I moan, satiated and oh-so-satisfied.

As I come down from my orgasmic high, I catch sight of him, as he lifts his head up, his blonde hair perfectly mussed and a lust-filled glint in his dark brown eyes.

"God, you're so fucking beautiful."

He shifts up the bed and lays down next to me, wrapping me his arm around me, pulling me close to him. He silently traces idle circles on my shoulder with his finger, as I cuddle into him. I want to voice all the unsaid things between us, but something tells me this isn't the time. I'm content with lying here naked with my real-life rockstar and it had to be enough, for now.

# 24

## Jax

There are moments that define us as people, the joyous, the sad, the elation, the pure inconsolable agony, rage, love, hate and pure carnal lust. As I lay here with Zeppelin, I think of all the moments in my life where I've felt all of these feelings, but nothing matches up to the way I feel right now, the warmth of a woman next to me, the scent of her Jean Paul Gaultier Le Belle perfume invading my nostrils, the remnants of her orgasm damp on my chin. For the first time in three years, I was content, but I wasn't sure how to feel about it. It excited me and terrified me all at once, I wanted to let her know it wasn't just her that was falling, but the thought overwhelmed me. I wasn't ready to say those three words to someone who wasn't Ruby, not yet anyway.

"What'cha thinking about, Handsome Jack?" she says brightly, as she rests her chin on my pec and I find myself smiling fondly at her nickname for me.

"How many different ways I can make you come," I say seductively, shutting down any form of communication, as I climb on top of her, blanketing her beneath me. I straddle her, as I take a few moments to take in my surroundings.

Her bedroom has a grey geometric print feature wall above her Queen size bed. The white gothic headboard is elaborate and decadent. Next to the bed, are two white lacquered gothic bedside tables with silver knobs, with a picture of her with a dark-haired male on top. The rest of the walls are light grey and are covered with a series of nine, what look like book covers and metal wall plates with what I'm assuming are characters from her books. The window has a grey dreamcatcher hanging in the centre, with grey blackout blinds and a slate grey carpet completes the room, which doesn't look girly at all. My eyes shift to the white gothic headboard and the intricate leather and lace mask that hangs from it. I've seen it somewhere before, but I can't quite put my finger on it.

I reach over to run my finger across the delicate material, as memories of the night at the masquerade ball assault every corner of my mind. Zeppelin was the mystery woman I had sex with. *Fuck my life.* I look down at her, waiting expectantly, her lip trapped between her teeth and her blonde hair mussed.

"Did we... were you... have we had sex before? Were you the woman from the masquerade ball?" I ask, my voice level, but my thoughts all kinds of mixed up. She seems taken aback by my direct question, as her smile fades and she looks up at me, her silver eyes wide and turbulent.

"Jack, I can explain." I curse long and low, not knowing how to feel. I had no right to feel betrayed; I was the one who omitted the truth from her, that's why we were here in the first place. But, at that moment, I knew I couldn't be here any longer. I climb off her as if she's burned me, taking a second to sit on the edge of the bed, I drop my head into my hands. I feel the bed dip and I know she's close because I can feel the warmth radiating from her.

"Jack?" she says softly and she's careful not to touch me.

"Don't, just fucking don't," I snap, keep my gaze focused forward.

"I was going to tell you!" she says exasperated. I shake my head, as I get up from the bed and haphazardly start pulling my clothes on.

"Jack, please! Don't do this!" Her voice is small and filled with desperation. I zip up my combat trousers, pull on my t-shirt and jam my feet in my boots in complete silence.

"Are you really going to just walk out? Without even letting me explain?" she asks incredulously and I run my hand through my hair.

"What's there to explain? You don't fucking get it! We had sex with each other unknowingly, were you ever going to tell me?"

She sighs.

"Of course, I was going to fucking tell you! That night will be etched in my mind for eternity! You made me feel things, Jack! Things I haven't felt in five years, the last man broke my heart beyond fucking repair! Do you think it was easy for me? Do you?"

Her voice shakes with emotion, and I start to soften a little. *Come on, Chase, stop being a prick.*

"As soon as I fucking laid eyes on you, I was drawn to you like moth to a flame and I fucking hated myself for it, because you made me forget that Ruby existed!" I admit and try desperately to swallow back the lump that has formed in my throat.

"You intoxicated me, you... bewitched me and I didn't even know your fucking name! You were a total stranger who had me feeling things I hadn't felt in so long. It excited me, but it made me feel sick!"

She balks at my statement, and I shake my head, willing her to listen to me.

"I'd committed the most intimate act with a woman that wasn't her, but no other woman has made me feel like that in three fucking years, Zeppelin! That revelation in itself scared the absolute shit out of me! Do you think I wanted to hide who I really was from you? I felt fucking guilty! It felt like I was cheating on the only woman I've ever loved! Do you know what that's like?"

The tremor in my voice betrays me, as she starts to pull on her clothes.

"Yes, I do as a matter of a fact! I haven't been with a man for five years because of it! The guilt fucking crushed me! But deep down, it was the guilt that was keeping me alive! So, don't stand there and tell me I don't know what it's like!"

She swipes angrily at the tears that have tracked their way down her cheeks. I scrub my hands down my face, suddenly feeling physically and mentally exhausted. *Fuck me.*

"I convinced myself I didn't want to know your name; I was content with it just being a random hook up and I didn't want more than what had happened between us. But the truth was, I wanted so much more, so much more than I could offer at that moment in time. I was an absolute mess, I'd just had this revelation and there was nothing I could about it, no one I could talk to about it! The boys have all got their own shit going on and I'm supposed to be the sensible adult, because you know, I'm a dad now."

She buttons up her black and red cherry print shirt and regards me intently with careful, guarded eyes.

"I want to be reckless; I want to throw caution to the wind like I did when life was simple and straightforward, but I have to consider Thea now, I won't introduce temporary women to her."

She visibly stiffens at my words.

"Hear me out, she deserves stability... I'm all she's got, what I'm saying is... I-I don't want... whatever the fuck this is between us, to be temporary. My life is hectic and full-on on a good day, it's not easy juggling a three-year old, touring, performing in front of thousands of fans on a nightly basis and trying to maintain a sense of normality. I'm just asking for some time, that's all."

She moves closer to me, and I can feel her hot breath tickling my cheek, as she cautiously wraps her arms around my neck. She looks up at me as if asking for permission and I step into her, giving her the green light. I reciprocate her embrace, enveloping her in my arms, as she begins stroking the hair at the nape of my neck. My heartbeat pounds in my chest like a harsh drumbeat, as I come to the stark realisation that she is the woman I need to put me back together and with her in my arms, I had finally made peace with that.

# 25

## Zeppelin

I wanted to experience what it was like to date Jackson Chase in real life. If we worked on our relationship, it could blossom into something more, but the look in his eyes when he found out I was the woman he had sex with in the club that night, was more than I could bear. I hadn't intentionally deceived him; we were both at fault in one way or another and I wanted to make it up to him.

After he left last night, I went to sleep wondering if our relationship was strong enough to survive. Relationships were based on trust, and we had both inadvertently deceived each other. We had already gotten off to a bad start and I wasn't entirely convinced that we could move past it. We were both to blame, but somehow, I hated myself for it.

**ZepW92:** I'm sorry x

**HandsomeJack0304:** I know x

I wasn't sure what that meant, but I managed to fall into a dreamless and restless sleep, with one thought at the forefront of my mind *'will Jackson Chase ever really be mine?'*

*\*\*\**

The next morning, I wake with a sluggish start and decide to take a shower. Taking a shower is my favourite way to start the day. The sting of the almost too hot water, as I stand under the spray, it invigorates me and awakens me in a way that nothing else can. After my shower, I'm getting dressed to start my day, when the hum of TV in the background snaps me from my reverie.

*"Brody "Snake" Hart, one quarter of popular rock band Rancid Vengeance, has been involved in a horrific hit-and-run accident. Notorious bad boy of the band has hit headlines in recent weeks for his blossoming romance with troubled Hollywood movie actress Raleigh Storm. Storm, twenty-nine, is currently starring in 'Rocked', directed by controversial British*

*movie director, Damien Valentine. Hart, thirty-four, was identified as the victim at the scene and rushed to a nearby hospital. Sources close to the band say, "he's in a critical, but stable condition." Police are urging the driver of the other vehicle to come forward and are encouraging witnesses to contact their local constabulary with vital evidence. A spokesperson for Rancid Vengeance has been contacted for an official statement. However, the extent of his injuries are said to be severe and potentially life-threatening. The band's future has been thrown into turmoil and speculation has begun on whether the band will continue touring without Hart, or if touring with cease and shows cancelled, disappointing fans worldwide. Stay tuned for more in the coming days."*

I look up at the TV to see Raleigh Storm leaving the hospital, she looks visibly upset, her eyes watery and red rimmed. With her lilac hair and her unusual amethyst eyes, she was making waves in Hollywood. She was a presence that couldn't be overlooked due to her undeniable beauty and her immense acting talent, she was an upcoming force to be reckoned with. She is being shielded by Sam Newbolt, his sheer size eclipses her, as the crowd of paparazzi surround them. My eyes are drawn to the way he makes his thick, tattooed bicep a barrier between her and the crowd surging towards them.

I let my mind wander to what it would be like if Jack and I ever went public with our relationship, we would be public property, our lives front and centre. It was relatively small time with Abel, we were photographed a handful of times together, but with Jack it would be on a much larger scale. Rancid Vengeance are hot property and huge on the rock music scene. They are one of the most famous rock bands in the world and have been for almost two decades.

I finish getting dressed and run my fingers through my hair, my thoughts interrupted by a soft tap on the door. Jericho starts running in and out of my legs and wagging his tail wildly. I laugh at his excitement and stroke his ears.

"You know very well who it's going to be, Mister!" I say with a chuckle, as I head to the door and swing it open. I'm greeted by a set of silver and rose gold balloons, I smile softly as Rian peers between them with a brown paper bag, a cupcake with a candle in the centre and a large grey and white chevron striped bag at his feet.

"SURPRISE!"

He sings brightly and I cup my hands over my mouth in shock.

"Happy Birthday, baby girl!"

Today is my thirtieth birthday, I'm not really big on birthdays. My dad killed himself on my fifteenth birthday and ever since then, it has kind of tarnished the sentiment with each year that passes.

"Rian! Oh my God! You shouldn't have!" I squeal and he rolls his eyes dramatically.

"Oh yes I bloody should! You deserve to celebrate being on this earth for another fabulous year!" he says with a kick of his leg and a theatrical sweep of his hand.

"Now, are you going to leave me standing out here like a spare prick at a wedding, or are you going to invite me in?"

I step out of the doorway and help him carry everything inside, closing the door behind us with a loud click. Rian sets the food down on the kitchen worktop, the smell wafting through the flat making my stomach growl reminding how hungry I am. He spins around to face me with his hands firmly placed on his lean hips, as he regards me intently with narrowed eyes.

"You look... different."

I try to remain indifferent, but he points his finger in my direction.

"Did you get laid again?" he asks and I throw my hands up in the air in exasperation, avoiding his eyes.

"*For fucks sake*, Ri! Why is my sex life, or lack thereof, such a topic of great interest to you?"

He laughs.

"Because it's tragic and practically non-existent!"

He moves back over to the worktop and pops the cork on the Bucks Fizz, he takes out two champagne flutes out of the cupboard and sets about pouring us two glasses. When he's finished, he hands me one and we clink our glasses together.

"Cheers to the birthday girl! Happy thirtieth, beautiful!"

He blows me a kiss, as I lift my glass in the air and take a sip, the bubbles instantly popping on my tongue.

"Stop being so coy and spill the tea!"

I puff out a long, laboured breath. *He's going to find out eventually, so I may as well tell him.*

"I finally met Jack."

His eyes widen and his mouth drops open.

"Shut the front door! Really? When? You kept that quiet! So... what's he like? Is he fit? Did you fuck his brains out, is that why you're so..."

He points his finger and makes a circle in the air. I down my drink in one gulp and he almost chokes on his.

"Was it really that bad?"

I put my glass down on the worktop with a little more force than necessary.

"It was going so well, until I opened the door and Jackson fucking Chase was standing there!"

I don't meet his eyes, as he lets out a bark of laughter.

"I fucking knew it! So, did you?"

He makes a crude gesture with his hands and I bite down savagely on my lip.

"You did! You little slut!" He squeals and we both burst out laughing.

"We didn't have sex, but he gave me quite possibly the best fucking orgasm I've ever had. We were about to fuck, when he recognised that bloody mask hanging off my headboard! He figured out I was the woman from the masquerade ball, it was fucking awful, Rian! Quite possibly one of the worse nights of my life! I slapped him and shrieked at him like a banshee for lying to me and pretending he was someone he wasn't, when I was no better than him! We had a huge row! It wasn't the perfect, romantic meet cute I envisioned."

I put my hand to my head and as I think back to last nights' events, shame fills every inch of me.

"He's quite possibly the hottest guy I've ever met, he's sweet and he's so...sincere. He's nothing like Abel, in fact they could be more worlds apart if they tried, but now I'm not sure if he wants to see me again, then if that wasn't bad enough, I fucking told him I'd fallen in love with him!" I admit shamefully and Rian gasps.

*"Fucking hell!"* He wraps his arms around me and I breathe him in.

"It's all such a fucking mess, Ri," I mutter into his chest and he soothes me, as I allow the dam to break. I start to sob and standing in the middle of my flat in Rian's arms, I don't know if I'll ever be able to stop. *This is all such a fucking mess.*

# 26

## Zeppelin

Rian and me eat breakfast of Eggs Benedict with copious amounts of smoky bacon in relative silence, sitting on the floor in front of the coffee table, the TV a soft hum in the background.

*"Worldwide rock phenomenon Rancid Vengeance have released a statement concerning guitarist Brody Hart. Hart, thirty-four, notorious for his wild on and off-stage antics. Highly publicised bad boy of the band has thrown the bands' future into turmoil, as the victim of a horrific hit-and-run. Rancid Vengeance have released a statement regarding recent developments."*

As I look up at the screen, I am greeted by the sight of all three members of the band Sam, Jax, Lucas, and the band's manager, Michael James Richmonde III, or M.J as he is more commonly known. Jax is a sight to beholden, he instantly holds my attention and he pushes every single one of my hot buttons. I can't take my eyes off the screen, as I place my fork noisily down on the table. Rian reaches for my hand in a gesture of reassurance. His long blonde hair flowing to his shoulders, looking like something off a high-end shampoo advert and oozing sex appeal. He stands a few inches shorter than Sam, their body types couldn't be more different, Jax's body is lean and defined, without looking too bulky, compared to Sam who looks like he could bench press four of me and Rian, without even breaking a sweat. Jax is wearing dark blue skinny jeans, a white v-neck t-shirt, showcasing his collection of ink, including the bright, bold yellow buttercup which spans his throat, as a tribute to his late fiancée Ruby and white Converse hi-tops, his expression sombre. Cameras are flashing wildly, and as the rowdy chatter of the press and news reporters dies down, Sam steps forward, clears his throat and begins to speak.

*"In light of Brody's accident, as a band, we have decided to postpone our current UK tour indefinitely while we focus on other projects. We can't apologise enough for letting our loyal fans down, but as a band, we don't feel it's*

*the right thing to do to continue touring without Brody. We're not just a band,*
*we're a family and family always comes first. Any tickets will be reimbursed or*
*can be used at any future events. Updates will be posted on our website and*
*social media. Any questions, please direct them to our manager M.J."*

He nods curtly, offering a brief glance to Jax and Lucas, they both offer
him nods in return. The cameras continue to flash wildly and the press
catcall to the band.

"Phew! Those boys are hot with a capital H! *Fuck me,* baby girl, do you
need a cold shower? *Jesus Christ!"* Rian says with a chuckle, as I let out a
long sigh and lean back against the sofa.

"He's really got to you, hasn't he?"

Rian's face turns serious and I glance up at him.

"I don't know what to do, Ri."

My heart clenches in my chest, causing a physical ache and it takes
everything I have not to burst into tears. He turns to face me and cups my
face in both of his hands.

"Listen to me, I'm not letting you wallow in your own self-pity,
Zeppelin! It was meant to be a surprise, but you and me are going out on
the town tonight to celebrate your birthday! We're going to paint the town
neon pink! No arguments!"

I open my mouth to protest, but the look he gives me in return makes
me think better of it. *Happy birthday to me.*

***

I stare at my reflection in the mirror and my halter neck fire engine red
dress shows off every curve on my svelte body. But instead of feeling
self-conscious, I feel empowered and for the first time in twenty-four hours,
I feel great. My eyes are smoky and dramatic, with a cat-eye flick and my lips
match the colour of my dress. My hair is styled poker straight and I finish
my look with my old faithful black peep-toe Christian Louboutin sky-high
heels. I pick up my black leather clutch bag and head over to the door. I
open it and I'm greeted by Rian, in a pair of skinny jeans so tight they look
like they are sprayed on, a white shirt open at the collar and a pair of simple

black shoes to finish his outfit. His hair is perfectly styled into a soft quiff and the diamond stud in his ear glints, as the light catches it.

*"Wow!* You look fucking stunning, baby girl! You scrub up well!"

We both laugh, as we link arms ready for a night of celebration.

As we enter Neon Nights, the beat of Ed Sheeran Bad Habits blasts through the speakers. This isn't the first time we have frequented this establishment, the last time being the night I had my first steamy encounter with Jackson Chase. He rocked my world just as hard as I rocked his and I still couldn't stop thinking about him. I have been checking my phone constantly all day, for any calls or messages, but there has been nothing. To say I'm disappointed and beyond hurt is an understatement. As Rian hands me a drink, I try to push that thought to the back of my mind and focus on drinking, dancing and celebrating my thirtieth birthday with my best friend.

The night goes by in a blur of drinking, dancing and giggling with Rian. I'm buzzed from the countless glasses of wine and shots I've drank, but I'm enjoying myself. I deserve to let my hair down once in a while and as one song fades into the next, one of my favourite songs starts to play. I make my way through the throng of people and onto the dance floor. I start to move my hips to the pumping remix of *Maroon 5 Sugar*; I lose myself in the music. My skin starts to prickle and the hairs on the back of my neck stand on end, as a familiar tattooed arm slides around my waist. My back is to his hard, muscular chest, as we move in time to the music. He is moving fluidly with me, he moves his mouth to my neck, the scrape of his beard against my skin and his hot breath causing goosebumps to erupt all over my body.

"Zeppelin," he whispers and my name is like a love song on his lips.

"Jack." My voice comes out a breathy moan.

"What are you doing here?" I ask, curiosity getting the better of me.

"A little birdy called me and told me it was your birthday."

*Fucking Rian.*

"Don't be mad at him, love," he says with a chuckle, as if reading my mind and he pulls me closer to him. He grinds his hips into me to the beat of the music, the song fading from Maroon 5 into Britney Spears Toxic.

"Jack, I-I..." I stutter, but he shushes me, spins me around and crushes me to him. The move is possessive, almost as if he is staking his claim. I chance a peek up at him from beneath my lashes and he looks ever the rock star. He is wearing a flannel red, white and black checkered shirt, rolled up at the sleeves, a pair of black ripped skinny jeans and black Doc Marten boots. His blonde hair is tied up in a neat man bun and his goatee beard neatly trimmed. At that moment, it's as if time ceases to exist, it's just him and me, staring up at each other. The look he gives me is reverent and so full of tenderness it makes my heart slam against my rib cage. He takes my hand in his and places it on his chest, I feel the steady rhythm of his heartbeat, as we sway slowly to the music.

"I was a fool to think I could just walk away from you..." he mutters so softly I barely hear him over the pulsing beat surrounding us.

"Let me take you home, no funny business, I just want to hold you."

With those words, I find myself agreeing, in the arms of my gentle rock star.

# 27

## Jax

The measure of a man determines the fundamental worth of a person, of how he lives and how he dies. As I stand here with Zeppelin in my arms, swaying to the music, it's as if it's just her and me in the room. No one else exists beyond us and for the first time in three years, I was allowing myself to think about the future. *Our future.* I didn't want to be remembered as a father who spent his years alone, by my daughter, or any other children I may, or may not have. That thought kept me awake at night, which is why I couldn't stay away from her a moment longer. After her best friend Rian called me earlier, he sounded genuinely concerned for his best friend, who was celebrating her birthday alone and I somehow felt responsible for that.

"Jackson Chase! Jackson Chase from Rancid Vengeance is my boyfriend!" she slurs, enunciating the S' and giggling childishly. I try to stifle my smirk, as she looks up at me, closing one eye to focus. *She's adorable when she's drunk.*

"Handsome Jack!" She sings at me and I burst out laughing.

"You're an adorable drunk, love!" I say with a chuckle and she bops me on the nose.

"You're so fucking hot! How did I get so lucky?" she compliments, as we're joined by her friend, Rian and he nods curtly in my direction.

"We good?" He asks sternly and I nod back in return.

"I've got her, I'll take her home. My car's outside, I promise I'll look after her."

He points his finger in my direction.

"Damn fucking straight you'll look after her! We'll have a huge problem if you don't and your face won't be so pretty!"

It's obvious he's trying to sound threatening, but he just ends up sounding like some drunken knobhead spouting off some empty threats. I get that he's being protective of his best friend and he might be wary of me, but I'd rather hurt myself than hurt her.

She stumbles into me and I catch her in my arms easily to stop her from falling.

"Oopsie!"

She pulls a face and she squeals, as I scoop her up, The crowd dispersing, as I stride with purpose and carry her out of the club.

"I'm taking you home, love."

Rian follows us and as we get outside, the fresh air causes her to shiver in my arms.

"Jack, I don't feel very well. Put me down, please put me down," she says in a panicked rush, as I set her down and lean her against the wall. She vacates her guts all over the pavement and Rian groans, muttering about her being a lightweight. I rub her back soothingly.

"I've got her, mate," I say resolutely, giving him no room to argue, as a photographer leaps out of nowhere. *For fucks sake.* The '*click, click*' of his camera shutter sets my nerves on edge, as Kai moves into position and ushers the wiry photographer away from us. He lifts his hand up to his ear and speaks in a clipped tone, nodding curtly in my direction.

"Okay, give me a call if you need anything at all," Rian says, suddenly sounding a little unsure of himself. Zeppelin stumbles to try to regain her balance and composure. I grab her around the waist to steady her and she falls into me, placing her hand on my chest. She looks up at me and she couldn't look more beautiful if she tried.

"*Fuck,*" she curses and I take her hand in mine, placing a tender kiss on the back.

"Call me in the morning, baby girl," Rian calls and she salutes, giggling girlishly, as I carry her to my navy-blue Tesla Model 3, flanked by Kai who is a few steps behind. I sit her in the passenger seat, she leans back in the seat and lets out a small sigh. I buckle her seatbelt, go around to the driver's side.

"I'm taking her back to my place."

Kai nods.

"I'll follow, I'll remain two car lengths behind at all times."

I slap him on the back in a friendly gesture. Kai Hunter, or 'K' as he is more affectionately known, served in the military for several years, before being recruited by Cole, as a trusted member of our team. At six feet seven inches tall, he is extremely muscular, with broad shoulders and narrow hips. He looks like he should be on the front cover of Men's Health Magazine. His blonde hair shaved close to his head and his indigo eyes make the women look twice, but he's happily married to his wife Gabriella and has a daughter Brooke, who he adores. As fathers to daughters, we have a lot in common and he is a loyal part of the Rancid Vengeance family.

"I'll see you back at Vengeance Manor, Jack."

He salutes in my direction and I flash him a wink, as I get into the car. Zeppelin's head is resting against the window, her shoes kicked off haphazardly in the foot well.

"If you need to throw up, let me know, and I'll pull over," I say softly and she turns her head, blinking up at me with heavy eyes. Her silver eyes sparkling in the moonlight. Her profile is striking, her cheekbones defined and her nose perfectly straight. Her blonde hair, a few shades lighter than mine, her lips look like they are begging to be kissed, but I try to push that thought to the back of my mind and focus on pulling away from the kerb to make the journey back to Chislehurst.

She looks at me from the corner of her eye and offers me a beaming grin.

"Handsome Jack."

She lets out a sigh and I move my hand from the gear stick to reach for her hand.

"Happy birthday, beautiful."

She offers me a soft smile, my heart slamming violently against my rib cage and my stomach somersaulting. *Wow, that feeling takes me by surprise every time and I can't explain why.* She doesn't say anything else, as she leans back in her seat and soon she drifts off to sleep.

***

When we pull up to the circular driveway, I stop the car, pull up the handbrake and turn off the engine. I'm glad to be home, as I unclip my seatbelt, Kai pulls up behind me. The glare of his headlights temporarily blinding me, I open the car door, get out and go around to the passenger side. I open Zeppelin's door and lift her gently out, carrying her in my arms and kicking the door shut with my boot.

"All good, Jack?"

I nod curtly.

"Cheers, Kai, I've got it from here."

He flashes me a smile, as he walks across the driveway, his shift done for the night. Zeppelin snuggles closer to my chest and I plant a chaste kiss on her forehead. I take out my keys, open the door and instantly the open plan foyer is flooded with light. I carefully make my way up the stairs and I'm about to open my bedroom door, when I hear a creak. *Fuck.*

"Daddy."

I turn and Thea is standing there in her animal print pyjamas, her hair sticking up in all directions, rubbing the sleep from her tired eyes.

"Hey, sweetheart, you should be in bed!" I chastise softly and she looks up at me puzzled.

"Daddy, who's that lady?"

*Shit, this is not fucking happening! Why did I think this was a good idea to bring her back here?*

"She's just daddy's friend, sweet pea, she's very tired, she needs to go to sleep."

I'm aware of how lame my excuse is, but it's late and it's all I've got right now.

"Can you sing to me, Daddy?" She asks with a yawn and I chuckle.

"Course, baby, give me a second, yeah? Go back to bed, I'll be in in a few."

She nods and goes back into her room. I open the door to my bedroom, lay Zeppelin down on the bed and make quick work of undressing her, careful to leave her underwear on. I lay her head on the pillow and pull the covers up over her. I toe off my boots and go quietly into Thea's room, finding she has already fallen asleep. I'm going to have a hard time of explaining to her in the morning, but that was a problem for another day.

# 28

## Zeppelin

I wake the next morning with the hangover from hell. My head is pounding, my throat feels like sandpaper and I suddenly don't remember getting home. I'm in an unfamiliar bed, in my underwear, and I sit up to look around the room. I don't recognise the decor, or any other surroundings and fear settles in my gut. *Did I meet someone last night? Did I come home with someone?* I try desperately to remember, as my heartbeat starts to quicken. *I can't remember. Why can't I remember?* My eyes move around the opulently decorated bedroom and my greedy eyes land on Jack standing in the doorway of an en-suite bathroom. A towel slung low on his lean hips, revealing the perfect *V* on his lower abdomen. He looks delicious with rivulets of water running down his perfectly sculpted washboard abs. He has a towel in his hand, as he towel dries his long-wet hair.

"Good morning, love." His voice is low and gruff, as relief floods through me and my pussy starts to throb violently at the sight of him semi-naked.

"Morning," I say almost nervously, the air feels as if it has been sucked out of the room.

"How are you feeling?" he asks, as I clutch my head, feeling sorry for myself and he chuckles softly. *I don't do hangovers very well.*

"There's two aspirin and a bottle of water by the bed, love."

He points towards the dark wood bedside table. I reach over, gulp down the water and pills immediately, offering my thanks. The cool water instantly soothing my dehydrated throat.

"I'm so sorry, I don't remember you being at the club, or you bringing me home," I ask, my voice filled with shame and I take another long sip of water.

239

"Rian called me and told me it was your birthday. I thought I'd surprise you, we danced, you threw up outside the club, and I brought you back here."

I squeeze my eyes shut briefly and apologise.

"I'm so sorry, I'm an awful drunk, Rian calls me a lightweight! I don't get out much and besides, we were celebrating," I explain and he dismisses me with a wave of his hand.

"You don't have to explain yourself; you are actually an adorable drunk!" he says on a laugh and I find myself smiling along with him.

"You can grab yourself a shower, love. I'll go and make us some breakfast, I need to be back at the hospital in a few hours, but I'm all yours until then."

He flashes me a wink, as I swing my legs out of the huge iron four-poster bed.

"Thank you, I'm honoured!"

I tiptoe across the bedroom, planting a gentle kiss on his stubbled cheek before slipping into the sleek, modern bathroom. Shedding my underwear, I turn on the shower, testing the water with my hand until it's just right. A glance in the quirky sunburst mirror stops me cold, I look like a fucking train wreck. Mascara smudged into full-blown panda eyes; hair matted like I've been dragged through a hedge backwards. *Brilliant work, Zeppelin. Truly inspiring.*

I step under the steaming spray, letting the hot water melt away the hangover clinging to me like a second skin. I linger longer than usual, scrubbing my hair with Jax's fancy products, trying to coax myself back to something vaguely presentable. When I finally emerge, towel-wrapped and slightly less feral, I feel almost human again, ready to take on whatever chaos the day throws my way.

I pad across the plush carpeted floor bare foot into Jax's bedroom; to find he's left out an oversized Rancid Vengeance t-shirt and a pair of running shorts on his bed. *Bless his heart, he's so thoughtful.* I make quick work of dressing; towel drying my short hair and make my way down to the kitchen. I don't have time to take in my surroundings, as my eyes home in on every inch of Jax's lean body. His hair is tied up in a messy top knot and it oddly suits him. He's on the phone; he has the phone resting between his ear and his shoulder and cooking breakfast at the same time with a spatula in his hand. I take a seat on one of the tall bar stools at the slate grey marbled kitchen island and take a few moments to observe him. It makes him seem more normal somehow, more human just going about his daily life and not the famous rock star who everyone wants a piece of. It must be so hard for him to switch off from Jackson Chase, guitarist in Rancid Vengeance, to Jackson Chase, single dad.

"Hmm, okay, perfect, sounds good, when do I start? Hmm, I can come into the office later this afternoon. I need to go to the hospital to see how Brody's doing, I know, I know. Look, we'll talk later, yeah, I'll drop Thea off with Marnie and I'll call you when I'm on my way. Okay, bye."

He hangs up the phone and he offers me a lazy grin.

"Feeling better, love?" he asks expectantly, his head cocked to the side, and I nod.

"I feel a little more human now, thank you."

I say on a nervous laugh and he smiles softly.

"You're most welcome."

He serves us both breakfast consisting of bacon and scrambled egg on white buttery toast—it looks delicious. He takes a seat on the opposite side of the island, and we both tuck into our breakfast in silence, observing each other at intervals. We are interrupted by the sound of tiny footsteps across the wooden floor.

"Daddy!"

I turn to see a little girl with pale skin, bright, wide, inquisitive hazel eyes and her short dark brown hair framing her face. She is wearing animal print pyjamas, Jax places his knife and fork carefully down on the counter, sliding off the bar stool towards her. He swings her up easily in his muscular arms and she clings to him, idly playing with the hair at the nape of his neck.

"Morning Princess!" He greets her brightly, his eyes dancing with amusement. He looks younger than his thirty-three years and I quietly watch their interaction with rapt attention.

"Daddy, that's the lady from last night! You said she was tired; did she sleep well? She's pretty!" she babbles and I laugh out loud, as both of them turn towards me.

"Thea, this is daddy's friend Zeppelin." Jax introduces me and I wave awkwardly in her direction.

"Zeppelin, this is my daughter, Thea," he says almost shyly, turning to face me, studying my reaction.

"You've got a funny name!" She giggles and Jax frowns.

"Hey, don't be rude, Princess, that wasn't nice. Now say sorry to Zeppelin."

She pouts dramatically and looks up at me.

"Sorry, Zepp-a-lin!" She sings and I find myself grinning right along with her. *She's a cutie.*

"Do you want some breakfast, Princess?" Jax asks Thea and she shakes her head.

"Marnie is taking me to the beach with Freddie and Zacky," she squeals excitedly and Jax laughs.

"Sometimes I think you have a better social life than I do, cheeky chops!" he muses, as there is a soft tap on the door.

"Give me a second, then I'm all yours."

He flashes me a wink and my pussy floods with slick heat. *Will he always have that effect on me? I certainly fucking hope so!* He heads over to the door and I hear chatter, the sound of tiny footsteps and the squeak of shoes. A few moments later, the house falls silent and Jax resumes his place at the kitchen island.

"Sorry about that, that wasn't the meeting I had planned in my head. She woke up last night when I bought you back here, she sort of...caught me in the act, so to speak," he explains, biting his lip, a look resembling guilt on his handsome face.

"Don't apologise, I'm sorry I got drunk, I'm so fucking embarrassed," I say on a long, low groan and he laughs.

"Don't be embarrassed and stop apologising, I didn't mind taking care of you, although I think your friend Rian might have had something to say about it," he says on a frown. *Rian, shit, I was supposed to call him to let him know I got back safe.* I curse softly and slide off the bar stool, my bare feet hitting the floor with a slapping sound.

"*Shit!* Where's my phone?"

I curse in a panicked tone. He swallows a mouthful of scrambled eggs and points over to my bag hanging on a coat hook.

"I was supposed to call Rian to let know I got back here safely, he worries, bless him."

Jax nods and I pad over to my bag, take out my phone and notice twenty-three missed calls, five voicemails and ten text messages. *Fucking hell.* I don't listen to or read any of the messages, I just bring up Rian's number and dial, it rings twice before it connects.

"Thank the fucking Lord! I had you lying in a ditch somewhere, passed out at the side of the road, murdered by a sadistic serial killer! Where have you been, baby girl?" he says in a panicked rush. *Dramatic as ever.*

"I'm so sorry, Ri, I meant to call, but I passed out drunk, I'm still at Jack's," I say quietly, turning my back to him and hoping he doesn't hear.

"Oooh, I want all of the sexy details when you get back! You dirty stop out! I can stop worrying now I know you're okay. Jericho is with me by the way, but this old Queen now needs her beauty sleep, I've hardly slept," he says with a long, drawn-out yawn, his voice laced with amusement.

"Don't you fucking lie to me, Rian St James!" I say on a laugh, and he lets out a hum of satisfaction. *At least someone got laid last night.*

"You caught me, baby girl! I've hardly slept for a different reason! Danny Debonair."

His voice a few octaves higher than before and I'm happy that my best friend has found someone.

"You're going to tell me all the gory details when I get back! Fancy a movie night? My choice! And we can order takeaway, your choice!" I ask expectantly.

"Sounds perfect, babe! I'll see you in a little while, call me when you're back home. Don't do anything I would! Love you!" He sings, as the line goes dead. I shake my head in exasperation and put my phone back in my bag, as I turn around Jax is casually walking towards me. His grey jogging bottoms hanging low on his hips, his feet bare and his plain black t-shirt clinging to his muscular body. He stops in front of me, our eyes locking and I can't look away. The look in his brown eyes temporarily disarms me and makes my breath catch in my throat. My heartbeat quickens, as he reaches over to tuck a strand of my hair behind my ear.

"Alone at last." His voice is deep and low, filled with all the wicked things I was desperate for him to do to me. Standing in front of me looking like that, made me want to jump his bones. But another part of me wanted to take time to get to know him, to get to know his body, what turned him on, what made him tick. I didn't want to rush things between us, I wanted to take things slow, but with him being inches away from me, I wanted to throw caution to the wind. I wanted him to take me, all of me, whatever the cost, I didn't care because in this moment, he was mine, he was mine to do with as I pleased. I wanted him to pleasure me until I saw stars, until the only name that was on my lips was his. He places his hand on my cheek, and I lean into his touch, taking a moment to just feel his hand on me.

"Jack," I breathe, as he presses his forehead to mine. Wordlessly, he seals his lips over mine in a kiss that claims me as his and steals the breath from my lungs. I lose myself in all things Jackson Chase as he deepens the kiss, his pierced tongue probing mine. He pulls me closer, and I stumble awkwardly into him, drunk on him. I didn't want to stop feeling the way I did when I was with him, he made me feel whole and even though there was a long way to go, I was willing to take a chance on him. We deserved a chance at happiness, and I would do everything in my power to make sure that was a reality.

# 29

## Zeppelin

We make it to Jax's bedroom, it's a tangle of limbs and we're both naked in record time. I'm eagerly anticipating his hard, firm body pressed against mine. His brown eyes are smoky and blazing with a fiery heat. He licks his lips as his eyes travel over my body, and I'm suddenly filled with an unwanted apprehension. I don't want him to see me naked, because if he sees me fully naked, he'll see the raised, mottled pink burn scars all over my back, which looked like someone had dripped candle wax on my back. I had gone through several skin graft operations to lessen the impact on my mental health and my self-esteem. But no amount of operations would erase the deep-seated trauma associated with the suffering I endured in the yacht fire that killed Abel and his band members on that fateful day all those years ago.

Jax wraps his arms around me, running his hands up and down my back, my boobs squashed against his chest. I can feel his steel erection between us, pressing into my lower abdomen. I tense when his large hand lingers a little too long on the taut skin, my heartbeat quickening, as he pulls away briefly. A questioning look on his face, but he doesn't say anything. He leans forward, softly brushing my lips tenderly with his, but the intimate moment between us is lost, as repulsion spreads its way through my body like a poison and makes my stomach roil violently. The scars that marred my body weren't beautiful; they were ugly and reminded me of a time in my life that I would rather forget. I shove against him, and he instantly releases me, I take a few steps back putting some distance between us. A frown line jumping in between his eyebrows.

"Zeppelin, what's wrong? Did I do something? We can go as slowly as you need to, just say the word." His voice is filled with such sincere concern; I am suddenly so overwhelmed with sheer panic and the sadness envelopes me. My chest feels tight, my breathing erratic, my heart is pounding, and my blood roars in my ears. Jax is standing gloriously naked in front of me, a look of concern marring his chiselled, rugged features. His furrowed brow tells me he feels way out of his depth, as gut-wrenching sobs overtake me, he goes to step forward with his arms outstretched, but I hold my finger up, halting him in his tracks, not allowing him to move closer to me.

"Zeppelin, please, talk to me, *Jesus fucking Christ!* Look, we can just talk if you're not ready?" he states incredulously and I can't find the words to explain this fucked up situation. I open my mouth to speak then close it again, unable to coherently string a sentence together. Sobs violently wracking my body causing me to visibly tremble, I shakily get dressed in silence careful not to expose my back to him. He drops down onto the edge of the bed, pulling his boxers on, hanging his head in defeat. My heart slams against my rib cage at the stricken look on his perfect face.

I jam my feet into my black and red cherry print Vans, avoiding his gaze as I gather the rest of my things.

"I-I...I need to go home." I manage to choke out, as tears roll freely down my cheeks. He gets to his feet and pulls on his jeans, nodding curtly as he picks up his phone from the bedside table.

"Hey, Cole, it's me, I need you to take Zeppelin home for me, please? Yeah...sure, no worries...yeah, thanks man, appreciate it...hmm...see you in a sec...bye."

He swipes the screen, ending the call. He clears his throat before he speaks.

"Cole's sending Trey one of our bodyguards to drive you home," he says flatly and I nod.

"Thank you," I say with a sniff.

"It doesn't have to be this way, love. Just stay and talk to me, something tells me that you've got secrets just like I have. Seems we're not so different after all."

I shake my head vehemently. *He doesn't need to know all the ugly, gory details of the yacht accident.* He sighs.

"Fine, have it your way."

He runs his hand through his hair, as his phone vibrates.

"Trey's outside."

As soon as he finishes his sentence, I turn on my heel and rush out of the house. He doesn't deserve the broken version of me, he has his own demons, he doesn't need to hear the horror story that keeps me awake at night. I take the stairs two at a time and land at the bottom, taking my bag from the hook next to the door. I turn to see Jax shirtless with his jeans still unzipped, his hand tucked into his pocket. The look he gives me breaks my heart a little more, as I reach for the door handle.

"Zeppelin."

My name is like a love song on his lips, and I press my clammy forehead against the cool wood of the door, briefly closing my eyes.

"Goodbye Jack."

I pull the door open and walk across the gravel driveway. I climb into the back of a black BMW X5, I slam the door behind me and as soon as the door closes, I give in to the all-consuming grief and sob all the way home.

*** *

*Our scars tell our story, of lives half lived and our journey so far.*
*It's nothing to be ashamed of, just a road map of where we've been and where*
*we're heading...*
*I'm sorry*
*J x*

I run my fingers across the neat, flowing, script-like penmanship on the note card in the huge bouquet of red roses. They were delivered by courier this morning, I wanted to call him to say thank you, but all that was replaying in my mind on a constant loop was the look on his face when I carelessly shoved him away from me. He deserved to know the truth, but I wasn't ready to tell him the horrors of my past. *Would it make him see me in a different light? Would he still want me after I told him the ugly truth?* My heart was sprinting in my chest, as I read the words over and over again. My finger hovered over his number on my phone, but every time I went to dial, I lost my nerve. I had spent the morning cleaning my flat within an inch of its life and I had spent the rest of the day sitting at my desk trying to write but getting wildly distracted by thoughts of God-like rock stars and by the time evening came round, I hadn't written a single sentence.

I had settled on the sofa with a glass of wine and a few episodes of Arrow, when there is a light tap on the door. Jericho starts barking and jumping up the unopened door. I get up and pad over to the door bare foot, patting his head.

"It's okay, buddy, it's probably just Rian," I softly placate him, and he sits down beside me, taking on the role of my protector, with his furry chest puffed out. As I open the door, I'm not prepared for the sight that greets me. Jackson Chase in all his glory. He's wearing tight black jeans, which leave nothing to the imagination, a dark blue denim shirt open at the collar, with the sleeves rolled up to reveal tattooed, corded forearms, white Converse trainers and his long blonde hair loose, a black bandana secured around his head. I swallow a few times as I take him in, and he leans casually into the door frame. My thoughts scatter, as his shirt rides up a few inches to reveal his tattooed abs.

"Zeppelin."

His voice low and rough. I look up into his brown pools of sin and I'm rendered mute, as he flashes me a dimpled grin.

"I think we've got some... unfinished business," he says seductively, moving a little closer to me. His scent of Diesel Only the Brave invades my nostrils, and I can't think straight when he's within touching distance, I want him too much. I take a few deep breaths to steady myself and seemingly come to my senses.

"I said all I needed to yesterday," I say flatly, my voice void of emotion, he smirks and nods coolly.

"If I remember rightly, you didn't say anything at all, you just left me with a painful hard on, which wouldn't go away. You seem to have that lasting effect on me, sweetheart."

The way he calls me sweetheart turns me into a desperate mess of want and I can't stop thinking about the way his magic fingers made me come over and over again. He cocks his eyebrow, as I drop my gaze to the floor.

"Keep thinking those thoughts, because I'm not going anywhere until you talk to me. At least tell me why you fucking ran out on me like a bat out of hell. Your mood swings give me whiplash, love, and not in a good way. One minute you want me and the next minute you run like I mean nothing to you, why Zeppelin."

He reaches up to cup my cheek in his hand and I lean into his touch, relishing in everything Jackson Chase.

"Please, I'm not above begging, just talk to me."

I take a few steps back and he drops his hand to his side.

"It's not important, it's in the past, Jack, we all have demons, it's best to leave them where they are, in the past," I explain and he shakes his head.

"Bullshit, that's not good enough, we were naked for fucks sake! We were about to have sex, and you just ran! With no explanation, how the fuck do you think that made me feel? I never usually have that effect on women! Tell me why, Zeppelin?"

He raises his voice a few decibels, frustration clear on his beautiful, chiselled face.

"Because no one can hate me more than I hate myself, Jack! What happened all those years ago, it... damaged me, it fucking broke me! I can't bear to look at myself in the mirror, it disgusts me, it makes me feel sick! I'm not the same person I used to be, and my scars remind me of that!" I shout and I swear he growls.

"You're not the only one with fucking scars, Zeppelin!"

He opens another button on his shirt and haphazardly shoves the shoulder to the side revealing an angry round, but jagged scar, the skin purple and raised. I remember watching the news at the time and couldn't imagine the chaos that must have ensued.

"I got shot! My fiancée died! She got shot in the head! They kept her alive long enough for her to give birth to Thea! How the fuck do you think that made me feel? The woman who was going to be my wife! She took her last breath, and my daughter took her first! How twisted is that! A life for another! Some days I can't look at her because it fucking hurts! So don't you stand there and pretend like you're the only one with scars, with an ugly past!"

His voice is filled with such emotion it makes my heart hurt for him. I'm about to speak again when I hear loud footsteps approaching.

"Oi, dickhead! What the fuck are you doing here?"

Rian spits angrily and Jax moves out of the doorway, spinning around to face him.

"That, mate, is none of your fucking business," Jax says casually, emphasising the word '*mate*' and Rian laughs bitterly.

"It is my business when you're upsetting my best friend, now I suggest you get the fuck away from her, before I make you."

Rian's voice low and menacing. I've never seen Rian like this before, it's a side of him I never knew existed. Jax cocks his eyebrow and nods, his shoulders squaring, as if to say challenge accepted. He's at least a good few inches taller than Rian and he takes one step forward until they're toe to toe. Jax looking down on Rian, his eyes full of angry fire. This could turn ugly if I don't stop them, so I step out of the doorway and put myself between them, pushing Jax's firm chest, but he doesn't budge.

"Jack, stop, please," I plead, as I turn to face Rian.

"Rian, babe, please."

I turn my turbulent silver eyes to him, and he nods, pinching my chin between his thumb and forefinger.

"I came as soon as I heard raised voices, are you sure you're okay?"

His Welsh lilt softer now and I nod. Jax steps back and I'm bereft at the loss of contact, my hand dropping back to my side.

"This isn't finished, Zeppelin," he says with such conviction, as he turns to leave, striding down the corridor.

"Jack! Wait!"

He stops, I think he's going to turn back around, but he doesn't and carries on walking. The sight of him walking away too much to bear, as my legs buckle underneath me and I sink to the floor, wailing sobs wracking my body. *Being in love shouldn't hurt this much.*

# 30

## Jax

I've lived in the madness of Rancid Vengeance for almost two decades. It's hard to remember who I was when all of this began. I was just an ordinary boy, who loved to play music. As I'm staring at my reflection in the mirror in my dressing room, I don't recognise the man staring back at me, he's worlds away from that shy, boy next door. As a band, we're taking some time out of the music industry while Brody recovers from his accident. We're all pursuing solo projects, it's long overdue, Sam's writing new material for the new album and he's collaborating with Jett Powers from Skarlett Ribbon. He's just started writing a column for a music magazine. Lucas is pursuing his passion of photography, he's started writing a memoir to help people, specifically kids, who have dealt with grief and abuse. I've been asked to be a guest judge on a panel of a talent show, *'UK's Finest.'* Our manager M.J, is the executive producer and it's his passion project. It's in its ninth season and every year, he asks a variety of artists to be guest judges and to be mentors for the contestants. After we announced we were taking some time out, M.J asked me if I would consider being on the judging panel and I reluctantly agreed.

Today is the first day of filming and I couldn't be any further out of my depth if I tried. Phoenix King, the manager of Devils Henchman. She's the driving force behind frontman, Draven Michaels, arch-rival of Sam. Phoenix is tall and slender, with an hourglass figure to die for. She has long red hair, styled into loose waves, wide green eyes, and full red lips. She has a cluster of star tattoos around her eyebrow, curving onto her cheek. She speaks with a soft, breathy, Southern American drawl. She is one of the regular judges, alongside M.J, who is the head judge.

I'm one of the guest judges with radio DJ and TV presenter Bernie Lomax. Bernie is around six foot one inches tall, with black spiky hair, dark brown eyes and a full beard. He hails from New Zealand and speaks with

251

a prominent Kiwi accent. He is famous for his wild on-air and on-screen antics, he is outspoken with a razor-sharp wit, dry sense of humour and sarcastic nature. He is also famous for his trademark Hawaiian shirts, which should look ridiculous, but they oddly suit and compliment his personality. I'm in the dressing room waiting for my hair and make-up to be applied when M.J enters the room.

"Jack! Morning, so glad you could be with us today, man. Good to see you, how's Brody?"

He asks in his familiar American accent.

"There's been no change, they don't expect him to come around anytime soon," I explain, a sombre tone to my voice and he pats me on the shoulder in a gesture of reassurance, as the door swings open. Bernie strides confidently into the room, wearing a long black trench coat, dark jeans, a blue, pink and yellow Hawaiian shirt, sunglasses and a large cup of coffee in his hand.

"Fuckin' hell! This time of the day should be illegal! I'm hungover to shit!"

He drops down into the chair next to me and a takes a sip of his coffee.

"Ah fuck! Probably shouldn't have said that while the boss is here!"

He laughs and I find myself smiling along with him. He turns to me and offers me his hand.

"Bernie Lomax." He introduces him and I take his outstretched hand.

"Jax Chase, or you can call me Jack," I reply and he smiles.

"Pleased to meet you, Jackie boy."

We are interrupted by M.J's phone ringing and he answers. He speaks in a clipped tone for a few minutes and ends the call abruptly.

"Danny's just called in sick, he's asked a friend of his to cover for him today. A guy called Rian St James."

I curse under my breath. *Jesus fucking Christ, what are the odds that it would be Zeppelin's best friend. Could my day get any fucking worse?*

After she left my place a few nights ago and I drove to her flat in a vain attempt to get her to talk to me. We both said some things we didn't mean, and she won't return my calls. I haven't heard from her since and her silence is killing me. I'm starting to think our relationship was doomed from the beginning. *What could have happened to her that was so bad?* I push that thought to the back of my mind and try to focus on the present. I lean back in my chair and kick my feet up on the table in front of me. *Looks like it's going to be a long day.*

***

A few hours of shooting the shit with Bernie, the dressing room doors swings open and in breezes Rian. He's wearing black skinny jeans, an off-the shoulder black t-shirt tied at his midriff and a black trilby hat. He beams at Bernie, but when his eyes land on me, his smile falters and he looks to the doorway behind him, whispering to someone. I'm not prepared as the person comes into view, dragging a metal suitcase behind her, Zeppelin. *Fuck my life.*

She looks like a fucking Goddess, wearing a distressed, ripped denim skirt, black and red cherry print Vans, a white and black striped t-shirt, her hair styled straight, framing her beautiful face. Her silver eyes widen, as she looks across at me and we both seem to be rendered speechless.

"I had no idea he was gonna' be here, baby girl."

Rian turns to Zeppelin with a stricken look on his face and she shakes her head in disbelief. M.J takes in the situation unfolding and looks between the three of us.

"Is there a problem here?" he asks and I look at her, but she refuses to meet my gaze.

"No, no problem at all, mate," I say with a smile, hoping he believes the lie and Bernie chuckles throatily.

"You've fucked her, haven't you?" His gruff voice is filled with amusement.

"Too clingy, was she? Or just a disappointment in the sack?"

Zeppelin's mouth drops open in disgust, as she spins on her heel, leaving the room. *For fuck's sake.*

"Well done, dickhead!" Rian exclaims, as he rushes out of the room after her. Bernie takes off his sunglasses, laying them down on the table in front of us.

"Something I said, Jackie boy?" he says wryly and I stifle a smirk, as M.J burst into a fit of giggles.

*"Jesus fucking Christ!* Here's me thinking you were the sensible member of Rancid Vengeance!"

I laugh right along with him. *Sensible one? He couldn't be further from the fucking truth if he tried.*

# 31

## Zeppelin

The glitz and glamour of being on a TV set isn't all what it's cracked up to be. There are people rushing around at a hundred miles an hour, talking into headsets in clipped tones, the live studio audience applauding on cue when a red-light flashes *'applause'* and the contestants being rounded up like herds of cattle. When I woke up this morning, this certainly wasn't how I imagined my day going. Rian called me last minute and said he had been asked to stand in for Danny Debonair on a TV talent show, as lead hair stylist. He asked me to tag along and be his *'assistant'* for the day. I had never been an assistant in my life, but I think the nerves got the better of him and I reluctantly agreed as a source of support for my best friend, never in a million years did I think I would bump into Jax again. I was still licking my wounds from a few nights ago and he was the last person I wanted to see.

I'm stood awkwardly at the side of the stage watching the array of performers have their moment in the spotlight. A young woman with tanned, olive skin around twenty-five steps onto the round centre stage in front of the four expectant judges. She's around five foot six inches tall; she is wearing a long, flowing white maxi skirt, a floral Bardot top, which exposes both of her shoulders to reveal flawless skin. Her long dark hair tumbling down her shoulders, secured in a matching floral headband. Her feet are bare, as she secures an acoustic guitar strap across her slender body. She adjusts the microphone and attempts a nervous smile, looking out to the audience. M.J looks at her, a casual smile on his face.

"Hey! And who do we have here?"

He asks a little too over-enthusiastically and she clears her throat.

"Hi! I'm Noa, I'm twenty-six and I'm originally from Tennessee, but I live in Croydon."

Her accent a mixture of Southern American and British, it sounds odd, but it suits her quirky, bohemian style perfectly.

*"Wow!* That's awesome! So, what made you want to audition for UK's Finest?" Phoenix asks, her overly botoxed face expressionless and unmoving.

"Music is my biggest passion; I've always wanted to perform and what better platform than UK's Finest." Noa says with a nervous smile, as the audience clap and cheer for her. As I watch her awkwardly nod, I can't help but root for her.

"The stage is yours," Jax says casually with a curt nod. The glaring stage lights dim and the strains of Rancid Vengeance *'An Angel's Kiss'.* The all-out, driving rock anthem has been replaced with a slow, haunting, acoustic melody, played on guitar by Noa. She takes a few steps forward, resuming her place at the microphone and begins to sing.

*"You broke down my guard, shattered my defences. You're my mistress of destiny; I am a master of my own universe. You're my diamond in the rough, a heartbeat in my perpetual darkness. I was the boy who tried to heal a broken heart with a shattered mind and a shattered mind with a broken promise. Like a hurricane, you cure my soul of pain; I've never felt like this, there's no end to this bliss. Our worlds collide with an angel's kiss."*

My eyes wander over to Jax and I watch him lose himself in the music, his eyes closed, nodding his head from side to side and his feet tapping in time to the music. She plays the guitar effortlessly, her voice hitting every note perfectly and all too soon, the song is over. The audience are all on their feet, cheering and applauding her. She takes a bow, and I can't help but cheer for her too. M.J beams, clapping his hands excitedly and turns to Jax.

"Jax, over to you, buddy."

Jax nods and puffs out his cheeks, as if he can't believe what he just witnessed.

"Wow! Just wow! You had the audience eating out of the palm of your hand! That was special! After being in the industry for as long as I have, as part of Rancid Vengeance, it's been almost two decades. I have to say I'm a little jealous of the upcoming artists just starting out. It's the appeal of the fame, performing in front of thousands of fans on a nightly basis, there's nothing quite like it. It's addictive, ya know, I used to busk before we made it big, it was a massive stepping stone for me, I've paid my dues as a performer. But you... you're so, so talented, I feel like you've paid your dues too? Am I right?"

He asks her thoughtfully with his head cocked to the side and Noa nods, a look of pure awe on her face. Her eyes wide and glossy, I can almost see stars in them.

"I might be somewhat biased because you just sang the absolute hell out of a Rancid Vengeance song! But you deserve your time to shine, Noa and I want you on my team."

The concept of the show is each judge chooses four people to have on their 'team'. The teams are mentored by the judge and a guest mentor, which is usually a famous music artist and each week they go head-to-head in a song battle. Week by week the audience and the viewers vote for their favourite and the final four go on to the final. If the judge wants the contestant on their team, they press a green button to signal.

"You're something special, Noa. Your voice is unique, like nothing I've ever heard before, you're a breath of fresh air. You took our song and put your own spin on it, for that, I salute you."

He stands up, saluting her with a beaming grin on his face. The pure passion in his voice renders me mute and I can't tear my eyes away from him. He pushes his green button, and audience erupts into rapturous applause.

"Welcome to Team Chase!"

He steps out of his seat, rounding the judges table and makes his way up onto the stage. He throws his arms around her and lifts her from the floor, whispering something in her ear. She clings to him, sobbing softly into his shoulder. He looks over, catching my gaze and I offer him a small smile. He flashes me a wink and I can't look away. The moment lasts a few seconds, and I'm filled with renewed hope that our happy ever after is still possible.

\*\*\*

I feel a nervous kind of energy once filming is over for the day, as Rian catches up to me while I'm walking down the corridor.

"Hey, Zep, wait. I've been looking everywhere for you, baby girl!" he says with a chuckle.

"Well, now you've found me!" I reply with a smirk, and he walks slowly next to me, linking my arm with his.

"So, do you fancy going out to celebrate?" he asks expectantly, as I throw my head back and laugh.

"Celebrate what?"

He narrows his eyes and looks at me as if I've just fallen from another planet.

"Celebrate me being fabulous and a job well done, of course!" he exclaims in a pitch so high only dogs could hear. He stops in the corridor and does a theatrical twirl. I roll my eyes and shake my head exasperated.

"Sure, let me get my stuff and I'll be right there." I laugh and he nods.

"I'll go and wait in the car."

I nod in return, as he turns to walk away, blowing me a kiss. I blow him one back and head into the dressing room. The door is ajar; I don't bother knocking and just walk in. Jax is leaning casually against the dressing table, startling me as I come to a halt in front of him, my steps faltering. He doesn't say anything, he just watches me silently, regarding me intently, as I go about grabbing my bag. I bend down and when I'm upright, he's standing behind me.

*"Jesus fucking Christ,"* I mutter, placing my hand on my chest.

"So, you're not going to say anything about what happened the other night?" he says matter-of-factly.

"What's there to say that hasn't already been said?" I snap back and he laughs bitterly.

"The fucking truth for a start, you owe me that, Zeppelin."

I cock my perfectly plucked eyebrow.

"The truth, wow, that's rich coming from you, seeing as you started our relationship by not even telling me your fucking real name!" I bite out and he nods coolly, folding his muscular arms. I can't help getting distracted by the bulge of his tattooed biceps and swallow a few times to compose myself. *Come on, Zeppelin, focus!*

"Ah, so that's what this is about?"

He nods, dropping his arms and tucking his hand into his pocket, lowering his head. He lets out a long-drawn-out sigh before continuing.

"This life, the fame, being in the spotlight, it was never supposed to be permanent! You don't get it! Do you think I want this life for my daughter? I don't want her growing up terrified some photographers going to shove a camera in her face! It was only supposed to be temporary, we've all got a shelf life, Zeppelin."

The defeat in his voice apparent.

"All those months when we spoke online, that was the happiest I've been in a long time. I had no baggage, I was just Jack, ordinary Jack. The fame, it lingers and follows me around, it hangs around my neck like a fucking noose! I could quite happily hang up my guitar right now and walk away from it all. I want to walk away from the fame and live a quiet, comfortable life, knowing the difference we've made to someone's life through music. Hearing people's stories of why they listen to our music, what our music means to them. It humbles me massively knowing the impact we've had."

Listening to him talk so passionately about his music, explaining his actions, gave me a true glimpse into the real Jackson Chase. But there was still so much we had to learn about each other and our lives.

"So don't stand there and act like I'm the one in the wrong when you're hiding things from me too!"

He points his finger accusingly in my direction.

"We've all got things we're not proud of, chapters in our lives that we don't want to read out loud but at least throw me a fucking rope!"

I'm about to speak, when M.J strides confidently into the dressing room, without knocking.

"Jax! That was a fantastic choice, buddy! TV Weekly is on set; they want to do some interviews and take some pictures for this week's edition."

He nods, as M.J looks between us.

"I'm not interrupting anything, am I?"

Jax glances at me and then looks back to M.J.

"No, not all."

He states nonchalantly, turns and walks away, leaving me dumbfounded standing in the middle of his dressing room wondering what the fuck just happened.

# 32

## Zeppelin

As I make my way out to the car, I decide I don't want to go out and celebrate, I just want to go home. I want to close myself off from the world and forget about this horrible fucking mess just for a little while. *Why couldn't Jax understand that I had my reasons for not telling him about my tragic background.* I understand that to move forward with our relationship, both of us had to purge the ugly truths of our pasts, but I wasn't ready. I wasn't sure when, or if I would ever be ready to share that with him. I was conflicted, but I manage to convince Rian to take me home and once I shut the door in the privacy of my flat, it was only then I allowed the tears to fall.

I ask Alexa to play my playlist, as the upbeat sound of *Rob Thomas One Less Day (Dying Young)* echoes through the flat, breaking the eerie silence. I pour myself a large glass of cool white wine and place it on the coffee table and sit on the floor in front of the sofa. Jericho settles himself beside me and I pull the large photo album from underneath the sofa. I reach for my wine and begin to flip through the album, stopping on a familiar photo that I hadn't allowed myself to look at for so long. I was twenty-five and very much in love, in the photo I stared up at him, Abel Creed. The smiles on our faces so genuine, we looked at each other with so much love, it hurt to look at it. My fingers caressing the photo softly, remembering the day so clearly in my mind.

My fingers tighten around the glass, as I flip to the next picture. A picture of all four of us, in Italy, posing and smiling in the sunshine, in front of the yacht that went up in flames on that fateful day. Me, Abel, Rico and Shep, me cuddled into Abel's side, wearing sunglasses, a short white sundress, black diamante studded flip flops and my hair in loose, tousled waves around my shoulders. We all look so fresh faced and so carefree, just a group of people enjoying their trip, little did we know then that would be the last time. Tears began to fall, as one song faded into the next, *Lewis Capaldi Someone you Loved*, the lyrics like a thousand knives to my already fragile heart. I allow myself to flip through the rest of the photo album and start to think that I'm grateful for the hand that life has dealt me. I have a roof over my head, a job I love, a best friend who means the world to me, but I can't help thinking of the life I had before. The life I had before was unpredictable, it was exciting, and I craved to be that carefree woman again.

At that moment, a flash of inspiration hits me like a Boeing 747, and I get to my feet, Jericho lifting his head up at the sudden movement. I sit down at my desk and open my laptop. As soon as it loads, I open my book, and the words flow like a torrent in my over-active mind. My fingers fly over the keys, and all sense of time seems to abandon me. All that exists in my head is the words and the profound love story of Montana and Dustin. By the morning, my ninth book is finally finished.

*** 

After pulling an all-nighter writing and spending most of the day sleeping, I'm woken to a loud pounding on the door. Jericho leaps on the bed, barking wildly, rousing me from my slumber. I grumpily swing my legs out of bed and pad across the flat to the door, rubbing the sleep from my eyes. I open the door and I'm greeted by Jax. He never fails to render me speechless, I'm suddenly wide awake and I'm very aware of this perfect male specimen standing expectantly at my door in all his tattooed glory.

"I'm done waiting, Zeppelin." His voice is gruff and filled with such emotion it makes my heart slam against my rib cage.

"I've proved that I'm fucking incapable of staying away from you," he admits with a frustrated sigh, and I lick my lips, as my greedy eyes roam all over his lean physique.

"Keep looking at me like that and I don't think I'll be able to control myself."

His voice low and filled with all the wicked things he wants to do to me. His eyes lock with mine and I can't look away, I'm frozen to the spot, as he reaches over to tuck an errant strand of hair behind my ear. I feel the familiar slick heat pool between my thighs and in that moment,

I'm done waiting too. I boldly bunch the front of his t-shirt in my fist and pull him closer. He stumbles into me and slams his hand on the door to steady himself, his thick, tattooed bicep flexing. I steal a glance at his chiselled features, his sculpted cheekbones, his strong, heavily stubbled jaw, his brown eyes filled with fiery heat. *He's so fucking hot, how did I get so lucky?*

"I'm done waiting too, Jack, I want you. I'm tired of fighting it."

My voice doesn't sound like my own, as I drag him inside, slamming the door behind us. He stalks forward, until he's so close to me, I can feel his hot breath on my cheek. The scent of *Diesel Only the Brave* invading my nostrils, it's intoxicating...*he's intoxicating.*

He doesn't say anything, as he crashes his lips to mine, wrapping his hand in my hair and gently tugging me towards him. He deepens the kiss, his tongue caressing mine, as he slowly strokes the roof of my mouth. I can feel his tongue piercing, as he continues to kiss me with such passion and fervour, moving his free hand down to cup my breast. He gently kneads it in his large hand, briefly pulling away from our kiss and pressing his forehead against mine.

"Zeppelin, tell me you want me, tell me what you want."

His voice rough and his breathing laboured, as he strokes my nipple and I let out a soft moan.

"Jack, I want you, please, I want you to fuck me," I admit shamelessly, my voice filled with desperate need, and he takes that as the green light, as he lifts me up and I automatically wrap my legs around his lean waist. He strides across the flat, kicking the door of my bedroom open with his boot and depositing me in the middle of my Queen Size bed. He stands at the foot of the bed, unbuckling the belt on his jeans, kicking off his boots haphazardly and pulling his jeans off. He is wearing a pair of tight grey Calvin Klein boxer shorts, which contrasts against his lightly tanned skin.

"I want you naked, Zeppelin, I want to see all of you," he demands, his voice filled with dark promise, and I do as I'm bid, taking off my pyjamas until I am lying on the bed completely naked. He growls low in his throat, and he hasn't taken his eyes off me once, as he strips off his t-shirt. The sight of his naked tattooed torso momentarily disarms me, and I lick my lips hungrily. He's standing there looking delicious, as he slowly climbs on the bed and positions himself between my thighs. My breasts feel heavy and ache to have his hands on them, the throbbing between my thighs almost unbearable.

"I want you to touch yourself," he commands, as I slowly move my one hand down my abdomen and down to my pussy, gently rubbing and teasing my wet folds.

*"Jesus fucking Christ,"* he grinds out, as he watches me carefully, his erection straining painfully in his boxer shorts. I push a finger inside myself and moan aloud, rolling my nipple with my free hand, as I begin to quicken my pace, the slow build-up of my orgasm blossoming deep within me.

"Jack, oh God! Jack! I'm so close!"

I can feel my orgasm cresting to the surface, my heartbeat quickening, as my breath comes in sharp, gasping pants.

"You look so fucking hot right now, don't stop," he says gruffly and smiles his panty-dropping smile, as I continue to fuck myself with my fingers. He looks at me with pure, unadulterated want in his deep brown eyes, which are smoky with desire.

"Come for me, Zeppelin, I want to watch you come," he commands gruffly, and with those words, my orgasm tears through me, like a thunderclap of pent-up sexual energy.

"OH GOD! JACK! I'M COMING! OH FUCK! JACKKKK!" I scream out in pure ecstasy and as I come down from my orgasmic high, Jax moves closer to me like a hungry lion about to pounce on its prey. He straddles me, his muscular thighs either side of me, trapping me beneath him, pressing his hard body into mine. He leans down to kiss a burning trail from my neck and across my collarbone, the feel of his beard against my bare skin causes goose bumps to erupt on every inch of my body. Everything about this man is addictive and I wasn't willing to give up the habit, at least not yet.

# 33

## Jax

She looks perfect spread beneath me, ethereal, almost like an angel. Her skin soft and flawless, her breasts pert, an intricate lace design tattooed on her sternum and her nipples standing to attention. I yearn to have my mouth on them, and I can't seem to tear my fucking eyes away. *She is the epitome of female fucking perfection.* I didn't plan on turning up out of the blue, but I couldn't stop thinking about her. I have to claim her as mine, I don't care that she has secrets, and I don't care that she's keeping things from me. I've fallen for her just as hard as she's fallen for me and I can't seem to stop myself.

"So beautiful," I whisper softly, as her greedy eyes roam over my body. I pull my boxer shorts off, my erect cock springing free and she eyes it carefully.

"God, I want you so fucking badly, Jack!" she pants impatiently, as I stroke my cock a few times.

"Condom?" I ask, as she reaches over to open the drawer beside her bed. She hands me the foil wrapper, and I tear it open impatiently with my teeth, rolling the rubber onto my almost painful erection. *I'm fucking solid.* I push her legs open wider, positioning myself between her thighs. She cries out loud, as I thrust my cock deep inside her, allowing her to adjust to my length.

"Okay?"

Concern lacing my voice and she looks up at me expectantly, her silver eyes wild with lust.

"Oh God! You feel so fucking good! Don't stop! Please, don't stop!"

Her voice breathy and desperate, as I thrust deeper inside her almost urgently, my cock sliding easily out of her wet heat. She mewls softly, spreading her legs wider to accommodate me.

"OH GOD! JACK! JACK! OHHH FUCKKK!"

My name leaves her lips like a prayer, as I increase my pace.

"You feel so good around my cock, Zeppelin, it's like you were made for me," I say gruffly, and she shifts her hips up to match me thrust for thrust.

*"JESUS! FUCKKK!"* I curse, as she wraps her legs around my waist, pulling me in deeper. Her hands start to roam over my back and shoulders, as my pace quickens.

"Oh God! Don't you dare fucking stop! Please, make me come, Jack! Make me come!" she pants, her eyes locking with mine, silver on brown.

"It feels too fucking good, love."

I push my cock deeper into her, feeling my cock bump her cervix, as I drive in and out of her slickness, building up a punishing, unrelenting pace. I can feel her pussy undulating and clenching around me, squeezing me in the most delicious way. She's moaning softly, biting down on her lip, her head thrown back in pure ecstasy.

"I can feel you, you're close, so fucking close." My voice is a rough whisper. She's trembling with pent-up desire beneath me, gripping my biceps almost painfully. Her breaths coming in ragged pants, I can feel her pussy rippling around me. I know she's almost there and with one sudden movement of my cock, her orgasm detonates from deep within her.

"JACK! Oh God! I'm going to come!" she yells with pleasure, as I drive my cock into her with an expert swivel of my hips and she writhes beneath me.

"I've got you, Zeppelin, that's it, come for me," I encourage her softly, as she screams out, her orgasm flooding through her like a tsunami.

"FUCK! I'M COMING! JACK! OH GOD! JACK! JACK! I'M COMING!" she cries, as I explode into her at the same time.

"ZEPPELIN! JESUS FUCKING CHRIST! I'M COMING! FUCKKKKK!"

We both ride out our orgasms, as I empty my seed inside her, and her legs fall limply either side of me. I collapse on top of her, trying not to crush her, her lithe body trembling and twitching with post-orgasmic aftershocks, as I pull out of her.

I roll over onto the bed next to her, tucking her closer to me. I silently wrap my arm around her, her head resting on my chest. For the first time in a long time, I feel content just lying here with her, I reach for her hand and place it on my chest, my hand resting on top of hers.

"Your hearts beating really fast," she says with chuckle, and I look down at her, her blonde hair perfectly mussed, her silver eyes sparkling, she's stunning. I shift a little, moving my hand to rest on her back and she flinches, as if I have burned her, ruining the moment almost instantly.

"Jack," she warns, untangling our limbs and perching herself on the end of the bed, exposing her back to me. I sit up, the raised, mottled pink burn scars on her back and I start to wonder what happened to her. I move closer to her, dropping kisses across the rough skin and she shivers as my lips move over her scars.

"Don't, please don't," she whispers and I continue to kiss a burning trail across her back and shoulder blade, as she moans softly, tipping her head back.

"So fucking beautiful."

I lift my hand and trace across every inch of her scars with my fingers, letting her know I'm not repulsed by them. She squeezes her eyes shut and traps her bottom lip between her teeth, her head resting against my chest. I lean down peppering her neck with soft, gentle kisses, while my fingers roam across her back.

"Jack." Her voice is thick with unshed tears.

"Shhh, I've got you. Do you trust me?"

I ask and she nods against me, as I shift her backwards onto the bed. She's lying on her front, her body trembling.

"I'm going to take you from behind."

She lets out an audible gasp as I grip her hips, moving her into position. She doesn't object as she lifts her bum in the air. *Fuck, could she be any more perfect?*

"Are you on birth control?" I ask boldly and she hums her answer, as my hand snakes down her stomach and to find her swollen clit. She moans long and loud, as my finger swipes up her wetness.

"You're so wet for me," I grind out.

"Jack," she whimpers.

"I'll take care of you, love."

I move away from her aching cleft and rub the head of my cock against her slick entrance, entering her on a loud moan. She pushes back to meet my every thrust, establishing a rhythm, as I pound her up the bed, causing the headboard to bang against the wall.

"OH GOD! THAT FEELS SO FUCKING GOOD! JACKKK!" she screams, as I tighten my grip on her hips, impaling her on my waiting hardness. Her pussy feels like velvet with nothing between us, as I reach around to circle her nub.

"Jack! Oh God! Please, please, make me come! I want to come all over your cock!" she yells and I chuckle softly.

"Your wish is my command, beautiful girl."

I increase my thrusts, the pace almost frenzied and frantic.

"Oh Jack, please, please, don't stop, I need to come! Please!" she pleads almost desperately, as I move in and out of her slick heat. As my pace quickens, I can feel her squeeze her inner walls around my cock, and I gasp at the feeling.

"Play with your pussy, make yourself come around my cock!"

She reaches down to play with herself, as we both near climax. Her breathing coming out in ragged pants, as I feel the moment her orgasm reaches its crescendo.

"Jack, Oh Jack! Jack! I'm coming!" she screams, as I growl out my own climax.

"*FUCKKKKK!* Oh shit! Zeppelin, I'm coming!"

My breath comes out in ragged pants, as wave after wave of pleasure barrels through my entire body. I pump my hot seed inside her, as we both tremble with tiny post-sex aftershocks. I still, as she collapses spent on the bed. I pull out of her and as I do, she shoves me out of the way, leaping ungraciously off the bed. She rushes into the adjoining bathroom, and I'm left still semi-erect, wondering what the fuck just happened.

# 34

## Zeppelin

The gut-wrenching sobs that wrack my entire body, as I collapse in a heap in front of the toilet bowl, my stomach roiling violently. I empty the contents of my stomach and vomit into the toilet, as the door handle rattles.

"Zeppelin, open the door."

His voice calm. *Why the fuck did I have to expose my scars to him?* He didn't react the way I was expecting him to, but it still opens me up to questions I can't give him the answers to. He'll know what a monster I am and once he finds out the truth, he'll walk away.

"I'll wait here all day if I have to, but I'm not going anywhere."

I press my damp forehead against the cool tiles next to the toilet and briefly close my eyes. I'm suddenly exhausted, both mentally and physically.

"Is everything okay in there? Please, open the door."

I get unsteadily to my feet and catch sight of my reflection in the mirror above the sink. *I look thoroughly fucked.*

"Please, can we just talk about this?" he asks, his voice steady, as I tear off three sheets of toilet paper, wipe my mouth and flush the toilet. I run a brush through my hair and swing the door open, his concerned gaze locks with mine. He's sitting on the edge of the bed in his boxer shorts looking as if he has just stepped out of Calvin Klein advert. He's all clean lines, his shoulders broad, his hips are lean, his biceps thick and in perfect proportion with the rest of his perfect masculine body. I bend down to pick up Jax's discarded t-shirt and pull it on, the material soft against my skin. I move towards him bare foot across the soft carpet, almost apprehensively.

"I'm a work in progress, Zep. But I'm fucking trying, for you, for us. I don't know how to be in a relationship these days and I know I keep fucking up, but please, don't give up on me, on us."

His words cut deep, as a tear rolls down my cheek.

"Whatever happened, whatever...whoever hurt you, you can tell me in your own time, I won't push you, I'm so fucking sorry."

He swallows hard, dropping his head into his hands and I step between his legs, wrapping my arms around him. He envelopes me in his strong arms and my next words take me by surprise.

"My ex-boyfriend was a rock star, and he died in a fire."

He stiffens as I say those words and I pull away from him, instantly trying to put some distance between us.

"Zeppelin, *Jesus Christ!* You can't just say something like that then pull away from me!" he says incredulously, as he drags his hand through his long hair.

"How can we be in a relationship when you don't even trust me enough to tell me the fucking truth?!" His voice is a few decibels louder, as I allow five years of grief to come spilling out.

"Because I feel responsible for his death! Okay? Because I'm fucking ashamed, Jack! It haunts me! Even after five years!" I yell, jabbing my thumbs in my chest, before continuing.

"We argued right before he died, and I never got to say sorry! He died thinking I fucking hated him! My ex-boyfriend was Abel Creed from The Poison Puppets, and I despised the person he turned me into. He refused to commit, he cheated on me time and time again and I took him back like a weak, pathetic idiot! In my head, I put him on a pedestal, as if he was the perfect boyfriend, but he was a selfish motherfucker who let the fame go to his head. That's the ugly truth, Jack!"

Jax remains still, as he listens to me recount my relationship with Abel.

"We were together for four years and in the end, I didn't even recognise him, he wasn't the charming, genuine, loving man he was in the beginning. He was manipulative, the fame swallowed him up and spat him out, he didn't care who he had to tread on, or fuck, to get to the top. I was the only one who stuck around when everyone else from his old life abandoned him. He had just finished a European tour on the night of the accident, Abel asked me to join them, the band's manager called in a favour from Nolan Wilder, some rich billionaire type. Abel got so drunk, he was a mean drunk, I caught him with his pants down, we argued, and he started shouting about how I was holding him back and forcing him to settle down, he told me he felt trapped. It wasn't the first time we'd had this argument, but I burst into tears, and I started yelling about how I felt he chose his career over me. I felt so lonely, and I wanted to him to commit, but he stormed off, telling me it was over."

I swipe angrily at the tears that have tracked their way down my cheeks. *I don't look at Jax, I can't, I don't want to see the pity in his eyes, or even worse disgust.*

"I wanted to give him a chance to cool off and I ended up chatting to one of the other band members girlfriends, I-I can't remember her name, it was so fucking long ago. We chatted, we did shots, and we were so drunk. I passed out and woke up hungover to the smell of smoke, it all happened so fast. The yacht had three floors, we were on the top deck, the rooms were at the back. There was only one way out, I had to make it to the front of the yacht. The fire was wreaking havoc, the heat was so intense and spreading quickly, I was fucking terrified, thick smoke filled the area where I was and I couldn't see in front of me. The flames licked hungrily at the polished wooden deck, I thought that maybe there would be lifeboats or something, but I was panicking and disoriented, I felt like I was suffocating. My lungs felt like they were burning, I couldn't breathe, but I knew I had to get out of there. I managed to find a towel on one of the sun loungers, I soaked it in a champagne bucket, put it over my head and ran towards the front of the yacht. Unbeknownst to me, that's where the fire had spread to. I knew I'd be dead if I turned back, so I kept as low as I possibly could and just made a run for it, the flames engulfing and burning my skin. I managed to get to where I needed to be and I didn't know what to do, I think I was in shock, or in a blind panic, I don't know, it all happened so fast. By that time, the yacht was consumed and ravaged by the inferno, it was like something out of a horror movie. I jumped overboard to put the flames out, I don't remember what happened after that. I remember coming around in the back of the coastguard's boat and I was in so much pain." I sob, as I remember the worst night of my life.

"Ever since it happened five years ago, I haven't been with anyone, or at least no one who really mattered. It was like I was punishing myself for Abel's death, after the accident, I locked myself away for a long time, I shut myself off from the world because I was disgusted with myself, I hated myself. When I looked in the mirror, it wasn't my reflection staring back at me, I didn't recognise the person I had turned into. I was hollow and haunted, I suffer nightmares, it got so bad I was terrified to fall asleep. My Nan and Granddad were my source of support; I couldn't have gotten through it without them. I received a substantial amount of compensation from the accident and my Granddad suggested using it to buy my own place, so I took his advice and here I am."

I manage a small smile, but Jax doesn't say anything for long moments. I observe him and I couldn't help the deep-seated fear that had settled itself in my gut. That after listening to me recount and relive the horrors of my not-so-distant past, he would just get up and walk away. My stomach roiled with each second of silence that passed, I was relieved when he clears his throat and begins to speak.

"This changes nothing between us, Zeppelin." His voice is level and filled with such conviction my heart soars. In that moment, the depth of feeling I feel for this man is like nothing I have experienced before, and I didn't want it to end. I wanted forever with Jackson Chase.

# 35

## Jax

Listening to her account of how she survived something so horrific, I can't imagine what she must have gone through, what she must have endured. It made me want her even more, I was in awe of her bravery, and I think in that moment, I found myself falling just as hard as she had. She silently drops down onto the bed, her silver eyes filled with raw sadness, and I lie down, patting the space next to me and encouraging her to lie beside me. She does as she's bid and I tuck her under my arm, pulling her close to me. Her skin warm and soft beneath my hand, as she snuggles against me, as if she can't get close enough, the connection crackling between us. She throws her leg over mine and tangles our limbs together, her bare legs rubbing against mine.

"I'm so sorry you had to go through all of that alone," I whisper, as she reaches for my hand and I let her.

"I wasn't really alone, I had my Nan and Granddad, but I felt so stuck in my own head, ya know? I just shut myself away because my confidence had taken a hit, but I knew deep down it wasn't doing me any good. I was in a dark place, and I refused therapy at the time. I made the decision to focus on finding my own place and moving somewhere where no one knew me, where no one looked at me with pity in their eyes."

She explains. *I can relate to that, after the events of Vegas, we were all so overwhelmed by grief. But everywhere we went, it was all people wanted to ask us about.*

"I get it, I really do, more than most."

I try to reassure her, but she won't understand fully unless I explain the true extent of that fateful day.

"After Vegas, you couldn't open a newspaper or open a news website without seeing what happened. It was front and centre for months, it was like I was being tortured from all angles, I'd just lost my fiancée, and I was functioning on three hours sleep a night because Thea wouldn't settle. I felt like the world's worst dad; I'd failed Ruby by not protecting her and I'd failed every single one of the boys by not being the hero. For the first few months, it felt like I was reliving that single moment over and over again, on a constant fucking loop. We lost nine people, people who had been in our entourage since the beginning, our family," I explain and even after three years, I still can't believe the events that unfolded that day. She squeezes my hand. I relish in the comfort of the warmth of her hand in mine, as she continues to listen intently.

"I don't remember much, but I remember the continuous loud popping noises from behind me, it resembled a loud engine backfiring. At first, I didn't even realise I had been hit, I don't know if it was because of the adrenaline and my fight or flight instinct, but I didn't feel a thing on impact. It was only after I felt the warm trickle of blood and when the adrenaline finally wore off, it became the greatest pain I had ever felt in my entire fucking life. The only way I can describe how it feels, is like your body is being scorched from the inside out. I managed to take a few steps back, there was just utter chaos going on around me, but I collapsed to the floor, I thought for sure I was dying. My whole life flashed before me, I started to contemplate all the shit I'd ever done that led me to this exact moment, I thought about all the people I had ever wronged or hurt in any way, and I thought of Ruby and our unborn child. That's all I could focus on, then the popping noises ceased, and this eerie kind of silence washed over me. The next thing I remember was waking up in hospital."

I try desperately to push the horrific memory to the back of mind, as she moves her head to rest on my pec and looks up at me. Her silver eyes full of sympathy.

"It wasn't your fault," she says softly and I shake my head vehemently.

"You don't understand! I couldn't fucking protect her, protecting her was my job, it was my duty! She was carrying my child!" I say incredulously, a few decibels louder. We've spent countless hours going over and over that horrifying day in minute detail. Reliving every gun shot, every scream, and the dull cacophony before everything went black.

"Jack, you were shot! You did all you could! You've been carrying around that guilt for three years, it's time, you need to let go," she says carefully and I briefly squeeze my eyes shut. I know deep down she's right; I know it wasn't my fault, but I've carried around that guilt like a lead weight for three long and painful years. I had spent countless hours in therapy with Kalvin unpicking and analysing that night. But no one truly understands the impact it had on all our lives, individually and as a band.

"You know the last thing I remember? The last thing I heard. Ruby screaming, it wasn't just any ordinary scream, it was a scream of pure terror and that's what fucking keeps me up at night! I'm damaged, Zeppelin, Rian was right, we're not good for each other."

I laugh bitterly, as I sit up, pulling away from her, untangling our limbs and perching myself on the edge of the bed, still wearing just my boxer shorts. I scrub my hands down my face, suddenly feeling exhausted, as I feel the bed dip behind me.

"Rian has no fucking right to say if we are, or aren't good for each other, shouldn't it be my opinion that counts? I'm damaged too, Jack! Don't you get it? It wasn't just a coincidence we matched, and both ended up in that chat room all those months ago, it was fate. We can heal each other, Jack, but we have to start being honest with each other, or this will never work."

Her voice almost pleading, as I'm instantly transported back to three years ago.

# Past

# Jax

*I am awoken by the melodic sound of birdsong. As I stare blankly and aimlessly at the ceiling, I think to myself how dare those tweeting little fuckers be so happy when our lives have been turned upside down. I've lost the woman I was going to spend the rest of my life with; it still doesn't seem real. I'm numb and still struggling to wrap my head around the whole fucked up situation. Every time I close my eyes, it feels like I'm reliving it all over again. The deafening sound of gunshots still ringing in my ears, the terror-filled screams, the metallic scent of blood permeating my nostrils, causing me to gag and sit bolt upright in my uncomfortable hospital bed. The sharp ache in my shoulder causing me to audibly wince.*

*The silence that envelopes the stark, sterile hospital room seems fitting for my sombre mood. The door taps softly, and my head snaps up from my sorrow-filled reverie.*

*"Come in," I say so quietly I'm not sure they hear me, but the door swings open and a doctor, Sam and Sam's older brother Brandon walk in. The click, click of the doctor's heels across the floor set my nerves on edge.*

*"Mr Chase?" The tall blonde female doctor breaks the silence.*

*"The police are here; they'd like to ask you a few questions."*

*The fury that boils in my veins at that moment is evident, as I swing my legs out of bed and get unsteadily to my feet, ignoring the agonising pain that rips through my shoulder blade. I make my way to the door and lean heavily against the frame, breathing deeply, as I catch sight of the two police officers. One in full uniform and one wearing a black suit are standing outside Peyton's room across the corridor.*

*"Mr Chase."*

*His prominent New York accent clipped, as they both nod curtly, and I move out of the room, with Sam and Brandon following close behind.*

*"How fucking dare you show up here with your questions, have some god damn respect! My fucking fiancée has just died!" My voice is hoarse and thick*

*with unshed tears. I am about to launch into a full-on tirade when Brandon casually steps forward, his hand tucked into the pocket of his dark jeans.*

*"Jackson," he says sternly and Sam joins us, squeezing my good shoulder in a gesture of reassurance. Brandon takes charge of this situation, as if he were born to lead.*

*"Look, we're all a little on edge right now, tempers are frayed, emotions are high, so I don't think answering your questions is going to solve anything. I get that this is a serious police investigation, but our family and friends have been injured, some of them didn't make it, but please give us the space we need. At least until things have calmed down, we're not going anywhere, not anytime soon, his fiancée is no longer with us, and his newborn daughter is in the neo-natal unit. I can assure you and give my solemn word that we will co-operate, just not right now, but you know where to find us?"*

*The uniformed officer stares Brandon down, until he realises, he isn't backing off, nods curtly and walks away. I cock my eyebrow, impressed at Brandon's diplomacy and he shrugs nonchalantly.*

*"Well, one of us Newbolt's had to have inherited the diplomatic, cool, calm and collected gene, it certainly wasn't going to be this fuckin' clown," he states wryly and Sam narrows his eyes on his older brother. As I look between the two of them, I see the stark resemblance. Brandon is a little on the more rugged, less put together side, his dark hair, the same shade as Sam's, pulled up into a messy man bun. Sam on the other hand, looks pale, his eyes red rimmed with tears. I can't imagine what Sam and his family are going through right now, knowing it was his older sister Savannah that set all this in motion in some twisted act of revenge for J.D.*

*"How are you holding up, man?" I ask, breaking the uncomfortable silence. He presses his lips into a straight line and shakes his head.*

*"I can't get my head around any of it, it makes me physically sick to think that my sister, the girl I grew up with, did this to our fucking family! I'm so fucking angry, Jax. I can't comprehend the chaos she created, on our wedding day of all days and Peyton doesn't know about Ruby yet," he confesses and my eyes widen, as he hangs his head in shame.*

*"What? You haven't told her?" I ask and he shakes his head, running his hand through his hair.*

*"How the fuck do I tell the woman I love more than life itself that her best friend is dead? How can I be the one to blow her world apart like that? How can I be the one to put that look of pure heartbreak in her eyes? I can't, I just can't, Jax, I can't. We've lost eight people, Cole might never walk again, Jesus fucking Christ! I can't bring her world crashing down around her, she doesn't deserve that, not now."*

*I laugh bitterly.*

*"Do you think my world hasn't come fucking crashing down around me? I lost my fucking fiancée! The woman I was going to marry! I've got a daughter who hasn't got a mother! How the hell am I supposed to raise her on my own, Sam!"*

*I raise my voice, and I can't seem to put into words how I'm feeling right now, I'm numb, overwhelmed and completely consumed by grief. I keep thinking that this is all a bad dream and any second now I'm going to wake up, but the cold stark reality jumps up and punches me full force in the gut. Ruby's gone.*

# Present

## Jax

I'm snapped back to the present by Zeppelin sliding her arms around my waist and I take a few moments to revel in her warm touch; her softness pressed against me. She rests her cheek on my bare back, she doesn't say anything, she just drops a trail of kisses across my shoulder blades and down my spine. My head falls back limply, and I briefly squeeze my eyes shut at the feel of her lips on me.

"Just feel, Jack, no more talk of the past, it's you and me now," she whispers against me, as she spends long moments caressing and touching every inch of my body.

"Let me worship you, let me do to you what you do to me, I want to drive you crazy, I want to drive you wild with pleasure."

Her voice low and seductive, as she tackles me down to the bed until I'm flat on my back and she climbs over me to straddle my hips. She's naked and watching her hovering above me, backlit by the natural daylight coming in through the window, she looks like an angel. *An angel sent to help me love again.* My heart slams against my rib cage at the thought, but I push that to the back of my mind and just focus on her. She pulls my boxers down my legs and discards them. She leans down and her lips land on mine, our kiss raw and intense, as our tongues sensually dance, my piercing stroking the roof of her mouth. She pulls away and directs my cock into her already soaking wet pussy, not bothering with foreplay. I'm so turned on; my dick is rock solid, and I can't think straight. I can only focus on the pleasure she's bestowing upon me. She drops down onto my steel erection and I roar out loud. She looks down at me, her silver eyes glittering, a satisfied look on her beautiful face. I skim my hands over her slender body, as I move to grip her waist, her skin heating with my touch.

"Oh God! Jack, you feel so fucking good!" she moans, as she lifts herself up and drops back down onto my cock, increasing the pace with each precise measured drive. Her perfect breasts bouncing, as she establishes a punishing rhythm. I grit my teeth; she feels almost too good.

"That's it, oh fuck!" I growl, and in one swift movement I roll us so I'm on top. She's spread beneath me, and I haven't felt like this in a long time. Three fucking years to be precise, I'm actually enjoying the moment, the feel of flesh on flesh, the feel of her velvet cunt around my cock. I press my body against hers, as she lifts her leg wrapping it around my waist allowing me to go deeper.

"Zeppelin, oh fuck you feel amazing! Jesus Christ!" I curse, as she writhes underneath me, I build up a rhythm and she meets me thrust for thrust.

"OH FUCK! JACK! JACK!" she yells, as I feel my cock bump against her cervix. I'm fully aware I'm not wearing a condom, but I'm too lost in the moment, drunk on lust.

"OH FUCK! I'M CLOSE! I'M SO CLOSE! JACK!"

I quicken my pace, then slow, alternating between deep drives and leisurely thrusts. Her breath hitches in her throat and she plays with her nipples, rolling them between her thumb and forefingers.

"I want you to come for me, Zeppelin, I want the neighbours to know my fucking name! Come all over my cock!" I demand, both of our faces covered in a thin sheen of sweat.

"OH GOD! DON'T YOU DARE FUCKING STOP!" she pleads, almost desperately. My strokes becoming more frantic, slipping in and out of her slick, aching channel. That's all it takes to tip us both over the edge.

"OH FUCK! I'M COMING! FUUUUCCKKKK! I'M COMING! JACK! JACK! OH GOD! JACK!"

she screams, as her sex ripples around me. My impending orgasm right behind hers, as I growl out my climax.

"JESUS! ZEPPELIN! FUCK! I'M COMING!"

I pump my hot seed inside her, as she milks every last drop of my release. Her inner walls contracting, as we both shudder with tiny aftershocks. I still and she goes lax beneath me, waiting for our breathing to return to normal before I pull out of her. I flop down on the bed next to her, exhausted and sated. I look down at her and she looks perfectly fucked, her hair a dishevelled mess and her cheeks pink. I pull her into my side, wrapping my arms around her, relishing in the post-sex haze. I feel a wave of contentment wash over me and an inner peace I've never felt before. In that moment, I was the happiest I've been in three long years.

# 36

## Zeppelin

In that moment, we both went from being emotionally unavailable, to satiated and content lying next to each other after a marathon round of lovemaking. I felt like we had turned a corner, and we at least understood each other a little better after our heart to heart. What I suffered in the yacht fire doesn't compare to what he must have gone through that day in the chapel in Las Vegas. It made my heart hurt for him, but we were both lucky to be alive and we had found each other amongst the wreckage. That had to be enough for now.

After Abel died, I was sure I would never love again, I thought my heart would never recover, I was resigned to the fact that I would never truly heal from the trauma it bought with it. As the time went on, I thought about it more often in those times I spent in my own head and eventually in therapy, I came to the conclusion that whenever, or whoever you love, it will hurt, love hurts and that's a sad fact of life. I don't think what I felt with Abel was love, whatever I felt for him, there wasn't a word for it, it was lust maybe, infatuation at best. The events leading up to his death, I felt him slipping through my fingers, day by day, minute by minute, hour by hour, he was slipping further away from me. He delegitimised the word love for me and turned it into a dirty word. As the years went by, I began to realise I had built a prison around myself, those impenetrable walls were my safe place, and my mind was my own worst enemy. Behind those walls, there is still a shadow of who I was before the corruption of experience, and I owed it to myself to honour the person I used to be before grief consumed me.

I deserved my happy ending, I deserved the ride off into the sunset with my Prince Charming because I had survived, *I survived*. My nightmares used to be laden with demon voices of placing blame, but now the guilt that I felt, was no longer at the forefront of my mind when I woke up in the mornings and it was no longer the thing that plagued my slumber at night. I was grateful for the hand I had been dealt, but because of the deep-seated trauma I had suffered in the yacht fire and with my high-profile relationship with Abel Creed. I was always waiting for other shoe to drop and catapult me head first back into the depths of hell. Over the years I always avoided and shied away from relationships, but something about Jack made me want to break all of my own rules.

My thoughts are interrupted by a light scratching on the door and Jax sits up, looking across at me curiously, leaning back on his elbows. I have to stop myself from drooling over how hot he looks lying naked in my bed, freshly fucked, his abs tight, his tattoos on full display and his shoulders broad. *He really is model worthy.* I swallow hard and I can't help but wanting him again. I shift my gaze away from him and move my attention back to the scratching on the door, as I chuckle softly.

"It's just Jericho, he wants attention, that's all," I say playfully, swinging my legs out of the bed, I pull on Jax's discarded t-shirt and pad across the floor bare foot to the door. I open the door and Jericho gallops in like a big furry horse. I climb back on the bed and Jericho leaps on the bed. He regards Jax with a wary curiosity, sniffing wildly and dropping down on the bed, his large paws stretched in front of him. Jax reaches over to him and lets Jericho sniff his hand investigating this stranger who has invaded our space. Jax looks over to me and I smile softly at their interaction.

"Trust me, if he didn't like you, he would have let you know by now!" I say with amusement in my voice, as Jericho shifts his furry body and climbs into Jax's lap. Jax scratches his ears and fusses him, as Jericho plants a long, wet lick on Jax's face. We both laugh.

"He likes you; you've got the Jericho seal of approval!"

I watch them with rapt attention for a few precious minutes, wishing I could freeze this moment and keep it with me forever. Jax is distracted by petting Jericho and stroking his fur, I strip his t-shirt off until I'm naked again. I throw it haphazardly onto the floor, taking a second to finger comb my hair.

"Ahem..."

Jax looks up and his mouth drops open. He curses under his breath, and he can't take his eyes off me.

"I want you again, Jack." My voice is dripping with pure seduction, Jericho lets out a whine and leaps off the bed, as I tackle Jax down to the mattress.

***

After waking up next to Jack the next morning, after an endless night of unbridled passion. I roll over and feel a delicious soreness deep inside me, reminding me of our X-rated activities. A smile spreads across my face, as I look over at Jack who is still asleep. Even in slumber he looks good enough to eat, the duvet lying across his abdomen, as I observe him unhurriedly. His vivid tattoos popping against his lightly tanned skin, my eyes move up to the tattoo that spans his neck and throat, I can't help but feeling a pang of jealousy, as I look at the bright yellow buttercup and the words '*Breathe in, breathe out, it'll be OK, one step at a time.*'

I carefully lift up the cover and crawl under the sheet, settling myself between his legs. I fist his cock once and take it deep into my throat. He groans low in his throat, and he reaches down to place his hand on the back of my head, lifting the cover. I lick up and down the length of his cock and run my tongue over the thick mushroom-like head. I look up at him through my lashes and he grins lazily, his hair sleep mussed and his eyes dark.

"Good morning, Mr Chase," I say around his cock and flash him a wink. He chuckles softly, as I continue to bob my head up and down, taking him further into my mouth.

"Good morning to you too, *Jesus fucking Christ,* your mouth feels so good."

He grunts, as I lick and suck his length and I can feel his cock twitching with his pending release. I cup his heavy sacs in my hand, and he bucks his hips up, causing me to gag, but I don't stop. I look up at him, his thrown back in pure unadulterated ecstasy. He fists my hair in his hand; the pleasure mixed with pain makes me wet with want and I rub my thighs together to create a friction. *I need him inside me again.*

"FUCCCKKK!" he barks, my mouth sliding down on his entire length, taking him to the hilt.

*"SHIT!* I'm going to come! *FUCK!* Zeppelin! I'm going to come! FUCKING HELLLLL!"

He breathing quickens and I continue sucking, as he spurts his seed into my mouth, yelling and jerking, shuddering out his release. I swallow every drop and lick my lips; a satisfied grin spreads across my face. He opens his eyes and the look on his handsome face floors me right there.

"Wow! That was one hell of a wakeup call!"

We both laugh. *Oh yes, it was indeed.*

# 37

## Zeppelin

The weeks and months that followed, we spent as much time getting to know each other and we made love on a nightly basis. We were closer than we had ever been, I couldn't help but think it was a little too perfect, but I had pushed that thought to the back of my mind and was enjoying every stolen moment I could with Jax. Brody had been transferred to a private hospital and was still in a coma, they were becoming less hopeful as the days went on that he would come through it.

Jax was still filming 'UK's Finest' and he was down to his final act, the young woman, Noa Vega. She was exceptional and I had been secretly rooting for her ever since that first time I had witnessed her first audition. The past few months we had spent at my apartment, never at Jax's house in Chislehurst in Kent. It hurt, but I understood his reasons why, he didn't want to introduce me to his daughter as his girlfriend, not yet. But tonight was the night, he was taking me back to his house and I couldn't be happier.

I was stood at the side of the stage, waiting for him to finish up filming. I mostly kept to myself because I felt oddly out of place, after spending some time in the spotlight previously with Abel, I had gotten used to being an ordinary woman again. The last few months, we were careful not to be seen out in public together and so far, it had been a success. I'm standing at the side of the stage wearing a pair of dark blue dungarees, white Converse and a white t-shirt underneath. My hair was styled in loose waves and secured in a navy headband.

"Hey." A soft American voice startles me from my reverie. I turn to see who it is, and I'm greeted by a six feet three-inch male. His hair is light brown, almost blonde and styled into a fauxhawk, shaved at the sides. His lightly stubbled jaw made him look ruggedly handsome. His tan is golden, his physique ripped, and his hips narrow. Like Jax, he is covered in tattoos with full sleeves. He is wearing black ripped skinny jeans, a plain black vest, a denim jacket and black biker boots. The diamond earring in his ear glints, as the stage light hits it and he cocks his head to the side, regarding me intently. His face looks oddly familiar, but I couldn't place where I had seen him before.

"You must be the famous Zeppelin?" he says with a playful tone to his American drawl, as he chews some gum. I find myself smiling right along with him.

"Your deduction skills are exceptional; you would be quite correct!" I quip and he chuckles softly, offering me his tattooed hand.

"Lucas, but you can call me Luke. I'd like to say I've heard a lot about you, but I'd be lying!" he states wryly and I take his offered hand. *Ah, this must be the famous Lucas Landon, drummer in Rancid Vengeance and Jack's best friend.*

"Zeppelin, officially, it's a pleasure to finally meet you, Luke," I say genuinely, instantly feeling comfortable and at ease in his presence.

"I hope you don't think I'm talking out of turn, but you're good for him, you know," he says matter-of-factly and his statement takes me aback. His jaw going ten to the dozen chewing his gum. He narrows his eyes briefly and regards me intently for a few minutes, but it doesn't feel awkward or uncomfortable, his presence is calming.

"Sorry, I don't mean to be rude, but I'm just good at reading people, he's got his sparkle back, before you came along, he was... dead behind the eyes."

He makes an elaborate gesture with his hand, and I don't know what to say. I'm rendered speechless by this man stood in front of me.

"You're probably thinking I'm some sort of weirdo and I have no right judging your relationship, but he's special, he's...he's my family, after everything he's been through, he deserves some happiness."

There is a melancholic tone to his voice, and it makes my heart hurt for him. There must be more to his relationship with Jax than I'm yet to discover. I'm about to speak again when we're joined by Jax.

"Hey Luke, how ya doing, man? Everything good, yeah?"

Luke nods and smiles.

"Yeah, all good."

Jax looks between us and narrows his eyes on Luke.

"I see you've met Zeppelin?"

Luke laughs and slaps Jax on the back.

"Don't worry, I haven't let out your deepest darkest secrets...yet!"

He flashes Jax a wink and I find myself smiling at their easy, friendly banter.

"Don't sweat it, man, it's all good! I like her!" Luke states enthusiastically and Jax rolls his eyes.

"Go on, fuck off! Noa is waiting backstage for you."

Luke's expression changes and his jaw tightens, but he doesn't say another word as he turns to leave. I cock my eyebrow and Jax shakes his head, leaning a little further into me, his arm braced on the wall.

"So, now I've got you all to myself, what to do with you."

He smirks wickedly, as I silently pushed my fingers through his long hair and held him in place. It was one of those rare moments that even though the world was carrying on around us, it felt like it was just him and me, frozen in time.

Backstage was shrouded in shadow, but I could see his profile backlit by the bright stage lights. I allowed my greedy eyes to roam over his features hungrily, as if committing every part of him to memory. He was beautiful, his jaw deep set and sharp, his nose slightly crooked, his cupids bow prominent and his lips thin but slightly parted. His imperfections remind me that despite the fact that he was a world-famous guitarist in a rock band, he was still human.

I had fallen for him hard, and I didn't regret a single second of it. He was my second chance at righting the wrongs of the past and healing my heart in the process. He was...everything and even though it was early days, I knew deep down I wanted a future with him.

I press my lips to the hollow of his throat and breathe him in. He smells of Diesel Only the Brave and something uniquely Jackson Chase. As my lips explore his throat, I feel him growl against me and thrust his hips into my lower abdomen. I feel his erection, hard, I move my hand down to cup him and he lets out a long groan.

*"Jesus fucking Christ!* I wish we could just get out of here, so I can fuck you like I need to, but I don't know how long I'm going to be."

His voice guttural and so full of wicked promise it made the throb between my thighs almost violent.

"I'm a patient woman, Mr Chase, I can wait for you to ravish me, as long as you make it worth my while."

I flash him a cheeky wink and he presses his forehead to mine, moving us until my back collides with the wall.

"You drive a hard bargain, Miss Williams, however, I'm sure I can meet your... demands!"

He moves his lips to my neck, and those kisses started a fire within me that no one else could ever ignite. The tickle of his beard caused my whole body to erupt with goosebumps, as his hand slips into my hair and the other hand holds my hip with a firm pressure. He nips, hot and hungry at my neck, his touch electrifying every nerve in my body.

"Oh God, Jack!" I let out a soft moan.

"Shhh, I'll take care of you."

He moves his hand to the side opening of my dungarees and reaches for the waistband of my pants.

"Jack," I warn.

"What if someone sees us?"

He smirks.

"You need to be quiet, but trust me, relax, I've got you," he reassures me softly and I don't stop him; I'm too far gone. He moves his hand further into my pants, as his fingers gently tease my slick, aching folds. I'm silently begging for his fingers to touch me, and he slides a long, calloused finger inside me, and I moan with pleasure. We are tucked in a dark area between the stage and the dressing rooms, I can hear people rushing around, but I pay no attention. All I'm focused on is the pleasure he is bestowing upon me.

"Shhh, you're going to have to be quiet, sweetheart," he whispers and I'm trembling against him with white-hot desire.

"Oh, God, Jack!"

I bite down on my lip, as he lazily slides his finger in and out of my wet pussy while I whimper. My head thrown back against the wall. To any by passers, we just look like we're a couple, sharing a warm embrace.

"*Fuck*, Zeppelin, you feel so good."

He strokes my nub in deliberate slow circles, and I try desperately not to let out a long moan of pleasure. I gasp as he plunges two fingers deep inside me and I can't help the cry of pure pleasure at the feel of him deftly twisting his calloused fingers in and out of my soaking wet heat. He places his other hand over my mouth, as he increases his pace with each measured movement, finger fucking me thoroughly and driving me towards my release. My breath is coming in short, sharp bursts, as he quickens his momentum, moaning softly around his hand at my orgasm building deep within me. I feel the familiar flutters of my pending orgasm and my pussy floods as he continues punishing thrusts of his two fingers inside me, every nerve in my body tuned into Jackson Chase.

"I've got you; your pussy is so wet for me; I want you to come. Come hard for me, Zeppelin."

With a few more expert twists of his calloused fingers, the first hard tremor of my orgasm hits me like an earthquake. My breath coming out in sharp, urgent gasps, as I cry out around his hand. He milks every ounce of my release from me, leaving me a desperate mess of want, my legs buckling beneath me. He catches me easily and I cling to him, as he snakes his arms around me, pulling me against him to stop me from falling.

"JACKSON! JAX! WHERE'S JAX? HE'S NEEDED ON SET! JAX!"

Our moment is interrupted by the sound of Rancid Vengeance's manager M.J impatiently calling his name. Jax sucks my juices from his long finger, and it takes everything in me not to moan out loud at the erotic sight.

"Duty calls, beautiful!"

He pulls his finger from his mouth with a pop and flashes me one of his signature grins that I love so much and leaves me wanting more. *So much fucking more.* But good things come to those who wait, right?

# 38

## Zeppelin

It was silent on the journey to Jax's house in Chislehurst, Kent. I was stuck in my own head at the thought of meeting his daughter properly. It was the first time I was being introduced to Thea Chase as her daddy's girlfriend. I was nervous to say the least, I was sick to my stomach, and I was fully aware that it could cause an issue between us if she didn't like me.

On the approach to the large looming black gates, I was reminded of how different our lives were. This was beyond luxury, all four members of Rancid Vengeance lived-in purpose-built properties in Chislehurst, Kent. The land surrounding it was at least twelve acres, and they all lived in ten-bedroom mansions in a very private and heavily guarded gated community, aptly named '*Vengeance Estates.*' The houses are built in a spacious semi-circle, and they all live in close proximity to each other. As we pull up in the circular, gravelled driveway with a large fountain in the centre, I look up at the house in awe. *Wow, it really is worlds away from my tiny apartment in Notting Hill.* The house looks like a large, rustic, grey brick farmhouse, with large sash windows and a navy-blue wooden door. The steps leading up to the property are grey stone and as the car comes to a halt, Jax reaches for my hand.

"Don't look so nervous, sweetheart, Thea's going to love you!" he says with a beaming grin, as he lifts my hand up to his lips and places a kiss on the back.

"What if she hates me, Jack?"

He turns to me, his thumb stroking my hand softly.

"She won't hate you; I promise. Plus, she's three years old, I don't think she knows how to hate!"

I wanted so desperately to believe his words of reassurance, but I couldn't help but feel she was going to think I'm trying to replace her mother. I tried to push that thought to the back of my mind, as Jax gets out of the car and comes around to my side to open the door. He helps me out of the car, kicks the passenger door shut with his boot and takes my hand in his, leading me up the steps and into the house.

*** 

As I step inside, the large marble floored foyer is flooded with light. The house is modern, open plan and the large living space has light grey walls with dark slate grey accents. A large dark grey L-shaped sofa dominates the space, as does a large TV mounted on the wall with glossy grey cabinets either side and underneath. The walls are adorned with pictures of Jax and Thea, there is a picture of Jax with a striking, dark-haired woman, she is beautiful. She's smiling wide and they both look so happy and carefree; I assume the woman is Ruby. My heart slams against my rib cage and that pang of jealousy rears its ugly head. I know I shouldn't be feeling this way, but I can't help feeling inferior to the woman in the photo.

"Welcome, make yourself at home." Jax's voice interrupts my thoughts, which I'm grateful for and I flash him a reassuring smile. I hear idle chatter coming from the kitchen, followed by the sound of tiny footsteps approaching.

"Daddy!" Thea squeals, running full pelt at Jax and he catches her easily in his arms, swinging her up.

"Hey, Princess! Daddy's missed you!"

He beams and covers her face in kisses, causing her to giggle girlishly. It's adorable to watch their interaction and I can't help but grin as I observe them.

"Thea, daddy wants you to meet someone," he says softly as she turns towards me. She has pale skin, bright, wide, inquisitive hazel eyes and her short dark brown hair frames her face. She is the image of the woman in the photograph; she is wearing blue jeans and a pink Rancid Vengeance t-shirt.

"Thea, this is daddy's girlfriend, Zeppelin, you met her before, remember?"

She nods, twirling her hair around her finger.

"Hey Thea, it's really lovely to meet you, your daddy has told me lots about you," I tell her and she smiles shyly.

"Zeppe-lin, see I 'membered," she babbles and I look at Jax, as he laughs.

"Yes, you did, good girl! She's daddy's new girlfriend, is that ok with you?"

She pauses for a few moments and then she nods, wriggling for Jax to let her down. He sets her on her feet, and I let out the breath I didn't realise I was holding. She runs towards me and comes to a halt in front of me, I drop my bag, as she regards me intently with those inquisitive eyes, before she holds her arms out for me to pick her up. I lift her into my arms, and she wraps her arms around my neck.

"I'll be right back."

Jax flashes me a reassuring wink, as he heads up the stairs leaving us alone. When Jax is out of sight, she looks up at me, with her finger in her mouth.

"Are you going to be my new mummy?" she asks and the tone of her small voice breaks my heart. I swallow back the lump in my throat, before I answer her.

"No, sweetheart. No one will ever replace your mummy, but we can be best girls, if you want to?" I say, to placate her and she grins, removing her finger from her mouth.

"Like me and Aunty Peyton?"

I nod and she mirrors my action enthusiastically. In that moment, I had once contemplated having kids with Abel, but neither of us were equipped emotionally to handle raising a child. We were young, stupid and didn't have the first clue on what it would take physically and mentally to be parents. But with this little girl in my arms, she gave me hope that one day, me and Jack would give her a brother or sister and that thought warmed my heart.

We spent the rest of the evening eating takeaway pizza, watching Disney films, laughing and enjoying each other's company. I was lying on the sofa wrapped in Jax's arms and Thea had fallen asleep in his lap.

"I think tonight's been a success, Thea loves you!"

He laughs and I find myself smiling right along with him.

"She's adorable, I was terrified she was going to hate me!" I admit and he places a kiss on my forehead.

"That was never going to happen, look, I need to put her to bed and then we can finish what we started earlier." His voice is low and gruff, as he shifts, lifting her into his arms and taking her up the stairs.

He's gone for a few long minutes and when he joins me again, he's shirtless and wearing a pair of grey jogging bottoms which hang low on his lean hips, revealing the deep set 'V'. I lick my lips at the sight of him. He moves closer to me, and I can feel his warm breath gust out against my face as I take in his devastating, savage beauty. From his model-worthy, God-like features to the defined set of his tattooed biceps. His dark eyes are hooded and blazing with white hot lust, as he cups my breast in his large hand, ghosting his finger across my nipple, and I bite my lip, softly mewling.

"Jack." His name is a plea on my lips.

"Your pleasure is all mine tonight, Zeppelin, I'm going to take you right to the edge until you're begging for your orgasm, I want you to know that it's just you, you own me, you own my pleasure, you own my fucking heart."

His voice sounds thick with emotion, as I reach out to stroke his cheek. He leans into my touch and places his hand on mine.

"You captured my heart from the very first words, Jack."

He climbs on the sofa and lays me down beneath him. Heat blossoms through me, the throbbing between my thighs is almost unbearable.

"I need you naked, Zeppelin. Now."

He commands and I do as I'm bid, unbuttoning my dungarees. Our moment is interrupted by his phone vibrating on the table in front of the sofa. He looks over at the screen and leaps ungraciously off the sofa.

"*Shit*, I have to get this, babe, I'm sorry."

He picks up the phone and puts it to his ear. I can't help the disappointment that washes over me, as I observe him pacing up and down the living room.

"Hey... yeah... yeah, oh shit, okay, erm... yeah... hmm... I'm on my way. Thanks, love... I'll be straight there... okay, see you soon, bye."

He hangs up the phone and I'm unprepared for his next words.

"Brody's awake."

# 39

## Jax

After three months of hoping and praying Brody would come around from his coma, our prayers were finally answered. I didn't know how to feel when Peyton called me to tell me the news, and I felt like an awful human being for even thinking it. I drove to the hospital on autopilot, leaving Zeppelin to stay with Thea. The journey there had me feeling all sorts of edgy, I hated hospitals. I was aware my fear was irrational, but the innate fear of hospitals was a dark presence at the edge of my peripheral vision. The closer I got to my destination, the acid rose in my throat, my stomach roiled and my hands clammy on the steering wheel. My fight or flight instinct was strong, the adrenaline coursing through every nerve in my body gave me the energy and strength I needed to face my fear head on. But the unease that crept its way up into my subconsciousness felt like I was drowning and desperately gasping for air. As the building comes into view, my head spins, as the noose I had been running from all this time had tightened and I felt like I was being strangled. I claw at my throat one handed, as I swerve to avoid oncoming traffic, the car horns instantly snapping me out of it. I screech to a halt at the kerb outside Weymouth Street Hospital, the private hospital that Brody was moved to when he was put into a medically induced coma to allow his brain and his body to heal.

The entrance is full of paparazzi and journalists. *For fucks sake.* They heckle and cat call to me, the cacophony of excitable chatter, as I step out of my Jaguar F-Pace. I press the key fob to lock the door, and a heavy-set journalist leaps out of nowhere, blocking my path.

"Jax! Is it true Brody's awake?"

I am momentarily blinded by the wild flashing of the flashbulbs and the *'click, click'* of the camera shutters sets my nerves on edge. I'm fully aware I'm vulnerable without security protection.

"Jax! Is Brody the father of Raleigh Storm's baby? Or is the baby a product of a one-night stand with Carter Leonard?"

The incessant questions cause me to clench my jaw and my heartbeat start to quicken. *Fuck my life, not again.*

"Jax!"

I look up to see two of our security team and relief washes over me, my heartbeat returning to its normal speed. Kai and Trey push their way through the throng of paparazzi wearing their signature Men in Black suits and earpieces. Kai grabs my arm and Trey touches his ear.

"Yes, boss, we've retrieved Chase." His voice is low and clipped, as Kai pulls me through the crowd and escorts me into the hospital reception area. I let out the breath I didn't realise I was holding, and I look up at him, grateful for their intervention.

"Cheers, man," I say gratefully and Kai nods curtly.

"Anytime."

I'm flanked by Kai and Trey, as we make our way silently up to Brody's room. Unexpectedly, I see Sam fly out of Brody's room.

"MOTHERFUCKER!" he yells, pounding his fist repeatedly into the coffee machine, as I approach.

"FUCKING COCKSUCKER!"

He runs his hand savagely through his dark hair, his other hand grazed and bloody.

"Sam? You good, mate?" I ask cautiously and he looks at me but doesn't say anything for long moments. His nostrils flared and his broad shoulders heaving.

"You're bleeding," I say and he hangs his head, ignoring my statement.

"He doesn't have a fucking clue what he's done, Jax. He's put every single one of us through absolute hell these past three months and he doesn't give a shit! He's so blasé about the whole thing, acting like everything's normal, when it's so far from fucking normal! I'm so fucking angry with him; he could have died!" he grinds out through gritted teeth, his voice gruff.

"He doesn't seem to comprehend that there are fucking consequences for his stupidity! I can't be around him right now! This could have ended so differently, but he's alive and I'm truly grateful to whoever for that, I really am. After everything we've been through, after all the people we've lost."

The tone of his voice sets me on high alert, as he starts pacing and running his hands through his hair. I think he's in the tight grip of another episode, but I don't say anything. *Not out loud at least.*

"This is Brody we're talking about; his actions never have fucking consequences because we've enabled him over the years, again and again! We've been part of the lies, the cover-ups after every rehab stint, after every relapse, how many more times can we wipe his arse, Sam! How many more times before we say enough is enough! I know you two are close, but come on, wake up and smell the coffee! He's a law unto himself! He's a God Damn train wreck!"

I raise my voice a few decibels louder than necessary to get my point across.

"I'm not a fucking idiot! Don't you think I know that? After every relapse, I'm terrified that that's going to be it, game over. He's got no one else, Jax, we're all he's got."

I scrub my hand down my face.

"Stop making fucking excuses for him, Sam! For Christ's sake!" I say through clenched teeth and Sam leans his head on the coffee machine, his arm braced above him.

"I'm so fucking tired, Jax. We've had three months to rest and pursue other projects while he's been in a coma, but I'm exhausted."

He sounds defeated, but as I move closer to him, we're interrupted by Raleigh flying out of the room. The noise of the door banging against the wall echoing around us. She's sobbing and she walks straight into Sam's arms, he wraps his arms around her. The sound of her gut-wrenching sobs, as she clings to Sam for dear life.

In the months since Brody and Raleigh have been together, Raleigh and Sam have developed a blossoming, unbreakable bond, mirroring that of Peyton and Brody. He has supported her through the past three months and she's now five months pregnant with twins.

"Hey." Sam's voice is husky, as he tilts her chin up to face him. He towers over her, and she has to crane her neck to look up at him. I observe their exchange with rapt attentiveness, feeling my phone vibrating in my pocket, but I ignore it.

"Sweetheart, look at me."

Sam wipes the tears from her eyes with the pad of his thumb, and she sniffs.

"I spent every day by his bedside, praying to anyone who'd listen for him to wake up. I've wanted this for so long and now I've finally got it, I don't know what to do, or how to feel. Does that make me a bad person? Oh God! It does, doesn't it?"

She bursts into floods of uncontrollable tears, as Sam pulls her into his chest and he flashes me a look. I nod curtly, pulling my phone out of my pocket, seeing I have a missed call from Zeppelin. I swipe the screen to life and dial her number. She answers on the third ring.

"Hey, is everything okay?" I ask softly, suddenly uber aware of my surroundings.

"Hey yourself, yeah everything's fine, Thea woke up asking for you, but I managed to settle her, and she's fallen back to sleep. I just wanted to check everything was ok. You left kind of abruptly, is Brody okay?"

Her voice laced with concern, and I take a deep breath.

"Thanks for settling Thea back down, and yeah, he's doing fine, as far as I know, I haven't been in to see him yet, part of me doesn't want to after what he's put us through. But I'll be home soon; I feel terrible for just rushing off like that," I admit and she chuckles softly.

"Well, you better get back here and make it up to me then, Mr Chase."

Her voice low and seductive, I find myself smiling at her words.

"I'll be home soon, sweetheart."

"I'll be waiting, naked in your bed," I growl, adjusting myself in my boxer shorts.

"What the fuck are you doing to me, Zeppelin?"

Sam looks up and cocks his pierced eyebrow at me, as I clear my throat, turning away from his watchful gaze.

"Look, I have to go, sweetheart. I'll call you when I'm on the way home, see you soon, bye."

We say our goodbyes and I hang up the phone, spinning around to see Sam leaning against the wall with his hand tucked casually into his pocket.

"Something you want to tell me?" he says with an amused tone to his voice, and I sigh.

"I left Zeppelin with Thea at my place... fuck, she's..."

I puff out my cheeks, not knowing the right words to say to describe the depth of feeling I feel for Zeppelin.

"She's like that oasis in the desert when I'm dying of thirst, she's like the life raft when I feel like I'm drowning in grief... I feel like it's time to move on from Ruby and she's the woman I want to move on with. She's so different from Ruby, she's the complete polar opposite and it's new, it's exciting and... refreshing," I admit shamelessly and Sam regards me intently.

"I'm so happy for you, man, I know how difficult it's been for you, for all of us. Losing Ruby was hard on all of us, I can't imagine what it's been like for you, but if anyone deserves to be happy, it's you."

His gruff voice full of sincerity and I smile at the sentiment.

"Thanks, mate, that means a lot," I say genuinely, as Sam slaps me on the back.

"So, when do we get to meet this blonde bombshell who's ensnared the boy next door?"

I roll my eyes and we both laugh.

"Soon," I promise and he nods.

"Now, fuck off, go home to her, I'll call you if anything changes."

He flashes me a wink and I turn to leave, firing off a quick text to Zeppelin letting her know I'm on the way home. Optimistic that this new chapter is going to be a good one, even if it doesn't include Ruby Logan.

# 40

## Zeppelin

I was unapologetic of my feelings for Jackson Chase because for the first time in five years, I didn't need to hide who I was around him. I didn't need to beg for his attention, I didn't need to change my appearance to suit his image, and I didn't need constant reassurance because I was the one he was inevitably coming home to. I was no longer that needy, immature, attention seeking young girl who was obsessed with keeping up appearances. I was a mature adult who didn't need her feelings validated anymore because Jax wasn't Abel Creed.

I was at Jax's ten-bedroom mansion in Chislehurst, Kent, lying in his King size bed naked, anticipating his return. The thought of his lean, naked, tattooed body pressed against me, incapacitated me where I lay. I trembled with nerves as I waited, my nipples puckered into hard, erect buds and my pussy oozed moisture. He had been gone most of the night and I had about three hours of sleep, but I wanted him with a fierce passion. The sun had come up a while ago and I prayed Thea would stay asleep long enough for me to fulfil a deep-seated need.

I'm not sure how much time passes, but I hear the sound of a car crunching across the gravel, and I swallowed hard, positioning myself in the middle of the bed and fluffing my hair. I wasn't what you would call body confident, I was comfortable in my own skin, but my insecurities stemmed from my scars across my back from a time in my life I would rather forget. I hadn't been naked in front of a man that wasn't Rian in five years before Jack and I was still trying to get used to it. It was hard for me at first and that's why I felt the need to do this for not only him, but for me as well. It empowered me in a way it never had before and it was me taking back that small, but significant piece of me I lost that day.

I hear the door click shut and the sound of footsteps coming up the stairs. My heartbeat quickens with each step he took, each one of my senses on high alert. I hear a soft click of the open and close of a door and I'm acutely aware of the moment he opens the door to his bedroom. His breath catches, as his eyes land on me completely naked in his bed.

*"Jesus fucking Christ,"* he mutters, his eyes roaming over my naked form, hungry and lust filled. He comes to a halt at the foot of the bed and watches me carefully for a few precious moments.

"So fucking beautiful," he grinds out, the outline of his erection on his jeans straining against the zip. His gaze intense, as he wordlessly starts to undress. He's stood before me gloriously naked in record time and I lick my lips at the sight. I desperately try to maintain my composure, but as soon as he climbs on the bed, I tackle him, pushing him down so he's lying beneath me.

I mount him at a reverse angle, so my pussy is directly over his mouth, as I face the headboard and press my wetness against his face. I grind against him, and he responds by taking my engorged bud into his mouth and sucking it, then licking, repeating the motion over and over again. I moan long and loud, as I grind harder against his mouth, his pace increasing and my hips bucking downward, creating a rhythm to match his expert tongue. It takes every modicum of control for me not to grind too hard against him, I didn't want him to suffocate.

"Oh God! Jack!"

I feel my juices running over his chin, as I move backwards, straddling his hips and lowering myself over his waiting cock. His cock was pulsing as my warmth enveloped him and gripped him tightly. A simultaneous intake of breath from both of us fills the room, as he pushes his hips up to meet me. He pushes into me so deep my eyes start to water, but I don't stop.

*"Jesus Christ*, Zeppelin, you feel so fucking good!" he hisses, as I continue to ride him, the motion rhythmic, but becoming more and more desperate with each rise and fall onto his steel erection. He moves his hands up to grip my hips to control the pace, my orgasm building, my body begging for release.

"THAT'S IT, JACK, FUCK! MAKE ME COME, JACK! PLEASE MAKE ME COME!" I yell, trembling against him, desperate to come. He reaches down, his thumb finding my swollen clit, circling it slowly, as my orgasm tears through me like an explosion of pleasure behind my eyes and I see stars.

"JACK! I'M COMING! I'M COMING! OH GOD! FUCK! I'M COMING! JACK!" I scream his name, as he grunts his release and he tenses beneath me. His breathing hitching, as he comes long and hard. The pulsing of his cock forcing his hot seed to coat my insides and I was fully aware that we hadn't used a condom again, but I was too caught up in the moment to care. I climb off him, feeling the warmth of his release to run down my inner thighs. I lay down next to him and he pulls me into him, wrapping his arm around me. He presses a soft, tender kiss to my forehead.

"That was one hell of a greeting!"

We both chuckle softly.

"I aim to please."

I flash him a cheeky wink, as he gets up and walks into the bathroom, leaving me bereft at the loss of contact. He returns a few minutes later with a warm flannel and gently cleans me up. I find myself smiling at his care and thoughtfulness. Once he's finished, he returns the cloth to the bathroom and settles himself back down next to me, tucking us both underneath the covers. I fall asleep deep in the knowledge that I was fiercely in love with Jax Chase, and I had no doubt in my head that the feeling was reciprocated.

*** 

I wake with a start to an empty bed and stretch out like a cat, a beaming grin spreading across my face.

"Ah, there's my favourite smile."

My eyes land on Jax, freshly showered, a towel wrapped around his lean waist and rivulets of water beading on his tattooed chest, his blonde hair damp.

"Good morning, my beautiful girl."

My heart melts at his words and I chuckle softly.

"Good morning, my handsome rock star."

I greet him with a wink, and he laughs, as he pads across the carpeted floor bare foot. He sounds so boyish and so carefree when he laughs. He doesn't do it often enough, I muse, while admiring his fine physique.

"Thea's with Marnie, Freddie and Zach for the day, tonight is the finale of UK's Finest. I have a hectic day ahead, my schedules pretty packed, but you're more than welcome to come hang out at the studio?" he asks expectantly and I smile at his thoughtfulness. *He really is perfect in every way.*

"As exciting as that sounds, I've been neglecting Rian and Jericho, I should go home and spend some time with them."

He nods.

"I've had your names put on the V.I.P list for the finale, you're more than welcome to bring Rian along."

He moves closer to the bed and plants a tender kiss on my lips. In a lithe move, I rip the towel away from his waist and yank him down to the bed, allowing ourselves to indulge in one more passion filled session before I'm tossed back down to earth with a thud.

On the way home, my phone constantly vibrates in my bag, Rian's name flashing up on the screen. I cut him off each time he calls. I'm in the car with one of Rancid Vengeance's security team, Kai. He has blonde hair shaved close to his head, deep, piercing indigo eyes, and at least three days' worth of rough, blonde stubble on his chin. He is at least six feet seven inches tall with broad shoulders, narrow hips, and he is extremely muscular. He is wearing an expensive black suit, tailored perfectly to fit his large frame, consisting of a white shirt, black tie, black trousers and a black jacket that stretches across his impressive ample shoulders. I allow myself to admire his profile as I sit in the front passenger seat, he's extremely friendly and easy to talk to. We idly chatter the whole way home about anything and everything, a sense of dread settling in the pit of my stomach, as we pull up outside my apartment building. I say my thanks to Kai for the lift and head upstairs, greeted by Rian pacing up and down the corridor outside my place.

"There you are! Where the fuck have you been!"

He throws his arms up the air in despair, his usually neat hair dishevelled, and he looks a little less put together than usual. His grey jogging bottoms hanging off his narrow hips and his white t-shirt crinkled.

"You know where I've been, babe!" I state incredulously with a sigh, exasperated at his unnecessary and irrational behaviour.

"Yeah, too busy being banged by your fuck boy to notice anything or anyone fucking else in your life! This isn't you, Zeppelin!" he blurts out, a venomous tone to his voice. My mouth drops open at his crass statement, as I lash my hand across his cheek.

"How fucking dare you! I've finally met someone I want to actually spend time with, in real life, might I add! Anyway, you didn't give a shit about me when you were getting your needs met by some random! What's the matter, Rian? Did he finally see you for who you really are and dump you?"

His mouth opens and closes at my blatant insult, aware that I'm being a bitch, but how dare he accuse me like that. I move around him and unlock the door to my apartment, Jericho jumping up at me as soon as I enter my apartment.

"Hey buddy, I've missed you too! Has Rian been looking after you?" I coo, petting his head and fussing him. Rian stomps in behind me and slams the door, Jericho starts barking and growling at the loud noise.

"Hey, it's okay, I'm here now," I soothe Jericho softly and Rian spins around to face me.

"Yes! The answer's yes! Danny fucking dumped me! Are you happy now? I fucking needed you and you were nowhere to be found, Zeppelin! I needed a shoulder to cry on! He broke my fucking heart, and I needed you!"

He bursts into uncontrollable floods of tears, and I throw my arms around him, suddenly feeling like an awful human being for abandoning my only friend in his hour of need.

I spend long minutes comforting him, listening to his gut-wrenching, soul-destroying sobs makes my heart hurt for my best friend. We spend the rest of the morning siting crossed legged in the middle of the living room, eating breakfast consisting of Eggs Benedict, with bacon, drinking copious amounts of coffee and catching up on what's been going on in our lives the past weeks. After a lot of laughing, crying and everything in between, it's like our disagreement never happened. Our gossiping session is interrupted by a sharp rap on the door. Rian cocks his perfectly plucked eyebrow at me, taking a small sip of his coffee.

"Are you expecting someone baby girl?"

I shake my head curious to who could be at the door. I get up and make my way over to the door, opening it tentatively. I'm greeted by a bored looking courier wearing a red jacket and black wireless ear buds. His jaw chewing gum loudly and furiously, he offers me an electronic device.

"Sign here." His voice is flat, I sign his device and hands me a large white box, wrapped with a black ribbon. I take it and kick the door closed with my bare foot. Rian claps his hands excitedly.

"Yaaaayy! I love surprises!" he says in a singsong voice, as I lay it down on the sofa and begin to unwrap the ribbon. I'm stunned into silence as I lift the tissue paper, my mouth agape. I pull the beautiful red dress from the confines of the box and hold it up. It's a long, red strapless gown with silk roses across the neckline. It's gorgeous, a black box falls out and I pick it up. I open the velvet box, and I gasp at the platinum necklace with a matching red ruby, encrusted with diamonds. It reminds me of the 'Heart of the Ocean' from Titanic, but the red version. Rian wolf whistles.

"Fuck me, he's got amazing taste for a rock star."

I stick my tongue out at him, and he laughs.

"Please tell me I can be your best man at the wedding!" he squeals and I roll my eyes.

"Let's not get carried away, Ri!" I say with a nervous laugh, and he scoffs.

"If that isn't the man you're going to marry, you're even more deluded than I thought! I know I acted like a jealous lover in the beginning, but that was only because I fucking care about you, Zeppelin, I love you! You're my best friend, I just want you to be happy, and it looks like Handsome Jack makes you happy. Any man that puts a smile on your beautiful face has my vote!"

He plants a kiss on my forehead.

"Sooo, are we going to make ourselves look fabulous for our moment in the spotlight, or what?"

He strokes his chin and the answer to that question is hell yes!

# 41

## Zeppelin

As I study myself carefully in the large square mirror and I notice my eyes have their familiar sparkle back, I'm the happiest I've been in five long years. I'm finally content with my life and I'm hopelessly in love with Jackson Chase. My smile is genuine, as stare at my reflection in the mirror while sitting at my white gloss dressing table, applying some red lipstick. My blonde hair expertly styled by Rian into soft waves, I feel fabulous, and I look a million dollars. The red dress hugging my curves and accentuating my figure, the ruby necklace sitting at my throat sparkling and glinting proudly in the light.

"*Fucking hell,* you look... *shit,* I'm speechless, baby girl!"

Rian's voice full of praise, as Jericho circles me, letting out a single bark to let me know he too approves of the way I look tonight.

I straighten and smooth out my dress, the dress' plunging neckline makes my boobs look amazing and I feel confident. Rian and me spent the rest of the day pampering and preparing for the finale of UK's Finest. Jax's final act, Noa Vega was in the final and I was so happy that she made it. After watching her blossom from that shy girl, into a confident powerhouse, I had my fingers crossed that she was going to win. I look up at Rian, he is wearing a black suit, consisting of a black silk shirt, a black blazer with elaborate feathers on the shoulders, black skinny jeans that look like they have been sprayed on and black sparkly loafers. His eye make-up is dark and dramatic, his hair styled into a neat, back combed quiff. He reminds me of Adam Lambert, and I smile to myself at the comparison. Rian offers me his arm as the door knocks and I take it, grabbing my clutch bag on the way. I swing the door open, and I'm greeted by Kai, he salutes coolly. We head out, ready to face the world as Jackson Chase's girlfriend.

***

I step out of the black Bentley to blinding camera flashes, it sets my nerves on edge, and I know now how Jax must feel living his life in the glare of the paparazzi's lens. Rian steps out behind me and places his hand at the small of my back, it instantly calms my racing heart.

"I got you, baby girl," he whispers so only I can hear him, and we pose on the red carpet for the eager photographers, the click, click of the shutters and the loud cacophony of the press calling out to us.

"Is it true that you're Jax Chase's new girlfriend?"

My heartbeat starts to accelerate, but I manage to block them out, focusing on putting one foot in front of the other and making my way down the red carpet. Kai is a few steps behind us, his earpiece in place and his sunglasses shielding his eyes. We make our way into the large, modern glass building that houses the TV studio, it is filled with people. I recognise a few familiar TV, movie and music stars amongst the crowd, as I have Rian's hand in a death grip.

"*Fucking hell*, I bet you give one hell of a hand job, baby girl!" he quips and I cock my eyebrow at him, flashing him a smile. I turn and that's when I spot Jax, he is wearing a black suit, with a black v-neck t-shirt underneath, his neck tattoo looking especially vibrant, his blonde hair styled, and his beard neatly trimmed. He poses for the paparazzi, as if it's second nature to him after years in the spotlight. He's casually standing with one hand tucked in his pocket, but he's acting as if they aren't really there. His brown gaze shifts and land on me, I see his Adam's apple bob as he swallows hard.

"*Fuck,*" he mouths, as he makes his way over to me. Rian nods curtly and steps to the side, leaving us alone.

"*Jesus Christ,* I... I can't get my breath, you look... *fuck*... you look absolutely ravishing. I knew red looked good on you, but holy *shit*..." he says and I find myself blushing at his compliment, both of us acutely aware that the press and paparazzi are observing and analysing our every move. The flashes firing continuously, as he moves his hand to the small of my back. As soon as his hand makes contact, I feel like I'm on fire for him.

"Keep thinking those thoughts." His voice is low and seductive, as I swallow hard. He ushers me towards the entrance to the studio, and I notice he doesn't stop to entertain anyone who tries to get his attention.

"I didn't get to say thank you for the dress and the necklace."

I subconsciously lift my hand to my throat to check if it is still there.

"You're most welcome, call it a late birthday present."

He smiles his devastating smile, tipping my chin up to face him and planting a tender kiss at the corner of my mouth. He leads me into the vestibule of the TV studio; it is a hive of activity. The bright studio lights temporarily blinding me, he leads me through the backstage area and down a short corridor. We come to a stop outside a dressing room door with his name 'Jackson 'Flash' Chase' in big, black, bold letters. He opens the door and gestures for me to step in ahead of him, I walk into the unusually neat dressing room. He follows me inside and shuts the door with a click, as I take in my surroundings.

There is a large, white glossy dressing table, with a huge mirror with bright spherical shaped lights around the edge. There is a white leather chair in front of the table, a rail of men's clothes to the right and a large sofa to the left. There are various make-up and hair products scattered across the table. He pulls up his sleeve and checks his smartwatch. I cock my perfectly plucked eyebrow curiously.

"I'm just trying to figure out how many times I can make you come before I have to be back on set."

His voice rough with pure, pent-up need and my pussy floods at his words. He moves closer to me like a lion stalking his prey, he swipes the make-up and hair products onto the floor, clearing the table with a loud crash. I audibly gasp, as he lifts me effortlessly onto the surface and I feel his warm breath on my cheek. He smells like Diesel Only the Brave, mint and something uniquely Jax Chase.

"Take off your knickers," he whispers against my mouth and presses his lips to mine. His tongue probing mine, as he deepens the kiss. The softness of his lips and the scratch of his beard is a total contrast, as he pushes himself further into me. His erection digging into my lower abdomen and the low rumbling sound he makes, lets me know he's just as turned on as I am. I reach under my dress to take off my black, lacy knickers. I hand them to him; he pulls away from our kiss and he shoves them into his pocket with a wink.

"Lift your dress and spread your legs," he commands and I do as I'm bid, lifting my dress and spreading my legs.

"You look fucking stunning in that dress, as soon as I saw you you made me want you. *Fuck,* Zeppelin, what are you doing to me?"

I'm not sure if the question is rhetorical, but I don't get to answer, as he skates his hand across my bare pussy and shoves his finger into my slick heat.

"*Fuck,* I knew you were wet for me, I can smell your arousal and it's so fucking addictive."

I moan softly, as he builds up a rhythm. I lean my head back against the mirror and let out a moan. I'm burning for him, as he continues to alternate between finger fucking me and stroking my engorged nub.

"I want you to come hard all over my fingers, Zeppelin. Show me how much you want me."

I writhe beneath him, as he introduces a second finger and pushing deeper.

"OH GOD! JACK! FUCK!"

I pant, as his calloused fingers twist deftly inside me, his thumb circling my swollen clit.

"Come hard for me, Zeppelin. That's it, baby, come for me."

His words are my undoing, and I scream as his rhythm increases.

"FUCK! JACK! I'M COMING! OH GOD! JACK! I'M COMING! I'M COMING!"

I find myself panting and moaning impudently for him.

"That's it, I want to watch you come. Come for me, baby. Eyes on me."

My eyes lock with his, silver on brown as my orgasm tears through me. He squeezes every ounce of pleasure from me, and I shiver with tiny aftershocks beneath him.

"Mmmm." I hum my appreciation, and he chuckles softly.

"One," he whispers, as he moves between my legs. I moan long and loud, as his tongue swipes up my sensitive folds.

"OH FUCK, JACK!"

I grab a fistful of his hair and throw my head back in pure ecstasy. His tongue gloriously assaulting my pussy in the most erotic way. I tighten my grip on his hair, as I briefly close my eyes, focusing on the pleasure.

"Oh God, that feels so good. Don't stop, please, don't stop."

My breath comes in short, sharp bursts, as he quickens his momentum, a second orgasm building deep within me. His tongue piercing flicks over my sensitive swollen nub, and I feel the all too familiar flutters. My pussy floods as he continues his punishing lashes.

"I'M GOING TO COME! JACK! OH GOD! JACK! OH GOD! I'M COMING! I'M COMING!"

With one swift brush of his tongue, my orgasm tears through me like an explosion, as wave after wave of pleasure surging through me like a tidal wave. I free his hair from the confines of my fist, and I catch sight of him as he lifts his head up. His hair perfectly mussed and a lust-filled glint in his glittering brown eyes.

"Two," he says with a wicked smirk and in that moment, as I come down from my orgasmic high, I couldn't be more in love with this man.

# 42

## Zeppelin

We made it to six before Jax had to go back on set and I was sore in the most delicious way. He escorted me to my V.I.P seat in the audience, whispering all the wicked things he wanted to do to me once we were alone. I was wound so tightly, I almost thought I'd unravel right there in front of an audience of three thousand people.

The pounding, electronic beat of UK's Finest theme tune blasts through the TV studio, the deafening sound of the crowds screams and rapturous applause, as the judges emerge from a rising podium in the centre of the stage. Phoenix King, the manager of rock band, Devils Henchman emerges in a long, decadent, lacy crimson gown, to match the shade of her hair. She's holding hands with M.J, the music mogul and manager of Rancid Vengeance and Jax. Jax has changed into a black tailored suit, it fits his body as if it were made for. He is wearing a black shirt and a matching black tie with a neon pink skull print, his long blonde hair perfectly styled, and his beard expertly trimmed. Bernie Lomax is standing casually on the other side of Jax with his hand tucked into his pocket. He is wearing an equally as sinful suit, with his trademark Hawaiian shirt, his black spiky hair mussed and his full beard neat. The judges all bow gracefully and make their way down the steps to their seats for the remainder of the show.

The crowd's applause continues, as the show's presenter steps onto the stage. Cynthia Del Rey is a veteran TV presenter. Her bubbly personality and eccentric presenting style is what sets her apart from all the other TV hosts. She is tall, slender, with the skin the colour of espresso. Her long, straight jet-black hair styled into a high ponytail, her lips stained red and her signature gold tooth, as she beams at the audience. Her dark eyes dancing with excitement, she is wearing a short black glittery dress with sky high matching black heels. The audiences' applause dies down, as she moves the microphone up to her mouth to speak.

"Good evening! And a warm, Great British welcome to UK's Finest!"

She tilts her head back and stamps her heels on the stage gleefully. She straightens and continues her introduction.

"After a country wide search and weeks of auditions, it's certainly been a whirlwind and a drama-filled few months. But we've made it to the final, can you believe we're down to the final four contestants!" she says enthusiastically, as the crowd cheers.

"For the first time in UK's Finest history, every judge has an act in the final! So, judges, how does it feel to have made it to the final?" She addresses the judges directly and Jax grins.

"I can't believe we've made it to the final! I'm super excited for tonight! We've got some very special performances coming up and some amazing guest artists!" Jax says with a chuckle and Cynthia laughs. *It isn't just me that's affected by him; he's magnetic and his sweet persona shines through his infamous rock star exterior.*

"What about you, M.J? Are you excited for tonight's' show?"

M.J smiles coolly, his sandy brown hair, with a quirky grey streak and his forest green paisley print suit making him look like the legendary rock star manager that he is.

"Of course, I'm excited, Cynthia! I can't wait to see what all four acts have to offer! They need to step up their game if they want to be in with a shot at being victorious on UK's Finest! As Jax said, we've got some very special, super talented guests to duet with our final four and all I can say is it's going to be a wild ride! Let the show commence!"

M.J says with a bright white smile and the crowd goes wild, as Cynthia steps forward.

"Now, let's welcome our four, super talented finalists!"

All four finalists emerge from the sliding doors at the back of the stage. All four are holding hands and grinning widely, the camaraderie between the four easy and friendly. I can't help thinking that there must be an element of rivalry, as there can be only one winner out of the four contestants.

"Ladies and gentlemen, please welcome onto the stage, Noa!"

Jax stands up for his act and claps enthusiastically. She looks equally as stunning as she did on her first audition and she waves to the audience with a wide grin.

"AJ!"

Bernie stands up, whooping loudly and pounding the air with his fist. "Baylee-Bliss!"

Phoenix stands up and nods curtly at her act, clapping daintily.

"And finally, welcome onto the stage, Chance!"

M.J stands and bows gracefully for his act.

"Ladies and gentlemen, your final four!" Cynthia yells excitedly and the crowd erupts into a rapturous applause.

"Now! For tonight's first finalist! Welcome to the stage Noa!"

A video montage of her time on the show, from her very first audition to her last performance a few short weeks ago. She steps on to the stage, wearing a gypsy style white dress, her hair secured with a white head scarf around her long hair and her feet bare, a nod to her first audition. A piano rises from beneath the stage on a large white podium. Noa gestures praying hands to the audience and she takes her place behind the white glossy baby grand piano. The audience break out into an applause, as she begins to play. The haunting melody filling the venue, as her fingers fly over the keys with grace and expert precision. I recognise the song as 'Still Breathing' by Rancid Vengeance. I watch her with rapt attention, as she leans forward into the microphone.

*"I've been slow dancing with your ghost again. He holds me, oh he holds me like he's barely there. I hold him like he's all I've got, but I'm still breathing, still breathing. Oh, I will wait until all the stars die out, for you, for you, but I'm still breathing."*

As she leads up to the chorus, an impressive guitar solo echoes around the studio and there is a collective gasp from the crowd, as Sam Newbolt steps out onto the stage, flashing Noa an encouraging wink. He casually saunters onto the stage, his fingers moving up and down the fretboard of his custom galaxy Schechter Blackjack, as if he were making love to it. His eyes fixed on her, as he comes to a halt in front of the piano. He is wearing a plain white v-neck t-shirt, stretched over his large, muscular body and showcasing his collection of tattoos. He is also wearing black leather trousers that are so tight they look like they're spray painted on him and black motorcycle boots. His raven black hair is styled into his usual messy spikes; he is clean shaven and without his usual stage make-up of dark eyeliner. His eyes are an intense, sparkling emerald, green under the bright stage lights and I can see why all the women go crazy over him, he is a sight to beholden. He begins to sing with Noa, their voices in perfect harmony.

*"I've been slow dancing with your ghost again. He kisses me, oh he kisses me like he's barely there. Barely there, but I'm still breathing, still breathing. I will wait until the stars die out for you, but I'm still breathing. I count to three, still breathing, our hearts beating now in time. Still breathing, barely breathing..."*

Noa plays an epic piano solo, joined by Sam on electric guitar. The two instruments in sync, as the closing strains of the song fill the auditorium and fades. The crowd erupts into a thunderous applause; the euphoria is palpable. Sam offers his hand to Noa, and she steps out from behind the piano bench, her eyes glossy as she takes a bow, Sam's face breaks out into his signature dimpled grin, and he offers his applause. Jax is on his feet, clapping and pumping his fists. His enthusiasm is infectious, as I join in with the crowd. Cynthia comes onto the stage; she kisses Sam on the cheek and hugs Noa.

"*Wow!* Ladies and gentlemen, please give a warm UK's Finest welcome for Sam Newbolt from Rancid Vengeance!"

The crowd goes wild, cheering, screaming, and stomping their feet. Cynthia laughs and Sam beams, taking a modest bow.

"We have a lot of Rancid Vengeance fans in the audience tonight! Jax, over to you! You must be so proud!"

Jax breaks out into a full-on smile.

"So, so proud right now! I can't stop smiling! Noa, you've completely transformed from your first audition, you were a shy, wallflower who didn't realise how good you were! That's why I wanted you on my team, I saw something in you, I saw your true potential and that right there, is the reason why you're in the final! That was amazing! Literally beyond words! I can't describe what I'm feeling, and I know it's not easy being the first act. I might be biased, but I think you're in with a real shot after that performance!"

The crowd break out into applause.

"Sam, how was that for you? What are your thoughts?"

He moves closer to Noa and slings his arm around her shoulders. His sheer size eclipsing her slight one.

"When Jax asked me to duet with Noa, I said yes instantly. Like Jax, I saw her first audition and it totally blew me away! She's definitely a star in the making, that's why shows like UK's Finest are a platform for talent like this! It was an absolute honour to perform alongside you, sweetheart and I wish you all the luck!"

He kisses her on the cheek, takes one last bow and turns to exit the stage.

"Ladies and gentlemen, give it up one more time for our special guest, Sam Newbolt from Rancid Vengeance!"

As the audience break out into another rapturous applause, I think to myself that I couldn't be happier to share this night with Jax.

# 43

# Zeppelin

After all four acts have performed, there is a short interval while the votes are counted and verified. The lavishly decorated red and gold bar area is a who's who of the TV, movie and music world. I can't help the starstruck look that spreads across my face. Rian chuckles softly, as he hands me a glass of champagne.

"You're such a dork!" he says with a dramatic eye roll, and I take a sip of my drink.

"Isn't that...?"

My words die on my lips, as Rian nudges me and I almost choke on my drink.

"*Good fucking Lord,*" he mutters and I follow his gaze.

"*For fuck's sake,* Ri, you knew there was a possibility he could be here," I grumble, as his eyes land on Danny Debonair and I swallow the rest of my champagne in one mouthful. I place my glass down on a nearby table and tug my dress down.

"I need to go to the ladies," I announce and Rian doesn't acknowledge me, his attention turned on Danny. I turn on my heel and head for the toilet, muttering my annoyance.

I'm so wrapped up in my ire that I don't notice my wrist being seized and I stumble on my heels, as my heartbeat kicks up a notch. I'm pulled into a familiar, hard, muscular chest and I look up into the lust filled hazel eyes of Jackson Chase.

"I haven't been able to keep my eyes off you in that dress, you're a sight for sore fucking eyes, Zeppelin Williams." His voice is low and gruff, as he cups my cheek. His warm breath on my neck, the familiar smell of Diesel Only the Brave all contributing to the throbbing ache that has settled itself between my thighs.

"How does it feel to know that every man in this building tonight wants to fuck you? Does it turn you on?"

I bite down savagely on my lip at the dominant and possessive sound of his voice, as I press my thighs together anxiously. *This was a whole new side of him, and I was oddly turned on.*

"You're desperate to come, aren't you? I can smell your arousal, you smell... delicious, how would you like it if I pushed my finger deep inside you and circled your swollen clit until you couldn't take anymore"

He nips my earlobe and moves the slit of my dress to the side, walking his fingers down to rest between the apex of my thighs.

"I can feel the heat between those gorgeous thighs."

I swallow hard and a small moan escapes from me.

"Shhh, quiet, love, I'll take care of you, how does it feel knowing that I own every inch of you, Zeppelin? I know which buttons to press to satisfy your every need, your every desire, your every dirty little fucking fantasy."

His gruff voice washes over me and I rub my thighs together more furiously, desperate for the pending climax I can feel deep within me. Jax chuckles softly and runs his rough calloused finger down my neck, across my collar bone and down my arm. His touch feels like electricity, like my skin is burning for him to take me.

"Jax," I whisper, aware that my voice sounds breathy and full of need. My body is on high alert, humming and vibrating for Jax.

*"Jesus*, you look so hot right now, all hot and desperate for my cock to slide deep inside you, I'm craving to have you beneath me."

I turn my head to face him, and his hazel eyes are blazing with lust.

"I...I need you, Jax," I manage to pant out.

"I wish I could lay you down in front of all those people and fuck you like I need to, Zeppelin."

He buries his face in my neck and kisses a searing trail down my neck. The softness of his lips, a stark contrast to the roughness of his beard lightly scratching my skin.

"I need to lose myself inside you," he says against my skin, and I hear someone approaching us, softly clearing their throat.

"Ahem..."

Jax chuckles and I feel my face flush with embarrassment.

"Sorry to interrupt, mate, but you're needed backstage, the votes are in."

He presses his forehead to mine.

"Hold that thought."

With a chaste kiss to the corner of my mouth, he's gone, and I'm left a panting hot mess staring after him, desperate for the orgasm he so willingly promised. *Well fuck.*

***

Cynthia steps back out on to the stage, long, straight jet-black hair loose and cascading down her shoulders. Her lips stained red and her signature gold tooth, as she beams at the audience. She is wearing a hot pink dress with match sky high heels, and the audience goes wild, as the four finalists step out onto the stage with their celebrity duet partners.

Noa is with Sam Newbolt, Baylee-Bliss is with Draven Michaels, Chance is with Jett Powers and AJ is with Lyla Hudson.

"Good evening and welcome back to UK's Finest! We scaled the length and breadth of the UK searching for homegrown talent! After weeks of auditions and a week of live shows, it's bought us to tonight. Our four finalists sang their hearts out with their celebrity partners and the votes have now been counted and verified!"

The crowd applaud, as Cynthia is handed an envelope. She opens it and takes it out, her expression neutral.

"In fourth place, is..." She pauses for longer than necessary and I find myself rolling my eyes at the over-the-top theatrics.

"AJ!"

AJ, a six-foot tall, with bleach blonde hair shaved close to his head, one eye blue and the other brown, with cute deep-set dimples in his cheeks. He has a nose ring, and he is clean shaven, he has the boy band look about him and I find myself smiling at the comparison. He steps forward with Lyla, takes a bow and leaves the stage to rapturous applause.

"Commiserations, AJ, in third place this evening, is..."

Cynthia pauses again and the final three wait with bated breath.

"Baylee-Bliss!"

Selective gasps from the audience, as she bursts into tears, comforted by Draven who looks genuinely devastated. She is ushered off stage, as Noa and Chance move closer, so they are side by side.

"Now, we're down to our final two."

Cynthia looks over to the judges.

"Jax, how does it feel for your act Noa to be in the final two?"

She asks him and he puts his hands together in front of his mouth.

"I can't describe how nervous I am right now! I'm grateful and honoured to have an act in the final two. My first time as a guest judge, I can't put into words how proud I am of you, Noa and the dice will fall where they fall. Good luck, sweetheart!"

He flashes her a wink, as Cynthia moves to stand between Noa and Chance.

"The winner of this years' UK's Finest is..."

She looks down at the card for a moment and I bite down viciously on my nail, nervous to hear the outcome. Rian reaches for my hand, and I let him take it.

"Noa!"

Noa drops to her knees, a look of pure shock and elation on her face. Jax leaps out of his seat and runs onto the stage, pulling her up from the floor. He wraps her in a hug and they both jump up and down with excitement. Gold ribbons fall from the ceiling and onto the stage.

"Guys, Noa, you're the winner of UK's Finest! The prize is a million pounds and a guaranteed record deal with Vengeance Records! How are you feeling right now?"

She pulls away from Jax, as Cynthia thrusts the microphone towards her.

"Oh my God! I can't believe it! I'm so, so grateful to everyone, especially to Jax and to Sam for believing in me. Up until yesterday I wasn't sure I could get up on stage and perform, but with the guidance and encouragement from these guys, I couldn't have done it without you! Thank you so much, thank you for voting for me, for mentoring me! I'm...speechless!"

Jax hugs her again and Cynthia moves the microphone over to him.

"I'm genuinely lost for words! I honestly can't believe it! For all of you who voted, who supported us all, I want to say a huge thank you from the bottom of my heart!"

The audience is on their feet and in that moment, all I want to do is celebrate the win with the man who has captured my heart.

# 44

## Zeppelin

I flash my V.I.P access card to the large, burly security guy at the backstage door and he drops the rope allowing me through. I smile my thanks to him and he nods curtly. I walk down the corridor, my feet screaming in my heels and as I head further I hear raised voices.

"What the fuck do you want from me, Luke?"

A distinctly female voice yells frustratedly.

"I don't fucking know! I can't give you what you want, Noa! I'm not capable of it! I can't help the way I feel!"

I recognise the male voice as Lucas from Rancid Vengeance, my curiosity piqued.

"You willingly had sex with me knowing full well I couldn't give you anything more than that! I don't want to hurt you, Noa! That's the last thing I want!"

The door to the dressing room opens and I stop dead in my tracks, trying to stay out of sight.

"You broke my fucking heart, Luke!" she sobs, as both of them come into view, Noa's hand lashes out and slaps Lucas across his cheek.

"You know what! We're fucking done here!" he shouts and storms off down the corridor, as Jax comes to a halt in front of me.

"There you are! I've been looking all over for you!" His voice is laced with amusement.

"Take me to bed, lover boy!" I groan, my feet protesting, as he looks down at his smartwatch and lets out a sigh.

"I wish I could, beautiful, but I've got some interviews to do, and the after-show wrap party."

I can't hide my disappointment, as he takes my hand in his.

"I'll make it up to you, I promise."

He drops a kiss on the back of each of my hands and I understand that he has certain duties to fulfil. A few moments pass between us, Jax doesn't take his dreamy hazels off me, as we are joined by Sam and Peyton Newbolt. I'm the first to break eye contact, as I turn to face rock's power couple. Peyton looks stunning, her dark hair with purple and electric pink flashes is perfectly tousled on one side and shaved on the other side. She is wearing an off the shoulder black mini dress, which emphasises her slender figure, fishnet tights and knee-high black Doc Marten boots with red roses stitched into the sides. Her make-up is natural, but her eyes are smoky with a dramatic cat-eye flick. Her lips are stained red, as Sam wraps his thick, tattooed arm around her. His sheer large size eclipsing her slight one, she regards me intently, as she looks up at Sam. He drops a kiss on her forehead and turns his attention to us. Jax wraps his arm around my shoulder and pulls me closer to him, as if he is making a statement to his long-time friend.

"Ah, you must be the famous Miss Zeppelin that we've heard absolutely nothing about!" Sam says wryly in his familiar husky tone that drives all the women wild. Jax narrows his eyes on Sam and looks from him to Peyton, the atmosphere palpable and somewhat awkward between us. I decide the break the silence and paint on a smile.

"Hi! I'm Zeppelin, it's so good to finally meet you both!" I say a little too enthusiastically and offer my hand to Sam. He looks at my outstretched hand and shakes it courteously.

"Sam, pleasure to meet you too, finally! We actually thought you were a figment of his wild imagination!" Sam jokes and Jax bristles beside me. Peyton steps away from Sam and he looks at her with questioning eyes, as she slowly shakes her head, her blue eyes glossy.

"I-I'm sorry, I-I-I can't."

She rushes off down the corridor and my mouth drops open wondering what the fuck just happened.

"Well, that didn't go as well as I planned!"

I try to lighten the mood and Sam shakes his head.

"It's nothing personal, sweetheart. I should go after her, we'll catch up in a little bit."

He nods curtly, flashing me a wink as he sprints off down the corridor in the direction that his wife went in.

"I'm so sorry," Jax whispers and I shake my head in disbelief.

"Did I do something wrong?" I ask, desperately trying to keep the emotion from my voice.

"Zeppelin, look at me."

He steps in front of me, tilting my chin up to face him. I swallow back the lump in my throat. *I just want to get to know the people closest to him.*

"Peyton was best friends with Ruby; they knew each other since they were kids, practically their whole lives. It's nothing personal; it's just hard for her that's all. We all experienced a devastating loss, Peyton most of all, she was like a sister to her. I haven't been with anyone since...you know, you're the first woman I've cared enough about to introduce to the people closest to me."

He explains, as a tear tracks its way down my cheek. I swipe it angrily away, cursing my stupid emotions to hell.

"*Jesus,* please don't cry, I can't apologise enough, I'm so sorry."

His voice thick with emotion.

"It's not you..."

I shake my head, composing myself with a sniff.

"Don't fucking carry on that sentence, it's not you, it's me, right? Don't make excuses for her, Jax! I'm not trying to replace her! I'd never do that! Thea asked me if I was going to be her new mummy the first time I met her, so don't stand there and pretend like you haven't thought the same! I'm a poor replacement for the only woman you'll ever love!"

I yell, as he drops his head into his hands, attracting the unwanted attention of the people surrounding us. *Shit.*

"No! You're putting words into my mouth! God, why didn't you tell me about Thea? *Jesus fucking Christ,* Zeppelin! You need to tell me these things!"

He drags his hand through his hair, and I take a step back from him. I shake my head, my words caught in my throat, as he squeezes his eyes shut. Suddenly and completely out of nowhere, I seemingly come to my senses. I *can't* be here, as every emotion barrels its way through my body. Sadness, confusion, disappointment and to some extent even guilt. I lift up my dress, turn and rush down the corridor to the sound of him calling my name.

I push my way out of the TV studio and the rush of cold air instantly chills me to the bone. A doorman moves into my path and tilts his hat. I can't see his face properly because the tears swimming in my eyes makes my vision blurry.

"Miss? Do you need a taxi?"

I offer him a watery smile and nod. He sweeps his arm out to the side gesturing for me to go on ahead, on autopilot I put one foot in front of the other and stop at the kerb, as a taxi pulls up. The doorman opens the door, and I climb in, nodding and smiling my thanks, unable to speak. If I speak, I'll break down and I can't allow anyone to witness that. I take a breath and settle back into the seat, giving the driver my address, as we smoothly pull away into the night.

The journey back to my place is uneventful and as I step on the kerb, my feet screaming in protest. I toss some cash at the driver and rush up the steps, pushing my way into the safety of my building, the heat a stark contrast from the chilly night air. The click, click of my heels across the marbled floor the only sound, as I press the call button for the lift. I bounce from one foot to the other impatiently, as I continue to stab the button. After what seems like a lifetime, the lift arrives, and I step inside. I slip my shoes off and settle myself back against the mirrored wall, catching sight of my reflection. My cheeks flushed, my eyes brimming with unshed tears and my hair slightly mussed from the bite of the wind outside. The lift comes to a halt on my floor, and I shuffle wearily out into the carpeted corridor, suddenly feeling exhausted. My heels hanging off my slender finger, I come to a stop outside my apartment and rummage through my bag looking for my keys. I locate them in seconds and put the key shakily into the lock. I step into my apartment, turn the light on and set my bag down on the white glossy console beside the door. I drop my shoes at my feet with a thud and it's then I allow the events of the evening to settle at the forefront of my mind.

I lean back against the door and slide down on to the floor in a sobbing heap, as Jericho comes bounding towards me, whining and whimpering, nuzzling my wet, tear-stained cheek. I hear my phone ringing, but I'm too consumed by grief to acknowledge it. I had the first meeting with the rest of the Rancid Vengeance family perfectly planned out in my head, I just wanted to make a good impression on the people who mean the most to Jax and as the tears relentlessly fall down my cheeks, I allow myself to wonder will I ever have a happy ending.

***

I sobbed long, loud and well into the night. The hiccupping, soul-destroying sobs of despair, as the grief enveloped me in its tight grip. I just wanted it all to stop, I was simply exhausted. I wanted to be in relationship with Jax, and I wanted to enjoy the honeymoon period, I wanted to enjoy spending time with him, making love to him and spending time with the people he called his family. I started to wonder if I would ever be good enough for him, I didn't want to replace Ruby, I would never do that. That chapter of his life was closed, and I wanted to be his next chapter, his happy ending.

I struggle to process the events of the evening, and I can't comprehend Peyton's reaction. It was made a hundred times worse that Jax didn't jump to my defence and I resented him for that. I'm not sure how much time passes, but I flinch as I hear a loud pounding on the door at my back.

"Zeppelin!" Jax's loud, annoyed voice echoes through the door, as Jericho leaps up and starts barking wildly.

"Zeppelin! I know you're in there!"

He continues to pound his fists on the door, but I can't move, I'm rooted, frozen to the spot. My heart is racing, and the blood is roaring in my ears. Jericho circling and growling as if ready to attack.

"Open the fucking door!"

The door handle rattles vigorously, startling me into action. *Come on, Williams, pull yourself together.* I get shakily to my feet, take a few moments to gather myself and to calm down my furry companion with a few comforting pats to his head and scratching behind his ears. I take a deep breath and pull the door open. I'm greeted by a less than put together Jax, his tie loose, his top two buttons on his shirt undone and his hair hanging loose limply around his shoulders. He's leaning into the doorjamb, his biceps thick and his chest heaving.

"*Jesus Christ*, Zeppelin, don't fucking do that to me ever again! You hear me? You ran off knowing I couldn't damn well come after you!"

His voice rough and full of anger. *You deserve every ounce of his anger, you selfish bitch.*

"I-I'm sorry."

It takes everything I have inside of me not to burst into tears again. I take a few steps backwards and open the door wider, as he saunters casually inside and closes the door with a click behind him.

I drop down heavily onto the sofa, still wearing the red dress he so kindly bought for me.

"I'm not a bad person, Jack, I'm not trying to replace her. I would never do that; she'll always be a part of your life."

I sniff, as he shakes his head.

"I know and I'm sorry I didn't leap to your defence, Peyton is still so consumed by grief for her best friend, I don't think she's ever truly gotten over it, none of us have and I don't think we ever will," he explains, as I drop my head into my hand's emotion overwhelming me and burst into uncontrollable floods of tears. I hear the sound of his soft footsteps across the carpet, as he gets down on his haunches in front of me.

"Hey, please don't cry," he says softly, as he reaches up to stroke my face and he wipes away my tears with the pad of his thumb. I lean in his touch, as I briefly close my eyes and relish in the feel of him. His touch sends electric shocks through my entire body and lights me up from the inside out. His warm hazel eyes lock with mine and I can't look away, I don't want to because of the intense feeling he evokes in me every time he's near me.

"Jack."

His name on my lips is a breathy whisper and the emotion at the forefront of my mind at that moment, wasn't grief, or sadness, it was something entirely different. It was...the carnal urge to fuck.

"I want you to fuck me, Jack. I need you to take it away, please," I plead with my eyes, as the needy thrum between my thighs becomes almost unbearable. I need him to erase the events of the evening, I want to forget it ever happened. I want to lose myself in him and by the possessive look in his eyes, he knows it.

"Jack," I mewl softly, as he moves his hand to the nape of my neck and presses his forehead against mine.

"Don't say things you don't mean, Zeppelin, because I've thought of nothing more since I made you come over and over and over again."

His voice dripping with pure sex and that's all it takes for me to tackle him to the carpeted floor of my apartment.

I crush my lips to his in a searing, white-hot, bruising kiss. Our tongues performing a sensual, erotic dance. My breasts feel heavy and ache to have his hands on them. My pussy floods violently, as every one of my senses was on high alert and tuned into everything that was Jackson Chase. It's a race who can get naked the fastest and I win as I kneel naked before him. He shakes his head, as he lets his shirt drop to the floor and unzips his trousers.

"Keep the heels on," he demands, as he takes off the rest of his clothes allowing me a few moments to admire the view of him gloriously naked. The heat radiating between us, hot and heavy, as he moves his mouth back to mine, devouring me. I was just as hungry as he was, his tongue plunging between my lips, tasting me and taking what he wants. His hands dive into my blonde hair, his urgency and need just as potent as my own. I needed to feel the press of his hard, chiselled abs against me, the need to touch, to be touched almost overwhelming me.

Every single one of my five senses tingled, as a surge of heat settled itself deep in my core, as the contours of his body hard against my softness was so perfect it made me want to weep. I could feel his erection solid between us, as I moved to straddle him. His back against the sofa, as I reach back to hold his cock and lower myself down onto him. I'm aware he's not wearing a condom, but I'm too far gone to care, I'm too caught up in everything that is Jackson Chase. We both let out a moan of pleasure, as the deliciousness of his cock inside me is almost too much to bear. I feel my pussy expand to accommodate his length, a feeling of fullness settling deep inside me. I raise my hips up and down, starting painfully slowly and building up to a punishing crescendo in time with our laboured breathing. He reaches up to cup my breasts, his long, calloused fingers rolling and tugging at my already erect nipples.

"Harder, Jack, harder!" I beg, as he moves his hands to grip my hips and I relinquish all control, as his pace becomes frantic and urgent. He thrusts deep, plunging in and out, driving me towards the release I have been desperately craving since he teased me earlier.

"*Oh fuck!* You feel perfect around my cock, Zeppelin. Look how we fit together," he breathes and I throw my head back in ecstasy, letting out a scream. His thrusts become faster and harder, as I feel his cock bump my cervix and he's so deep my eyes start to water. He looks up at me with those hooded hazel eyes and his hand snakes down my flat stomach to find my swollen clit. He rubs my engorged nub in lazy circles, and I can feel my orgasm rising. I arch my back to create a delicious friction, as his relentless rhythm becomes urgent.

"That's it, sweetheart, fucking come all over my cock."

That's all it takes, and I shudder out my mind-altering orgasm, as it ripples and detonates through my entire body.

"JACK! OH GOD! JACK!"

With one more unrelenting thrust, Jack shouts his own release.

"FUCK, ZEPPELIN! JESUS! FUCKKKKKK!"

I fall forward, collapsing, spent on top of him. Our sweaty bodies pressed against each other, as we are both left breathless and panting, post-orgasmic and spent. After a few minutes, he lifts me up, pulling out of me and I feel the remnants of his hot seed running down the insides of my thighs. The realisation has me crashing back down to earth with a thud at our blatant carelessness, but that was a problem for another day. I intended to enjoy another night of blissed out passion with my hot rock star.

# 45

# Zeppelin

I wake up feeling deliciously sore and open my eyes, noticing it's still dark outside. I sleepily reach over, and I'm met with cold sheets and an empty bed. *Well shit.* I can't help the hurt that hits me full force in the gut. *He didn't even stay the night; he just left without a word. Arsehole.* I fell asleep in his arms, content that he was in my bed, after a marathon love making session. It wasn't just fucking this time; it was actual real-life love making. It was slow, unhurried and I felt the unbreakable connection between us that hadn't been there previously.

I swallowed past the lump in that had formed in my throat and tried to go back to sleep. After an hour of tossing and turning in the dark, I swing my legs out of bed to the sound of Jericho softly snoring and curled up like a furry ball, in his dog basket in the corner of the room. I pad across the floor bare foot and open the door; I almost jump out of my skin when I see Jax sitting on the sofa bare chested and in his boxer shorts. Relief washes over me that he didn't just leave me in the middle of the night.

*"Jesus fucking Christ*, you scared the shit out of me!" I whisper with a chuckle and my hand placed on my chest, fully aware that I'm still completely naked.

"Sorry, didn't mean to scare you, sweetheart. I couldn't sleep, Brody had a seizure earlier on today and what with the finale of UK's Finest, I haven't had a second to contemplate what that means for us as a band and for him," he says with a sigh.

"Brody's got a brain injury and they're not sure if it might be permanent, Sam's in the midst of another bi-polar episode because he's stopped taking his meds, Lucas is sleeping with anything with a pulse because he's so hung up on Nick fucking Slade. I'm...exhausted, Zep, I don't know how much longer I can do this. I don't know how much longer we can keep painting over the cracks and carrying on like nothing's happened, ya know? I shouldn't even be telling you any of this, but there's no one else and I'm fucking terrified."

He admits, leaning forward, his elbows braced on his knees and seeing him so...forlorn and so out of sorts, makes my heart hurt for him. *He's been going through all of this alone and you've been so wrapped up in yourself you didn't even notice. You selfish bitch.*

"I might not be part of your world, at least not yet, but I'm here for you," I tell him, sincerely and genuinely, suddenly feeling terrible for not noticing he was struggling sooner.

"Thank you," he whispers, as he flicks his gaze up to mine.

"I want you to be a part of my world, I've never wanted anything more. I know it wasn't the meeting we planned with Sam and Peyton, but I want you to meet the people who are important to me-officially," he babbles nervously and I find it endearing. My heart feels almost too big for my chest at his statement, and I find myself nodding my agreement. I move closer to him, offering him my hand.

"Come back to bed, Jack."

He takes my hand in his and we both fall asleep happy in the fact that we are taking the next step in our relationship.

***

I wake the next morning to a raised voice, and I can't help myself from listening to his angry tirade.

"Are you for fucking real, right now... He's been in a coma for three months and now he's all of a sudden redeemed of all his wrong doings... Come on, Sam... Don't be a dickhead all your life! He's been in a coma, that doesn't mean he's had a fucking personality transplant... He's not accepting visitors, fine, but he's gonna' be a dad for Christ's sake... It's about time he took responsibility for that... Yeah and he'll hurt her like he's hurt the string of women before her... Because he can't say no! We've been complicit in his antics for fourteen fucking years, Sam... No, you fucking listen to me... No, I can't do this anymore... No, no, no! Look, I need to go, I'll be back soon..."

I hear a frustrated shout the sound a low muttering, as the door to my bedroom opens with a click. I pretend to be asleep, as I feel the bed dip.

"Good morning, beautiful."

I open my eyes to his smiling face, as if the conversation from a few moments ago didn't happen. He's shirtless and his jeans are hanging open, the waistband of his boxers peeking through.

"Good morning, Handsome Jack."

He beams at my nickname for him and leans down to kiss my forehead.

"There's coffee in the machine, but I have to go, I have a meeting with M.J to go through the terms and conditions of Noa's contract," he says with a satisfied grin, and I find myself smiling right along with him. *I'm so happy she won; she deserved it.*

"Congratulations! I didn't get to say it last night," I say genuinely.

"Thank you, I'm over the moon! I can come back later if you want. Or I can send a car for you? We can go out to celebrate, finally!"

I nod in agreement.

"That would be nice."

I smile, as I swing my legs out of bed and pad into the kitchen. I see a piece of paper poking out from under the front door, my heart sinks and my stomach drops. *Fucking hell, not another one.* I bend down to pick it up and open it with shaky hands, my back to Jax as I try to hide it from him.

*Tick, tock, tick tock, time is running out.*

*The truth will come out.*

I stare down at the message, assembled with various newspaper and magazine cuttings. I feel the colour drain from my cheeks, as I go to screw it up, but Jax moves closer to me, stopping me with a gentle brush of his hand.

"What's going on? You look as white as a sheet." His voice is filled with concern.

"I-It's nothing."

I stutter, as he takes the piece of paper from me with a cock of his eyebrow. *You're not fooling anyone, Williams.*

"What the fuck, Zeppelin? Who's sending these?" he says incredulously and I lean against the sofa to steady myself.

"I-don't know, it started just after I moved here."

I squeeze the bridge of my nose, feeling a dull throb start in my temples.

"Why didn't you tell me about this sooner, sweetheart?" he asks softly and I shake my head, trying to quell the tears I can feel burning behind my eyes.

"I-I didn't want to worry you; you've got enough going on," I say in a rush and his mouth forms a straight line. I know he's keeping his mouth shut, as he towers over me and lifts my chin until I look up at him. The look in his hazel eyes serious, as he pulls his phone out of his pocket. He doesn't take his eyes off me, as he swipes the screen a few times and putting it up to his ear.

"Cole, hey, it's me... yeah... look, I need a favour, please... I need you to look into something for me... Yeah, I've got a meeting with M.J, but I can drop by after I'm done... cheers, man, thank you... really appreciate it, see you soon... yeah, bye."

He hangs up the phone and slips it back into his pocket, zipping up his jeans.

"Cole's going to look into it for me, are there any others?"

I move past him and kneel in front of the sofa, reaching under and pulling out a shoe box. I open the lid and place it on the sofa cushion. Jax looks inside at the piles of notes, cursing long and low in his throat.

"*Fuck me*, Zeppelin. There must be hundreds of them, *Jesus*. You've been dealing with this on your own for too long, it's not safe for you here."

I roll my eyes at his words and his puffs out a breath at my obvious nonchalance.

"It's been going on long enough, I'm sure if something was going to happen, it would have by now! Besides I'm a big girl, I can look after myself."

He drags his hand through his hair.

"That's not the fucking point! Look, maybe you should come and stay with me for a little while? At least until Cole can get to the bottom of who's behind this?" he offers and I shake my head.

"Jack, you're overreacting! This is probably just some nut job fan, thinking they're being funny, it's no big deal," I say with a dismissive wave of my hand, hoping that I come across more confident than I feel inside.

"This isn't a fucking joke, this is serious, Zeppelin! Your safety is my number one priority right now, and I need to make sure you're safe."

He squeezes his eyes shut, as if to rid himself of his previous thought.

"I have Jericho and Rian is just upstairs, stop worrying. I've got it covered."

I try to placate him, as I move closer to him and plant a chaste kiss on his lips.

"Okay, fine, if you don't want to stay with me, I'll have CCTV and twenty-four-hour surveillance set-up. I can't imagine my life without you in it; it makes me physically violent to think someone out there wants to harm even a hair on your fucking head."

My heart melts at his need to protect me and in that moment, I couldn't be more in love with him.

# 46

## Jax

After a long, drawn out, but productive meeting with M.J, Noa Vega is now signed to Vengeance Records, and I couldn't be prouder if I tried. I couldn't wait to work with her and for her to succeed in the music industry. She deserved a chance at super stardom, she was talented, down to earth and one of the most humble human beings I had ever met.

Following the revelation that Zeppelin had been getting threatening letters, I had made some phone calls to put measures in place to make sure she was safe. I couldn't lose another woman in my life; I wouldn't survive it again. It made me physically sick to think someone would want to harm even a hair on her beautiful head. I wanted to protect her with every fibre of my being, and I had the resources to do that, even if we couldn't be together all the time.

I head down a light grey corridor with grey slate flooring all the way down with the shoe box in my hands, as if it were a bomb about to explode. I tap the door, and I hear Cole's deep rumbling voice.

"Come in."

I swing the door open and step into the room. There is a bank of small flat screen TVs mounted on the wall, and Cole is sitting in front of them with his feet up on the desk, his hands casually behind his head. He's wearing black dress trousers, a white shirt with two buttons undone.

"So, what have you got for me then, Jax?" Cole asks and I hand him the shoe box. He places it down on the desk in front of him, swinging his long legs down onto the floor and grabbing his cane. He leans heavily on his cane, as he flips the lid to the box open, examining the top few letters.

*"Jesus fucking Christ,"* he mumbles.

"There must be hundreds of them," he muses and I observe him carefully, as he tips the shoe box upside down until the piles of letters hit the desk.

"So, can you look into it for me, please?" I ask hopefully and he turns to face me.

"I can try, what do we know?" he asks.

"Not a great deal, she's tight lipped about the whole thing, I don't know how much more I can take, Cole, I've fallen for her harder than I should have, but I feel like I've barely scratched the surface."

I hang my head in shame, and he squeezes my shoulder.

"I get it, man, I do, you feel like you're betraying Ruby, and you think history is going to repeat itself?"

I nod, trapping my bottom lip between my teeth.

"I can't lose anyone else, Cole, we've lost too many people already," I say with a sigh, and he hums his agreement, uncomfortably uncrossing his leg and leaning forward.

"Do we have a start at least? Is there a crazy ex with a grudge?"

I shake my head.

"Her ex is dead, he was Abel Creed from the Poison Puppets, died in a yacht fire five years ago. Her ex's family blamed Zeppelin for the death of their son, so we could start there."

Cole nods and lets out a rich, rumbling laugh.

"*Fucking hell*, Jax, you boys will be the death of me!"

I smile.

"We like to keep you on your toes."

He rolls his eyes.

"I've heard that before! Right, leave it with me, man, I'm on it, I'll let you know if I find anything."

I slap his shoulder.

"Cheers, mate, I really appreciate it."

He nods curtly and I turn to leave the room.

"Let me know what you come up with."

Cole salutes and I leave the room, shutting the door behind me with a click, hopeful that Cole will find something.

***

During the weeks that passed, I found myself getting closer to Zeppelin, we had entered the honeymoon period of our relationship. We were spending almost every night together; she was bonding with Thea, and it warmed my heart that they were getting along so well. The shit had hit the fan with Brody and Raleigh after she found out he had been having a four year long affair with Lorna Lavelle. I was vaguely aware of her, but we had never met her in person. It was a car crash that you couldn't tear your eyes away from. Brody was discharged from hospital a week ago and he had fallen into a deep depression. He had shut himself off from the world and refused to come out. Sam had tried to reach out, only for his messages to remain unread and his calls never to be returned.

An intervention was needed, which is why me, Sam, Lucas and Lenny are currently outside his house. Sam pounding on the door with his clenched fist.

"HART! I KNOW YOU'RE IN THERE, YOU PRICK! OPEN THE FUCKING DOOR, OR I'M GONNA' BREAK IT DOWN!"

Sam's husky, booming voice fills the silence, as he continuously raps on the door. The pounding getting louder and louder.

"HART! OPEN THIS MOTHERFUCKING DOOR, OR SO HELP ME GOD!" Sam yells, his whole body vibrating with rage. I place my hand on his shoulder, and he flinches.

"Sam, he doesn't want to see us, mate, leave it, yeah?"

I try desperately to placate him, as he turns to face me. His eyes a dark forest green, and the look in my friends' eyes worries me. I try to push that thought to the back of my mind, as he shoves me back with his forearm and his foot connects with the door. The splintering of the wood piercing my eardrums and sending the door hurtling against the wall with a deafening thud. *Fuck my life.* We all enter Brody's house, our footsteps across the marble floor the only sound, as we all head up the stairs and swing the door of his bedroom open. It smells like sweat and the musky scent makes my stomach roil.

"For fuck's sake!" Sam mutters, as he flings the duvet cover away from Brody's body and we loom over him. He is curled into a foetal position, as Lucas states.

"Dude! It fucking reeks in here!"

He pulls the curtains open and pushes the window open, daylight flooding the room, as Brody lets out a whimper.

"*Jesus fucking Christ*, boy," Lenny says gruffly and as he says those words, Brody bursts into uncontrollable floods of tears.

We all set about clearing up the mess in the house, taking a room each. It takes a couple of hours, but it no longer smells and it's spotless. Brody enters the kitchen, as I'm finishing up wiping the counter tops. His movements are slow, and he looks so different to the way he did a few weeks ago. He is wearing blue, white and black checkered pyjama bottoms and a v-neck black t-shirt. His feet are bare, and his dark hair is flat and longer, as it falls haphazardly into his eyes. He has a visible scar that stretches from his hairline to round the back of his head. He has grown a short beard, and he looks freshly showered, but it doesn't hide the vacant look in his silver eyes. His face is pale, and he has dark circles underneath his eyes.

"Why do you hate me, Jax?" he asks out of the blue and I'm taken aback by his question. *Where the fuck did that come from?* I take a few moments to contemplate my answer, and I turn to face him. He's leaning against the worktop; he's unsteady on his feet and his legs are shaking.

"I don't hate you, Brody, I actually feel sorry for you. You were dealt a crap hand in life and I'm sorry for that, I really am. But that doesn't give you carte blanche to do whatever the fuck you want, whenever you want, without consequences, because that's not how real life works!" The tone of my voice is incredulous, as he audibly sighs.

"Do you think I don't know that! My brain is like scrambled egg right now and I can't remember how to do the one thing that grounds me and brings me joy! I'm terrified the damage to my brain is going to be permanent and it makes me feel useless! The mother of my children fucking hates me and the funny thing, I don't blame her for it, because I hate me too!"

He raises his voice, but squeezes his eyes shut briefly and blinks a few times.

"Oh, come on, spare me the pity party for one! You were sleeping with another woman throughout your entire relationship! What did you expect, no fucking wonder she hates you! You bought all this on yourself, Brody!

There's no one else to blame, but yourself!" I yell, jabbing my finger angrily in his direction.

"Don't you think we've lost enough people in our lives? You're careless, reckless and you couldn't keep your dick in your pants! That's the truth of it! We've spent three fucking months praying you'd wake up, Raleigh is growing not one, but two humans inside of her, she doesn't need the stress!" I explain and he has the sense to balk at my angry tirade.

"Do you know what keeps me up at night, Jax? Do you?"

He moves closer, holding onto the counter for support, breathing heavily.

"I hid underneath one of the pews in that chapel that day and I saw that bullet pierce Ruby's skull; I saw the moment in slow fucking motion. I tried to help her, I did, I tried to reassure her, I was fucking terrified."

I can't comprehend the weight of his words, and I shake my head, pretending I just didn't hear what he said.

"Shut the fuck up!" I shout, but he shakes his head and continues, despite my pleas for him to stop. I can't listen to this; it takes everything inside of me not to put my hands over my ears to stop the words from leaving his mouth.

"I was covered in her blood, but it all happened so fast. Some of it was a complete blur, but I lay next to her and held her hand, I stroked her stomach and I and I told her everything was going to be fine. I fucking lied to a dying woman!"

He bursts into tears and starts to sob, and I shake my head vehemently. Praying to all that's holy that none of what he said is true.

"No! No! You're lying! You shut your fucking filthy mouth, Brody Hart!"

He moves closer to me on unsteady feet, until we're practically toe to toe.

"It's about time you knew the truth, Jax, that's what keeps me up at night, that's why I'm in therapy! Because I can't come to terms with what happened that day and we never talk about it! I have P.T.S.D and my brain has turned to mush since the accident. I can't...I can't...I can't do this anymore."

He lets go of the countertop and collapses to the floor at my feet. My whole body is trembling with anger, with grief and with utter disbelief that he was the one who was with Ruby at the end.

"It should have been me! I should have been the one that was there with her at the end! I should have been the one whispering words of reassurance, not you! Why did it have to be you?" My voice is full of vitriol, as I lean down.

"You didn't have the fucking right to say those words to her! You're a pathetic fuck up, Brody! It should have been you that died that day! Not her! Not my Ruby!"

I know I'm being a complete prick, but I can't help the hatred that spills from my lips, as I watch the sobs wrack every part of his body.

"IT SHOULD HAVE BEEN YOU!"

I jab my finger in his shoulder, as Sam and Lucas come flying into the kitchen. Sam grabs me from the one side, Lucas grabs me from the other, practically lifting me off my feet and dragging me away from him.

"JAX!" Sam bellows.

"THAT'S ENOUGH, JACK! IT'S DONE!" Lucas shouts, as I desperately try to break free of their iron hold.

"GET THE FUCK OFF ME!"

They drag me into the living room and launch me onto the sofa. I leap up from where I landed and Sam pushes me back down. His muscles bunching and flexing, as he holds me in place.

"What the fuck, Jax?" he says through clenched teeth.

"Did you know he was the one who was with Ruby when she was shot? Did you?" I accuse, his mouth agape and he shakes his head.

"I had no fucking idea."

All of the fight seemingly drains from me, and I sag in his hold, he lets go of me, observing me with cautious eyes. I lean forward, my arms braced on my knees, and I sob. I sob for the woman I loved, I sob for my daughter, and I sob for the life we should have had together, as a family.

# 47

## Zeppelin

Writer's block is when the words go away. *Entirely*. There is nothing in your head, no words, nothing. When you lie down in the evening and think of your characters, there is nobody there. The film has ended, the credits have rolled and there is just a blank screen, where the action once was. My imaginary friends weren't talking to me, for the first time ever, I'm completely alone and I didn't like it one bit. I had submitted book nine to my publisher weeks ago and in between edits, rewrites and the release date, I usually have another book on the go. But this time, there was nothing. I had been too wrapped up in my own real life love story with my hot, Norse God-like rock star.

I'm sat at my desk, with a glass of wine, staring at a blank screen wishing the words that I know aren't there, to magically appear in front of me and show me the way. *Luke Combs Six Feet Apart* is playing softly in the background, as I take off my glasses and try to rub away the headache that I can feel building behind my eyes. I tuck my legs underneath myself, as I hear a soft tap on the door. Jericho starts circling my chair, wagging his tail wildly and letting out a series of barks. I roll my eyes and smile to myself, as I scratch his ears.

"It's probably, Rian, as usual, silly dog!" I say with a chuckle and a shake of my head, as I pad across the flat bare foot. I open the door expecting it to be Rian, but I'm surprised when I look up into the turbulent hazel eyes of Jackson Chase. His eyes are red rimmed, as he leans his shoulder heavily into the door frame.

"I-I'm sorry, I..."

He lets out a strangled sob and practically collapses into my arms. I just about catch him and smell the stench of alcohol on his breath.

"Jax?"

He shakes his head vehemently and I flash him a questioning look. He glances up at me, his eyes brimming with tears.

"I don't like it when you call me Jax."

He sounds so boyish and vulnerable my heart hurts for him. He's in clear emotional distress, as he buries his face in my neck.

"Beautiful Zeppelin. My Zeppelin," he murmurs, as I pull him inside, closing the door behind us.

"Do you want to tell me what happened?" I direct him to the sofa, and he drops down heavily, his head flopping back.

"What happened?"

He laughs bitterly, I've never seen him like this before, and it sets off alarm bells.

"Brody was with Ruby when she was shot, he was the one whispering words of reassurance to her while she lay dying, when it should have been me!"

He jabs his thumbs into his chest, and my mouth drops open at his revelation. *I know his relationship with Brody hasn't been the best over the years.*

"That fuck-up was with my Ruby!" he grits out angrily, as he leans forward and drops his head into his hands. I don't know what to do, or say to make it better, so I sit down next to him. He lifts his head up and cups my cheek in his hand, moving closer to me until I can feel his warm breath on my cheek.

"Jack, don't do something you're going to regret in the morning," I breathe softly, as he lets out a small sigh. *I'm trying in vain to be the sensible one, even though I want him to satiate my burning desire for him.*

"The only thing I regret is lying to you at the beginning, I should have been honest from the start and I'm so fucking sorry for that. Truly, please forgive me."

He closes his eyes and presses his forehead to mine.

"You've got nothing to be sorry for, but I forgive you," I whisper without hesitation, and he flashes me a lazy, drunken grin, which is adorable. I find myself smiling right along with him, as he presses his lips to mine. His kiss immobilises me, it's reverent and so soft. I'm frozen in place, terrified to move and end this tender moment between us. I let him explore my mouth with his, I let his hands roam every part of my body, aware that he's drunk and probably won't remember any of this in the morning, but I'm too far gone to stop it.

I moan softly into his mouth, as I feel a sudden rush of heat between my legs. His tongue performing an erotic, sensual dance with mine, it's lazy and unhurried, as if he has all the time in the world to worship me. I silently plead with him, to take me right there on the sofa, but he shakes his head slowly.

"I need you, Zeppelin."

He pulls me to my feet and leads me into my bedroom, laying me down on the bed, undressing me with care. After he's finished, he strips until he is deliciously and gloriously naked in front of me. I'll never get tired of the sight of him, all taut, muscular with hard clean lines. He kneels between my thighs, fisting his cock a few times, as his erect cock finds my entrance, pushing in gently. He shoves forward into my slick channel, and I cry out.

"OH GOD! JACK!"

He buries himself deeper inside me, I arch my back towards him and he rewards me with a sharp swivel of his lean hips. His thrusts become slower and unhurried. *He isn't fucking me tonight, he's making love.*

"Does that feel good, baby?"

His voice laced with seduction, and I hum my approval, wrapping my legs around his waist. He moves in and out at a painfully slow pace, with each measured plunge, I feel the familiar flutters of a pending orgasm. My soaking wet sex rippling around his hard length.

"That's it, Ruby, come for me."

My eyes widen and my heart slams against my rib cage, as I hear him yell another woman's name. But not just any woman's name, the woman he was going to marry. I lift my hips off the bed and with some effort, I manage to buck him off me.

"GET THE FUCK OFF ME!"

I scream, as he hits the floor with a thud, realising his mistake and shaking his head.

"*Fuck! Fuck! Fuck!* I'm sorry, I'm so sorry, Zeppelin."

I sit up, pulling my knees up to my chest and wrapping my arms around myself. I was a fool to ever think that he would ever be mine.

"Zeppelin?" he whispers softly, a stricken look on his handsome face.

"There's always going to be a third person in our relationship, Jax! And I don't think I can handle that; my heart won't handle it. I've fallen in love with you, but I'll never be enough! I'll never be her!"

My voice thick with unshed tears, as I swing my legs out of bed and start to dress. I pull on my clothes, quickly and haphazardly. He doesn't say anything for long moments; he looks so broken and desolate. The look in his eyes almost shattering my resolve, but I remain strong and resolute.

"Get out." My voice is icy and void of emotion, as I try desperately to hold onto the crippling hurt I feel. His head snaps up, as he gets unsteadily to his feet.

"Zeppelin, please, I'm sorry, I'm so fucking sorry."

I shake my head.

"You can shove your fucking sorry up your arse, Jackson Chase! We're done!"

He moves closer to the bed, but I don't meet his gaze. I can't, if I do, I'll give in to my body's insatiable, uncontrollable need for him and only him.

"You don't mean that, please, just talk to me. I made a stupid fucking mistake! Zeppelin!" he states incredulously and I laugh bitterly.

"You yelled out another woman's name while we were having sex, Jax! What the fuck did you think I was going to do? Pat you on the head and say everything's fine! Because it's not fine at all! I get that you still love her, I do, but it's not healthy, you've spent three years mourning her, never moving forward with your life. Maybe this is the wakeup call you need because I'm done, I won't be second best to a fucking ghost!"

His eyes widen at my statement, and he looks as if I have just slapped him across the face.

"That fucking stings, Zeppelin! You of all people should know what it feels like, you lost someone you loved too!"

He runs his hand through his long, blonde just fucked hair, and I drop my gaze to the floor.

"Zeppelin, please, don't do this."

He moves forward until he's within touching distance, he tilts my chin up to face him, but I don't stop him.

"Fucking look me in the eyes and tell me we're over, Zeppelin. I need to hear you say the words out loud."

His voice low and so full of emotion. I shake my head, unable to speak the words. There are a few moments of uncomfortable silence, as I drop my head into my hands.

"Jack, I'm sorry, but I can't be with you. Not now."

My lip quivers and my voice shakes as I say those words. He lets out a laboured breath and looks up to the ceiling as if it will offer him the answers he seeks.

"Do you think it was easy for me to get involved with someone else after what happened? Do you?"

He raises his voice a little and I wrap my arms around myself, as if to hold the broken pieces of me together.

"I had to come to terms with the fact that the next woman I entered into a relationship with wouldn't be Ruby! And to hear that Brody was the one who was with her at the end! That breaks my fucking heart! I've spent three years grieving, trying to get my head around being a single dad and how to navigate my life without her in it. Then to find out that while I was unconscious, while I was on the floor of that fucking chapel bleeding out, Brody of all people was the one who was whispering words of reassurance to my fiancée! It should have been me! So don't you dare fucking sit there and act like the holier than thou, scorned little princess, when you've not been so forthcoming with the truth either!"

He states bitterly and I balk at his tone, as he takes a step back from me.

"Get the fuck out!"

He laughs sardonically, as he starts to dress and I avert my gaze so that I'm looking anywhere but in his pained hazel eyes. He's genuinely sorry and so full of remorse, but I can't allow myself to continue our relationship while there's a third person ever present. Even though she's a ghost haunting every facet of our unbreakable bond.

"I-it's over, Jack, I'm sorry." My voice wavers and the words threaten to choke me, as I swallow back the tennis ball sized lump in my throat.

"So that's it? We're over, just like that?" he asks and I nod.

"I can't do this anymore, Jack. I can't."

My silver eyes finally lock with his and he nods curtly, pressing his lips together into a straight line, while tucking his hand into his pocket.

"Goodbye, Zeppelin."

He leans forward to press a kiss to my forehead and I briefly close my eyes, willing the threatening tears I feel burning behind my eyes to fuck right off. I know if I open my eyes and watch him leave, I won't be able to hold them back, so I keep them closed. As soon as the door slams shut, it's then that I allow the dam to break.

# 48

## Jax

During the weeks that passed, the stark and shocking realisation of the fucked-up situation hit me like a freight train. Zeppelin avoided my calls, my voicemails containing my sincere apologies and left all of my messages unresponded to. *Why the fuck did I yell out Ruby's name while in the throes of passion?* I genuinely had no answer for that, and I had lost all hope of a reunion, as it had been announced that we were embarking on a sixty-two date UK and European tour.

The *"Vengeance – I'm not Dead"* tour sold out in eleven minutes, breaking our previous records. I was attending twice weekly sessions with my therapist, Kalvin and I felt like I was making real progress. I was finally coming to terms with the fact that Ruby was gone and I owed it to myself, my daughter and Zeppelin to start living my life after three long and painful years. Unpacking my excess baggage made for some emotional therapy sessions, but I was determined to lay Ruby to rest and begin the next chapter of my life.

Brody had been arrested for the murder of his ex-girlfriend, Lorna Lavelle and her husband, Stefan. It had taken a few weeks to investigate further, and all charges were dropped due to extenuating circumstances. Clear evidence pointed to Stefan murdering his wife, after her four-year affair with Brody. Stefan restrained Brody, stabbed him and Brody retaliated in self-defence.

Rancid Vengeance were front and centre again, but I was unsure of how much more we could take, as a band and as individuals. Our private lives weren't private anymore and I blamed Brody for it all. Tonight, we were performing a sold-out gig in front of a crowd of twenty thousand dedicated and die-hard fans at the o2 arena in London. This was our first gig since Brody's accident, and I was pumped to be back. I was excited to play after six long months.

The day is spent rehearsing and sound checking with the rest of the boys, but Brody's mind was somewhere else. I pull out my earpiece and stop playing, lifting my arm up in the air to signal a short break. We all move casually to the centre of the stage as a group, Sam, Brody and Lucas looking at me questioningly.

"Brody, what the fuck was that man?" I blurt out and he doesn't seem phased by my words.

"I-I dunno', mate, I'm sorry," he stutters, as he lets out a laboured breath and I regard him intently. His face is pale, he has dark circles underneath his eyes, and he has lost a significant amount of weight.

"Look, are you sure you're ready for this?" I ask diplomatically and he's silent, as he sets his guitar down. He turns and runs off the stage like a bat out of hell.

"Well done, dickhead!" Sam yells gruffly and I grab him to stop him from going after Brody. He looks at where my hand is gripping his bicep and cocks his eyebrow.

"Something you want to share, mate?" Sam says cockily, glancing between Sam and Lucas, as Sam runs his hand through his hair. I let go of his arm and he starts to pace the length of the stage.

"How fucking long are we going to keep cleaning up his mess, Sam!" I ask, breaking the awkward and uncomfortable silence. Sam stops pacing and looks at me, his green eyes full of fire.

"For as long as it fucking takes! For as long as there's breath left in me! He's been abandoned his entire life, Jax! I'm not going to abandon him! He fucking needs us!" Sam says through gritted teeth, and I laugh bitterly.

"He doesn't need us! He's a fucking liability, Sam! When are you going to admit it! He's not ready to perform tonight!"

Sam's jaw starts to tic and his eyes narrow.

"He's going to be a dad of twins, for fucks sake! It's about time he grew up and took fucking responsibility for once in his God damn life!"

I continue, as Sam places his hands behind his head and looks up to the sky.

"Don't you think I don't know that? We can't lose any more of our family, Jax, we can't. I won't survive it, we've been through enough, so I can't give up on him."

His gruff voice turns to a whisper, and I barely hear him, as I fold my arms across my chest.

"It's commendable, I get it, I really do. But are you sure he's ready to perform tonight? He's literally had to learn all of our songs practically from scratch again. It's your call, Sam."

Sam growls, as he moves towards the microphone stand and places his earpiece back into his ear.

"He'll be fine! End of. We need to go again!"

He says into the microphone, and I shake my head in disbelief. *We'll see.*

*** 

The mass of Rancid Vengeance are screaming out their familiar chant.

"Vengeance, Vengeance, Vengeance."

There is no feeling quite like it, the tumultuous hum around the venue and the atmosphere is palpable.

"Do you want to raise a little hell with us, London?" Sam growls huskily into the microphone. I find myself smiling at his uncanny knack to command an audience, he has them eating from the palm of his hand and despite our differences, he is a devout professional.

"*Wow!* It's so fucking good to be back after all this time! Give me a riff, Flash."

Sam turns to me and flashes me a wink. I wink in return and nod once.

"We owe these guys a show, right?"

Sam laughs into the microphone and the crowd scream.

"Let me fucking hear you, London! YEEAAHHHH!"

The cheering is so loud, and the screams of adoration drive me to play as I've never played before. I start to play the opening riff of '*Rock Me*.' I turn to Brody, and he looks vacant, his trembling hands poised on the fretboard of his guitar. He begins to play and he misses a note, as I catch his blank gaze.

"What the fuck, man?!" I mouth and he shakes his head, muttering his apologies. Sam turns to him with a furrowed brow, he stops playing, sets his guitar down in front of Lucas' drum kit and rushes off stage in a blind panic. *Fuck my life.*

We make it to the end of the song, and our first comeback gig is temporarily halted, as Raleigh goes into premature labour. It all happens in a blur, as we make it to the hospital, escorted by our security team. Raleigh was prepped for surgery for a caesarean section due to a placental abruption and pre-eclampsia. By the early hours of the morning, the Rancid Vengeance family had expanded by two, with the addition of Bowie Hendrix Hart and Azalea Iris Hart.

# 49

## Zeppelin

The weeks that passed, Jax wasn't far from my thoughts, but the fragile, ugly truth of it is that I couldn't be with him, no matter how much I loved him. I loved him with a fierce passion, but I was terrified that I would become second best to his dead fiancée, and I wouldn't put myself through that. After Abel, I was resigned to the fact that I would never find love again, but Jack changed that for me and made me believe in real love. I listened to all of his voicemails and read all of his heartfelt messages, but I couldn't bring myself to respond, I just wanted to feel something other than heartbreak.

My ninth book titled *'Swan Song'* was released and I threw myself into my book launch. I was attending book signings, and I was promoting through my social media accounts. I had something other than Jackson Chase to focus on and I was grateful for the reprieve. I've just finished a virtual interview for a book group on my social media when my phone pings another voicemail from Jax. I pick up my phone, staring at it like it's grown two heads and might jump up to bite me. I swipe the screen to life and I'm about to listen to his message, when there's a tap on the door. Jericho leaps up from the sofa and his tail starts wagging wildly, his tongue flopping out of his mouth. He starts to circle my chair, and I roll my eyes at him.

"How many times do we have to have to have this conversation, buddy?" I mutter, as I scratch his ears and pat his head. I get to my feet, as he lets out a single bark and I pad over to the door, swinging it open expecting to be greeted by Rian. I'm taken aback when I look up into the familiar hazel eyes of Jax. My eyes roam over his body, his muscles bulging and more prominent than the last time I saw him. The veins in his arms thick and his tattooed forearms corded. His waist is leaner, his shoulders broad, his thighs thick and powerful. *He's definitely been working out.* I involuntarily lick my lips at the sight of him in all his glory. He looks delicious, I stand still observing him for the longest time and I'm fully aware I'm gawking at him, but I can't seem to help myself after weeks of silence. *He truly is a sight for sore eyes.*

"Zeppelin." he drawls lazily and I look up at him through my lashes, as if it's the first time I have laid eyes on him. My hungry gaze scans his face, as he moves his arm up to rest on the door

"Are you going to invite me in, or are you going to stand there eye-fucking me?" His tone is cocky and laced with amusement. I quirk my perfectly plucked eyebrow at him, as he steps closer to me. I can feel the palpable sexual tension thick and radiating between us. The scent of Diesel Only the Brave, mixed with something uniquely Jackson Chase invades my nostrils and intoxicates me in every way imaginable. As soon as I looked into those hazel eyes, I knew I was fucked. I knew the weeks that had passed hadn't dulled my feelings for him, they had only made me fall deeper and made me want him even more. Despite my own protests, I listened to every single message he left and read every word. He moves closer to me, and I can feel his hot breath tickling my cheek, as he wraps me in his strong, muscular, tattooed arms.

"Jack," I breathe, as he buries his face into my neck. The scruff of his beard lightly scratching against my skin.

"*Christ*, I've missed you," he declares and we stand there, both mute just looking at each other. He lifts his head and crushes his lips to mine. The unexpected feel of his lips teasing mine after so long, causes a rush of heat between my legs. He pulls away briefly, resting his forehead on mine and cupping my face in his hands.

"I'm so fucking sorry, Zeppelin."

His voice thick with emotion, it makes my heart constrict in my chest.

"The last thing I wanted to do was hurt you. I know I fucked up, but I'm eternally sorry, please let me make it up to you."

I swallow past the lump in my throat and stroke his beard, which is longer than the last time I saw him. I'm fully aware that I haven't invited him in, so I pull him inside and shut the door behind us.

He turns us and pushes me against the door, taking both of my hands in one of his and holding them prisoner above my head. He kisses a burning trail from my neck and across my collarbone, as his free hand skates down to cup my breast. The feel of his lips on mine, the all too familiar heat between my thighs becomes a persistent throb. I crave his body desperately, I was addicted, and I had no willpower to kick the habit, at least not until I'd had my fix. The urgent need emanating from every inch of him, as he presses his lips to mine, lazy, measured and painfully slow. I writhe against him, his grip on my hands firm and he chuckles softly.

"Shhh, soon."

Our perfectly synced breaths become ragged, and desperate, as I feel his heart pounding in his chest. He pulls away from our kiss and presses his forehead to mine. I can feel the slick heat pooling between my legs, a fierce ache blossoming within me. I can feel his solid erection between us pressing into my lower abdomen, as he reaches underneath my t-shirt to pull the cup of my bra down and his thumb strokes my nipple into a hard-erect bud. I moan aloud and focus on the feel of his hands on me after all this time. I'm so full of desperate hunger and only he can satisfy my intense need. My pussy is aching for him to be inside me, my pulse is racing and I'm burning with desire for him.

I can feel his hard body pressed against me and I wanted to run my fingers over his rigid abs. I wanted to devour every single inch of his perfect body. I had an unquenchable thirst for him and only him. He kissed my neck feverishly, creating a moist path of hungry nips upward, until his lips met mine. He still held my hands prisoner above my head, I wanted so desperately to touch him, to explore his God-like body.

"Jack, please," I whimper.

"What do you need, beautiful girl?" he whispers against my lips.

"I need you, please. Oh God, I need you!"

Heat surges through every part of my body and my blood began to pound in my veins. I could feel the unreserved fire and passion sizzling between us, as our bodies melted together as one. My full breasts press against his hard chest, as he wedges his thigh between mine, encouraging me to spread my legs. His hand travelling down and slipping underneath the waistband of my knickers. I cry out on a half sob, as he pushes his middle finger inside me, finding my sensitive nub with his thumb, and strokes in slow, gentle circles, fraught for my release.

"Jack, I need you to fuck me, please, please, Oh God, I need you to fuck me!" I pant, breathless and desperate for him.

"Patience, sweetheart. I want you to come for me first."

His voice rough, as his finger circles my engorged clit. I writhe against him, his grip on my wrists still firm as he increases his momentum.

"That's it, come for me, Zeppelin," he commands, and that's all it takes to tip me over the edge of orgasmic oblivion. Violent tremors fill me, as I find my release screaming Jack's name. He releases my hands, as he reaches down to unzip his jeans and pulls his boxers down, his erection springing free. I pull my shorts down, it's frantic and frenzied. He lifts me up effortlessly in his arms.

"Wrap your legs around my waist, beautiful."

I do as he says, as he impales me on his waiting stiffness. I gasp at the feeling of him filling me to the hilt, as I mewl softly in his ear. He moves me up and down in a painfully slow, leisurely pace.

"Don't stop, Jack, please, don't stop," I beg, as he lifts me up and impales me again, pushing me further up the door causing a dull thud. His pace quickens and I'm on the precipice of another orgasm, as I feel the familiar flutters somewhere deep inside me.

"*Jesus fucking Christ,* Zeppelin, you feel... fuck, you feel so good... I-I don't think I can hold it, fuckkkk!"

I clench my inner muscles around his cock, and he spurts his hot seed inside me, causing my orgasm to explode at the same time.

"Jack, I'm coming!"

He growls out his release and he stills for a moment, coming down from his orgasm. The only sound in my apartment is the sound of our laboured breaths. He moves lithely into my bedroom with me in his arms. He pulls out of me and lays me down on the bed, as he climbs in beside me. He shifts me carefully, so I am tucked under his arm. I lay my head on his chest and soon, I am a slave to sleep.

# 50

# Zeppelin

I am woken the next morning by the sound of loud pounding on the door and continuous threatening barks from Jericho. I blink my eyes open, temporarily blinded, as I adjust to the daylight flooding into my bedroom, as I unwrap myself from Jax's sleeping form. He stirs, slowly, opening his eyes and staring blankly up at the ceiling.

*"Fuck me,* what's all that bloody racket?" he grumbles, his voice thick with sleep and filled with irritation. I swing my legs out of bed, my bare feet hitting the soft carpet, I pull on Jax's discarded shirt from last night. I take a moment to breath in the scent of him, instantly calming me, as I proceed to investigate where the noise is coming from.

"There's someone at the door, that's all," I explain, pulling the shirt closed, as I pad into the main vestibule of my apartment. Jericho starts circling me wildly, as I open the door and my eyes shift down to the floor. They land on a large package, wrapped in brown paper and neatly tied with twine at my feet.

"Who was it, love?" Jax shouts from my bedroom, as I snatch the box up and bring it inside, taking a moment to look up and down the corridor, the long corridor quiet and empty. I kick the door shut behind me with my bare foot.

"It was just a delivery that's all," I call out to him.

"Go back to bed, I'll be in in a sec."

My words seem to placate him, as he doesn't respond further and I place the box down on the worktop in the kitchen, curious as to who has sent me this mysterious box. I haven't ordered anything, at least I don't think I have. *Although I couldn't recall ordering anything, sober at least. I have been known to make drunken purchases every once in a while.* I eye the box curiously; it looks unsuspecting and whoever sent it, took care in making sure it was wrapped neatly. My curiosity grew, wondering what contents hid beneath its cardboard interior. I move towards the box; I untie the twine and carefully begin to unwrap the brown paper. My heartbeat quickening and my inquisitiveness growing exponentially with each second that passed. I pull the box open and peer inside, as I'm greeted by the severed head of my best friend Rian St James. The atmosphere is thick and palpable, I feel like I'm going to throw up. I let out a blood-curdling scream, as I stare into his gazeless eyes and my world goes dark.

THE END

Stay Tuned for the epic conclusion with Dark Truths

Coming soon...

www.ingramcontent.com/pod-product-compliance
Lightning Source LLC
Chambersburg PA
CBHW060414030726
47495CB00003B/574